HEMLOCK AND AFTER

Angus Wilson was born in the south of England in 1913. A part of his childhood was spent in South Africa, and he was then educated at his brother's school in Sussex, Westminster School and Oxford. He joined the staff of the British Museum Library in 1937. When the War came he helped towards the safe storage of the British Museum treasures before serving the rest of the War in Naval Intelligence. It was while trying to emerge from a period of depression and near-breakdown that he began to write short stories in 1946, a collection of which, *The Wrong Set*, was published in 1949. This met with immense critical acclaim, and was followed a year later by a second collection, *Such Darling Dodos*. In 1952 his short critical study *Emile Zola* was published and was followed in 1953 by *Hemlock and After*, his first novel and one of his best known works. In 1955 he resigned from the Museum in order to devote his time to writing, and in 1963 became a part-time lecturer at the new University of East Anglia in Norwich, subsequently becoming Professor and Public Orator. He was made a CBE in 1968 and knighted in 1980.

His other novels are *Anglo-Saxon Attitudes* (1956), *The Middle Age of Mrs Eliot* (1958), *The Old Men at the Zoo* (1961), *Late Call* (1964), *No Laughing Matter* (1967), *As If By Magic* (1973) and *Setting the World on Fire* (1980). His third volume of short stories, *A Bit Off the Map*, was published in 1957 and a critical auto-biographical study, *The Wild Garden*, appeared in 1963.

Angus Wilson died in 1991. Among the many people who paid tribute to him on his death were Malcolm Bradbury: 'He was brilliant in the real sense of the word. He shone and he was very theatrical. Lectures were packed'; Paul Bailey: 'He was the kindest of men. I am not the only younger writer who is indebted to him'; and Rose Tremain: 'Angus Wilson was a great novelist and a profoundly lovable man'.

HEMLOCK AND AFTER

HEMLOCK AND AFTER

ANGUS WILSON

St. Martin's Griffin ⚎ New York

Library of Congress Cataloging-in-Publication Data

Wilson, Angus.
    Hemlock and after / Angus Wilson.
        p.   cm.
    ISBN 0-312-15544-1
    I. Title.
    PR6045.I577H43   1997
    823'.914—dc21   97-5836
                                                     CIP

First published in Great Britain in 1952 by Martin Secker and Warburg Ltd.
Published in Great Britain by Penguin Books in 1956.
Reissued in Great Britain by Penguin Books in 1992.

First St. Martin's Griffin Edition: June 1997

10   9   8   7   6   5   4   3   2   1

TO ANTHONY
most gratefully

Contents

BOOK I

1. *The Prophet and the Locals*   9
2. *Country Matters*   31
3. *Family Favourites*   47
4. *Progressive Games*   67
5. *Camp Fire Cameos*   87

BOOK II

1. *Confidence and Confidences*   111
2. *Life-loving Ladies*   127
3. *Up at the Hall*   145

BOOK III

1. *In Sickness and in Health*   187
2. *Epilogue*   221

The events of the novel take place in the summer of 1951.
The principal characters in order of their appearance are:

BERNARD SANDS — *a novelist*
ELLA SANDS — *his wife*
MRS CURRY — *a lady of many interests*
JAMES SANDS — *their son, a barrister*
SONIA SANDS — *his wife*
MRS RANKINE — *a local lady*
HUBERT ROSE — *an architect*
NICHOLAS — *the small son of James and Sonia Sands*
BERTHE — *a French nurse*
ERIC CRADDOCK — *employed in a bookseller's shop*
RON WRIGLEY — *a Cockney boy living in the country*
MRS WRIGLEY — *his mother*
ELIZABETH SANDS — *a journalist, the daughter of Bernard Sands*
BILL PENDLEBURY — *a writer, brother of Ella Sands*
ISOBEL SANDS — *a lecturer in English, sister of Bernard Sands*
LOUIE RANDALL — *a lecturer in Statistics*
CELIA CRADDOCK — *a lady from Virginia living in Esher,*
 mother of Eric
ALAN CRADDOCK — *a school inspector, her son*
TERENCE LAMBERT — *a stage designer*
SHERMAN WINTER — *a theatrical producer*
EVELYN RAMAGE — *a hostess*
CHARLES MURLEY — *a civil servant*
SIR LIONEL DOWDING — *a gentleman of influence*
REV. BILL MACGRATH — *a clergyman*
MR GREENLEES — *a young poet*

Hemlock and After was Angus Wilson's first novel, and it created a sensation on its first appearance in 1952. Wilson had already established himself as a writer with two highly praised volumes of short stories, but this work secured his reputation as the most daring novelist of his generation, the *enfant terrible* of post-war fiction. After more than a decade of wartime patriotism and post-war austerity, Britain was in need of something new. The country had been patting itself on the back and singing its own praises for long enough. There was no longer any need to appeal to the virtues of family values, to the heroism of the fighting man, to the self-sacrificing domesticity of women guarding the home front. The battles had been won. The time had come for the English to look at themselves more critically, and this is the novel that showed them the way.

The action takes place in a fictitious small English village called Vardon, not too far from London, the kind of comfortable setting familiar to generations of readers from Jane Austen and Trollope, from Mrs Gaskell and Agatha Christie. But Wilson tells a tale of corruption and deceit, of sexual abuse and blackmail, and he describes a social world which was changing rapidly into something quite unrecognisable to earlier generations. He turns the pastoral idyll inside out, presenting us, in the figure of the procuress Mrs Curry, with one of the most monstrously comic and wicked characters of British fiction. She may live in a cottage of tea-cosy charm, but her plump exterior conceals depths of unpleasantness beyond the dreams of an Agatha Christie murder mystery. Her protégé Ron foreshadows generations of delinquent youth, and the suave and civilised lawyer Hubert Rose represents perversions which were then rarely mentioned outside text books or crime reports. Wilson has evident relish in exposing the truth behind stereotype and sentimentality: he enjoys poking fun at our own preconceptions and prejudices. And this is a very funny book.

It also has its serious themes. At the centre of the novel lies the complex relationship between writer Bernard Sands, his tormented wife Ella, and Bernard's young lover Eric. The treatment of homosexuality and bisexuality has an unprecedented frankness, sympathy and subtlety. The book appeared when homosexuality was still a crime—homosexual acts between consenting adults would not be legalised for another fifteen years, when the Sexual Offences Bill was passed in 1967—and the frisson of danger which some of the characters experience was recognisable to many. Some of Wilson's first readers, including W. H. Auden, E. M. Forster, and Stephen Spender, were as alarmed by the book as they were impressed by it, for they all recognised that for the first time the world of the closet homosexual was being opened to public view. Spender in particular, a lifelong friend of Wilson and himself a married bisexual, must have seen something of his own dilemmas in the portrait of Sands. Yet he and others recognized that this was a moral book as well as a sensational one. It sought to redefine the boundaries of gender, and indirectly it offered hope to those who refused to or could not accept the old definitions. Some of the questions which it raises, concerning the age of consent, concerning questions of sexual responsibility outside the structures of marriage, have not been answered yet. The debate continues.

A pioneering work, then, but also an intensely enjoyable one, in which Wilson gave free rein to his talent for bizarre crowd scenes of Saturnalian extravagance, to his love of the grotesque, to his delight in repartee. Yet despite the satiric flights of fancy, the anti-village of Vardon, based in part on the village of Little Hadham where Wilson spent some of the war years, was—and remains—a very real and recognisable place. This is England, whether we like it or not. A few of the novel's first reviewers did not like it at all, but their cries of indignation were drowned by the chorus of praise. It made its mark. *Hemlock and After* is one of those rare works, a novel of historical importance, which remains as lively and readable and relevant now as it was when it was first published.

HEMLOCK AND AFTER

BOOK I

CHAPTER ONE

The Prophet and the Locals

OF all the communications that Bernard Sands received on the day of his triumph the one which gave him the greatest satisfaction was the Treasury's final confirmation of official financial backing. He looked back over his long years of struggle and victory, against authority in all the guises which the literary world could lend it – publishers, editors, critics, cultural committees, the reading public – and noted with a certain surprise that he had almost come to take his ultimate ascendancy for granted. The earliest victories, of course, had cost him the most in self-discipline and in intellectual determination. For a Grand Old Man of Letters it had become fairly plain sailing; even, he reflected with satisfaction, for a Grand Enfant Terrible, though he instantly reminded himself of the histrionic dangers – the knickerbockered, bearded, self-satisfied, quizzing air – of the position he had won in English life. If he had forced from the public and the critics respect and hearing for his eternal questioning of their best-loved 'truths', he must never allow them to feel they were indulging the court jester. They should continue to take from him exactly the pill they did not like, and take it without the sugar of whimsy. Beneath his lined, large-featured face a certain bony determination asserted itself as he thought with satisfaction of his proved strength and independence; the habitual irony of his large dark eyes was replaced by an unusual serenity. If on occasion he mistrusted his own powers, it was not a mistrust that he intended others to share.

All the same, the Treasury letter was a pleasant reminder of the esteem in which he was held. To meet authority at its most impersonal level had been a new experience for him, and he had felt a certain interested speculation in how far his deep convictions would carry him against the world of Kafka's 'they'. And now *that* little bogey had been exorcized with the rest! He turned once more to the letter and savoured the phraseology that satisfied by its unfamiliarity his constant thirst for new facets of human behaviour.

Dear Sands, he read, *I am pleased to be able to tell you that official agreement has now been given to the grant for Vardon Hall. The subsidy is, as we agreed, provided for a trial period of three years, at the end of which it will be subject to review; but we accept your view that during this period of probation the committee should be autonomous. In agreeing to this, we have, of course, taken account of the fact that the authorities of the various Universities and private bodies which have lent their support to the scheme have accepted the same conditions. I understand that their agreement is based upon the memorandum that you addressed to us on May 12th of this year. As we anticipated in our last conversation, there was little disagreement with your general advocacy of the need for financial aid being given to younger writers, or with your particular arguments in favour of the purchase and maintenance of Vardon Hall as a centre to provide leisure and support for them. You were right, however, in believing that there would be greater opposition to your view that the Hall should be managed by the writers themselves and to your insistence that the committee should act only as an advisory body; in the last resort, however, feeling was quite unanimous that your own position and authority overrode any doubts that might be felt on this score. I hear that this was also the feeling of the Universities and the Arts Council. Your memorandum, in short, has been accepted in its entirety.*

The letter of protest from various local bodies, which you anticipated, was received. They were acting on behalf of a Mrs Curry who wished to purchase Vardon Hall for use as a hotel. You may be interested to know that this protest has not been entertained.

May I conclude by adding my personal wishes for success. After our conversations of these last months, I have inevitably been deeply impressed by the importance which you attach to the scheme in relation to the future of English letters.

        Yours sincerely,
        Stephen Copperwheat.

So much, thought Bernard, for Mr Copperwheat with whose curiously official personality relations had at first been so prickly. It was, nevertheless, very gratifying to an anarchic humanist to have the State eating out of his hand, even when the fodder was taken with such primness.

The sound of his wife's voice broke the satisfaction of his mood. Watching her descend the stairs – her eyes blinking, her hands trembling slightly – he felt an exceptional hatred of the neurotic misery which cut her off from the rest of the world. He would have been so happy to have had her share in his triumph.

Despite his knowledge that she could not really participate, 'Ella, my dear,' he cried, 'even the Circumlocution Office has come round. The Barnacle Tites have decided to do me honour.'

Ella's furrowed face twitched as she tried to focus on his words. 'Have they, dear?' she said uncomprehendingly. 'I'm not surprised.' Then, making a supreme effort, she added, 'Is it to do with Vardon Hall?'

'Yes,' he said. 'We're assured of the Government grant.' Searching for links of memory, 'It's foolish, I know,' he said, 'to feel so pleased, but in a way it's the first new field for so long in the barren stretches of eminence's desert. Do you remember the first notices of *Nightmare's Image* and how I could hardly take "prep" from the excitement of it?'

But it was clear that Ella's mind could not easily return to his first novel, to the slavery of the preparatory school.

'Don't let us keep the local gentry waiting,' Bernard cried hastily, a little too loudly. 'The least I owe my son is his freedom to show me off to the country-gentlemen commuters. They need a Roman holiday.'

At the return of the accustomed bitterness to Bernard's voice, his wife seemed about to speak, but although her lips trembled a little, she made no sound and followed him out of the front door.

As the car sped past the trim yew hedge and the carefully distanced hollyhocks of Mrs Curry's cottage, Bernard received a blurred glimpse of her mountainous figure, seated in a cane chair on the wide front lawn – a gigantic moored airship swaying and billowing in the light summer breeze, all a pretty pastel mauve that only emphasized the soft, cushiony flesh around it, with no satisfactory point of definition for the eye save the famous crown of red-gold hair. He felt rather than saw that she bowed a stately, old-world inclination of her swollen, baby-faced head, and guessed at the hard, sweet smile of her round, outsize blue eyes. His victory over Vardon Hall had ended, perhaps for ever, that more intimate wave of the little, fat, dimpled, and beringed hand. It gave him great satisfaction that the speed of the car prevented his returning the greeting.

'For all the phoniness of that woman's personality,' he said to his wife, 'she is in some way genuinely evil. Apart, I mean, from all that play-acting psychic nonsense she puts across to frighten people.' He regretted the observation as soon as he had made it. Any suggestion of forces that were not clearly definable was one of the hundred topics that had still to be avoided in talking to Ella, although her breakdown was conventionally regarded as having come to an end six years ago.

He need, in fact, have had no anxiety. Ella was far too pre-occupied with the terror of driving the car. The doctor had insisted that she should do anything for which she felt an inclination. 'She'll find her own way back to life,' he had said solemnly; 'but, whatever you do, don't let the alarms of affection scare her off the roads she chooses.' She had no inclinations, no wishes, could find no roads to choose. However, she did feel an urgent need not to be fussed over, to be left alone; and to simulate desires of some kind seemed the best means of maintaining isolation from her nearest and dearest. The momentary expression of a wish to drive the car again – such feelings and wishes ran through Ella's head all day in constantly changing patterns – had apparently given great pleasure to her family, the more so since the irrational guilt which they felt for her distress could in some degree be expiated by the panic that, at one time or another, they all experienced from her erratic driving. To the car, then, she was committed; and if, at times, her terror made her regret bitterly this particular road to life, she cared too little for life itself to face the bother that a public revocation would involve.

Bernard could only guess at this. Glancing for a moment at the strained, weather-beaten skin round her tight-drawn lips, the lined temples across which strands of her sun-bleached hair had straggled, he recalled telegraphically his knowledge of her inner unhealed anguish, his own complete impotence before her agony. It would, indeed, have pleased some of his critics and rivals to note that a novelist so eminent for his psychological insight should be so completely without a key to his own wife's terrors. Ella had retreated into an underground cave whose pale, albinoid flora and fauna were less real than the vast shadows they cast on the high rocky walls around her. So much he could visualize and no more. Eventually, he hoped, these pretence escapes, these illusory signs of recovery would turn into reality for her, as her gardening had, perhaps, already done. The psychia'rist would then claim chance as a well-planned victory, another of the little empirical successes that might yet make psycho-analysis the science it pretended to be. This whole reflection came to him in the code word 'Ella'; for of any memory of her before her breakdown he had now only quite occasional visions.

Satisfied that his wife had not heard his injudicious remarks, he settled down to consider the growing apprehension of evil that had begun, this summer, to disrupt his comprehension of the world. Vera Curry, an elephant figure of Mabel Lucie Attwell chubbiness before her vulgar, picturesque tea-cosy cottage, was a cinch, of course, for a symbol. Nevertheless, it was not only the dramatic contrasts of her appearance – that alone would only have been ludicrous; nor could this evil be entirely explained by her lust for money and her more sympathetic, if more repulsive, lust for men. There was beyond all this a sprawling waste of energy in malice for its own sake that could not be quite satisfactorily dismissed as thwarted power. It was not only accumulating disgust at the endless malevolence which fell in honeyed, lovey-dovey words of beauty from her cupid's-bow lips that made him feel her to be a natural destroyer, pitted against life itself. Hypocrisy, though deeply distasteful to him, was not a necessary companion of his new conception of evil. He had felt it also recently in Sherman Winter, whose stock-in-trade in the theatre world was unconcealed bullying; and in others. He smiled as he thought of the recent reviews of his novel, *The Player Queen*. 'Without losing any of his sense of life's irony, without sacrificing his honest acceptance of human tragedy and failure, Mr Sands has at last won to a wider view of life, a realization that the real conflict lies beyond the contemporary scene. . . . ' And old Grendall with his 'Refreshing, if unexpected, source of renewed hope and affirmation in living. Mr Sands has given a sadly needed testimony to the endurance of the human spirit, and he will reap his reward by finding a place in that great traditional stream of the English novel, in which the humour and the pathos of humanity are forever embodied.' Even intelligent James Ramsay had capitulated. 'Insistence upon values,' he had written, 'is now so *à la mode* that one inevitably anticipates insincerity, all the more sickening because it is too often unconscious. *The Player Queen* is happily at times both spiteful and frivolous, but it has, too, a note of certainty that is reflected in a more complete mastery of style.' And all this, Bernard reflected with amusement, proceeded from an irrational preoccupation with evil that was probably the result of nervous anxiety. 'Anyhow,' he declared aloud, 'I'm not going to become a Catholic, so they can put that in their pipes and smoke it.' He anticipated with pleasure the disappointment they would feel at his outmoded libertarian management of Vardon Hall. There would be none of the neo-authoritarianism, none of the imposition of dogmatic spiritual values upon the writers, for whom he had fought to secure Vardon Hall against all bidders as a comfortable and secure refuge in which to practise their art. Yet some such autocratic imposition of his personality upon the younger generation would no doubt have delighted the literary world as a fitting apogee to the career of an erstwhile humanist who had now won through – how they delighted in such Buchmanite phraseology – to a fuller, richer sense of values. Very well, he decided, he would give them not just plain liberal humanism, but something

14

of the anarchy which had so fascinated him in his youth. He thought with relish of their future chagrin, and then reflected wryly that it would be no doubt the young writers themselves who would regret the lack of standards or dogma which he would offer them. Nor would it be only the intellectual young who would wish him to assert the unfair, unreal rights of age and success, his own young – James and Sonia, in particular – would even forget some of their hostility to him and accord him grudging respect if he were only to act the great Panjandrum, the Grand Old Man of Letters. As for their friends, his own dear neighbours, the mass of business and professional commuters to London who formed the 'gentry' of Vardon, they would, no doubt, forgive even literature if he offered them some sign of 'living up to his position'.

As if to give his thoughts a concrete reality, a confused babble of careful *bonhomie* greeted Bernard as the car turned into his son's short drive.

'O God,' said Bernard, 'Sonia's busy broom seems always to have swept up the dregs of our dear local gentry.' He spoke the last word in inverted commas. 'Don't bother too much to like them.'

Ella's faded blue eyes smiled. 'I don't really notice them like you do,' she said, 'so I don't have to work so hard at universal acceptance.' She was pleased to make even so slight a contact with her husband. Little poisoned darts of remorse for her estrangement from him were by now the only weapons that could pierce her armour of neurosis; he was, after all, so continuously gentle and kind; and, again, it was rather appalling to be wasting an intimacy that so many people would have felt to be a great privilege.

Their son James, towering above his guests, a crane among the common waterfowl, sloped down upon his parents. The stoop, so ungainly in adolescence, so evidently an attempt to disguise the isolation into which his great height had plunged him, now only added to the generally 'distinguished' air in which his ambition was clothing him. He seemed, with his shoulders bent forward, perpetually to be rising in court. He kissed his mother's cheek and held her elbow with the courteous guidance he had used ever since her illness. In Ella's foggy picture of life this courtesy stood for her loss of him, Sonia's triumphant presence, another of the steel walls against which she had ceased to batter, not from resignation but from tired weakness.

Sonia met her mother-in-law at the edge of the lawn. 'I'm sorry about all these people,' she said. 'Don't tire yourself with them.' Her pleasant, easy voice – so sharp a contrast to the edgy, jolly, class-conscious voices of most of the party – was not modulated to avoid their hearing. As with all her actions, it was by instinct that she succeeded in making herself audible only where she intended. Ella's memory went back to the twenties, when Bernard was still running the prep school. There had been one or two such young mothers, whose confident and natural manners had made her socially uneasy, whose jumpers and skirts, carried so gracefully, had made her carefully chosen coat frocks seem common. Hard little bitches, she reflected with satisfaction, whose competence had not saved them from messy divorces. The reiteration of Bernard's reassurance from her daughter-in-law's lips infuriated her. She ignored the remark and, advancing towards a young couple she already knew, made a desperate effort to push through the mesh of anxieties which wound round her consciousness.

'How nice to see you again,' however, was all that she could manage to produce, and, seating herself in the deck chair that the young man had vacated for her, she focused her eyes a little above his wife's head while the conversation went on around her.

Sonia, turning to a group behind her, continued her inter-rupted conversation. 'I think perhaps,' she said, 'I could face it better if it wasn't that wonderful yellow colour. Somehow I find all those fish bones and bits of old bread so disappointing after the way it looks.' And, when the others protested 'you ought to have had it with real *langouste*, as we did in Bandol,' and con-tinued, 'Do you remember, darling, the place where the waitress looked like a tart?' 'Not a tart, darling, a *poule de luxe*,' Sonia simply said; 'I expect I just don't like saffron.' Let Ella stew in her own self-centred, neurotic juice, she thought, and then realistically – there was nothing Sonia enjoyed so much as a piece of histrionic 'realism' – it's a pity she doesn't die, it would be better for all of us if she were dead.

'The news about Vardon Hall is good,' said James to his father. It was all he could bring himself to say. It was impossible to estimate how far this whim of his father's might damage his own position locally, spoil his chances with the local Conservative Party office, ruin his career. The very thought of his father's quixotic behaviour – that no doubt was the charming, knighterrant way he would like to regard it – made the veins in his temples throb with anger. All his life he seemed to have been crushed beneath the weight of Father's career, and now, at last, when he was free and was building his own future, that 'noble old fighter' could not deny himself this extra gratification, this selfish piece of charming idealism. 'Bernard's always spoiling for a fight. He'll rise from his death-bed if there's an injustice to attack,' Aunt Isobel had said with tears of pride in her eyes. This time, at least, he had hoped against hope that his father would be beaten. He flushed with the unfairness of life. Bernard, who knew what his son was thinking, could only say, 'Yes, I'm very pleased.'

But the topic was not to be avoided. Though Bernard was instinctively distrusted by the local gentry, as, with the disappearance of the last few estates, the mixed collection of commuting civil servants, barristers, and stockbrokers, and a smaller intermingling of local farmers felt themselves to be, they yet enjoyed the presence of a public figure among them. If only he had lived up to his position, had specialized in good food, a good cellar and a 'philosophy of life' that took you above everyday things, they would not have minded his talking over their heads, would even have welcomed the reassertion of their prejudices in terms that were a bit out of their depth. They would have liked affirmation of their private conviction that the grievances and grudges they felt against a changing social order should be considered the reawakening of spiritual values. As for the faint rumblings of sexual unorthodoxy, many of them would have been glad to evidence breadth of mind, so long as the testimony was not asked too publicly. 'Spenlow was telling me the courts are choc-a-bloc with these cases every day, wasting the time of the police. If it wasn't for this damned Nonconformist government the law would have been changed long ago,' they would have said; or their wives, 'Darling, don't be so egotistical, just because you like one thing. . . . It's pathetic, really, more than anything else.' If only he wouldn't pour out all this undergraduate rubbish, would be a little more responsible, in fact. Nevertheless, almost all of them remembered occasions when they had 'got on so well' with him, when it had been 'amazing what an intelligent interest he took' or 'how amusingly he could sum the others up'.

It was a young farmer, one of those especially convinced of an understanding with Bernard, who now brought public attention to the unfortunate topic of Vardon Hall. 'Congratulations, sir,' he said. 'When do you hold the Victory celebrations?' Bernard registered the penalties one incurred for showing off one's powers with the shy. He remembered that the 'sir' had seemed to him a pathetic imitation of public-school behaviour, gleaned from out-of-date novels. He also remembered flattering the young man by entwining his stories of rags at the local agricultural college with his own Cambridge reminiscences. A charming, if rather pathetic, snob, he had thought him. Now, he just seemed a snob. As for the boyishness, Bernard now could see only an oaf. As always, however, his conscience turned in reverse. His own snobbery seemed far more disgusting. He sat down by the young man's side in expiation.

'Oh,' Bernard smiled, 'it's a victory of the mind, you know; they're only celebrated by clean living and high thinking, unfortunately.' He was gratified by the farmer's smile to note how exactly he had remembered the level of humour to which the young man could aspire. He evidently believed that this was in a range beyond the reach of the rest of the company, though Bernard could have told him that he was wrong. But then the more intelligent men present probably had less charm. In any case if they both got pleasure out of the fake. . . . Warming up to the encounter, he pushed Vardon Hall and all that concerned himself aside with grinning modesty. 'What about the Morris Eight?' he asked. 'Do you still feel doubtful?'

'Oh yes,' said the boy. 'It's definitely no use buying a new car unless you can go into the fifteen-hundred class. If I was going for anything, I'd go for an old Rolls. In any case, *our* old bus will get by with a new engine. . . . '

But the diversion was not to succeed. The topic of Vardon Hall was too close to the hearts of everyone. It was the latest symbol of the war they were waging against a changing world. The war that, like the Cold War, was so frightening because so unfamiliar, so bound up with the ordinary process of living. One day the earth would tremble underneath your feet and nothing happened, the next day would seem so calm and yet the social seismograph registered an earthquake.

'I'm afraid I belong to the enemy camp,' said a youngish stockbroker, dressed in gentleman-farmer riding-breeches and hunting waistcoat. 'I don't think the district would have suffered from expanding a little.' He was slightly uneasy at taking a quick-profits view of the matter, for his position as a season-ticket country gentleman conflicted somewhat with his membership of a local tradesman's family, from whose chain of shops he still drew profits.

There was quick dissension among the business and professional men who had no local financial interest.

One barrister's wife said, 'I don't think I could have borne it if they'd made that terrible hotel and built those dreadful suburban villas. Can't you imagine them – Mon Repos, Wee Nook, and all the other horrors.'

'Betjeman's paradise,' laughed Mrs Rankine, who was literary.

The stockbroker's wife, who had only recently graduated from the suburbs into tweeds, sprang to her husband's defence. 'Isn't that a bit selfish?' she said. 'After all it would be nice to have a few *real* houses after all the never-never houses the dear Government have given us.' Her husband, who did not read the woman's weekly from which she had taken the phrase, looked at her with awakened eyes.

Support for the housing scheme came unexpectedly from little mousey Mrs Graham, who had married from farming into farming. 'I think it would have woken us all up a little,' she said. No one could guess how she longed to live in London.

'Please,' said the barrister's wife archly, 'can I go on sleeping?' Her husband looked away – Hilda's background showed sometimes in her coy manner.

Nothing was said, Bernard noticed, of Mrs Curry and her friends; even the most go-ahead apparently preferred to ignore the disreputable centre of their defeated hopes. His emotional sympathies immediately began to dramatize the situation. From Mrs Curry's cunning and audacity he built a woman of hard intelligence and courage, vulgar – evil even, if you liked – but with a will to power, an ambition outside the range of these pretentious money-grubbers who were ashamed of her.

'I'm glad, of course, that the housing scheme was defeated,' he said. 'Apart from caring for my own scheme a lot, I can never lose graciously. But it would have been interesting to see what Mrs Curry made of the Hall. She impresses me as having the vigour and the range of her immense personality.' The protest once made, the dramatic vision vanished. He knew exactly the sort of second-rate, profiteering road-house Mrs Curry would have made of Vardon Hall.

'Pretty easy to imagine, I should think,' a retired admiral mumbled, 'a high class knocking-shop.' He alone of the party was much older than Bernard, whom he despised as a typical canting usher turned writer.

'Oh, of course,' said Mrs Rankine, with a little laugh, 'I'd forgotten you'd been battling with that incredible woman. Is she as impossible as they say?'

'Do they?' asked Bernard, with a special little smile of intimacy for the questioner, which he had perfected for use when he was out of temper. 'Impossible for what, I wonder.'

It was more than James could stomach. The lack of consideration for himself implied in Bernard's aggravation of the situation overwhelmed him. He and Sonia were perfectly well aware of the vulgar stupidity of the greater part of these local people, quite as well aware as his father, but they were capable of a little civilized tolerance. It was typical of his father's endless self-deception. All this universal understanding, this Dostoyevskeyan emotional brotherhood, and, at bottom, he had nothing but utter contempt for nine-tenths of humanity; as for the other tenth he probably hated their guts for not being susceptible to his patronage. Thank God, thought James, *he* never aimed at understanding humanity. Indeed, the whole appeal of the law, his forte as a barrister, lay in his belief in justice. If people were too weak or too stupid to cope with life as it was, they had to be taught.

'Impossible, I imagine, in any sense which society can tolerate,' he said sharply. It was the sort of vague, conventional remark which he knew from experience would infuriate his father.

Bernard raised one heavy dark eyebrow, adding to the deep creases of lined, stretched flesh on his broad, bony forehead. His large dark eyes assumed his favourite 'mischievous' twinkle.

'Society, James?' he asked. 'Old Vardon? Vardon Bridge End? The Inner Temple? Or the Judges of His Majesty's Bench?'

James turned with disgust to open some more lager. It was enough that he had endured this in childhood – 'He can't keep order for a minute, Daddy, everyone simply loathes him.' 'Everyone, James? All the stern disciplinarians like yourself, of course, who want to be kept in order. But what about the anarchists? The boys who simply loathe order?' – If his father had remained a schoolmaster, everyone would have seen it for what it was – pedantic bullying; but because he happened to have a talent for writing, it became something quite different – 'gentle and ironic questioning of our most accepted values', 'teasing people out of prejudiced ruts' and all the rest of the nonsense. You could, it seemed, write whatever came into your head, contradict yourself fundamentally in every successive book, invent people who did things quite out of character, do anything but really think out what you meant, so long as you advertised yourself sufficiently as a humanist. In his anger, James opened one

bottle too clumsily, and the foam shot over his grey flannel suit.
'Blast,' he said loudly.

'Oh, I know all about goats,' Sonia was saying. 'People give
them the same recommendation as the billeting officers did with
evacuees – they're no trouble. For all I know it may be true of
goats. But then, like evacuees, they smell, and that's quite
enough for me.' Then, turning to a tall, youngish man, whose
dark good looks were running rather quickly to a jowl and a
porty flush, 'Are the Vardons terribly upset, Hubert?' she
asked. 'It must be awful to have a house that you think is
Baedeker and then see it turned down by the National Trust.'
She could have thrashed both James and Bernard for losing their
tempers in public. No doubt Ella had liked her men to be just
little boys who sulked if they weren't spoilt, but she preferred
adults. To change the subject, however, would have only made
them sulk more. She decided wisely to bring the defenders of
taste and beauty to her assistance. After all, if they, like the go-
ahead commercial group, were opposed to Bernard's victory,
it was a gap that could more easily be closed in a general benevolence towards culture.

Hubert Rose considered before he spoke. As he always
delivered *ex cathedra*, he liked a moment's silence before his pro-
nouncements. 'I think the old lady was rather riled. Thought it
rather impudent, don't y'know? And dear old Jerry, of course,
who hadn't the faintest notion of what was happening, took it as
just another example of the ghastly bad manners of to-day.'
Hubert Rose aimed at pastiche Edwardian in speech. 'Of course
the National Trust were perfectly right,' he chuckled weightily
for a moment. 'As a matter of fact, they came to me. One or two
of them were rather tickled with the project – 1720 house, right
period and all that, y'know. But as I pointed out, there was quite
a lot of bad design going about then, and Vardon Hall was one of
Kent's off days. It's high time this myth about eighteenth-century
design was knocked on the head. Though I'm sorry, of course,
that it should be poor old Mrs Vardon's head that suffered.' His
normal sneer changed to another that was intended for a smile.
'I'm delighted that Bernard's got his poets' home, myself. One

22

naturally feels alarmed at letting loose a lot of beards and sandals in the villages, but, as far as I know, most poets dress like bank clerks. A good few of them probably are, anyway.' He paused and swallowed his half-pint with gusto. Hubert was a great one for wallop and darts with the villagers in the local. 'Of course,' he went on, 'you can't rely on bank clerks, or their women-folk, nowadays, when they're on holiday. Three-quarters of them wouldn't be allowed on the beach at San Sebastian. Extraordinary what good sense the Catholic Church shows when it comes to aesthetics.'

If Hubert was not liked, he was felt to be all right. As a success-ful architect too, he knew what he was talking about. One or two of the lovers of the past, who had felt the National Trust's rejection of Vardon Hall as a personal affront, began to veer round. An Assistant Secretary at the Board of Trade, who kept up with modern poetry, said, 'It fills the gap we've all been so disturbed about. We can't bring the patrons back; we don't, God knows, want the State; so we have a nice little mixture of the two. The best sort of English compromise. Excuse me,' he added, smiling at Bernard, 'I know it can't have been easy for you with all this local objection. But then, that's rather English too. Always put up the maximum opposition to anything you see going ahead. It works out wonderfully in practice. I know *I* like nothing better than to watch any little bill the Minister's shep-herding through the House being opposed like hell, even if I've drafted it myself. It's amazing how right they are in the clauses they chuck out; especially,' and he laughed in self-deprecation, 'my own little pet ones. May I, in any case, as a former opponent, officially congratulate you?'

'Thank you,' said Bernard. The amazing provincialism of the man's views had rendered him almost speechless. Local opposi-tion indeed! And clearly they *all* believed it. After fighting the Arts Council, after weary hours at King's High Table and in All Souls' Common Room, after promenades in Neville's Court and Tom Quad, after portentous meals at the Athenaeum and catty ones at the Reform, after rallying what remained of Bloomsbury, *New Writing* and *Horizon*, after Treasury interviews and, God knew quite why, discussions with the Ministry of Labour – this fellow ought at least to know of those – he talked of *local* opposition.

'I'm completely selfish, I'm afraid,' said Mrs Rankine, rushing to the defence of culture, 'I know I'm going to have a chance of hearing music and readings and talks that I shouldn't have done otherwise and so I'm delighted.'

'Yes, so am I,' said Bernard, 'it's the Summer session – the concerts, talks, and readings – on which we rely to get a little of our money back. I hope,' he added, Peter Pan asking for Tinkerbell's life, 'that now we have been born, even if we were unwanted, you will at least help to keep us alive.'

There was a general murmur of assent. It was after all a distinction for the neighbourhood. There had been quite a correspondence in *The Times* and in the *Telegraph*, and some criticism in the *Daily Express*, so nobody present felt quite out of the national limelight.

'The papers have done you proud certainly,' said the stockbroker's wife, and then stopped, for she remembered a particular reason for being disturbed. The *Daily Express* had shown quite clearly that the whole affair was connected with this dreadful Peace Appeal; the *New Statesman* or *Reynolds' News* or some terrible paper had given it all away. Apparently the *Daily Worker* had taken it up and said it was just what the Government ought to be doing – thank heaven even they had at least got enough shame not to spend good money on nonsense like that – and that Russia had a number of such country houses for writers, only bigger and better than Vardon Hall.

There was a general hush. Mention of the newspapers had reminded many of the others of this disturbing political aspect of the new scheme. Bernard, guessing at their thoughts, was too annoyed to come to his own defence. Stupid lot of Fascists, he thought, and then smiled at his own prejudice. Even in an emergency, he reflected, even driven into a corner, not more than one or two would really act in a manner that could be described under the easy label 'Fascist': Hubert Rose, perhaps, out of cleverness; the young stockbroker and his wife out of stupidity; for the same reason, maybe, his boyish young farmer – here he smiled wryly again – but not one of the others. And yet many of the most intelligent of these men and women were ready at the slightest crisis to label him, or any other person whom they associated, however vaguely, with their anxieties, as Communist. He smiled at his own moralizing. It would not take much encouragement, he suspected, to have him on his feet, exhorting them all to unity in the face of common danger. But then, he decided, who could say where such unity lay? What would decide their choice in that threatened future when choice would almost have gone? These people thought Hubert Rose a 'sound' man, yet he could swear that the cleverness and the sneer concealed a far deeper hatred and inferiority than theirs, a ruthless fright that would have no consideration for ideas of liberty and humanity. But what did he know of his own son James, if his career were at stake? On his own 'progressive' side, too, he would swear to the innate decency of his sister Isobel; yet how did he know into what political enormities her failure, her defeated possessiveness, might eventually lead her. In the last resort, it would need intelligence, courage *and* pity in order to stand firm, and a little too much of any of the three would push one over the edge. Possibly it was this fundamental social distrust and unease that explained his irrational sense of evil in these last months. He suspected all the same that its roots lay deeper.

Bernard was recalled from his reverie by the sound of Sonia's voice.

'Personally,' she was saying, 'I'm so pleased that *Eliot's* given his name to the scheme.'

She was determined to take the sting out of her father-in-law's tiresome folly before she changed the subject. It was a happy stroke, for few of those present had not visited 'The Cocktail Party'.

Bernard's admiration for her persistence roused him to support her. 'Maugham as usual,' he said, 'has subscribed most handsomely.'

'I suppose you've got Priestley,' said Hubert casually.

Bernard was not so easily caught. He ignored the remark.

'Charles Morgan,' he said, smiling at Hubert, 'is unfortunately in France.'

Sonia saw her chance to put out to sea, away from the treacherous rocks. 'France?' she mused, 'how I wish *I* was.' Apart from motor cars and the iniquities of the Government there was no topic more likely to engage the company at large than 'abroad'. Before the war when motoring was easier and the Government was all right, 'abroad' had been very low down on their list of priorities. There had always been Switzerland, of course, and Cannes, or earlier, Le Touquet, if you were being grand. But it was to the old paradises of the intellectuals of the thirties that the new middle-class rebels from welfare England now turned their eyes – Provence, Burgundy, the small Riviera towns, Corsica, with the additional pleasure of Italy, which had been politically *verboten* to the nineteen-thirties progressives, and above all, of course, the newly opened up Spain.

'Oh dear!' said the barrister's wife, 'no abroad for us this year. I had so hoped to park Roger and Jeremy on their grandmother, but God wasn't on my side. I had the most wonderful letter from old Madame Peyrin, too. She called Humphrey "a quite gracious gentleman", which of course he *was* with her.'

Her husband removed his pipe for a moment. 'Anyone who can do *truite en gelée* as she can deserves all the gracious gentlemen she wants. I almost think I might make a trip on my own just for that trout.'

'You wouldn't get very far, dear, on your French. That, at least, has been some little recompense for the hell of having been at a girl's boarding-school.'

'Oh yes, you were all right in Tours or even in Burgundy with your French Oxford accent. But think how I came to the rescue in Marseilles.'

His wife giggled in remembrance. 'Humphrey has the most wonderful imitation of the Marseillais, just like one of those jokes about Marius in the Paris vaudevilles.'

'Derek's just as hopeless about speaking,' said another woman. 'There was an awful moment when he insisted on taking over at Périgord and I thought I wasn't going to get any truffles.'

'And what about Italy?' challenged her husband.

'Soldiers' slang,' laughed his wife. 'I feel sure half of what he said was simply filthy, if I could have understood it. All the same Cattolica was *heaven* – we're going there again in September. Nanny's going to take the children. I wish I could get her to come to me permanently, but of course she's getting frightfully old. I can see it in the way she spoils the children. When I think of the way she used to treat *us* as children!'

'We *have* to go to Cattolica,' said her husband, 'because Sylvia's fallen for the swimming professional.'

'And what about you and the padrona?' Oh! those dark Italian eyes!

'No holidays for us farmers,' said the boyish farmer ruefully, 'unless we take them in January.'

The commuting county gentlemen felt slightly embarrassed. They could not really claim that their vegetables or their poultry interfered with their holiday plans.

'What a shame!' said the stockbroker's wife. 'I can just imagine how you'd adore Bandol. That glorious bougainvillaea! and the sun! We're being very adventurous this year, someone's told us of a wonderful cheap hotel at Ivica, there's no need to speak Spanish. And, my dears, we're flying. I shan't have another stitch of clothing for years, but still . . .'

Burgundy, Provence, the Adriatic, the Balearics. Bernard felt as though he was transported back twenty or twenty-five years. Already, in his world, these places – Bandol, Cassis and the rest – were said to have been 'spoilt' by 1936. It was just the same when they got going on 'wonderful Regency pieces' or 'amusing Victorian *trouvailles*'. He hastily convicted himself of that worst of snobberies – chic snobbery. Happiness should be respected in any guise, and it was clearly their greatest safety valve from the self-pity and tension he had just been deploring. Nevertheless, to be honest he had to admit that he would not wish to be involved in these carefree Dornford Yates jaunts.

Mrs Rankine, of course, went one better. She had been to Lascaux.

'But perhaps the most impressive experience of all,' she said with studied effect, 'was not at Lascaux, wonderful though the cave paintings are, but at another group of caves where you sail on an underground lake. The complete silence, except for the sound of the oars, and the black, black water – I was terrified all the time, and yet I would have liked to stay there for ever.'

On the other side of the lawn, Ella had, at last, found a meeting ground with the Admiral's wife in the arrangement of herbaceous borders. 'It's eliminated wire-worm completely,' she was saying, 'and last year I lost almost every one of my lupins. I've got a new apricot shade this year. . . . ' Through the surface conversation which she could hear her own voice making, her consciousness now made contact, for the first time for many months, with an external image. Mrs Rankine's words slipped slowly through into her mind until miraculously they fitted into her own obsessive fancies. A liberation seemed to have come from a great distance away, yet with it came alarm, for this grappling hook which was clawing at her mind might be dragging her from a known safety of private agony into unknown danger. She was aware at any rate that any response must be carefully chosen, translated into conventional communicating terms. For a moment her lined face and blurred eyes seemed to tremble and flicker, then the words came in a rush which she tried vainly to check.

'The water, I suppose, must be very, very deep, and the ground beneath probably shelves, don't you think?' as if she didn't know! 'Arches, I mean, like the vault of the cave itself.' She wanted to continue, but Mrs Rankine began to answer, so she sat quite rigid and tried to set her trembling lips in a smile.

'I really don't know,' said Mrs Rankine, 'it's so deep, you know, that I'm not sure if *any*one knows.' She was a great reader of Virginia Woolf, and she saw the conversation as an important interchange by two women on a significant level.

But for Ella, the question was not one of interchange, but of certainty. She felt cheated when Mrs Rankine said that no one knew.

'What about the noise of the water washing against the sides of the cave?' she asked. 'You said there was only the sound of the oars. But can that really be so?' She spoke almost accusingly. 'How long would the echoes last, if you called out? Did you drop a stone into the water? The ripples must stretch endlessly.' She spoke like an eager child. It was Sonia's voice that made her realize her failure to step carefully enough. She had failed in communication, she must retire again into her own world and repair the disorder that this seeming contact had created.

'James,' said Sonia, 'I'm sure everyone's dying for a cocktail.' It was, she knew, quite artificial, but there seemed nothing she could do to repair the damage. If she had disliked Ella less, she might perhaps have managed her more dexterously, as she had Bernard. Somewhere within her she almost hoped that her abrupt cutting through of this outburst would upset Ella's balance completely. One could never tell with these half-crazy creatures. But though Ella's equilibrium was not shattered, the mood of the party was finally broken. Mrs Rankine saw that her interesting feminine contact was an illusion. There was some measure of surprise on every face. No, really, they must get along, the children would be back from the gymkhana. At last, the family were left alone.

As the last car turned the corner, Berthe, the French nurse, Sonia's greatest treasure, came into sight with the two children. 'Mummy!' shouted Nicholas, as he ran towards them. 'Granny! Miss Heppelstone fell from her horse and was badly hurt.' It was the most exciting, interesting thing that had happened this week. Even little Jennifer, who could only say a few words, expressed her pleasure by repeating them over and over.

Sonia's chance to punish her parents-in-law could not have come more aptly. Her thin boyish face hardened, she seemed like a pecking sparrow as she bore down on the children. 'Bed time,' she said sharply. '*Vous êtes bien retard, Berthe. Il ne faut pas les laisser s'enfiévrer comme cela.* Now say good night, Nicholas.' And then began the final torture of Bernard and Ella, as Nicholas and Jennifer made the rounds with courtly bows and little curtseys. 'Good night, Father. Good night, Grandfather.

Good night, Mummy. Good night, Granny.' The simple, happy days on Frinton sands seemed so far away from this – 'Shan't be a moment, Bernard,' James would call, and his sister Elizabeth, 'Oh, don't fuss, Mummy, get on with your book.' The contrast between those carefree days and this little circus of neo-Victorian discipline with Sonia cracking the whip was almost more than they could bear. Bernard attempted to soften the spectacle by drawing the children to him and kissing them. But Ella felt too guilty for her recent disgrace. She just sat quite still and tried to smile.

CHAPTER TWO

Country Matters

ERIC CRADDOCK leaned his elbows on the café table and stared at the mauve woollen wistaria set in the vase on the wall opposite. It was only a half vase and fluted. Like the rest of the walls of the café it was pink rough-cast shaded with silver. Nearby was a profile of a nineteen-thirties lady with a rakish black beret and golden hair running to a point on her cheekbone. He was, at present, in Florence, where the wistaria ran in thick dusty mauve showers from the balcony parapet on which his arms were resting. Though the youngest of Lorenzo's pages, he was loved not only for his beauty, but for his talents, which spoke of something more than mere talent. His verses, which seemed to crowd upon him faster than his pencil could write – the pencil remained an obstinate modern yellow – were, of course, in some degree the natural outpouring of his youth's fullness, but there were, Lorenzo said, sonnets here and there that were more than the overflow of boyhood's beauty. His treble voice in madrigal was judged the loveliest in Tuscany. But it was a certain gentle grace, not only of movement and of manner, but of spirit, that distinguished him from the other pages – a grace that spoke of nobler birth than that union between a passing *condottiere* and a lady of the court which common gossip gave to him.

Eric, biting into a hard meringue apparently made of plaster of Paris, began to giggle, and blew white sugar dust over the table. The nobler birth, he decided, was a little too much, and the treble voice. He wondered if his fantasy self would get younger each year, with hoops and marbles or whatever the boy of ten would have had at the court of Lorenzo, probably one of those olde worlde mummer's sticks with a horse's head. For oh the hobby horse! Remember what a big boy you are, said Humpty Dumpty. Remember anything you like, but don't cry. I am

twenty-one and a half years old, exactly. You needn't say exactu-
ally to me. But then, he reflected, it was exactly remembering
what a big boy he was, not a boy any more at all, in fact,
that *did* make him cry. Crying for my lost youth, he thought
tragically.

Carefully Eric arranged his belongings on the small table –
road map, dark glasses, sketch book, and copy of *Madame Bovary*.
He had read in a *Reader's Digest* that the process of arranging one's
thoughts in good order was often helped by an equally careful
ordering of external objects. Modern psychology, it had explained, was replacing the old-fashioned Freudian idea of the
unconscious controlling the conscious by a simpler, more
commonsense control of thought by action. Bernie had said it
was all balls, but at the same time it was Bernie who so constantly
urged him to control and limit his fantasies by achievement.
'From log cabin to White House, my dear,' Bernie had said,
'isn't done on a broomstick any more. And from bookshop to
Millionaire's Row is even less feasible, except *via* the bed, and
then it would only last a couple of years at most, *and* be pretty
hard work while it lasted. But a little work at French and German
plus a little influence and charm will make you manager in the
not-so-distant future, with a flat and more money on which to
dream and wake up with a less nasty bump. So,' Bernie had
ended as always, making a face at him, 'put that in your pipe and
smoke it.' So! Eric repeated to himself, in irritation, there's the
abbey to see first, because that's what you came for; not bother-
ing to look up in the guide book about triforium or clerestory,
unless your curiosity really bids you, and, at the same time, not
standing in a daze – St Albans' loveliest choir-boy drinking it all
in – but really looking at things. Then there's the sketch book,
though he doubted if Bernie really thought much of his sketches.
And, lastly, there was *Madame Bovary*, by which for part of the
time he was moved, thinking of his own pinioned wings, and for
part of the time disgusted, remembering that it was about a
woman and thinking only 'Silly cow! serve her right!' Practi-
cally all of the time, however, reading *Madame Bovary* was somewhat of a bore because of the need to acquire a vocabulary. He

noted with satisfaction that he had to-day forgotten the dictionary.

'Is it far to the Abbey?' he asked the cashier, although he knew it was just round the corner. From his mother, Eric had learnt the wonderful gift of drawing people out. By Bernie, he had been absolved from the guilty fear that this gift would no longer be wonderful if it was practised out of simple curiosity. It was, however, neither sheer desire for power nor pure curiosity that actuated Eric in his constant, darting flight of casual, brief intimacies. True, he sought the click of admiration, but he was only eager for it so long as he was held attentive to see how and when it would come; nevertheless there was, beyond this, not a positive belief that the important friendship was lying mysteriously round every corner, but a negative void which only a magical chance meeting could fill. He dared not, therefore, let anyone go by untried.

It was not, perhaps, surprising that his casual questions, often so inappositely produced, sometimes gave the effect of idiocy.

'Facing you, right outside,' said the cashier resentfully. She was seldom particularly busy, but she was always awake to the selfishness of holiday makers, who took this too much for granted.

'Oh! Golly!' cried Eric boyishly. 'Any idiot might have guessed from the name "Abbey Café". I hope most of your customers are a bit brighter.'

'Oh! that's all right,' said the cashier. 'As a matter of fact we had just the same name when we were out on the Watford Road.'

'Oh, have you only just come here?' said Eric. 'I *thought* the decorations were new. So many cafés look as though they wanted a lick of paint. I hate eating my food in dark, dismal places.'

'Six months next Thursday,' answered the cashier. 'It does look pretty, doesn't it? The silver seems to give the pink a bit of life.' She could see he was artistic.

'I think it's *charming*,' said Eric. He got quite a kick out of that sort of lie.

What a good-looking boy, thought the cashier. There was

something very distinguished about his dark eyes and fair wavy hair. A bit young, of course, but very sophisticated.

'It was all done by a real artist,' she said; 'I can't *tell* you what it cost!'

Eric saw almost automatically that here was not his El Dorado, meanwhile his vanity had registered the click.

'I can well believe it,' he said, pocketing his change, and, with one of his best smiles, he left the café.

Ron Wrigley was leaning against the railings of the Abbey lawn when he saw a young chap go by who gave him a quick but searching stare. He slowly finished squeezing a blackhead on his chin, then putting his hands in his pockets, he turned at his leisure and watched Eric walk up to the West door. 'Oh yeah!' he thought. 'I thought so. Not with all those beyootiful waves and that walk, you can't tell me.' Not that the old sweat-shirt and flannels looked very promising, but he had finished his little business for the day and there was an hour before the pubs opened. In any case, Ron, like Eric, was given to casual acquaintance, when he'd nothing better on. Man, woman or child for that matter, you never knew what there might be in it.

He let his mouth fall slightly into a lazy smile – or that's what they'd told him it was – and half closed his eyelids over what he knew from the familiar mirror was an insolent, knock-out look. He took out a cigarette and strolled over to Eric, who was trying vainly to study the details of the porch.

'Got a light?' he asked, in glottal Cockney. Eric fumbled nervously for his matches. Here was an acquaintance of which he felt in advance both too sure and too unsure.

'Thanks,' said Ron. 'First time you seen it?'

'Yes,' replied Eric. 'It's very fine, isn't it?'

'I wouldn't know,' Ron smiled sexily. There was a pause. Then, 'Do you live here?' asked Eric.

'What, in St Albans? This dump? I *should* think so. No; come over on a bit of business. Very nice too. What you do?'

'I run a bookshop,' said Eric.

'Oh! not much to that, is there?'

'We do very well,' replied Eric, which, considering that

Brandt & Ferguson was the best paying concern in Charing Cross Road, was truthful.

But Ron was getting bored. This was by no means in his usual line, and he was uncertain of the moves. 'Like a little walk?' he asked.

Eric hesitated. It was difficult to see a fellow-page here, but he was drawn on by desire and fright. He looked at Ron's high cheek bones with their strange covering of thick, dark down, and at his sleek black hair. 'All right,' he said.

He was disgusted at the precise, prissy tones in which he heard himself saying, 'It's lovely to be in the country.'

'Do you like it?' said Ron surprised. 'I live in the proper country. You'd like it where I live.'

'Oh,' said Eric, 'I thought you lived in London.'

'Yes, I'm proper Cockney, I know,' smiled Ron. He knew that one all right. That was a favourite one of old Ma Curry's – Funny Cockney Boy. 'Born in Stepney,' he went on, 'but we was evacuated, and I stopped there ever since.'

'Where is there?' asked Eric.

'Little Vardon. You wouldn't know it.'

'Oh, but I do. At least, I've never been there, but I have a great friend who lives there.'

'Oh!' said Ron, with careful lack of interest. 'Who's that?'

'He's a writer,' replied Eric, 'Bernard Sands. Do you know him?' The encounter seemed safer now, less *louche*.

'Oh yes, I know him. Special friend?' Ron asked. His attempt at a suggestive smile undid him. He only knew one kind of leer where sex was in question.

'He's an old friend of my family's,' replied Eric determinedly.

'I should think he'd like you,' said Ron, undeterred.

'Oh,' said Eric. 'Why?'

Something in the sharpness of his tone urged Ron to retreat. 'I should think anyone would. You look all right, you know.'

Eric did not reply. Ron felt that the time had come to settle questions.

'Want to go to a place I know?' he asked.

'It's rather late,' Eric hesitated. 'Is it far?'

'No. Ten minutes' walk. I don't do something for nothing, you know,' he added after a pause.

'I think I ought to get back really,' Eric said, and turned back towards the Abbey.

'Oh,' Ron said. 'Another time perhaps.'

'I hope so,' said Eric vaguely.

'Christ, I'm thirsty,' said Ron. 'Got the price of a drink?' Eric extracted half a crown.

'Make it ten shillings,' said Ron, a faint note of professional begging whine in his voice.

They were nearer the Abbey now, Eric felt safer. He laughed aloud. 'I haven't got ten shillings on me,' he said.

'Oh,' said Ron sulkily, 'well, make it five bob then.'

Eric produced two shillings. 'That's four and sixpence,' he said unnecessarily.

'It's not much,' said Ron, but then he remembered that little piece of information. You never knew what might be useful. Old Ma Curry would pat him on the back for that. He looked at Eric. Come to that, he wouldn't have minded.

'You're all right,' he said, putting his hand on the young man's shoulder. 'You done your National Service?'

'Yes,' said Eric.

'I bet it was the Navy,' Ron guffawed.

This sally, which he had thought up carefully as a compliment, was quite outside Eric's comprehension. 'No,' he said, 'Educational Corps. Have you done yours?'

'Not me. I'm too wide for bloody service,' boasted Ron. He had in fact been rejected on account of a defective lung. Outside the Abbey, Ron took Eric's hand. 'Pity we done nothing,' he said. 'The name's Ron.'

'And mine's Eric.'

'Eric what?'

With regained safety all Eric's interest in Ron had vanished, he felt only the insolence now. 'I've no intention of telling you,' he said, and turned on his heel.

'Bloody little pouff,' said Ron aloud.

Despite the hot June evening, Mrs Wrigley's first action on getting back to the cottage was to light the paraffin stove. The smoke filled the stuffy, airless little room. Mrs Wrigley's protuberant frog's eyes smarted and watered behind her thick steel-rimmed glasses. The smell of the paraffin spread to blend with the rank odour of stale sweat, the clinging scent from the half-empty tin of sardines on the table and the sickening, periodic whiffs mingled from bad meat and dog mess somewhere near the sink. These Mrs Wrigley did not notice. She took off her worn old red leather hat – disintegrating relic of the craftwork of some proud gentlewoman – revealing a close cropped mannish head of grey hair. She did not remove the old mackintosh which she wore over her bulky, shapeless form, although she was sweating with the long climb up the hill from the village. She put the kettle on the rusty gas stove which had been bought from some of Ron's winnings at the dogs only a year ago. While she waited for the kettle to boil she prodded with her boot at an old collie dog with sores that lay in a basket under the table. Then pouring the boiling water into a teapot full of dead tea leaves, she drew the sardine tin towards her and liberally sprinkled the contents with vinegar. Before she sat down to her meal, however, she turned on the wireless. Neither of the programmes being to her liking, she put a record onto an old gramophone with a greenish-white opaque glass trumpet. A high, trembling sound emerged which might perhaps have been more meaningful to a bat's ear. It was, nevertheless, in some curious way, unmistakably the work of Gilbert and Sullivan. To the music of the *Gondoliers* she began to eat her tea. When the selection from the *Gondoliers* was ended, she played 'Three Little Maids from School are We', and then 'The Ruler of the King's Navee'.

She was chuckling over this favourite song, indeed half choking in the attempt to laugh through the huge chunks of bread and jam with which she filled her mouth, when Ron came in. She gulped down half of the bread in her mouth and said, 'Keep quiet, can't you?' though her son had made no noise.

Ron's dark grey drape suit, grey poplin shirt and olive green tie – he had far too constant a vision of himself among the big

37

shots of the films he had seen to indulge in American-style blouses or ties – made a curious contrast to the setting of the room. Though there had been times in the last three years when he had shown open cracks in his suede shoes, mud-caked, frayed turn-ups to his trousers and tears in his shirts at the collar bone, money was coming in nicely now on commission from Mrs Curry, from the proprietor of the local cinemas who had other interests, from work on the side for one or two farmers, and from some odd jobs at greyhound tracks. What money came in went largely on clothes. Ron, preserving the creases of his trousers carefully, sat down to a tin of pilchards, then got up to boil a fresh kettle. Mrs Wrigley made no move to assist him, though she replaced *Pinafore* by 'Colonel Bogey', the only luxury she allowed herself from a strict fare of Gilbert and Sullivan. There were days, even weeks, when she spoilt Ron, devoting her time to giving him apple pies, and treacle suet, and mutton chops, but at present she was in one of her 'moods'. She had enjoyed a Wesleyan childhood, and, through the dirty fog of feckless slum living – the long rag-and-bone years of Stepney, and the lazy, odd-job existence of the country – a little pea-picking, a little mending, a little charring – faint rays of moral precept, of Sunday school saws, would shine from time to time, and she would feebly and grumblingly attempt to reproduce something of the pursed-lipped, self-righteous matriarchy of her own girlhood home. 'Penny wise, pound foolish,' she would say, or 'There's none so deaf as do not choose to hear,' or, more piously, 'Honour thy father and thy mother.' This last concept had been much with her recently, since she had read of the wool boom in Australia. The mother of eleven children, two of whom were out in Aussie, she felt sadly neglected. 'If they knew their duty,' she kept on thinking, or 'There's such a thing as duty though some seem to have forgotten it.' This mood of general resentment was kept aflame by the only employer she could still find to put up with her slovenliness and general dishonesty. Many a good jeremiad she had with Mrs Crawley, the incompetent mistress of a failing riding-school. Mrs Wrigley could not truthfully recall the very glorious past against which Mrs Crawley set the declining morals of to-day, but she suspected with good reason that Mrs Crawley could not either.

On certain evenings, when this mood was on her and she felt her rheumatism, Mrs Wrigley would upbraid Ron for his lack of respect and lament her own spoiling of him. Then there would be rows, occasionally leading to blows, in which she was by no means always the passive partner. This evening she contented herself with silence. Ron, too, was in dreamy mood, 'going places' on his looks and personality. After a while, the 'places' to which he aspired passed beyond the limits of his fancy. He made his way upstairs to a world of hair creams, unmade bed-clothes and suits neatly kept – from whole suits on hangers to flannel trousers and ties in presses. The images were fewer than he could have wished in this sacred temple, but what ministra-tions and rites he could offer them were devoutly carried out. Each, after all, was but an imperfect image, a poor iconographic attempt to portray the Absolute – that Absolute which stared back at him with 'lazy smile' and 'knock-out look' from the mirror.

Mrs Wrigley had finished her guzzling when her son came downstairs again. A full stomach and the airs of her favourite composer had put her into better, more talkative mood.

'Where was you to-day?' she asked.

'Over St Albans way,' replied Ron. 'Little business of Mrs Curry's.' He spoke of his employer in a more dignified form when addressing his mother than when talking to himself.

'Oh!' said Mrs Wrigley. She found Mrs Curry and her affairs beyond her comprehension, and, since Ron was not prepared to enlighten her, she preferred to treat them in a non-committal way that suggested a detached superiority. 'Didn't see no one over there then?'

Ron had already decided that the meeting with Eric should be kept to himself until he saw what its use might be. 'No. Why should I?' he replied.

'I don't know,' said his mother. 'Mrs Sands' brother's in the village. Arrived this afternoon. Wanting money, Mrs Crawley thinks. I'm sure I don't know.' Ron's uncommunicativeness was making her ponder once more on the prevailing absence of sense of duty. 'Where you going now?' she asked.

'Down to Mrs Curry's,' Ron answered; 'she's got a little party.'

'Oh,' said his mother meditatively, 'I can't see what she wants with a lot of *parties*. She's *religious*, isn't she?'

'Who said so?' asked Ron.

'Well, she is, isn't she?' pressed Mrs Wrigley.

'Yes,' Ron answered. 'But not what you'd understand.'

'I understand religion all right. I was brought up to it. Which was more than you was,' she added proudly. 'Anyway I don't have nothing to do with her. Always on about love. "We're just a village of love, Mrs Wrigley." ' The old woman mimicked Mrs Curry's genteel coo. 'Don't see what an old woman like her wants with love.'

Ron gave a guffaw. 'Not much different to the rest of us if it comes to that,' he said. 'Don't you start on Mrs Curry anyhow. The money what comes in here comes from her,' and, with this parting shot, he made his way out of the cottage.

Mrs Curry presided at the piano herself, her somewhat fat, stumpy fingers hitting the notes a little jerkily, but with plenty of feeling. Her round blue eyes smiled and smiled through the silver photo-frames, the jars of pot-pourri and the lovely soft masses of delphiniums and campanula. Everything was very soft about Mrs Curry, from the soft rose light which played around her soft pink features – not a trace of make-up or scent, just a dusting of powder and the fragrance of lavender water – to the soft dove-grey silk dress with a touch of old lace at the shoulders and the lovely soft red hair delicately set in an old-fashioned water-wave. Her voice was quite a light mezzo-soprano.

After a little sacred music there were usually one or two pro-fane ballads – 'And Did You not Hear my Lady come down the Garden singing?' or, 'I know a Bank whereon' – because Police Inspector Wragg, who was such an old and valued friend, had a very fine baritone voice. While she accompanied the Inspector, Mrs Curry kept her eye on the company to see that everyone had plenty to drink. She smiled and nodded to the two girls from London and the German girl who worked at Mrs Rankine's, to ensure that they replenished their glasses. She herself kept the same whisky and soda by her the whole evening, but she liked everyone else to drink liberally. There was always a slight hurdle when the Chapel gentlemen were persuaded to have their second, but after that they were usually only too happy to be 'cosy'. Love and smiles and cosiness were what Mrs Curry most believed in. She had never cared for jazz music, though she occasionally permitted herself a little ragtime for old times' sake, but there *was* an old dance tune of which she was very fond, it seemed to her to express so much that was valuable in life. Somehow, when she sang the words, 'Sweet Love nest, all cosy and warm', one got the feeling that there was something religious, or if not religious, what the Americans call 'ethical', a feeling of Higher Values and robins' nests in hedgerows and mottoes in poker work in the simple words. So it was, indeed, with so many of the slow, precise, cooing words that came from those little rounded lips. Sometimes, for example, she would give Ron's arm a little pinch and 'Naughty boy,' she would say, 'he's just a bundle of fun.' There were only two choices open to the hearer, either he might take it as a pretty, playful expression of some general beauty in human nature and the world around, or else it was a statement of such extreme obscenity that the mind reeled before it. Mrs Curry's words could never be taken in any ordinary sense.

This strange, double motif was carried out in much of the decoration of her house. Around the drawing-room, with its motley collection of chintz-covered couches with gay cushions, marqueterie tables and a lately imported striped chaise-longue – for Mrs Curry loved everything beautiful – there were hung upon the walls numerous bad watercolours. Some of these showed the last dying influence of Turner's later phase and were quite innocuous, but another portrayed a field of dancing daffodils into which a little girl had strayed without her clothes, or yet another a bluebell wood, misty and shimmering, in which two tiny naked children sported. 'So you've fallen in love with my

41

daffs?' Mrs Curry would say, and then quite suddenly, 'Poor little thing, she's lost her frillies.' Upstairs in the bedrooms the same theme was repeated more childishly. A little boy with a torn nightshirt trailed a teddy bear upon a lead – 'With a little bear behind' it was called; or, more coyly if possible, a little girl all stomach stood naked in the falling snow – 'I snude it was cold' read the title. It was quite horrible to hear Mrs Curry say, 'Naughty little things, they want a smack a bot, don't they?' But her *pièce de résistance* was a little china girl in a bathing costume lying on her stomach. This object had a removable lid revealing the buttocks. 'So you've found my naughty little imp,' Mrs Curry would say, and then taking the lid from the embarrassed visitor she would remark, 'Let's make her comfy again, dear. Now she's all tucked up for the night.'

While the Inspector was singing, Ron slipped in. Mrs Curry's mouth rounded, as though she was swallowing a fondant, but she continued playing. But, as the last vibrating, manly notes faded away, she left the piano and put her hand on Ron's shoulder. 'You're a wicked boy to be so late,' she said. Ron gave what he called his 'old one two' look. 'I went into the pub for some fags,' he said, 'and got talking to that old chap, Mrs Sands' brother. Wanted to come on here, but I wasn't having any. He was properly pissed all right.' Though Mrs Curry would never have uttered a dirty word, she had a wonderful faculty for passing them over, which put a lot of men at their ease. She dug her nails a little into Ron's arm. 'You old silly,' she said, 'I should have been glad to see him.' From the hard angry look in her eyes, Ron could tell that he had made a bad mistake. 'I heard something about old Sands at St Albans to-day that'll make you sit up,' he said to make up for his error. She was potty mad about the Sands family ever since that Vardon Hall business. Mrs Curry's eyes melted. 'What was that, you funny old thing?' she asked. 'Never you mind,' said Ron, all pinch and mischief; 'I might tell you later, if you're a good girl.' He was annoyed at losing control of his secret, and after all he was not sure what, if anything, there was in it.

Mrs Curry made a mental note that Ron should pay for

his impudence, but, meanwhile, her guests must be cared for.

She motioned a young man in flannels and a sports coat to the piano. A master at the local grammar school, he had come originally as an occasional visitor, but Mrs Curry had helped him when he was in difficulties over a bad run of luck at racing and he was now one of her 'regular boys'. A big, red-faced man now sang, in imitation of Sir Harry Lauder, 'Keep right on to the end of the road'. Mrs Curry included pluck and grit in her catalogue of virtues, but she laid greater emphasis on the softer ones like love and comfiness. The singer, however, was a Scots engineer who was very helpful to her with advice on investments, and she greeted his song with a special little clap of her hands. She noted with pleasure that Mr Warner was quite carried away by the song. There were tears in his eyes and his hand, which rested on Ilse's knee, was shaking. A little music brought out the best in all of us really, she thought. It was nice to know some one so successful had such a warm heart, just a big baby like all men probably, just a bundle of love. She'd been almost frightened to ask him down from London – a gentleman with so many business interests, but he had offered his help over her domestic service bureau – 'Everyone placed so happily' – whilst she had long been drawn to the correspondence clubs in which he was concerned – bringing lonely people together, with their funny little ways and whims, and making them cosy and happy. Ah! well, it showed how wise she was not to listen to people who wanted her to buy a big house, just because she had a little nest-egg put away. People didn't want grand places, they wanted peace and quiet and everything snug. The cottage and the bungalow at Angmering were all she needed. Of course, if she hadn't been cheated out of Vardon Hall. . . .

A tiny little frown of anger appeared on Mrs Curry's smooth forehead. 'Now, boys and girls,' she cried, 'what about some choruses? Don't move, Mr Warner, I'll put the whisky at your side. You get Ilse to teach you how to say *Ich liebe*. It's the same in every language, isn't it? We can do with a bit of love in this crazy old world, can't we, Mr Redfern?' 'We can indeed,' said the local draper – a Chapel man – whose butterfly collar had got stained with beer. 'If we don't have love we'll have war.' It was on the tip of Mrs Curry's tongue to say 'Why not?' but instead she put her arm round the waist of a thin, anaemic blonde whose orange lipstick clashed with her wine-red dress. 'This is little Coral, Mr Redfern,' she said; 'poor little dear, she doesn't seem to have anyone to love her. All dressed up and nowhere to go eh, dear? Sit down by Mr Redfern and make yourself cosy.'

As a matter of fact, Mrs Curry was very partial to wars. There was always such a real need for love in war-time. Of the two great ones, she had preferred the First – what with the Red Cross and the boys on Blighty leave – but the Second had been very nice too, with all the G.I.s and the boys in blue. These old choruses they were singing brought it all back to her.

She moved over to the piano to join in, her enormous body passing between the pretty little tables with miraculous ease. 'Pack up your Troubles', 'A Long, Long Trail', and 'The Little Grey Home in the West' were the tunes that brought tears to her eyes. But a party was a time for laughter and fun, so she obliged them all with 'What was it the Colonel told the Adjutant?' She was rather hurt when young Mr Cleaver, who ran the garage at Grayley and knew all about petrol, said, 'And now what about something we can remember?' She was happy, however, to join in the 'White Cliffs' and 'We'll meet again', and even in 'Buttons and Bows', but when they began to play Charlestons she decided to put her foot down. Why they should want to revive those ugly dances and dresses she could not imagine. The twenties for Mrs Curry had been a period of hard work, the foundations of her present success, not a time for nonsense.

'Well, who says it's time for a bit of fun and games?' she asked. 'What do you think, Mr Warner?'

Mr Warner, who was already having his fun and games on the sofa, was not quite sure that any more organized recreation was necessary, but he was in genial mood, so, 'Whatever you say, Mrs Curry,' he replied

Though Mrs Curry and the few of her guests who had also reached sixty had a natural taste for parlour games, it cannot be said that the younger members of the party were sophisticated enough to enjoy them for their period flavour. But it was not long before Ilse failed to guess an object in the room, and then Mr Warner found that he could claim a forfeit. After that people became more than ordinarily stupid and some of the forfeits took quite a long time. It went further than strip poker, really, and looked less ludicrous than postman's knock.

Ron's failure to guess the terra cotta group of putti arose from sheer ignorance, it was not in his nature to pay forfeits with good grace. Mrs Curry claimed her forfeit, however; she rather preferred coaxing unwilling horses – this evening he did not have to work very hard to play her off – Ron's simple policy was to give as little as he could. Mrs Curry, it is true, pulled him on to her ample lap in one of the big leather armchairs in the dining-room.

'You great big baby,' she said, but she contented herself with rumpling his hair and a butterfly kiss.

'Good news from St Albans?' she cooed.

'Old Potter's coming round. He's still fishing for the bloke's name, but I didn't say nothing. The kid's mum's O.K. though. I told him what you said about the bloke wanting a little party for 'er birthday,' Ron reported.

'Such a sweet idea. But he's such a sweet gentleman,' said Mrs Curry.

Ron guffawed. ' 'E give me this letter for you,' he added.

'What does it say, dear?' asked Mrs Curry.

'How should I know?' Ron answered.

Mrs Curry pulled the lobe of Ron's ear rather hard. 'Naughty boy,' she said. Then, running her finger along his down cheek-bone, 'What did you hear about old Sands, dear?' she asked.

'Oh! I just met a young chap what knew him,' Ron answered. 'Well?'

'We got talking a bit, that's all. Nothing to it.'

Mrs Curry's pinch was not as playful as her smile. 'Silly secrets,' she said. She thought for a few moments, then she said dreamily, 'Poor Mr Sands. It can't be a very loving home, with his wife so sadly all the time. Oh! well, it takes all sorts of love to make the world go round.' She looked very hard at Ron as she spoke, 'You must bring the boy to tea one day, dear.'

'Who said he was a boy?' asked Ron.

'I thought you did, dear,' replied Mrs Curry. 'Oh well, never mind. Life's too short to worry.'

After 'Forfeits' they played 'Sardines', which as Mrs Curry said was 'a nice chummy game'.

It was getting quite late when Inspector Wragg looked at his watch. 'Who goes home, eh, Vera?' he said. Mrs Curry gazed at him quite surprised. She didn't tell everything even to very old friends. 'Why, everyone, of course, Charlie,' she said, 'except poor Mr Warner, who's such a long way from home. We must make him snug here.' As they were all leaving, she said to Ilse, 'You'll stay a moment, dear, won't you? and help me put the room ship-shape so that it's nice and homey for Mr Warner when he wakes up in the morning.'

She sat up quite late going through the account books. Indeed, the lorry was collecting the early morning shift of railway workers when she went to her bedroom. She was sitting on her bed in a vast pink nylon nightgown – she had never become what she still called 'a pyjama girl' – and dwelling angrily on the triumphant court she could have held as mistress of the Vardon Court Hotel, when the muscles of her loose, billowing body stiffened rigidly. She knew at once what it was. She had had her great gifts too long not to take them as a matter of course, though with reverence. So often, too, these powers seemed to come to life when she thought of anything or anyone who had thwarted her wishes. This time it was so clear and immediate, 'in the room' as she liked to describe it, that she gave a little moan. She saw them both – Bernard Sands and his wife – and their faces had such terrible looks of misery, and, yes, you could only call it disgrace, that she tried to cry out to release herself from the vision. It was gone in an instant, and, as usually happened, Mrs Curry felt quite relaxed and soothed with its passing. She snuggled into bed and slept like a comfy old top.

CHAPTER THREE

Family Favourites

THERE were mornings when Ella woke as though the last ten years had never been. The shapes, the patterns and the noises which, since the beginning of her illness, had come to absorb more and more of her working concentration were scarcely memorable. Small objects, whose irregular form suggested a defiance of the carefully proportioned world on which her safety depended, reassumed their humble rôle in the household scheme, demanding no longer the full force of her attention to discover and outwit the subtle dangers contained in their divergence from the categorical harmony she had erected. More spacious scenes – the view across the hills from her bedroom window, the point where the drive turned sharply to the right by the syringa bush, the last apple tree that could be seen in detail before the general blur of fruit trees became simply 'the orchard' – no longer opened up to her endless vistas of spaces to be pursued and compassed by the fancy and so divested of their guessed, but unknown, perils. The cawing of the rooks in the nearby copse resumed its vaguely reassuring note of routine background. She could not even recall the jarring effect of its insistence that had troubled her moments of awaking ever since her illness, nor the depressing monotony of endless boredom which its persistence suggested; less still could she hear in its rise and fall those subtle barometric indications of portentous change which, on her 'bad days', her ears strained to catch and her senses to interpret. So distant did the care-ridden, dangerous, tight-rope world of her sick life seem to her that it was impossible for Ella not to feel that this was the beginning of the famous 'cure', the well-known 'recovery' – abstractions which, after years of discussion and contemplation, had become personified as the familiar yet remote personalities in a *cause célèbre* followed each day in the newspapers. 'Recovery' and 'cure', perhaps, seemed all the more imminent because the danger world was not quite vanished – a disappearance which would have savoured too strongly of the miraculous – but could be sensed in the remote distance, on the point, as it seemed, of fading for ever. It would in fact have been impossible for Ella not to believe in recovery on such mornings had they not occurred so often, and so regularly faded again the next day before a renewed battery of fears and suspicions, the more alarming because she seemed by her momentary lapse in vigilance to have forgotten the complicated and detailed strategy she had devised to fight them.

In the earlier years of her illness, when Bernard still attempted to enter her world by discussing these fears and perils at her own valuation, they had argued the possibility that these periods of happy acceptance were only further twists of her sick self, designed by their brevity the more completely to subject her to her world of illusion. But such discussions only alarmed Ella, who was never cut off from reality, for she knew that Bernard did not really accept her fears and problems at her valuation; and she was only involved in the further problem of deciding what was the real motive of his pretence, and of fighting her sick inclination to suspect that it formed part of a pattern of general hostile scheming against her.

For Mr Clark, the psychiatrist, they might be additional evidence that her illness, never a total dissociation, was not to be regarded as psychotic, but only as an acute neurosis, strongly defiant of all forms of assistance. For her family, and in particular for Bernard, they might still be welcomed as returns to normality which by persistence and courage might be prolonged until gradually they superseded her indulgent world of fears. But for Ella, who never for a moment doubted her own basic sanity, yet knew that the struggle was not to be solved by the Sunday-school ethics of discipline and self-control, they were welcomed both for the happiness they brought to herself and her family and for the respite they gave her from the exhausting mental struggle of her usual existence. What she could never communicate to the others was the greater reality of her fight against the perils and the fears that beset her. The symbols by which they came to her – the tunnels, the caves, the icebound oceans – were, after all, incidental. The dangers were real not only for her, but for all around her. *They* preferred to call them threats of war, of annihilation, of death, and so, by putting them outside their control, they believed they could avoid them. Yet, by the ingenious, endless campaign she devised, she alone was coping with them. She sometimes thought that it was her selfishness that had made her cloak evil in these concrete forms of rock and ice and unfathomable water for, at least, she could face and deal with their constant changes; while to be like the others – Bernard and Sonia and Elizabeth and even Mr Clark – was to be aware of peril, sudden and totally engulfing peril, always present a little beyond the perimeter of the world which their timidity preferred to choose as the real one, and then to build their sandcastles of creation, career, and love-affairs with the cliff-top cracking and trembling above them.

Elizabeth could tell that her mother was 'all right' this morning, as she heard her voice calling down the stairs in that interested, solicitous tone they had known so well before the War. To Elizabeth, who could never forgive herself for having stuck so patriotically to her job at Aircraft Production in those critical, mysterious months before Ella's breakdown, her mother's illness was always coincident with the War.

'Elizabeth,' Ella called, 'you've grown your hair, dear.' Elizabeth forbore to mention that for the last six week-ends on which she had come down from London her hair had been this length.

'Yes, darling. Do you like it?' she asked.

Ella walked round her daughter, considering the problem carefully. 'Yes, dear, I think I do. I'm not sure that Daddy will. He always liked that boyish cut so much.'

Elizabeth's mouth set, her rather long chin seemed more than underhung. 'Fashion, dear, waits for no man, whatever his taste. That's the view of the mag, and what's good enough for the mag is good enough for me.'

'Don't you find it rather tiring, dear?' asked Ella.

'Loyalty to the old mag? No, darling. You shouldn't have sent me to the co-ed, you know, if you didn't want an Arthur Marshall daughter. If you'd wanted the girl who slacks, who lets the side down, who crabs the Alma Mater, you should have put me down among the other girls, I'd have dished the dirt with the best of them. But not at Wrexley, dear. It was loyalty, loyalty all the way for us, with clean minds mixed in our paths like mad. That's why James is such an awful prig, bless him. Loyal to the Ministry, blast its guts, and loyal to the mag, that's me. As a matter of fact I believe I thrive on it.'

Ella thought, Bernard's right about Elizabeth, she's bored and she's getting to talk like a bore. She only said rather vaguely, 'Well, that's all right then, dear. Are you still doing contributors' cosmetics?' Terms connected with women's professions always seemed to be such ugly ones, she reflected.

'Cosmetic *distributors*, darling,' corrected Elizabeth. 'No, I'm off advertising copy. I'm doing a special feature now. Just the thing for you. What the Older Woman is wearing. I did a teesy-weesy piece yesterday about France and *la femme d'un certain âge*. How the old bitches would as lief go out without a stitch as without their *maquillage*, and how no one in their senses would look at them twice whichever they did. Only I had to put *that* dainty bit of copy into the W.P.B. All my real masterpieces go there. Anyway, none of it would be your cup, darling.'

'No,' reflected Ella, 'I never liked Frenchwomen. They have such mean minds. That's not a generalization for your father, darling,' she added, 'he hates that sort of condemnation and he's quite right.'

'I rather hate Bernard's broadmindedness sometimes,' said Elizabeth in a hard voice.

'Do you, darling? You're quite wrong,' said her mother, 'it's the only kind that isn't completely false.' It was bad enough that Elizabeth should have this deadening, smart career, but if it was going to make her embittered towards Bernard . . .

Elizabeth rushed to cover her outburst. 'One good thing, Mummy. I did the routine stores check for this article and Marshalls have got a genuine bargain in Irish tweeds. Just your little number – caked mustard and leafmould brown. No honestly, darling, I saw exactly the thing for you. Come to London and have a slap-up lunch with me on expenses. We'll eat ourselves sick on lobster at Prunier's and send you back complete with facial and house-gown.' She had so long pronounced these words in facetious Cockney that she could not now say them straight.

'That sounds lovely, darling. I don't see why not,' said Ella. Nor could she this morning.

Elizabeth kissed her mother. 'You shall have *two* peach melbas,' she said.

How she does fuss, thought Ella. She must know as well as I do that I shan't really go. Once again she reflected how lucky it was that her daughter had been kept away by war work in those first awful months of her illness. It did also occur to her that the failures in her daughter's personality might have been less had she been urged to come to her mother at that crisis, but she dismissed the thought; for even in moments of good health she could not easily accept her illness as a factor affecting any other lives than her own.

'Well,' said Elizabeth defiantly, 'is this the last we see of you for the week-end? Are the little pansy faces calling?' She felt a little stab of disgust. It was her usual manner of referring to her mother's gardening, but it had at the moment other, less acceptable connotations.

'Oh no, dear,' replied Ella, 'I shan't do anything in the garden to-day beyond what's absolutely necessary. I must have a long talk with Bill. It seems ages since I've seen him. Besides,' she added laughing, 'I want to find out why he's paying this visit. Although I think I can guess. I dare say this book he wants to do about Rhodes will be very good. It's a great pity no one will read it. He's not a good writer, but as your father says he's nothing like as bad as his failure makes him seem.'

Elizabeth felt quite indignant. She and Bernard had worn themselves to shadows while Uncle Bill maundered on last night and Mummy had just abstracted herself, and now it was 'I must talk to Bill.' Aloud she protested, 'But, darling, Uncle Bill sketched his ideas on Cecil Rhodes forty-four times at least last night.'

'I'm sure he did, dear,' said Ella, 'but I never listen to people when they're fuddled. I'll get his tray now and he can tell me all about it before he gets up.'

It was not really, Elizabeth decided, any broadmindedness that she detested in her parents, it was their bloody sensible censoriousness.

There was no doubt, however, of Ella's good health that morning. 'The hall wants a thorough clean out, Mrs Nourse,' she was saying to the village woman who, from her long service in doing the rough work up at the Sands', had acquired a position of autocracy that was seldom challenged.

'There's no sense in cleaning out when the front door's open day and night.' Elizabeth could imagine the snap of those tight, bloodless lips.

'Mr Sands likes the door open, Mrs Nourse, and I like the hall clean,' Ella's voice was firm.

'I do the hall Mondays.'

'Good,' said Ella; 'well, this week we'll do it to-day as well. And now I want Mr Pendlebury's breakfast tray.'

At the far end of the kitchen garden rose a line of poplar trees, and beyond stretched two large meadows that might with exaggeration have been described as parkland. Bernard had had most of the oak trees in these fields cut down, despite the shocked criticism of his neighbours. He had found their picturesque, gnarled antiquity all too reminiscent of the spurious, elfin charm with which Arthur Rackham's illustrations had so ruined the fairy tales of his childhood. Sheltered by the poplars from the east wind, he would sit here, when he was very happy, and gaze out over miles of flat land to the distant hills. The position was generally admired because it commanded so remarkable a view of the sunset, but Bernard preferred to sit there on a morning such as the present one, when the hard, blue, sunlit sky was clear but for a few wisps of cloud that moved swiftly with the strong wind. He ate an exactly ripe peach from the hot house. He hardly remembered a time of more complete bliss.

The exhausting preliminaries to the Vardon Hall scheme were at an end, and he had too few doubts of the scheme itself, or his ability to work it, to suppose that the trial years would be other than a success. He trusted that this essay in organization would still that itch for practical activity and reforming benevolence that seemed to assert itself so regularly and so forcefully in his life. He hoped that it would be assuaged for a good while. At fifty-seven he could not afford many more such exacting drains upon his creative energies, particularly since he noticed that his physical resistance was less complete – he tired easily and his heart murmured. To pretend, however, that the struggle to gain his own way had been wholly unpleasant would be untrue. He had, on the whole, enjoyed it; particularly in retrospect, now that victory seemed assured. Ella's good days he now accepted as a sort of bonus in life, a slight damper to those fires of guilt which no rationalized personal morality could wholly extinguish. To-morrow he would discuss the fruition of the Vardon Hall scheme with Terence who had planned each step of it with him. To-morrow, above all, he would see Eric. He even looked forward to anticipating his brother-in-law's request for money by some tactful gesture. If he remembered his recent preoccupation with evil, it was only to suppose it one more of the nervous symptoms which heralded literary pregnancy. He was probably about due for another novel.

It was lucky for Bernard that he was a constitutionally lean man, for neither his vanity nor his flirtatious, sensual nature would have kept him, as old age approached nearer, from 'going to pieces'. Spotted suits, scurfy hair, forgotten flybuttons, patches of stubble, and clotted bloodstains from shaving become both more usual and more noticeable as men grow older. In Bernard, they were not new. They had from youth been the neglected results of a total, energetic absorption in his immediate task. From youth he had been aware of them, and his vanity had set every charm of posture and movement to create a *panache* that would disguise them. Had he grown fat as he grew older, these tricks would no longer have sufficed, the untidy boy would have turned into the squalid old man. But with his lean, spare figure and his bony 'interesting' face, the large expressive eyes and the talkative hands could still set up a screen against malicious eyes that searched for signs of decay. It was rather his too-suddenly boyish movement, his too-consciously coltish gawki-ness, that, set against the knowledge of his years, were liable to arouse ridicule or malice.

Elizabeth was in as malicious a mood towards her father that morning as her brightly disguised boredom with life made possible. She had decided, after considerable argument with herself, to sit in judgement upon him. If she anticipated a certain secret, retributive pleasure from the task, it was, she had convinced herself, her duty; it was as yet obscured by the awkwardness of her peculiar errand. Bernard saw her approach with apprehension. There was a square ugliness about her jaw and her over-broad shoulders that the slightly too smart appearance, which the world of women's glossies had imposed upon her, accentuated without improving. He would have wished anyone a thousand miles away at such a rare moment of blissful relaxation, but he was too happy to regard even Elizabeth with more than vexation.

His divergence from sexual orthodoxy, though comparatively recent, was by now sufficiently fused with his personality to con-dition his general behaviour. With younger people, in particular, his natural boyishness was accentuated by a paederastic desire to bridge the years, which sometimes disastrously overstepped the boundaries of absurdity, particularly when it was not set in its necessary emotional framework, and, more often than he guessed, even when it was. He sprang from his deck chair as his daughter approached and sprawled on the grass, legs wide apart. Then turning lazily, as he supposed, on his side, he looked up at her with an amused, twinkling smile, and sucked at a piece of grass.

It was not altogether a fortunate performance, but it was all that Elizabeth could have wished to justify her long-debated dis-approval.

'Limbering up, Daddy?' she said. 'Doesn't the uric acid make it difficult? Or don't the deadly crystals give you their familiar message for the ageing?'

Bernard threw his head back and roared with laughter too hearty to suggest that he cared for the joke. The strained brightness of his daughter's speech confirmed him in his decision to try to probe and relieve the causes of her distaste for life.

A conversation in which each party is concerned to expose and help the other is not an easy one. It is inevitably marked by an apparent lack of give and take.

'Evelyn sent you her love. She asked me to one of her Do's last Tuesday,' said Elizabeth.

'Oh! I shouldn't have thought Evelyn's occasions were quite in your line.'

'They aren't. Her young men bore me silly. I just like Evelyn, that's all. I suppose I've got a teesy-weesy missionary urge to rescue her from their clutches. That's one of the things I don't like about those pretty climbing roses; once they get their tendrils round anyone they suck them dry.'

'I should have thought,' said Bernard, 'that if anyone battened it was poor old Evelyn. God knows she hasn't got all that much to offer to her faithful young men. The boot seems to me very much on the other leg.'

'Well I'm sure *les boys* would agree with you. They think they're doing Evelyn a hell of a favour by lending their beauty and grace to her studio.' Elizabeth's tone was becoming sharper. She ended with a snap, 'Since they profess not to be interested in women, I don't know really why we need consider their opinion.'

'My dear,' Bernard was slightly nettled, 'it's anyone's opinion. Poor darling Evelyn – and after all I've known her a good many years – has never built anything up inside of herself; the result is that at forty-five she's left standing, with a badge for being such a good scout, and a bagful of spare maternal impulses. It's the price that women, or men for that matter' – Bernard did not wish to ruin his case by antagonizing Elizabeth – 'pay in later life for being brittle and letting life bore them. It's the cardinal sin, I think, to let life bore you.' Bernard's humanism was not the less violently held because he had lately begun to doubt whether it was a totally adequate answer.

In the thrust towards 'straight talking', Bernard was getting much nearer to his objective than Elizabeth, and would probably have opened fire first had not Elizabeth's embarrassment and emotion forced her to discard the methods of ordinary conversation, and resort to accusation. She had, of course, been boiling up for so much longer than Bernard.

'Daddy,' she said suddenly, in a hard, clear, self-conscious little voice, and her eyes stared straight and brave before her, 'I heard something at Evelyn's which I feel I must talk to you about.'

Bernard's stomach heaved rather sharply, and then he felt very tired at the prospect before him, but he only said, 'Oh?'

'There was a man there, something to do with the theatre, rather an intelligent man, or perhaps it was because he was a bit older than the others that I found him easier. But like the rest . . . ' Elizabeth's combination of genuine distress and head-girl histrionics had completely robbed her of her special bright slang. She could not even bring out the direct references, which she had so determined not to evade when she had rehearsed the interview earlier that morning, let alone serve them up in her personal idiom in order to appear at ease. 'Like the rest he didn't know who I was, and he treated me, well, like any other queen's woman, dear.' She at last got out one of the terms, but it really made her seem more gauche than her straight embarrassment. 'He remarked on your absence from the gay scene. I didn't, of course, know that you were so often there. . . . '

'I'm not,' interrupted Bernard. 'It was Sherman Winter. And I think he *did* know who you were.'

'He couldn't have done,' said Elizabeth sharply. 'You see he went on to do what Granny would have called "coupling your name" with Terence Lambert's, and in no uncertain terms. Quite honestly, I didn't know what to do, but I think Evelyn must have heard, for she shoved us all round in a sort of lobster quadrille – only she may not have done, because she goes in for general post anyway. I lost touch with him, and, well that's that, as they say on the films. If it was on the films I should go on and say, "Tell me Daddy, it's not true, is it?" Only, thinking over various things and adding them up and so on, I realize, of course, that it is.'

There was a silence. Bernard felt a throb in his throat that might have led to tears. It was a reaction that made him feel both tired and old. 'Well, yes, of course, it is,' he said at last. 'I shouldn't have chosen Sherman Winter to present it to you, but that's my fault. And again I could say technically that it's not true about Terence. But, essentially, in relation to what you mean, yes, it is true.'

'I simply don't understand how any of it could have happened,' said Elizabeth, 'but that isn't my affair.'

'No,' said Bernard, 'it isn't. Though, if it's relevant, I could say I've made my attitude on the subject perfectly clear. In *Night Gleaning* and, again, in my essay on Goethe.' It was at times like these that the former schoolmaster showed most clearly in Bernard.

'Oh, theoretically, I know.' Elizabeth was impatient. 'It would have been pretty awful if you hadn't. I'm not medieval or something. I quite like queers if it comes to that, so long as they're not on the make like Evelyn's boys. I'd abolish all those ridiculous laws any day. But then, I don't believe in capital punishment, or at least I'm not sure, but *if* I didn't, I wouldn't immediately commit a murder.'

Bernard said nothing. The unexpected silence pushed Elizabeth into voicing thoughts she had been suppressing.

'It's not very pleasant for James or me,' she said.

'I can't see that it concerns either of you,' Bernard replied, then he added hastily, 'No, that's nonsense. It obviously must condition your attitude to me, and it might, of course, be a serious nuisance to you. For that reason, I'm glad that you know, and, as I'm sorry you should have heard in the way you did, I suppose the conclusion is that I should have told you myself.'

Elizabeth felt almost sorry for him. 'That would have made it worse if anything.'

'Yes, I'm afraid so,' said Bernard. 'Any attempt to merge two quite different social patterns is bound to have some embarrassing moments.' He was about to add a remark about the payment for living in a transition period, but he reminded himself that this was not a history class. 'But it would have been better to face them than this. As to you and James, I'm afraid I must say that I did consider the effect my life might have, and I chose to accept its possible harm to you. Harm to others is after all implicit in most decisions we take, and has to be weighed up when taking them. In this case, I thought that apart from prejudice, and that I'd already decided not to consider, the dangers to my family were not as great as the importance of my new life to me. A selfish, but to me necessary, decision.' Bernard remembered that these decisions had once been real and painful experiences to him, but he could not recall directly one single sensation he had undergone in making them. As a result, he felt that he could only use flat words which sounded even to himself like the cant that others would certainly call them. He struggled for a moment to break through the tough wall of failed contact and resentment that lay between him and his children. 'It would be too impossible a demand for sympathy to say that my family were the most painful aspect of what was a very unpleasant period of decision.' That, too, of course, was insincere; for since it had also been the time when he was in love with Terence, it had been a very mixed unpleasantness.

'Yes,' said Elizabeth, 'it would. I have no concern with how you made the decision. You had, as you said, a perfect right to decide, and what happened to us had little to do with it. I didn't mean to say that about James and myself. It's the sort of egotism that's bound to come into one's mind, but it shouldn't have been voiced. We're all quite separate adults and we can't rule our lives and wants by what's going to shock the others, unless we care so much that it will hurt us.'

Bernard had never felt closer to Elizabeth; he would have liked to touch her, but feared her reaction. 'If only,' he said, '*you* seemed to *want* something, one would know better where one was. Oh! James, I know, has his ambitions, but I judge ''wants'' a bit higher than that. But you, Elizabeth?'

'How do you know what I want or don't want?' Elizabeth cried in real anger. 'It would be jolly d. for you, wouldn't it?'

Her customary speech was returning with anger. 'My little head on your shoulder, "Help me, Daddy dear, to find life's place for little me". And you, the great Understander, you could say, "Tell me where it hurts, baby daughter, where's the great big pain?" You lost the right to that dainty little scene a very, very long time ago,' she ended bitterly.

There seemed nothing more to say. It occurred to Elizabeth that not a word had been said about her mother, yet in the preceding week it had always been as her mother's defender that she had planned this démarche. 'It's Mummy you should have thought of,' she cried. Bernard sat cross-legged on the grass, tearing a dandelion head to pieces. The deep lines in his sunken cheeks seemed to threaten a general subsidence of the whole flesh that would leave only his enormous dark eyes staring from the skull.

'I *will* not discuss that with you,' he said bitterly. And then once more he added, 'No, of course that's absurd. You have a perfect right to ask it. But remember, what I say has nothing to do with "a defence". My relations with Ella exist above ideas like defence or apology. Some years ago, Ella began to go away from me. Of the first of those years and the agony of them I can't speak; I think, by some mercy, I don't very well remember them. I tried to follow her, but I know now that's impossible.' He was about to add, 'You preferred to stay away', but he checked himself in time. 'I didn't change because of that, at least not integrally. I remained a person who is kept working, kept alive, kept whatever you like, by emotional and physical contact. You know all that, however little you like it. It's the answer to what you're asking,' as if, he thought, the problems of the years could be answered in a phrase. 'As to the choice of my life, Ella is a woman wholly without prejudice.'

Elizabeth considered for a moment, then she spoke slowly, 'I suppose you think all that. You've just done what you like, really, and then turned it into a sort of best-selling problem novel. Our talk hasn't been much use, has it? I shall act on Mummy's side,' she added, 'and now I shall go into Bantam and do the week-end shopping. I'd rather you didn't come with me.'

After she had gone, Bernard got up and walked into the kitchen garden. He followed with his eye the box hedge that surrounded the square plots of gooseberry and currant bushes. If he went to the right – talked to Ella to-day, when she was with him, and explained to her what had happened – if he went to the left – went to London and talked to Terence in clear, intelligent terms about his difficulties, and then bathed his wounds in his affection for Eric – it would all come round to the same point. A square wasn't much help, and there was no straight line. He was still considering when his brother-in-law bore down upon him.

Of Bill Pendlebury's 'going to pieces' there could be no doubt. His red, beery moon face, beneath the bald, grey-tufted head, oozed good nature or would have done but for his small, pouting, disappointed mouth. His old grey flannel trousers stretched barrel tight across his pot belly and broad buttocks, but even the old-school scarf tied round his waist could not bring them to a point where the top flybuttons could be secured. His short legs were like swollen baroque columns beneath his huge, broad trunk. For all his beer-sodden, over-indulged body, his broad shoulders and huge hands still had a gorilla strength. His eyes were small, very sensual, very intelligent and somewhat sly.

'Here are the old bastard's letters I was talking of last night,' he said, and his voice surprisingly was soft, blarneying, caressing. 'This one to Barney Barnato is absolutely characteristic – the note of patronage of the respectable rogue to the unpresentable pal, the doubtful facts and figures of the claim-jumper turned administrator – a more bloody cooked-up set of figures I've never seen even in a bucket-shop circular – and on top of it all, the wonderful Imperial moralizing note, the "God gave us our burden and we must shoulder it" tone, that was obviously the bit of cant or idealism in Rhodes, call it which you will, that we all need to make us tick. Now you can see why I must do Rhodes; he's such a full-size, all-round saintly bastard. Not one of those damned literary neurotics like Henley or Kipling who went in for Empire to make up for their lack of balls.'

For all the conscious element of toughly virile enthusiasm in Bill's manner, he was in fact constantly carried away by new subjects. He had a devouring interest in new personalities and facts, but once he had filled them with preconceived ideas about the past, his interest began to wane. He had made his dramatic picture, confirmed his beliefs and was ready to pass on. Unfortunately, it was usually in this waning stage that his biographies were written and their resulting machine-made, over-simplified presentation was as much a disappointment to him, with his memories of the early enthusiasm and the detailed preparatory work, as it was a comparative flop with the public. Originally a 'rolling stone' by inclination, with a genuine curiosity about unusual people and places, he had through failure and lazy indulgence become a professional purveyor of picaresque, sentimental cynicism. He played almost consciously the seedy rogue, and his stories, his much-aired wordly shrewdness and his touch of humour had the pathetic uncertainty of presentation that comes from having used them too often as a means of cadging. He prepared himself for the snubs of the successful so carefully that he inevitably received them.

Bernard, as usual, had decided on his 'line' so long in advance that he brought it out with insufficient preparation.

'You must get all this down while it's still hot with you, Bill,' he said. 'Would you find it easy to write here? If so, stay.'

Bill had been intending to lead up to this by elaborate paths. He was completely floored by so direct an offer, and immediately began to suspect patronage.

'I don't think all this comfort, you know, would help my particular little itch. All right for you. The bitch Goddess works with you. But if I'm to get the tick working – call it the divine fury, call it the creative urge, call it the subconscious, or what the devil you like – ' Bill specialized in these parades of alternatives. They presented an all-round, broad view of history. He had seen, it was suggested, too much of the world, read too much of the past to take account of the petty words that men used to describe their universal passions. 'I have to work *against* the grain. No morning tea, no orange juice, but a pair of kippers on the primus stove. You know the sort of thing, damned uncomfortable, and certainly no special virtue in it as some of these

W. H. Davies people seemed to think, but just my particular sort of poison.' If Bernard was in this 'understanding' mood though, he thought, he ought to be a honey for a loan. And really, he decided, he wished the old boy everything good; though a lot of his success was luck, he *could* write, which was almost like having wings these days. His children, too, were bloody awful bores, and as for Ella, well Ella this morning had been all right, but Ella last night, my God! Bill had the usual picaresque, sentimentalized view of domestic life as constant bliss, and he had, besides, been deeply shocked by Bernard's face as he came towards him up the garden. Bill could not bear to see anything hurt; when anyone he came in contact with got hurt, he made a practice of moving on. He called it 'travelling light through life'.

'If you think I could help by being here for a bit,' he said, 'just say the word, you know. After all, Ella *is* my sister, and to be quite honest, I felt a bit ashamed last night, that I hadn't shouldered more of the burden.'

The subject of his wife's illness was the last thing that Bernard wished to discuss at that moment, his brother-in-law the last man with whom he would discuss it at any time.

'There's nothing, thank you, that you could do, Bill,' he said. 'Time is what we have to rely on.' It was his stock cold shoulder to kind strangers.

'Yes, I suppose so,' said Bill. 'I'm not such an oaf as to think that these things are all my eye or anything of that sort. But psycho-analysis was after all conceived in the old days of Vienna, when the Hapsburgs, pretty women and neat ankles were going to last to eternity, and Freud naturally thought treatment could last as long. Unfortunately we don't believe in eternity now, although they tell me the moment you're atomized lasts a hell of a long time.'

'Ella is no longer under a Freudian analyst,' said Bernard.

'I see,' said Bill. 'What about this shock treatment? The Russians use it extensively. I know they're bastards, but they're very keen on getting people back to work quickly, whatever's wrong with them.'

'Ella,' said Bernard wryly, 'is not a Stakhanovite.'

'Isn't that a bit of the trouble?' asked B
are as real as hell, and I couldn't feel more
Ella's place, but there *is* quite a lot to be said fe
together and all the old moral stuff.'

'No,' said Bernard, 'nothing whatsoever.'
ning to get very angry.

Bill realized at last that he was being tactless. 'W   ..now
best,' he said, 'but I'm glad she's your problem not mine.'

It was a fatal remark. In Bernard's present state of remorse
about his wife, any reference to her which seemed to imply that
she was a passive object in life rather than an active human
being touched his conscience with red-hot irons.

'Beyond the fact that Ella is your sister,' he said angrily,
'there has not, as far as I remember, ever been any occasion
when you were called upon to show her any consideration.
Please don't trouble to do so now.'

'There's no need to throw my failure up in my face,' was
Bill's almost conditioned reply.

'Your failure,' said Bernard, 'if by that you mean your
material failure, has nothing whatever to do with it. If your
material needs of the moment are troubling you, you know
perfectly well that you have only to call upon either Ella or me.'

As soon as he had said it, Bernard realized that it was quite
indefensible, and, of more practical importance, it had probably
made it impossible for Bill to ask for the loan which he presum-
ably needed. Bernard was perfectly right, it had.

After lunch, Bill went for a quick one to the local pub. The
meal had been oppressive. Ella was disappearing into the distance
again, and the fears that accompanied this readjustment made her
at first silent, and then drove her upstairs to her bedroom.
Elizabeth gave a bright, strained account of her morning's shopping. Bernard said little, and then announced his intention of
going that evening to the flat in London. Bill attempted a monologue on religion and its importance to the least religious men
when in 'tight corners'. 'I suppose you can explain it by saying
that they reconstruct their nurses, or Proust's grandmother or
whatever you like, but I don't know that it gets you very far.

63

. ct remains that over and over again, men who've com-
etely forgotten about Allah or Jahweh or Baal-Peor or the
fierce old gentleman in a frock coat and whiskers that they
worshipped at the little Bethel. . . . ' Nobody listened to
him.

He would have liked to have acted on his injured pride and left
at once. But the fact was that he himself was in a very 'tight
corner', although he found no particular balm in thoughts of
God. The little manicurist with whom he had been living for the
last six months had walked out on him, and with her had gone
her manicurist's weekly wage, and now there was hell to pay at
the lodgings. There was no audience Bill liked better at such
times to restore his self-esteem than a pub audience. The audience he found was Ron.

'You missed a good party all right last night,' said Ron.

There was nothing about Ron that appealed to Bill. One of his
favourite saloon-bar topics was the advisability of reviving the
'cat' for young spivs. However, since the barmaid gave the
response of a deaf mute, he put aside prejudice.

'I certainly wouldn't have said no. Our little family party was
a dead loss. Are *you* troubled with a family?'

'No,' said Ron. He was uncertain of his approach, but his
great virtue on such occasions was directness. 'You'd like Mrs
Curry,' he said, and added, 'she'd like you too.'

'Wouldn't stop on there now,' Bill ignored Ron's remarks in
his eagerness to construct the story that would relieve his sense
of humiliation, 'but I've got to get a little question of money
settled. Never have money dealings with your family. Simply a
matter of their signing a document, and there's hell to pay.
Question of getting the money for a niece of ours, too, poor little
kid. I'd do it myself and say damn to them, if I didn't happen to
be so bloody short. . . . ' The audience was inessential now, for
Bill was in his stride.

Ron took very little notice of the long rambling story, but
when Bill paused, he said, 'You come and meet Mrs Curry.
You'll like her and she'll like you too. I dare say she could find
what's needed. She's very good with gentlemen who're tem-

porarily embarrassed.' Ron said the phrase without irony; he had learnt it in the course of his business.

Bill knew something of Mrs Curry and could guess the rest. His resentment to Bernard, however, and his pressing need made him put caution aside. Interesting type to see, he began to think, Wife of Bath, humanity built on the large scale, big faults and probably big virtues too, if he knew men and women.

Mrs Curry was in the garden, cutting lavender, when they arrived. 'I'm delighted to meet you, Mr Pendlebury,' she said. 'Is your sister a little better?' She did not wait for the answer. 'I live so quietly here, I hardly see any of my neighbours. But we're a loving village, *though* we don't see much of each other. I'm afraid it would be much too quiet for you. Last night's little party made a change, just a few boys and girls, you know, having a little fun. Nothing like London, I'm afraid. Do you like flowers, Mr Pendlebury?'

Bill began to explain, that though he didn't know the name of one flower from another, he had always . . . But Mrs Curry did not believe in wasting time. She was used to approaching the question of loans for strangers. 'You don't want to waste your time with old people like us,' she said to Ron. 'Shall we go in and have our little chat, Mr Pendlebury? I've got a bottle of fine old liqueur whisky. We'll have a tiny nip while we talk about your little business, and you can tell me whether it's any good.'

Before Bernard left for London, he wrote a letter of apology to his brother-in-law, enclosing a cheque for £50. Bill felt quite happy when he got back. Mrs Curry had been most understanding; as she said, she didn't know him very well, but she wasn't being as unbusinesslike as she probably seemed, because Mr Sands the novelist was good enough security for anyone. With Bernard's cheque in his pocket as well, Bill felt quite restored. A smaller man, he decided, would pay Mrs Curry back immediately, but he was big enough to know the importance of courage and capital in gambling. It was only amateurs who met the odds against them with too little of the ready; professional punters now . . . Bill had a great weakness for horses and an even greater idea of his capacity as a professional punter. He'd put a couple of ponies on a good thing he knew of, and keep the other fifty in reserve in case the old girl turned nasty. Come to think of it, the old girl's terms were both short and steep. He'd pay her off as soon as the race was over. Wouldn't do for the old boy to have a stink down here, and it could be a very nasty stink.

CHAPTER FOUR

Progressive Games

BERNARD looked down from the window of the flat on to
Bloomsbury lying embalmed in its Sunday death. The rows of
scarlet and lemon dahlias, the heliotrope carefully tended and
the little green chairs carefully painted for Festival visitors
decorated its stillness with a strange air of smartness – embalmed
in best Sunday clothes, no doubt, to accord with the conventions
of American visitors. From the ninth floor the sordid remnants
of Saturday lost the squalor of greasy paper, refuse ends, dirt and
spit which they showed to the pedestrian and merged into a
general impression of dust and litter. The district was dead but
recently, and these seemed the tag ends of life's encumbrance.
But already the corpse was stirring into maggoty life – a paper-
man distributing the sheets that, crumpled and tired-looking,
would add to the stuffy Sunday muddle of bed-sitting rooms and
lounges; knots of earnest foreign tourists collected for an 'early
start' on hotel steps; disconsolate provincial families already
straggling and scratchy at the day before them; a respectable
nineteenth-century couple, who Bernard hoped might be
Irvingites bent on worship in Gordon Square.

The image of trickling, crawling death satisfied Bernard, after
the terrors and claustrophobia of the night's mingled nightmares
and insomnia. He sat in his dressing-gown, drinking orange juice
at the kitchen table. The model kitchen had the white hygiene of
an operating room. But as he peered into the still-darkened
sitting-room, at the dim outlines of sofas, innumerable lamps
and endless rows of books, he determined that he would enclose
himself here until he had drawn on his reserves of courage and
calm.

Almost immediately, the telephone rang. For a moment he
thought of disregarding it, then the fears of obsessive affection

broke down his resolve. He caught his breath for a second, and felt a slight pain round the heart as he heard Eric's voice: 'Bernie? I'm speaking from a call-box. There's rather a thing going on at home.'

'Oh?' said Bernard, anxious not to betray his disproportionate anxiety.

'It's about the room. There's suddenly a great thing about my not taking it.'

'I see. Why, Eric? Last week you said your mother was so sensible about it.'

'Oh, Mimi's all right. She's wonderful as always. But Alan's been home and he's on about her being left alone. I suppose it *is* rather awful. . . . ' Eric's voice trailed away.

Bernard tried to sound neither angry nor stern, simply commonsensical. 'Eric, we've discussed all that. Firstly, Esher isn't far away. Secondly, no one wants to live life in their own right more than your mother.' This, of which Bernard was extremely sceptical, was his court card, so he played it with chosen casualness. 'Thirdly, you can't study properly at home. Fourthly, you yourself *want* a room, and that shows you need it.' Had it not been on the telephone he would have put in a plea for his own wishes. It was lovely having Eric to stay at the flat, but with Terence, his own family and Eric's to consider, it was also difficult.

'Yes,' said Eric, 'don't be cross. I'm going to stick to it. Only it *is* difficult, really it is. Alan keeps on about the expense.'

'The expense? I thought that was all settled. We agreed that it was much better to tell your family.'

'Oh! I have,' said Eric. 'Mimi's so sensible about it. But Alan doesn't like it a bit.'

'I see,' said Bernard in a depressed voice.

'Oh, not like that,' giggled Eric. 'Alan wouldn't think of that in a hundred years. You wait till you see him. No, it's just that he thinks it's all wrong not to be depending on yourself. I suppose he's right really.'

'Of course he isn't. Eric, really! All that too we've gone into at very great length.'

'Oh! I know. You're absolutely right. It's only that Alan makes me go all middle-class.'

'Well, don't.'

'Bernie, you aren't being very helpful. It really *is* awfully difficult down here.'

'Does all this mean you can't come to the Arts to-night?'

'No, of course not, Bernie.' Eric's voice became plaintive. 'That's all that matters to you – this evening and to-morrow evening. But when it's something important like the room, you don't want to help.'

'I'm sorry. I'm very tired. Of course I want to help very much. What can I do? Would it help if I saw your brother?'

'Well, yes, of course it would. That's what I've been trying to get you to say. I'd have got you to do so in half a minute, if I'd been with you. Oh! I do *hate* the telephone. Can you come down to lunch?'

It was this mood of naïve and happy self-revelation in Eric that most delighted Bernard. He replied, with genuine disappointment, 'Well, not exactly. I've got to lunch with my sister, and she's very touchy about being put off.'

'Oh,' Eric never liked the immediate impact of a negative. After a pause, he recovered and said, 'Well, it's sweet of you to say you'll come, anyway. When will you?'

'I'll come straight on from Isobel's. Say, tea-time – and then you can come back with me.'

'Oh! that's wonderful. I know Alan will fall for you.'

'Well, I can't say what I think about that until I've seen him.'

'Oh, not like that,' giggled Eric, 'at least I shouldn't think so. I suppose he *might*. But it wouldn't be a very good idea, I don't think. I must fly back now. Bobbie's used every lamp post within miles and he looks furious at waiting. I hate dogs, don't you?'

'Yes,' said Bernard.

'Mimi *will* be pleased to see you. She *loves* you.'

Bernard reserved his views on this, as he replaced the receiver.

Isobel Sands sat at her walnut escritoire. Three sorts of ink – blue, red, and green – were carefully arrayed before her. The

69

examination papers – folios – and her own crib notes – octavo –
were each in neat separate piles, weighted down with paper
weights. When she had read through a page of examinee's
answers she placed it carefully face downwards on a separate pile.
After she had read completely the answers of any one candidate,
she ticked off his or her name on a printed list at her side. She
kept a silver box of cigarettes, a silver match box and a yellow
and blue Hausmalerei jug of coffee within reach. She put two
small green ticks against A. Rodham's remark that in the last
resort Manfred and Childe Harolde must be valued more for
their place in the great continental Byron legend than for their
intrinsic worth as literature; but against the same candidate's
statement that in *Prometheus Unbound* Shelley attacked through
God the cruelty of man's impotence before the Natural Order,
she wrote in a small, neat hand, 'Does not the key lie more in
S.'s own psychology, e.g. the father image?'

She was profoundly bored, not so much with the candidates'
answers, which usually corresponded to the authorities – any
divergence she attributed to imperfect understanding rather
than original thought – but with the subject itself. As a professor
of English Literature she had no doubt that the whole field lay
within her control – not, she regretted, the more exact field of
Anglo-Saxon studies which, to her disappointment, she had been
foolishly persuaded to leave off after her tripos – but modern
literature from Sir Thomas Wyatt, and, in particular, of course,
her special study: The Romantic Movement. Though she never
quite admitted it even to herself, she had ceased to respond to
any work of literature soon after she began her academical
career. She had got her First partly through devoted application,
partly through an emotional absorption in poetry which had
faded with her youth. Her doctorate thesis on 'Natural Images
in Lake Poetry' had been completed largely through application
alone. She had for many years re-read at intervals the major
works of English literature in order to come to them with a
fresh eye, but each year of such re-reading had brought less and
less fresh ideas to her, and, when her little library was not avail-
able during the evacuation of the first years of the War, she had

happily relinquished so unrewarding a labour, never to return to it. She read such new works of criticism as appeared and occasionally marked passages for inclusion in her lectures. Otherwise her reading was confined to journalistic works on politics or history that had a 'left' flavour. In her opinion there were two possible approaches to English literature: exact, almost numerical examination of verse structure and images, and the detailing of dates of birth, college entrances or changes of address of authors – this approach she preferred for students unless, as was very rare, they were 'particularly brilliant' – or a philosophical approach, which suggested the underlying meaning of literature by the impressionistic use of a good deal of Hegelian terminology and a lot of figures of speech. Books with this approach she called 'important'. Few 'important' works of criticism appeared nowadays, though she had been very hopeful about Wilson Knight, until she found some concrete statements in his work; these, she felt, were 'rather shallow'. Of her own published works, a critical edition of the text of *Lamia* followed the first approach; 'The Essential Sublimity' and 'Glittering Eye – An Analysis of Narrative Symbol in English poetry', the second. At sixty, she usually said that literature now came second to life with her.

This Sunday morning she felt particularly averse to Wordsworth, Coleridge, and the validity of Crabbe Robinson's witness. Her mind was upon the same freedoms and liberties which had exercised Byron and Shelley; but so deeply had her enthusiasm in life become divorced from her 'subject' that it was only under the conviction that the cause for which she was sitting on a platform was a life and death one that she would be willing to quote the revolutionary poets in defence of it, as seemed appropriate to one in her official position. It was in defence of Liberty and Freedom, as they were threatened to-day, that she sought relief from the dead weight of the past. To-day, above all days, was too exciting for work. She was going to bring together her beloved brother, Bernard, and her brilliant new friend, Louie Randall, and bring them together for a very important purpose.

She put away the neat files of papers, closed the desk and prepared to fill in the time by bustling about the flat. Though her emotions and her energies were wholly given to humane causes, she believed, like her brother, in a comfortable, unostentatious material existence. The grey hair above her long, bony face with its horn-rimmed glasses was well cared for; her black cloth coat and skirt and white blouse were good and not without 'chic'. She was little and competently made up.

She prepared the meal herself – a good sherry from Harrods, where they knew her so well, a lobster mayonnaise – she prided herself on the consistency of her mayonnaise – two bottles of a good Sylvaner and an omelette, on which the Kirsch would burn with that cool, blue flame she so delighted in. A tin of Romary Bath Olivers for herself, of course, and for Bernard, who was a child in his indulgences, little hot fluffy French rolls with plenty of butter. Grumbling about rationing, when all that was needed was a little imagination, made her particularly angry. She did not, of course, expect people to have lobster every day, but even on one's own what could be nicer than Brie, brown bread and a raw onion, or a simple risotto? Poor Isobel! She would have been disturbed to know how many of the stockbroker's and barrister's wives at Little Vardon also prided themselves on their mayonnaises and their risottos, and yet how little it prevented them from grumbling at rationing.

She did not care for her brother's works, the earlier satirical ones seeming hard and frivolous – she felt that they did not do justice to the depth and courage of his humanity – the later ones faintly imbued with quietism; not alas! the admirable bustling quietism of so many Quakers with whom she had worked, but an almost unreal religious quality, which she had to admit seemed more and more to colour his personality. She attributed it to the tragedy of Ella's selfish retreat from life.

Isobel was deeply distressed at her brother's tired, grey appearance, his shortness of breath after the upstairs climb to her flat. But she had learnt, when still in her 'teens, that he could not happily receive her solicitude. He kissed her on the cheek – the mating peck of two bright-eyed, slender cranes.

Shy of personal rebuff, shy of their diminishing contact in the political field, she characteristically found herself diving immediately off the deep end. 'You look tired,' she barked gruffly. 'The American attitude would make anyone lose sleep. Isn't it criminal, Bernard? What can we do about it?'

She was as certain at sixty as she had been at twenty, he at fifty-seven was once more as uncertain as at seventeen. They had come back full cycle, Bernard reflected wearily. Smiling affectionately, he said, 'Attitude to what, Isobel? And who's ''we''?'

'Attitude about almost everything. But I meant, of course, Spain,' Isobel barked. 'And we's you and me and any decent, intelligent person who can still think for himself in this country.'

Bernard saw, as though on a newsreel, Isobel and himself at meetings and demonstrations, on platforms, on reception committees and collaborating over pamphlets. They had never been so close together as in those 'Spanish years'. He stroked her arm.

'Naturally, I don't find it easy to take,' he said, 'but it's only a small part of the whole thing.'

'We've got to make a stand somewhere, Bernard, and for once the issue must be absolutely clear to anyone.' She clung so desperately to her brother. Save for her friendships with younger women lecturers, of whom Louie Randall was the latest, she had made almost no personal contacts in her life.

'I don't think making stands is quite so easy as you think, Isobel,' Bernard said. 'You'll think I'm against you, darling, but I'm not. In a sort of way I'm even pleased that you're still so sure of what you think. But I don't think it's as easy as all that. And not being easy, I don't think amateurs should meddle, especially writers and professional people. Oh! and again, I don't think exactly that. But, for the moment, at any rate, I've got to work on quite little things which are basic – myself, for example.'

Isobel felt tears in her eyes. She almost burst out in anger, but then she reflected how tired her brother looked, really ill. She almost regretted asking Louie, though of course the issue was too big to consider purely personal matters. She could hardly bear to recall Bernard's wonderful stand over Spain in the years before the War; even Ella had been splendid in those days. She asked fiercely, 'What does Ella think about it all?'

Bernard tried hard not to smile at the note of jealousy in her voice. 'Oh! I think she's trying to work out these problems in her own terms.'

Isobel sniffed audibly and began to pour out the sherry.

There was some minutes' silence. Bernard's sympathy for his sister was mixed with a certain impatience at her self-centredness. I live in a world of never-grow-ups, he reflected, no wonder we are no use in the spheres to which Isobel herself attaches such importance.

'If I'm looking tired,' he said, 'it's probably because the last three months have been very strenuous. But I do really feel that getting Vardon Hall is one of my few achievements, you know. Of course, there's to be three years' trial, but I think we shall weather it. You don't know, Isobel, how desperately it's needed if writing's to survive in this country. Not only somewhere quiet where the younger writers – God help them – can go to work, but somewhere comfortable and really well run. And then, although there's certainly to be no community-centre atmosphere, it will be a help to have some meeting ground that isn't overlaid with clique snobberies. Getting the backing was about the thing I've least liked doing in my life, but if I'm tired, I'm rather happy too, my dear.' *Rather* happy was about it, he thought, so much seemed to have happened since last week.

Isobel stood like a gawky schoolgirl, her cheeks scarlet, 'Oh Lord! What a selfish pig I've been,' she walked over and kissed her brother's forehead. 'I'm so very pleased, Bernard, it's been the only good news I've heard for years.'

Lunch with Louie Randall was rather strained. Both women determinedly talked commonplaces in a way that puzzled Bernard. It was true that Isobel was always having these crushes, but there seemed to be something more in his introduction to this little, bright woman than Isobel's desire for her brother to meet her new friend.

Louie was younger than most of Isobel's recent friends – about twenty-eight, Bernard judged. With her *garçon* hair, her *bon*

74

copain handshake, striped sailor shirt, black cloth skirt, and jade green crêpe de chine scarf, she looked like a Saint-Germain American girl of a few years earlier. She spoke clearly, if a little loudly, with a slight North-country accent. If what she said was totally unaffected, it was also curiously dull. It was not, surely, Bernard thought, to hear estimates of recent programmes at the Academy and Studio One cinemas that he had been asked to meet her. Not even to deplore with her the reactionary atmosphere of L.S.E., nor to agree that Harold Laski was probably turning in his grave. In her capacity as a social science lecturer, Bernard felt prepared to bow to her superior knowledge on such a point.

Louie was slightly puzzled as to how to talk to the old man. She had looked at his books without pleasure; they seemed to her to be soft where they were not just clever for the sake of being clever. Social democratic wobbling. She had expected Isobel to open the subject, but she was unreliable too. Of course, they were both very old. All the same he appeared from all that was said to have done excellent work; surely he must have some feelings left. Certainly his name would still be a great draw for bourgeois audiences, and the question of peace called for a wider platform. Confronted by a strong black coffee ground by Isobel's own mill, she felt that the moment had come to speak.

'We need your help, Mr Sands,' she said in a disarmingly straightforward manner. 'You must be feeling as desperately worried as the rest of us. This business of Spain is just an example of the way things are going – Nazi Germany, Fascist Italy, De Gaulle, the Japanese war lords, they'll all be back with us any time now. People everywhere are worried to death, but of course you won't see that in the great free Press and you certainly won't hear about it from our *Socialist* government.' She wondered slightly if she was addressing him too much as though he was a child, but he gave no sign of impatience, only listened with his head slightly bowed. 'Some of us who feel strongly enough about it are trying to organize a meeting or meetings, if possible, to canalize middle-class feeling. The workers have their voice in the Trade Unions,' Louie almost smiled as she said this, 'but the middle classes are just as worried and they have every reason; but they've no solidarity, no means of expression. Their whole ethos prevents it. They'll come if there are people big enough, respectable enough, if you like, who have the courage to give them the lead. Will you take the chair at our first meeting?'

Isobel contented herself with saying gruffly, 'I think you should, Bernard.'

Bernard raised his head wearily. 'I'm honoured that you should ask me,' he said, 'but, of course, I should want to know a little more about the background of your movement.'

Louie was ready with figures and names. The figures Bernard could not understand. Of the names, however, he felt more certain – one or two scientists, a well-known actress, a Professor of History, two journalists, a former general, some clergymen – some of them gave him a glow of affection, some a slight sense of distaste, none a feeling of respect. His first thought was: They ought to have done better than this. Pushing his coffee cup away, he said, 'I see.' Then he went on, 'I should like to have appeared with so many old friends, but I'm afraid it's impossible. It would be as though I were to help officiate at a Roman Catholic Mass. The others know so much to be true which I'm fairly certain isn't. I'm sure all the things they want are exactly what I want – peace, social justice, freedom to create, full use of material benefits in safe surroundings – but there the agreement ends. It sounds quite enough, I know, but it isn't.'

Louie smiled. 'You prefer to wait until the atom bombs drop,' she said, 'and they certainly will, you know, on this tight little right little aircraft carrier.'

'I prefer nothing,' said Bernard. 'I only *hope*, like the rest of us. Hope that good sense, or fear, or better still compassion will prevail.' He felt angry with himself for his embarrassment at speaking so morally.

'Well,' said Louie, 'I hope you'll feel satisfied when you see the results of your hoping. Or perhaps like other escapists you think you'll go with the first bang.' She tried to control her anger; 'I'm sorry if I'm getting heated,' she said, 'but surely you, who know what our civilization has achieved far better than I do, can't see the whole thing go up in smoke and just shrug your shoulders.'

'I should see it go down in grief and agony,' said Bernard, 'but I doubt – I wish I could be sure, God knows – but at any rate, I doubt whether things necessarily happen in so millenary a fashion.'

'Well, I'm grateful at least for knowing exactly where you stand,' said Louie.

Bernard reflected with amusement that he too was grateful for her revelation of where she stood. She held out her hand in *bon copain* manner, with an ironical smile. 'May I congratulate you on all you did in the *past?*' she said. Bernard disliked the histrionic gesture, but he took her small, cool hand and said with equal irony, 'You have my full permission to liquidate me on the great day.'

'Oh,' said Louie, 'that isn't needed. If it were necessary, I should do so without your permission.'

'And what would you be afterwards?'

'Exactly the same,' she answered, laughing, then she looked more serious. 'As a matter of fact, if I had to do such things – and actually I don't think there will be much bloodshed when the time comes, the ruling classes only need a push to cave in now – but *if* I had to, I should naturally do what was required, but I should not regard myself as fit to do anything more of value.'

Bernard was at once repelled by the psychopathic background of this remark and impressed by its individual note of unorthodoxy. He was about to cry facetiously, 'Heretic!' when he suddenly felt an attraction towards this young woman. Mustering every charm at his command, he said, 'I don't know whether you could bear anything so escapist, but I should be very pleased to see you at the opening of Vardon Hall next week.' He regretted the emotional impulse as soon as he had spoken, but the bliss on Isobel's face quietened his fears.

Louie was clearly very pleased. 'Oh, I'm not the great Red beast, you know, tearing culture to bits, as I raven my way across the world,' she said. 'I admire your work there very much. The whole scheme has great potentialities. Thank you, I should like to come. And if your hopes should be replaced by something a little more positive, we'd still like to have you on our platform.'

Bernard thought that the moment had come to make a stand. 'I'm afraid that's quite unlikely,' he said.

All the same, Isobel felt very pleased that the meeting had not ended in anger. 'We'll go down to Vardon together,' she said to Louie, as she went with her to the door.

Isobel had her moment of intimacy with Bernard, too, as he left. 'How is your young friend, Bernard?' she said rather solemnly.

'He's getting on very well, thank you, Isobel,' he replied.

Looking at Bernard's tired features, she said, 'Remember, dear, youth can be rather thoughtless. I know,' she squeezed his arm, 'that you would never hurt any young man, but you mustn't hurt yourself, either.' She smiled at once warmly and sophisticatedly.

It was back in 1944, Bernard reflected, not long after the beginning of his *affaire* with Terence, that, one evening when he was still in conflict with himself about his duty to Ella, he had confided in his sister. She had taken his feelings for his 'young friend' very seriously and calmly. If, he thought, she were to see Terence how surprised she would be, and if she knew that Eric was now his 'young friend' how shocked. In this Bernard was quite wrong. Her brother's revelation had touched an unorthodoxy in Isobel that she did not realize herself, and, more important still, it gave her a special, private link with him. She had been most definite in her advice that he should not tell Ella.

'Eric! Eric darling! Where have you put Aunt Helen's jug?' Celia Craddock's silvery voice had a faintly plaintive note, as she stepped down from the little conservatory, where she 'did' the flowers, into the living-room. 'Mr Sands! I had no idea you were here yet. Why didn't you tell me, Eric?' And she stood statuesquely with the crimson roses held against the white of her graceful neck.

Bernard saw that she wanted to be drunk in, and, as usual, felt inadequate to the task. 'What heavenly roses!' he said.

'Yes,' said Mrs Craddock, 'or rather they will be, when I've smashed their stems and put them into water.' Beauty, she always believed, was more allied to breeding when wedded to everyday good sense. She saw quite enough genteelness in Esher never to allow a note of false delicacy to mar her manner. She wouldn't, of course, have been in Esher at all but for 'the house', such a strange, wonderful, yet unpretentious old house to find in the neighbourhood. A colonial-style white building with a veranda and a long conservatory, it stood in a large rambling garden, full of sudden surprises – magnolias, camellias, peach trees, even some agapanthus lilies. Perhaps it was something of her childhood Virginia, of which she retained the prettiest little Southern drawl after thirty years' absence, which so endeared it to Mrs Craddock, and there certainly hung about it, so low lying was it, a perpetual hot, damp mist. Even in winter it seemed close, and in summer Mrs Craddock lay on a chaise longue on the veranda fanning herself, until after the glowworms were shedding their pale light.

'Eric,' said his mother, 'take the roses, darling, and put them into water. It's much too long since I saw Mr Sands and I'm going to make up for it now.' She sat down in a cane rocking chair, which formed part of the 'Colonial' furnishing of the large, french-windowed room. 'The only way to enjoy life nowadays – and it seems to me England's tragedy to-day that so many people refuse to enjoy it – is to be able to drop anything at any moment if something nicer comes along. When I hear all these poor dears around here complaining that they never have any fun, I'm afraid I feel very superior. I know it's difficult, and it's boring and we'd like to have the old days back; but with a little method and a pair of hands – and let me tell you, Mr Sands,' she looked slightly arch, 'a good deal stronger back than men care to think women have – the chores can be done *and* you can have a good deal of fun. The secret's quite simple, fit the chores in when there's nothing more interesting offering itself, and don't pretend that things like arranging flowers aren't chores when they are.'

It was on the tip of Bernard's tongue to suggest that she should record this speech as a pep talk for 'Woman's Hour', but he realized that she was shy of him and would be less loquacious and less affected as the afternoon passed. He was exceedingly anxious to break down the mistrust between them, but he despaired of being able to offer her that male admiration which alone would quiet her uneasiness.

'What you do,' he said with great difficulty, 'seems to me so simply and yet so perfectly done.' As with any speech that he made to please her, he felt that he should have added 'dear lady'.

'Thank you,' she said with equal quiet dignity, 'but quite enough of these boring household details, which we wretched women are always boasting of not mentioning and then gabbling about for hours!' She bent forward her graceful neck, and, from the oval madonna face with its braided dark hair, the large brown eyes looked up at him. 'Tell me about Vardon Hall. *That* has been noble work.' Once again Bernard felt that something had been left out, she should have said, 'my friend'.

While he told her the details of the scheme, she looked up at him with absorbed interest, occasionally marking points by smiling or nods of the head. She was extremely interested; as interested, Bernard reflected, as anyone he knew, and a good deal more capable of appreciating his aims than most. But it was impossible for her not to lend that interest an air of insincerity, to act the intelligent woman, enjoying the good talk she had too long been cut off from. She accompanied her interest with too much pantomime, putting her finger to her lips to silence Eric when he came into the room, and then holding his hand to form a group – mother and son in rapt attention. Her whole life seemed to have been constructed for play-acting. Her beauty had never stood alone – it was the medium for her various rôles; the young Virginian bride, the so-deeply-in-love wife of the young Army officer, the so-tragic-and-plucky young widow. A series of romantic parts that came from Victorian fiction. Yet, in justice, Bernard felt that her beauty went on too long demanding because it had been too suddenly deprived. So too with her intelligence; she tricked it out, flirted with it so much, because life had never given her any proper use for it. A swan out of water, were it not that her grace and poise showed to greater advantage exiled in Esher from her true element.

When he had finished his account of the Vardon Hall scheme, she looked up at Eric, 'We shan't forget *that* experience, shall we darling?'

It was Eric's reaction to such questions that gave Bernard faith in him, despite all the iron clamps that tied him to his mother. 'Bernie enjoyed telling every word of it,' he said, 'and in any case, you haven't heard it all three times before like I have, Mimi.'

Mrs Craddock leant back her head and laughed. 'Of course he enjoyed telling it, darling, we all love to talk about our successes.' Then she smiled at Bernard, 'I think youth should be oh-so-cynical and oh-so-romantic, don't you?'

Bernard felt too disgusted to answer. He picked up a book from a small table at his side. '*Folksviende*,' he said; 'I didn't know you read Norwegian, Mrs Craddock. The things your mother can do!'

'Oh, I don't really. That's the trouble. I have a smattering of about six languages and don't really know any. But I felt in my bones that Archer didn't do him justice and I wanted to make sure.'

'And?'

'And I was right. There's something so direct, something so concrete about this Ibsen,' she waved the volume, 'that isn't there in the self-conscious stuff we're given on the stage.'

Bernard felt suddenly that it was somehow discreditable in him to be taking Eric and not Mrs Craddock to *Ghosts* that night. But he immediately reflected on the absurdity of the thought – however much she had missed the boat, he didn't want Mrs Craddock's company and he did want Eric's. As though to back up such a hedonistic reflection, he remembered that it was after all because of Mrs Craddock's desire to have only a smattering

of *six* tongues with a background of gracious living that Eric's
education had been suspended before he acquired *one*.

'There's something you can tell me,' said Mrs Craddock.
'I've been re-reading the Elizabethans after many years – how
good it all is! – but am I right in thinking that Webster is really
rather overrated?'

'I don't quite know what rating you have in mind,' said
Bernard, his hostile thoughts making him pedantic.

Mrs Craddock was disappointed. She had wanted direct confirmation of the individual candour of her judgement. She was
desperate to win some admiration from Bernard, however, so
'One of my usual silly generalities. How good he is for me,' she
said, looking up at Eric. 'Now let's see if I can succeed for once
in putting my thoughts into words. Yes, I think what I mean is
that. . . .'

It was only when Alan's voice was heard in the hall half an
hour later that both Bernard and Celia Craddock realized that
they had had an absorbing conversation, yet, so deep was their
mistrust of one another, that they were pleased at the interruption.

Quietly and efficiently, but for all that with an exit, Celia
Craddock went out of the room to get the tea, leaving Eric to
introduce his brother to Bernard.

'Bernie's done the penance of coming all the way down to
Esher to meet you,' said Eric.

Alan's rather stern, handsome features clouded, his mouth set
firmly. 'Don't be a snob, Eric,' he said.

Bernard smiled. 'I had forgotten that you were the valuable
influence that kept Eric from confusing art with snobbery.'

Alan's smile, when it came, made him seem far younger than
twenty-eight, but, if it was charming, it was also superior. 'I've
welcomed you as a distant ally for a long time. Though I confess
I was pleasantly surprised when Eric began to show a little good
sense at last. I had got the impression that simple Labour politics
were very much out of fashion in the literary world.'

'I hope,' said Bernard, 'that my books don't reek as heavily
as all that of the literary world.'

'I'm afraid I've never read them,' replied Alan with a simplicity that he clearly saw no need to render disarming. 'I only just have time to keep up with current affairs. Education is a full-time business to-day. I suppose that's why we haven't time to care whether our politics are dowdy so long as they're efficient.'

'It's refreshing to hear someone speak of the Government's efficiency,' said Bernard.

'Most people don't care for efficiency,' replied Alan grimly. 'The modified Socialism that's being carried out to-day is the only possible course, if we're not to founder.' The note of the successful A.B.C.A. lecturer, the rising Inspector of Education, sounded louder in his voice. 'As a matter of fact, I doubt if a Tory government could act any differently as things stand, whatever they might wish.'

'Then why does it matter which you vote for?' asked Eric.

'The government commands organized labour,' said Alan sternly, 'and any policy that is to succeed must carry organized labour with it.'

'Don't you feel,' asked Bernard, who was getting somewhat distressed, 'that it would be healthier for organized labour if it were to be more associated in its own government?'

Alan raised his eyebrows. 'Perhaps I do feel it, but it's not a feeling I can afford to indulge in a critical stage of social reorganization like our own.'

Bernard considered the snub. If he could really have believed that Alan was withstanding a deeply felt belief in workers' control out of motives of political necessity, he might have felt ashamed of his own frivolous idealism. But he felt justifiably sceptical. He must plead Eric's cause as soon as possible, he decided, if this opportune alliance was not to break from internal stresses.

Mrs Craddock's return with the tea trolley was a happy chance. There was no doubt that what she had done quietly she had also done well – Gentleman's Relish sandwiches, Fuller's walnut cake, a good Dundee, and Ridgway's best Orange Pekoe.

Bernard, who loved his food, felt quite warm towards her as she sat so gracefully dispensing hospitality.

'I hear you're not happy about Eric's room in London,' he said.

'Not happy?' Mrs Craddock sounded incredulous. 'But no! I think it's a wonderful idea. It's high time he had somewhere on his own. It will give him a chance to expand and, what's really rather more important, it'll give me one too.' She put her hand on Eric's knee. 'I don't really think it's more important, darling,' she said, and then smiling a little to herself she added, 'or, perhaps, I do. Did you really misunderstand me so much, Eric darling, as to suppose I didn't think it was a wonderful idea? But of course! If it can be managed.'

'But you said last week that the whole thing was settled, Mimi,' cried Eric.

'And what one says is immutable, I suppose, darling.' She turned to Bernard. 'Oh dear! Oh dear! When is the child going to grow up?' she asked, all mock wonderment.

'I must say I don't see why it *shouldn't* be managed,' said Bernard.

'Well, quite frankly,' Alan answered for authority, 'the expense. I don't know whether you know what Eric's getting. But I very much doubt whether he can pay for a respectable room in London out of it, let alone continue to contribute the small sum towards Mother's expenses, which, as a matter of principle, I think he should.'

Bernard would have liked to say much about this matter of principle, but he was saved from so doing by Mrs Craddock.

'Alan, darling, don't sound pursed up just because money's being discussed.' Such false gentility appalled her. 'There's no need to pretend that we don't know that Mr Sands has offered to pay for Eric's room.'

'It's very generous of you, Mr Sands,' said Alan, 'but I must say that I should be sorry if Eric accepted. It's entirely up to him, of course, but he ought to realize that if he doesn't stand on his own feet at his age, he'll lose his self-respect.'

'What a funny idea!' said Eric. 'I'm much too conceited for

that. If Bernie likes to give me the money, I shall be glad to have it. But I certainly shan't feel under any obligation. If I felt like it, I should spend it all on those woolly koala bears for the mantelpiece that Bernie hates so much.'

Mrs Craddock clapped her hands with delight. 'Bravo! Eric, bravo!' she cried. 'You want to have your cake and eat it. No, you mustn't be angry with him, Alan, it's exactly what I should say in his position. And really, you know, if it's going to make life fuller for him, I can't see why he shouldn't accept.'

'Good,' said Bernard; 'I'm sure you'll all be glad. It'll make all the difference to his continued education.' He looked at Alan for approval.

Alan was pensive. After the way his mother had urged him to dissuade Eric, he had looked to her for more support. 'I appreciate that point,' he said, 'but unfortunately there is something more important even than the night classes. I'm very much concerned about Mother's being left alone here.'

'Oh! Alan, really!' cried Mrs Craddock. Alan looked bewildered at her change of front, but she was conducting her own campaign now. 'I shall be *glad* to be on my own. Look at all the reading I shall be able to do. Of course, there are hundreds of little reasons for which I shall miss Eric.'

Yes, thought Bernard, hundreds of little errands and interruptions to his work.

'The coal's going to be rather a strain,' she made a little grimace. 'Oh dear! that awful boiler! and I don't know that I can face the hens, despite all those wonderful eggs. But otherwise I can manage beautifully, and you'll be with me at week-ends, darling. We'll just have to have a slightly different timetable, that's all. Anyway, I shall be able to think of you meeting people, going to concerts and opera. No, dear, if only for that, we must try it out and see.'

Bernard realized now that it was not jealousy for Eric but jealousy of him, of his opportunities, that moved her. It was just like the visit to *Ghosts*. Well, I'm not going to pay for a room for her, he thought. Nevertheless, he felt sorry for her. If she wasn't stuck down in this place she could be a live, interesting woman instead of an ageing Sleeping Beauty. But then, if she sold the house now, she could take a small flat in London easily, and, if she'd done it some years ago, Eric could have been properly educated. But of course, he reflected savagely, she would have had to take her place with her equals or superiors, and that would have been far less 'interesting'.

He smiled at her with almost open malice as he said, 'I hope you aren't jealous of my fondness for Eric.'

Mrs Craddock smiled back. 'Oh no! Of course not, my dear friend.' She had used the words at last, he noted. 'You see, I think we're rather alike. In our different ways, we're both in love with youth.'

CHAPTER FIVE

Camp Fire Cameos

IF it had not been such an intolerably hot evening, Bernard would have suggested remaining in their seats in the interval. He could see no point in a meeting between Eric and Terence though he had never hidden his relationships from either of them. They would, he felt sure, dislike one another, and he dreaded a little his own acquiescence in their criticisms. They would both be so perfectly right, and they would both so perfectly miss the point.

'It means a traipse upstairs to the members' bar,' he said, 'if we want anything stronger than fruit juice.'

'But I don't,' said Eric; 'I'm just thirsty, that's all.'

'You go then and I'll wait here.'

All Eric's feminine vanity was affronted. 'I don't think that's very polite,' he said. Terence would be quick to note that toss of the golden curls! thought Bernard, but he was easily mollified when Eric added, 'Besides, Bernie, what's the good of coming here, if I can't be seen with you. We might just as well not have come on the first night. Distinguished Mr Sands and a handsome young friend. Mr Sands' young friend, interviewed in his dainty little room surrounded by his teddy bears (how you'll hate that bit, Bernie), said, "I'm quite a child reely. I shot him because 'e done what 'e oughtn't".' Nothing in his relationship with Eric gave Bernard more pleasure than his easy inclusion as an older man in such nonsense conversations. He could imagine Terence's criticism. 'Of course you like it, dear, it's just the sort of warm whimsy that you probably used in your own little North Oxford nursery.' But what clinched Bernard's affection for Eric was his manner of switching from the 'nonsense' to youthful seriousness. 'Bernie, am I wrong or is the Mrs Alving too concerned to suggest that she's a bit of a bitch. It's easy enough for us to think

that, but I shouldn't have thought Ibsen meant it, quite a lot of
other things, perhaps, but not a bitch.'

'No, you're quite right,' said Bernard. 'It's an infuriatingly
self-conscious, clever performance.' And he took Eric's elbow
with extra pleasure to guide him through the crowded refreshment room. But it also occurred to him that Celia Craddock
might well have asked 'Am I wrong?' and been, in fact, equally
right. Her elbow, of course, would have been less interesting
to him.

Before Bernard met the full force of a meeting with Terence,
he sustained the lighter blow of a chance encounter with Hubert
Rose.

'I definitely think not Ibsen again, don't you?' said Hubert.
'If the mummers are going to amuse us, let them do it with a
certain richness, a certain vulgarity, don't y'know? But all this
sort of Rationalist press Sunday-school stuff, all right for callow
youth and so on.'

'Mr Rose, Mr Craddock,' Bernard said.

'How d'y'do,' said Hubert, and turned his back on Eric. 'By
the way, Bernard, another little victory for you. All the dear
locals at your feet. I was at a little gathering last night and it was
"Sands' wonderful scheme this" and "The Vardon Hall Scheme,
my dear, that". *The Times*, y'know, and T. S. Eliot, it's all too
much for them. Can't you see it all on the dear old 8.15 and down
at the "Ginger Cat" over the scones. I did my best to say you were
the biggest Bolshie since Aneurin Bevan, but I hadn't an earthly.
They'll all be out in force at next week's bun fight,' Hubert
flicked some ash from his dress waistcoat – he dressed very
strictly as a protest against all this dreary slackness, don't
y'know. 'And so shall I,' he added. Even when smiling with
charming self-mockery, his red face looked patronizing. 'Till
then,' he said. As he left, he turned and shook Eric's hand rather
slowly. 'Delighted to have met you, Mr Craddock,' he said;
'do hope we shall meet again.'

Terence had seen them coming and quickly wedged himself
securely in the crowd that was battling for coffee and lemonade.
His companion, Sherman Winter, however, advanced eagerly

towards them. 'Bernard my dear, Heaven!' Sherman's speech had not changed for twenty-five years. 'And with such beauty, double Heaven! Don't be cagey, dear, introduce!' When Bernard said, 'This is Sherman Winter, Eric. Eric Craddock, Sherman. I only hope you hate each other like poison,' Sherman only laughed and said, 'Pleased to meet you, I'm sure,' in Cockney. To see him like this, thought Bernard, anyone would think he was just another routine, harmless old queen.

Sherman was, in fact, quite fifteen years younger than Bernard and, in the right light, looked little more than thirty. He had fallen into a conventional, caricatured pansy manner when he was quite young and, finding it convenient, had never bothered to get out of it. He had more to do with his energies than to use them up on external personality. The manner, too, fitted well with his neither striking nor unpleasant pink face, his receding fair hair and willowy shape, which all passed unnoticed in the world he frequented. People judged him to have the accepted hard surface and the accepted golden, if limitedly golden, heart of his type. This, too, was convenient.

'Terence,' he said, 'is battling at the bar. It suits him to the ground. Pure Barkers' sales. Bless his little Kensington heart. Bernard, my dear, you look tired.' And as Bernard was about to speak, 'Oh I know, bitching me! Tired equals old. You must make him rest, dear,' he said to Eric; 'you know, feet up and forty winks. Not that I should think you'd be much good at making people rest,' he stared Eric up and down; 'you look a proper little fidget to me.'

Eric, despite all he had heard from Bernard, was obviously being lulled into cosiness by Sherman's conventionally malicious chatter. Bernard awaited uneasily the three or four brutal thrusts with which Sherman usually followed such a softening-up process when he was 'among friends'.

'My dear! what a ghastly play. I vow never to see it again every time, but back I come. I think it must be Pastor Manders, I can never resist a clerical collar. Actually I came with a purpose. My spies told me to see Oswald, and as I'm looking out for a piece we're putting on next winter, I foolishly came. Don't let

us speak of his performance, but let us definitely register dis-
approval of that snug little velvet coat, so bad with a spreading
waist line. My spies, as you see, are as faulty as our own dear
Secret Service, but at least I can cut *my* Supplementary Estimates.'

'I found the performance very moving,' said Bernard, and
then added, 'I expect it reminded me of my own student days.'

Sherman once again looked Eric up and down. 'So that's
what it is,' he said; 'I thought there must be *some* reason for it.'
Then, moving his eye deliberately from Eric's crew-necked
sweater to his corduroy trousers, he added, 'I never knew you'd
been an *art* student, Bernard dear. But then you're so versatile.'

Bernard decided that it was best to take the remarks at their
nastiest level, so he replied, ' *You* get around a bit, you know.'

' *Comme ci, comme ça*, as old Marie Lloyd must have said. But
I'm not *married*. That's what's so wonderfully versatile. Don't
you think?' he asked Eric.

Terence, who had been unable to absent himself at the bar any
longer, leaned over Sherman's shoulder. 'Don't bitch,' he said,
'I've brought four orange squashes, so I hope no one wanted
coffee.'

'Terence Lambert, Eric Craddock,' said Bernard. Both
young men said, 'How do you do?' and Terence added, 'I hope
you're hating the play as much as we are.' Eric, looking at
Terence's carefully done black hair, perfectly cut dark suit, lilac
tie and lilac cloth waistcoat, was far more frightened than he had
thought he would be. It was also some comfort that he felt he
wanted to giggle.

'I like it all very much except Mrs Alving,' said Eric. He
suspected that a simple, little-boy voice would annoy Terence
more than anything else he could produce, and, despite all
Bernie's praises of Terence, he felt quite certain that he must be
the first to annoy if he was not to be annihilated.

Terence found the reply as irritating as Eric had expected, but
he was determined to be nice, for Bernard's sake, so he merely
said, 'Oh did you? She was the only one I could bear. The others
were so stark. But Bernard will have told you already that my
taste has long ago been ruined by the clever-clever. It's the price

one pays for being on the social make.' Even if this frank approach didn't disarm little Miss Mouse, he thought, it would win Bernard's approval.

'Oh, is that what it is?' said Sherman. 'What did you make yesterday, dear, St John's Wood? It must be awful hard on the poor feet, climbing as slow as that.'

'Not now I've got *you* to help me,' said Terence.

'Be careful of Sherman's brotherly hand,' said Bernard, 'it's one step up and two pushes down.'

Terence was annoyed that Bernard should follow Sherman into discussing his private problems in front of Eric. 'Well,' he said, 'you're not really God's answer to a prayer for guidance, seeing as what you've got both your hands so full of sweetness.' Only by ending up in stage Cockney did he prevent himself from losing his temper.

Eric, who had been silenced for a few minutes by Terence's obvious desire to be pleasant, now felt released to come to Bernard's defence. 'Bernie seems to me to have as many hands as one of those Indian gods when it comes to helping,' he said. He meant it quite sincerely, but he instinctively made it sound twice as sweet for Terence's benefit.

'Oh Lord!' exclaimed Sherman. '*You* keep your hard centre pretty thickly sugar-coated, don't you?'

It was fortunate that the curtain bell sounded. They could only just manage four conventional smiles as they returned to their seats.

When Eric came in with breakfast on a tray to Bernard's bedside the next morning, he started all over again.

'I'm sorry, Bernie, I still don't see why you should have said that Terence was a nice person. Anyone can see he's attractive, but he doesn't even pretend to be nice.'

'No,' said Bernard; 'I said he was intelligent and honest, and within his rather tough code, kind, but nice I never said, and would never claim. As a matter of fact, he was trying to be as nice as he knows how last night. It was the worst of circumstances for you to meet in, and you formed the worst impression of each other. But on the whole Terence tried to behave better than you did.'

Eric was about to protest, then he buried his face in his coffee cup. He looked up again and said, 'Yes, I know. I'm sorry. I was frightened.'

'H'm,' said Bernard doubtfully. 'You do make things difficult for yourself, you know. If you're not despising people at the bookshop because they're not grand enough, you despise the people who go in for being grand because you think they look down on you.'

'I'm hopeless with people, but I *do* think I'm getting better. All the same I sometimes wish I could just stay down with Mimi and not have to worry about it. I think I'd be happier.'

'Yes,' agreed Bernard, 'I think you probably would be. With only your teddy bears and the old nursery relics to form a nice, acquiescent audience. It would, however, be a pity, I suggest.'

Eric got up and began to tidy the room. 'I know that's what you say. And I agree really that you're quite right. But there's another side to it,' he said, pummelling the chair cushions. 'Really, Bernie, that Mrs Hodges gets paid to do nothing in this flat. You go on sermonizing so much about coping with life that sometimes I think you're too busy poking moral lessons out of things to notice what really happens. Take last night's little meeting, for instance; that's a bit of life, if you like, but I can't see it did anyone any good whatever. It just left a beastly taste of spite and malice.'

'Yes,' said Bernard; 'trust Sherman for that.'

'He was just more honestly spiteful than the rest of us, that's all,' answered Eric.

'I've heard that before,' said Bernard. 'He was more honestly spiteful because he felt more spite. The rest of us wanted to behave decently, but he always manages somehow to shame everyone into being as spiteful as himself, and if they're not, he twists it round so that they appear as if they were.'

'You seem awfully frightened of him, Bernie.'

'I am. I feel very ashamed of my failure to control him last night. He's become a kind of symbol lately, he and a number of other people, for a lot of things I'm frightened of in life, chiefly because I haven't sorted them out yet, I think. I wish I could find some rather less second-rate symbols, though. It makes me look so stupid being downed by people like that.'

'I hate to see it,' said Eric.

'Thank you,' said Bernard.

'I'm not sure whether you should thank me really. It is chiefly that I feel let down, being with someone important that doesn't do his stuff.'

'I see,' said Bernard rather grimly.

'Well, I don't think you do really, because I like you for lots of other reasons much more. Only that *is* important. Oh dear! I wish you didn't make me preach so much. I might just as well have made friends with one of those clergymen who make passes on trains.'

'They probably moralize a great deal less and have a great deal more fun,' said Bernard bitterly.

If Terence Lambert did not aim at being 'nice', neither did he aim at making his very small flat appear 'nice'. He attempted rather to suggest that, though he had no means, no appearance of material support whatever, he did know the type of furnishing, or rather had that sense for bang-up-to-the-minute taste which, at a more affluent rung of the ladder, would have gained him more than a mere pass. There was, too, about his assemblage of bits of Baroque and Renaissance and scraps of Victoriana – some cadged, some on loan from friends with antique shops – a certain hardness of arrangement which further emphasized to the observer the qualities of mental toughness and determination by which he would ascend. He had long learnt that nothing assists success like the appearance of being one who is cut out to get it. There was usually one object, too, which suggested a *démodé* scheme out of harmony with the rest. It allowed the visitor to remark that progress had been made. At the moment it was a mustard carpet, last of a mustard and white 'Regency' set-up. 'My dear, I *know*,' he would say. 'You can't think how I long

93

to get rid of it. But at the moment I simply can't afford to.' Perhaps most remarkable, however, was his ability to avoid the mistakes which so many of his 'friends' with similar ambitions made. Though like the others he was 'clever with his hands' and not averse to the hand work involved in painting or varnishing, he never allowed a note of home-madeness or arty-craftiness to get into the flat, as Eric would have done. There were no home-made lampshades, no bits of Portobello Road junk cleverly tricked out; the Renaissance and Baroque were probably fakes, but proper commercial fakes, not pastiches made from silver paper, buckram and any old iron. He never allowed sentiment in the form of photos, teddy bears or memories of Mediterranean holidays to creep in, as Eric again would have done. And he never attempted Constance Spry flower-pieces. He knew that regular fresh flowers were beyond his means, and he rejected the 'tattiness' of dead mullion and withered sycamore berries.

He earned, as yet, very little money, and that very precariously. It was essential, therefore, to spend it carefully. The greater part went on really good clothes. The smallest item, perhaps, was food. He ate out at other people's expense as much as possible, and was perfectly happy to live on bread and marmalade, or ends of cheese, for the rest of the time. He gave two cocktail parties for a limited number in the year. Although his whole life was apparently concerned with sensual tastes – *objets d'art*, food and drink, clothes, travel abroad, sunbathing, and sex – he would have been perfectly happy to renounce any of these except clothes and sunbathing. The others, however, were the necessary background which his ambition demanded for his person when suitably browned and clothed. Like any other ambitious person whose work might have seemed more intrinsically interesting, it was really the day-to-day manoeuvres which absorbed his whole interest, and since, unlike ambitious barristers, trade unionists, dons, civil servants, or even social hostesses, there was no division between Terence's private and public life, no conflicting sex or emotion; he was in many respects a most successfully integrated person.

He produced a pot of tea and four ginger nuts for Bernard from the rather squalid kitchenette-bathroom which only friends completely in on his background were allowed to see. He hesitated before wasting four ginger biscuits, since they were going on to Evelyn Ramage's for drinks, but, as it was very unlikely that Bernard would eat them, he decided that it was better than to risk a long lecture on the sordidness of a career which made no provision for food.

Bernard had hardly sat down before Terence said, 'Cut last night, duckie. You say nothing about Sherman, who is bloody, and I'll say nothing about Miss Mouse, whose tiny head, though I'm sure unbowed, is faintly bloody too.'

'No, no, fair's fair,' said Bernard. 'You can't shoot your little bit of poison and then say the war's over. Miss Mouse's head – and I don't think Miss Mouse is very good really – was very much bowed before the prospect of your assault, in fact shaking with terror.'

'I,' said Terence, 'was profiting by long years of your tuition and practising kindness and compassion. I do it now like morning exercises or those beautiful thoughts which prevent American women from ever growing old. That's what I was doing, so there was no need for little Quake-in-his-shoes to quake at all. And as for Miss Mouse, let's face it, Bernard, mousey's the word. Very nice for those who like a bit of homespun, or a nice bike ride out to see the Norman Church with Devonshire Tea thrown in on the way home, but mousey. All the same, when I say very nice I mean it, and I'm very glad for you, Bernard. You can't do without a growing mind to play sandcastles with, and you've got one. So let's have no more grumbling. I want all the details of the last stages of the Vardon Hall Campaign, especially the Oxford and Cambridge bits, I know the literary-theatre world end, but all that ruthless tweed-and-pipe career-pushing and Common Room camp is a closed book. So tell me all.' Terence lounged elegantly against the mantelpiece, while Bernard talked, but he listened with avidity, as he did to the recounting of any manoeuvres involving personalities, saying occasionally, 'That was a wily one,' or 'Grand danger de mort there, I should think.' When

Bernard came to an end, 'God! they do sound bores,' he re-marked, 'but it would be amusing to cope with, and I'm very glad you got your way.'

While Terence washed up, Bernard looked round the room, engaging in a favourite pastime of reconstructing in exact detail the scenes of the past. . . . He was gazing thoughtfully at a papier mâché screen, when Terence reappeared.

'Take a good look,' he said; 'it's all but the last day in the old home.' When Bernard turned round in surprise, he added, 'Yes, I'm moving up to Hill Street.'

Bernard could not speak for a moment, then he gulped out, 'Sherman's?'

'Yes,' answered Terence, 'it stinks, I know. I've thought about it every way, but I simply can't afford to be faddy, Bernard.'

'You never have been,' said Bernard, 'but you don't have to make for the nearest sewer. Is it money, Terence?'

'Thank you, no. I do as I do. But I've spivved along on my own steam as far as I can go. Oh! I know I've got the right con-tacts in a way and God knows! I go where I wouldn't have dreamed four years ago. *And* I can keep myself going with a book jacket here, the jewellery and shoes for the last scene in *Lakmé* and an article on how to make last year's swimsuit look like Ava Gardner's. By the way I wish your Elizabeth liked me better. It's such a nuisance, because she *could* be so useful, and I think she's rather a poppet, if she wasn't quite so bright. And then, of course, I can usually manage a tart's holiday at Cannes or Ischia. But I'm twenty-seven, Bernard, and I must get settled. I *know* I could do the décor in a big way far better than all the old make-do-and-mends that are at it now, but the right *people* don't know it. That's where Sherman comes in.'

'Sherman,' said Bernard, 'will get what he wants and do nothing at all.'

'Of course,' replied Terence, 'I know that. But he has the people I need to know at his house, and he can't very well stop me getting to know them. I'm very much by way of making my own terms, you know. Sherman's been pressing me to go there far longer than he likes to press. Term one, by the way, includes my seeing anyone and everyone I want, when I want.'

'Thank you,' said Bernard sourly.

'God, you are a bore when you get on your moral dignity like that. You profess friendship and then when you have to pay the slightest price for it – and it's only prices that wound your dignity that *are* prices to you – you don't care a damn how you throw it back in my face.'

'I'm sorry,' said Bernard, 'I just don't think anyone who stays long at Sherman's will be much worth knowing. I thought, at least, that you'd learnt that that sort of open ruthlessness and cruelty were not only disgusting, but also calculated to put people off.'

'I know,' answered Terence; 'I've learnt a lot from you and I'm very grateful. Five years ago I could have been made into a boring, heartless climber whom everyone ran a mile from. But, thanks to you, I *have* grasped that a certain fundamental decency to others is necessary if one's to get anywhere. Maybe I like it that way better anyhow – but I prefer to think of it in terms of utility.' Terence stubbed out his cigarette angrily. 'Oh God!' he said, 'now I'm doing the golden-hearted tart. The boredom of you, Bernard. As if I couldn't stand up to Sherman's second-rate little act of the Fairy Evil, if I haven't been sucked down into your sticky well of high-minded treacle.' He looked at his watch impatiently. 'Come on. We must go. Evelyn's got a new inferiority – people always being late for her parties.'

'I'm not going to let you get away with it,' said Bernard. He felt more and more like the Rector of Stiffkey. 'Will you dine with me?'

'Sorry,' answered Terence, 'as your dear Elizabeth would say, "No can do." You must do something about that girl, Bernard. I'm invited to Violet Blackett's and it's the first time she's condescended.'

As they went down the very steep stairs from Terence's converted Queen's Gate, fourth-floor flat, Bernard said, 'Please, Terence, don't refuse to listen. Meet me later.'

'Oh dear!' said Terence. 'All right, I'll ring you.'

'I shan't be in this evening,' said Bernard.

'Well, *I* don't know,' Terence grumbled. 'I'm not going to say I'll come round, because I may not feel like it, and I won't say come here, because I may not want that either. I know,' he laughed, 'I'll meet you at Leicester Square at about half-past eleven. You can save a couple of poor boys from fatal steps while you're waiting.'

Bernard refused to be daunted. 'Very well,' he said, 'I'll be opposite the Empire.'

'We used to look very nice then, didn't we, Charles?' said Evelyn Ramage, as she showed the old snapshots to a group of gilded young men – the less young being the more gilded.

'My dear Evelyn, you look if anything more beautiful now,' answered Charles Murley, and he bent his long distinguished body to kiss her lips. It was a very long bend, for Evelyn was a very tiny woman.

'Don't advertise the loss of your faculties, Charles,' said Evelyn, and she laughed with a hard, brutal sounding note that showed nervousness and pleasure. 'I look the wizened old woman I am.'

Charles raised his head in the air, the nostrils of his aquiline nose were dilating; he looked very like a camel. 'Nonsense sweetie,' he said in that strange, blurted, stuttering speech which marks so many an ageing ex-beau of the nineteen-twenties; 'you were and are divine.' Some of the gilded young men took it up. 'Pretty as a picture, dear,' 'Quite my most adored woman,' 'On from triumph to triumph, duckie, *and* you know it.' Charles looked away in disgust. He found it annoying enough that Evelyn should surround herself with *ephebi*, but that they should associate themselves with his long traditional love-making with her was intolerable. Evelyn, perhaps, was no longer the urchin who seemed to have been running in and out of the legs of his love life since he came down from Oxford in 1922, but the appeal of her little, painted clown's face with the ridiculous pencilled eyebrows and high cheekbones was still quite sufficient to make him feel a handsome young aesthete again – a decorative young man, but always a womanizer. The perfunctory, ill-concealed patronage of the compliments of these inadequate second-rate young men – privately he thought all homosexuals, except one or two very old friends, inadequate and second-rate, though civilized tolerance forbade him to say so – seemed as much an affront to his own famous reputation as a Don Juan as it was to Evelyn's unusual looks. That she seemed so infatuated with these ninnies as to see nothing disrespectful in their treatment of her was the worst feature. It suggested to him that like so many of his contemporaries – Harry Norton a drunkard, Alice Lowndes always running after bruisers, poor old Janie shut up in her flat with her dark glasses, and Tim Rourke hanging about public lavatories – she was slipping downhill. He alone, of course, had a proper stable career at the Treasury and he smiled to think how much he had once envied them their freedom. Nevertheless, even if he was himself in no danger of slipping, his memories and his last real affections lay with these friends, and Evelyn's decline seemed to signpost the lonely road ahead.

When Bernard and Terence appeared in the doorway, Charles turned aside to examine some new records of Evelyn's; Bernard's behaviour he felt as the worst blow of all. Terence, however, was soon in chattering conversation with two or three of his contemporaries, and Charles felt able to greet his old friend. 'Bernard,' he spluttered, 'so you got the money out of us after all.'

'An indecently small part of what I asked,' Bernard replied. 'I think perhaps of all the revolting bodies of Barnacle Tites to whom I've had to grovel this summer, the Treasury was the most degrading. Do you know a man called Crumplewheat or Cripple-witch or something? He seemed to regard any literary enterprise as a sort of polite fiction for a brothel. At first he looked down his nose as though I'd said a dirty word in church, and in the end he got very matey in a sort of "Do you know this one old man" kind of way, until I thought he was going to pull out dirty post-cards from the drawer of his office desk. It was all because I mentioned the word poetry.'

'Stephen Copperwheat,' laughed Charles, 'you do him a tremendous injustice. He knows a phenomenal amount about the Augustans, as a matter of fact.' One of the minority of civil servants outside the Foreign Service to have a brilliant 'civilized' private life, Charles loved nothing better than to interpret the two halves of his life to each other.

'Thank you for your subscription, by the way,' said Bernard. 'You'll come to the official opening next week?'

'I simply don't know whether I can get away, but I long to hear more details of the great new Pantisocracy, or should I say the new Little Gidding?' Their chances of further conversation, however, were prevented by Evelyn's bearing down upon them with Terence in tow.

'Bernard, my dear,' she said, 'you can't let him go and live at Sherman's. The poor lamb'll be marked for life. And,' she said, turning to Terence, 'not any the more happily because it'll be in unshowable places.' Evelyn always feared that her young men would not remain faithful, unless she showed herself fully conversant with the inner details of their private lives. It was a mistaken assumption.

'I'm doing my best, Evelyn,' said Bernard. He did not wish to pursue the topic in front of Charles. 'You know Terence Lambert, don't you, Charles?' he said.

Charles made an effort for Bernard's sake, so: 'Yes, how are you? I liked your cover for that West African book.'

Terence was flattered. Though he had started as the least of Evelyn's young men, whom many even of the homosexual set thought embarrassing to be seen with, he was by now in a position to establish himself as an accepted member of the group of Evelyn's older, normal friends. Most of the butterfly spivs of the world from which Terence was successfully graduating would have passed Charles Murley over as a dreary bore, but Terence had profited by his intimacy with Bernard to gauge exactly the value of these older friends of Evelyn's. He never, for example, bothered about Gordon Raikes, of whom most of his set stood in awe, impressed by a name they knew on the Third or *The Critics*, but he was keenly desirous of propitiating Charles, whom he knew to be an old stalwart and a dispenser of judgements which counted in the inner ring of the literary world, though his name was unknown beyond it.

'If it hadn't been such a ghastly book,' he said. That judgement at least must be safe, he thought.

'*I* liked it.' Charles' stutter was brusque.

Terence could not have known that the author, now long settled in Jamaica, had once been a regular customer both at the 'Basque' and at the 'Eiffel Tower'.

'Desmond's written this book about the West Indies, you know, Bernard,' said Charles.

'No,' said Bernard, 'I've been out of real life this last two months with all this nonsense. I must read it. One never thought Desmond would write, but if he did, one knew it would be good.' With Charles, both Evelyn and Bernard slipped back easily into old loyalties and old phraseology.

'Not popular, apparently, with the younger generation,' Charles said.

'Oh, but Terence, you'd have loved Desmond,' said Evelyn. 'I think he was the *funniest* man I ever knew.'

'What did he do?' said Terence who was rattled and ready to make *gaffes*.

Bernard joined Charles and Evelyn in laughter.

'Darling,' giggled Evelyn, 'Desmond lived – I know, Charles, but really when people go so far away, I mean they might as well be, you know – Desmond lived, as I was saying, long before people began *doing* all the time.'

Charles looked at his watch. 'Must fly, sweetie,' he said, kissing Evelyn in turn upon both cheeks. 'Bernard,' he added abruptly, 'could you dine with me late at the Club, say a quarter to nine?'

'Yes,' said Bernard, 'I can think of nothing I should like better, Charles.'

With the departure of Charles, Bernard's company was in demand by other of Evelyn's old friends. Though he had, in fact not entered this twenties circle until 1928 or so, when its peak was already passed, he and Ella had soon become intimates of

Charles, Evelyn, and a number of others, and with the diminution
of the circle he was now regarded as one of its earliest members.
It was, in fact, a circle which stood him in far better stead with
his younger friends than the dowdy remnants of the nineteen-
thirties progressive world of which he had been a far more
integral unit. Terence, in particular, had delighted in Bernard's
place in this 'amusing' group of people, whose intricate web of
personal values and esoteric morality were not only important
to him as code groups to the cypher of social success, but absorbing also as a complicated puzzle on which to employ his wit. He
had used his native plausibility and address to forward himself
with them with considerable success. It was, therefore, all the
more painful to him when Bernard, as to-day, after exchanging a
few intimate civilities – a mixture of such apparent incom-
patibilities was the accepted hallmark of conversation among the
twenties survivors – slipped away to join in the languorous but
staccato gossip of the golden spiv group. Like many of the things
which teased Terence in Bernard's behaviour, he attributed his
refusal to ignore the 'camp' end of the room to sentimentalism.
He supposed that since Bernard knew many of these 'beautiful'
young men to depend upon their wits and their social success to
maintain themselves, he thought himself obliged to lend them
his support as a brother homosexual. Having himself at last, after
great struggle, almost succeeded in leaving the golden spiv
world behind, Terence did not realize that it still possessed
great attractions for so comparative a newcomer as Bernard.
There was first, of course, the simple attraction of youth, no
matter how over-advertised or how tarnished. There was also a
special interest for Bernard in this particular homosexual border-
land between respectability and *loucherie* during his present preoccupation with the nature of evil. He found in these young
adventurers a state of moral anaemia which he never tired of
trying to diagnose. They were hard and calculating yet often
without enough energy to pursue their calculations. They made
among themselves small groups of intimates to provide each
other protection against the toughness of society which their
own climbing invited. Yet they were so constantly measuring

the degree of affection which they could dispense to these chosen intimates without risking the charge of hiding conventionally and therefore ludicrously warm hearts beneath their tarty exteriors, that their deepest intimacies were themselves only shells. They pursued their complicated ambitions largely from a laziness which forbade less energetic ones. If the extremely intricate web of attenuated, self-conscious personal relationships which made up their lives had been spun in any meaningful shape, it would have required a moral system, however Machiavellian, whose working out would have been far beyond either their mental powers or the persistence of their concentration. They spun the web, in fact, with elaborate, meaningless, day-to-day threads, which fascinated Bernard by their complete lack of moral shape and their continuous personal, and therefore moral, consequences. Above all, however, Bernard asserted his powers to bridge the gap between the two ends of Evelyn's salon out of affection for her. Completely though she assumed or often actually was in total ignorance of this gap, it grew yearly and with each year the 'queer', more *louche*, more cosmopolitan element drove out, like the tough tree rats whose grace disguises them as grey squirrels, the older, more effete, more established, more indigenous, fauna. If it lasted a few years longer, thought Bernard, Terence would be scuttling over the side with the rest of the old order; he himself would remain to make havoc with the destructive invaders. It was after all only a question of which kind of rat you preferred to be, he decided bitterly.

Terence had hoped that Bernard would have left before Sherman arrived to collect him, but his hopes were deceived. Sherman, it is true, put in his appearance at the last moment. He would never have gone to Evelyn's but in pursuit of Terence. If the has-beens, as he thought of the older group, had been theatrical he might have enjoyed a little corpse-baiting; as for the young men, in general, the stage world offered him sport enough; but, until Terence was under lock and key, he continued to make his way with considerable ill grace to Middleton Square, whose lovely Georgian architecture, Evelyn always hoped, disguised her sinking income. He thought with a certain relish of the retribution which these tedious journeys laid up for Terence.

'Darling,' he greeted Evelyn, 'the Call of the Wilds. Here you are, dear, on your lone prairee, with Kensal Rise or Highgate or somewhere nice and handy for a really deep burial. How you do round up the same little dogies, dear, too! But not, Bernard, as one might have thought from your last night's aspect, the *last* round-up.'

Terence separated himself from an important 'catch' to remove Sherman before harm was done – 'If you really *could* let me see those Firbank letters. On Tuesday? No, I should *adore* it.' He smiled good-bye and rushed across the room.

Evelyn was rather self-consciously engaging the company, while Sherman, his pink face unusually flushed, was gesticulating to Bernard. 'Really, my dear,' he was saying, 'fun's fun, and I like mine feelthy, but you can't really suppose I would have dished the dirt if I'd guessed.'

'You would and did,' said Bernard, smiling at Sherman's discomfiture.

'Now, now,' said Terence, 'tempers. Bernard, my dear, what have you been doing to Sherman to make him blush?'

'He asked Evelyn after Elizabeth,' said Bernard, 'and I was saying what a pleasant afternoon she'd had repeating to me all his little stories about you and me.' He felt delighted at presenting Terence with the story so opportunely: how wise he had been not to use it earlier that afternoon.

'Of course I had no idea who she was,' said Sherman.

'Do we have to have this beastly little melodrama?' asked Terence, his lips set in anger. 'I shall make excuses for you at Violet's, Sherman. Just for to-night I'd like a little air that isn't straight from the sewer. See you later to-night, Bernard.' He kissed Evelyn and left the room, pursued by an expostulating Sherman.

'You fuss too much about power, Bernard,' said Charles Murley, leaning forward on the slippery horse-hair armchair and reaching for his whisky. 'We've known Tim Murdoch and

Bobbie and old Bartlett for years, both of us. Bobbie's pretty poisonous, God knows, and Bartlett's a fool, but they aren't any different, just because they've got comfortable rooms at the House and at Trinity.' His speech after the relaxation of a good dinner was less stuttering, more like the drawl of his youth. 'The same, after all, is true of Copperwheat. I knew him when he came straight from Liverpool. I respect him as much now as then, and no more. They and their masters aren't quite the same as they were a hundred or so years ago.' He waved his cigar at the portraits of Palmerston, Grey, Durham, Melbourne. 'Like the rest of us, they see bogies in the night. Of course *those* chaps did in *their* youth with Bonaparte, but I never believe they really did in '48. In any case the bogies weren't quite so real.' He pointed at a bust of Haldane. 'That's the first one that saw them properly as we do. Good man, that. But they've had to be tougher since then, and that probably does make them a bit more frightened, a bit nastier, a bit more ready to pinch the secretary where it hurts. Yes, I'll grant a slight inclination to misuse power, and it disgusts me. But what you seem to get so excited about appears to me the simple and proper use of authority. Naturally they were cautious of a scheme like yours, they have to look after large sums of public money or college funds. If the idea looks like succeeding in a year's time, they'll see that it goes on succeeding, but they can't take risks. I really can't see why you should expect them to.'

'I suppose I'm naturally anarchic,' said Bernard with a certain satisfaction. 'I'm not particularly happy with those in authority, although I get on with them all right. And I don't think they like me, really. It gets worse rather than better as I grow older.'

Charles was about to remark on the penalties of second-rate aberrations in middle life, but he checked himself. 'You lecture them too much,' he said laughing. 'You've never stopped being a school teacher, Bernard, and you try to teach these people what they know perfectly well but prefer to forget.'

'It's a good thing somebody is honest with them who's in a position to be so.'

Charles felt himself getting angry. 'I rather dislike all that

cant about honesty,' he said. 'That's what I can't stand about
Gide. You people want the pleasures of authority without any of
its penalties.' He sat back in his chair for a moment. 'How's
Ella?' he asked. 'I'd like to run down and see her one day. Is
that a thing *she'd* like?'

'I'm sure she would,' answered Bernard. 'Some days, of
course, she's still very unwell. Intensely frightened and unhappy,
you know. But in the main she's hideously bored, I'm afraid.'

Charles smiled. 'It sounds like a simple diagnosis of life to-day.
Mine at any rate,' he said bitterly.

'With authority to exercise?' asked Bernard.

'Yes, even with authority,' said Charles. 'It might be all
right in America. But here we can't do anything. We can only
sit back on our dignity and our longer experience and say, "We
know better", "Well well, we know" or "We could an' if we
would". It's probably more comfortable really, because bloody
little can be done about most of it anyway. Of course, that's not
perfectly true,' he added. He did not care for defeatist talk,
especially before Bernard. 'A lot has been done. But our part's
inevitably rather small. I have my other interests, of course. Did
I tell you I'd started on my work on Seurat again? I went over to
Paris this spring. A dreadful little man called Langlois from
Nancy has got hold of those drawings they found and is making
a fearful mess of the attributions. It could be frightfully interesting, but one's kept so infernally busy, and, then again, once
you're in on what's happening, it's difficult to cut loose.'

So much, thought Bernard, for the famous private life that's
supposed to differentiate him from other public servants. He
felt intensely depressed. It came to him that Charles was about
to say that he had an incurable disease, but in fact he only said,
'Well, I must be getting home, Bernard. I've some damned
papers to look at.'

As they went down the steps of the club, Bernard realized,
with amusement, that he had been supplying a suitable, dramatic
and literary end for Charles. Charles Swann, that was it, of
course. The name had led him to the antechamber of the Guer-
mantes' house. It was much more likely from the way he felt now

that he himself was Charles Swann with death so imminent. Charles, he hoped, would not be as embarrassed at the news as Basin and Oriane. But who could tell? He would certainly think any mention of it very bad form.

The evening seemed cooler. Almost anywhere but Leicester Square would have reflected its summer beauty. Here the hot orange and yellow lights only seemed to extend the day unnaturally. Ranelagh, Vauxhall, Cremorne had all faded out in seedy raffishness, but even in their last, gimcrack, stucco peeling hours they could never have had the sheer ugliness, the flat barrenness of Leicester Square or the Place Pigalle.

Bernard, waiting upon Terence's usual late arrival, noticed automatically, through his thoughts, the passers-by, noted as by habit their costume, walk, speech and even strayed occasionally from his thoughts into short dramatizations of their lives. Tourists, theatregoers, and prostitutes offered little to stir his imagination. A young man with a mackintosh on his arm stood by one of the telephone booths and Bernard, wondering at his carrying a coat on such a day, registered the deadness of his wooden features. The conversation with Charles had disturbed him from composing the arguments he would use with Terence. He decided to put the future interview out of his head and trust to his intuition. He stared rather vacantly at the passers-by, stretching his neck every now and then to search for an approaching Terence. The young man with the mackintosh was looking at him, he knew, but he disregarded him.

'Got a light, please?' He turned to see a thin-faced young man with long dark hair. He offered his box, and as the young man lit his cigarette, he noticed that he was smiling in confident, sexy invitation. 'Lovely evening,' he said, but Bernard turned away. This, he thought, is the kind of second-rateness from which Charles's embittered acceptance of his official station in life has preserved him. He realized that, for Charles, Mrs Curry and her little world of evil, Sherman's malice, Celia Craddock's prison-house of discontent, Louie Randall's pathological politics would be without interest; Charles had accepted the world of real power with its wider implications good and bad, and such second-rate failures were beneath his notice. Bernard began to construct his own defence: by not accepting the world of my position, he asserted, I have kept my imagination free as Charles cannot, and it is perhaps from these little stagnant pools beneath Charles's notice that the mists and vapours arise, which circle around his head like the bogies in the night he spoke of, like Hitler, like . . .

Bernard was startled from the wider, historical applications of his essay in self-defence by a firmly enunciating, slightly Cockney voice, 'Excuse me, sir, I'm a police officer. We are charging this man with importuning. I have had occasion to notice that he approached you a few minutes ago. I should be glad to know if you wish to offer further evidence against him.' Bernard's eyes were riveted upon the face of the young man with the long dark hair. His underlip was trembling, his eyes – over-large with terror – were on the point of tears. His arms were held tightly by the speaker. Bernard looked up at him. It was the young man with the mackintosh.

'Certainly not,' he said; 'he only asked me for a match.'

Two figures hovered vaguely in the background – another detective, no doubt, and the man who was charging him. 'Very good, sir,' the detective's tone was angry. As they moved away, the young man's terror woke into struggle and protest. Bernard stood cold with horror.

'My dear, whatever was happening?' Terence came up as the arrested man was led off.

'They've arrested him for importuning,' said Bernard in a dead voice.

'Oh God! how absolutely stinking! Couldn't you do anything to stop it?' All Terence's guilt at his desire to leave his louche past behind was being resolved in his fury.

Bernard did not answer. Terence gave him a quick look. 'Oh, my dear, I'm so sorry,' he said. 'Taxi!' he called, 'Taxi!' As they rode in the taxi, he put his hand on Bernard's arm. 'A drink and bed, I think,' he said, and when Bernard still did not answer he went on, 'It's absolutely beastly, I know, but there's nothing one can do. And it's so frightening, frightening for oneself, I mean.' But it was neither compassion nor fear that had frozen Bernard. He could only remember the intense, the violent excitement that he had felt when he saw the hopeless terror in the young man's face, the tension with which he had watched for the disintegration of a once confident human being. He had been ready to join the hounds in the kill then. It was only when he had turned to the detective that his sadistic excitement had faded, leaving him with normal disgust. But what had brought him to his senses, he asked himself, and, to his horror, the only answer he could find was that in the detective's attitude of somewhat officious but routine duty there was no response to his own hunter's thrill. Truly, he thought, he was not at one with those who exercised proper authority. A humanist, it would seem, was more at home with the wielders of the knout and the rubber truncheon.

BOOK II

CHAPTER ONE
Confidence and Confidences

ELIZABETH said, 'We all know those little girlish *moues*, those restless flutterings of the hands and eager, distorting smiles that are intended to be so captivating. How unbecoming they are and how exhausting for one's escort! The tragedy of it is that it is all so unnecessary. Nothing can surpass the poise and elegance of the mature and experienced woman, so long as she is content to let the calm detachment that comes with middle years speak through every line and movement of her body. What beauty there is in such calm repose, and how restful for the poor, tired man!' She ended her dictation and, turning to the secretary, added, 'And that, dear, should be practised over the sink. It should be done preferably in black velvet off the shoulders and a train. They tell me they've had some startling results in Potter's Bar.' The secretary, who lived in Finchley, wondered if Elizabeth thought she was the only member of the editorial staff who apologized for her copy by making jokes about the suburbs. Since all the others did so, and all supposed their attitude unique, she imagined that Elizabeth had the same illusions. Alone the editress took up a believer's attitude; she had so long supported the famous legend that no matter how clever people might be, they could not write for *Woman's Diary* if they had their tongues in their cheeks that inevitably she had to advertise her own faith.

The secretary, who was taking a diploma in Psychology, said curiously, 'Don't you ever feel split in two by your work here?' Elizabeth was up to that. 'Riven from crown to toe,' she answered, 'but then Careers Women are, aren't they, from birth, I mean.'

The secretary answered the telephone. 'It's Mr Terence Lambert for you,' she said, covering the mouthpiece with her hand.

Elizabeth was too surprised to know what to say. Her dramatic instinct came to her rescue. She was, after all, on Mummy's side. Frowning slightly, she leaned forward and said in a rasping voice, 'Would you say that I'm too busy to speak to him.'

The secretary reported that Mr Lambert said it was rather urgent. '*Rather* urgent,' said Elizabeth angrily. She picked up the receiver. 'Hello,' she said.

'It's Terence Lambert speaking.'

'Yes, I know. What is it?'

Terence's tone was businesslike. 'Your father's been rather ill. No, no, he's all right now. Yes, a heart attack. He wants to go down to the country. The doctor says it's quite all right, but somebody ought to go with him.'

'I see,' said Elizabeth. 'I'll come round at once.'

'Good,' answered Terence. 'I'll wait here until you come.' He was, in fact, waiting by the lift-shaft when Elizabeth emerged at the top floor. He looked, as usual, carefully dressed, so carefully as to give almost the effect of having been poured into his suit by machinery; but behind his recent, elaborate facial preparation she noticed that he looked drawn and tired. The fact that he might have been a 'good thirty' somehow made her feel less hostile to him.

'There's nothing to worry about,' he said. 'I made an excuse to come outside because I thought you would want to hear what the doctor said when Bernard was not there. It's not that there's anything Bernard hasn't heard, but only that you might have thought so if I hadn't told you on my own.' The incoherence of his speech, the momentary absence of the customary 'camp' once again calmed Elizabeth's hostility. It was the dislike of seeing Terence at the flat more than Bernard's attack that had possessed her in the taxi. She now felt the guilt of so unorthodox a priority. 'Did it happen here?' she asked. It was difficult to frame any questions that would not suggest an unbecoming probe into her father's intimacies.

'Yes,' said Terence, 'he looked madly tired when I saw him yesterday afternoon, and then he got involved in a squalid "thing" last night which seems to have put him in a terrible way. More than it would have done I'm sure if he hadn't been so over-strained already.'

Elizabeth sought with her look to establish a more definite identity for the 'thing' which had put her father in such a 'way'.

'An arrest,' said Terence, and then added, 'Nothing to do with *him*, of course. But he saw it happen, and I suppose on top of everything else . . . ' His voice faded away in puzzledness. 'Anyhow,' he went on, 'Bernard made me ring for a Dr Silverman, he said he was the family doctor. You must be the *oddest* family. But then, I don't know about doctors. Anyhow, *he* says it's simply a tired heart. Not angina or anything to worry about. He's given Bernard some pills and he's to rest as much as possible. I'm sorry I couldn't get hold of you sooner, but it was madly late last night when it happened. And I did my best,' he ended lamely.

Elizabeth found herself liking him now for his note of childish-ness. She suddenly felt with shame that she had interfered with-out sufficient forethought in her earlier talk with Bernard. She withdrew sharply, however, from so irrelevant a sentiment. 'I'm sure we're all very grateful,' she said.

Terence's dark eyes seemed to squint for a moment with anger. 'The family's approval for getting the family doctor. Perhaps I could have it all in what's called black and white from the family solicitor,' he said.

Elizabeth hastened to repair her error. 'No, really. Thank you. It was a very kind thing,' she said.

Terence looked embarrassed by this more sincere approach, though he had clearly wanted it. 'We had better go back now,' he said.

Bernard seemed very frail and tired. He slept for the first quarter of an hour of the train journey. When he woke, his eyes were brighter. Elizabeth simply smiled across at him, anxious not to disturb his rest. This invalidish treatment clearly decided him to resume authority once more. 'What about getting luncheon on the train?' he suggested. 'I don't fancy the sort of meal that Ella will have ready when she's on her own.' He insisted on a bottle of wine, 'however poor', at luncheon. Elizabeth felt as though she was seventeen again, being taken out to one of those special *tête-à-têtes* at which Bernard was always the charming host, the witty companion and everything was horrible. The artificiality of his approach to his children had been extraordinary in someone so easy and natural with the rest of his acquaintances. With herself and James his overtures had seemed always to savour of the *Sorrel and Son* sort of behaviour which he would have been the first to ridicule in anyone else. She only prayed that he would not raise his glass to toast her as on those girlhood 'special' occasions. His conversation, however, though competent and slightly over-consciously easy, was not apparently designed to bring her out, but rather to keep himself in. He seemed only too happy, when the meal was ended, to spend the last quarter of an hour reading his book.

When Ella was alone she always had a pot of coffee and a boiled egg or some cold tinned meat on a tray for her luncheon. She sometimes believed that this 'scrappy' way of living only added to the neurotic pressure of her existence. Certainly, the effect of these days of hastily put on clothes, quickly eaten snacks, and briefest possible attention to toilet was to increase her claustrophobic hatred of the little round of her life. Although the house was quite large, she tended to confine herself to one room until, with its accumulation of newspapers and books and unremoved plates, it seemed like a furnished cell provided for the more illustrious type of political offender. But to have enlarged her sphere would have necessitated distracting action. She needed all her concentration to balance on the tightrope between fantasy and reality and to make the decision between which of them was more 'real' for her at any moment of the day. She now of purpose walked this tightrope between the two, and walked with physical symptoms of anxiety – tightened stomach, blurred vision, and a mist around her consciousness – that made any unaccustomed action as exhausting and fruitless as the damming of a stream before an oncoming tidal wave. To sit in one room, though it ended as a prison, seemed safer; to sit, and on occasion to find outlet in the mechanical activity of gardening, seemed indeed the only safe means of getting by until the next 'good period'.

At the moment, however, this routine was broken for her by the unexplained and unexpected prolongation of her brother's stay. She always made – and it was part of her bargain with her sick self that she should so make – an effort to adapt herself to unusual circumstances, unless they occurred in one of those periods when fog so separated her from reality that all contact with others became impossible. To her brother she conceded such conversation as she could produce through the mist that surrounded her, normal meals and the organization of an appearance of listening to him which would not insult his intelligence. Had not such palliatives failed before, she might have been tempted, from the little sparks of curiosity and affection which their contact lit in her, to think this 'taking out of herself' was in fact the road back to life which she sought. Bill was convinced that it was so; and he gave what time was left to him from racing, Rhodes, and the growing attractions of Mrs Curry's household to devising means of restoring his sister's confidence; for, living entirely in himself, he automatically diagnosed his sister's sickness as his own.

'People talk a lot about Keats,' he said as he served the jugged hare. He often began his discourses with such general statements, but Ella, who received all conversation at random, was less surprised by them than most people. 'But, even if he had lived, it would probably have been to peter out as a five-day wonder. Now the man *I* envy,' here came the prepared fillip to Ella's self-confidence, 'is William de Morgan. To achieve success suddenly at seventy, produce the rabbit out of the hat, surprise everybody and leave no time for them to see how the trick was done. Imagine his feelings when *Alice for Short* was published. . . . '

'*Alice for Short!*' echoed Ella. It seemed a curious remark and she thought it only polite to follow it up.

'Yes,' began Bill, 'a brilliant book. Far more brilliant really than the Thackeray he adored.' Remembering de Morgan's theme of a wife in Bedlam, however, he stopped short, and made a mental note not to mention *Jane Eyre* either. 'I suppose,' he said, 'that this is the last house left in England where they still serve a decent damson jelly with hare.' Flatter a woman on her housekeeping, that was the thing. 'Red currant jelly's all very well, but it's a Victorian innovation, you know. It came in with the entrées, or side dishes, as they called them. They always had two – the brown and the white. Now, of course, everyone thinks it's an old medieval receipt or some such nonsense. Most of what the common man supposes to be traditional English is nine-teenth-century, middle-class invention to make the filthy age they lived in a bit easier to swallow. . . . ' While Bill rambled on, Ella remembered their father prosing in the same manner at the rectory table. Bill had been the rebel of the family and inevitably had ended by assuming his father's mantle. It was the kind of situation, she reflected, that was the core of the old 'psychological' novels she had read as a girl.

'I can always get you turkey eggs when you want 'em,' she heard Bill say.

It was difficult to imagine when she *would* want them, so she only said, 'Oh? Bill, who do you know who keeps turkeys?'

'The Rahab of the village,' replied Bill, 'Mrs Curry.'

Ella had early emancipated herself from the God of the rectory, but she had replaced him by a personal deity compounded of various aesthetic and hygienic preferences and a general sexual coldness which she called Discrimination. It had been, in the twenties and thirties, the common deity shared by herself and Bernard; by its worship they hoped to keep their vision clear for a more sensitive experience of life; on its altar they had sacrificed the intimacy of their children. Mrs Curry's name and reputation had dimly penetrated Ella's neurotic absorption as the archetype of blasphemous Lack of Discrimination. 'Oh, Bill,' she said, 'you haven't got to know *that* woman. Why! she's perfectly foul!' Ella almost lived again as she used this final curse in the commination service of the religion she had shared with Bernard. Joynson Hicks, Patrick Mahon, Lord Baldwin, Jimmy Thomas, Aimée Macpherson, Roehm, Ciano, Kipling, W. J. Locke,

Unity Mitford, Al Jolson, all had been in their day 'perfectly foul'.

Bill was quick to defend his new association. 'You've got no sense of the country, Ella,' he said. 'The English countryside is still basically pagan. That was something poor old Father never understood – he thought – God bless him – that a rowing blue, an East End settlement and a spot of Paley brought up to date by Gore would save the farm labourer's soul. He hadn't the faintest conception of the forces he was up against. The English country-side is still a matriarchy and a very old matriarchy. It's still com-mitted to the worship of Dea Mater, Isis, Cybele, the fruitful Virgin, the Witch of Edmonton. Call her what you will, she remains the most powerful force that primitive man knows. Here in Little Vardon you've got her perfect symbol, and all you can say is "she's perfectly foul". Of course she is, so were the rites of Cybele and Isis and the messing around with goats and bits of wax, but she's *with* life's stream and not against it, and so I say thank God for her.' Bill's loose red face shook with excite-ment as he composed the chapter of his book on the Great Mother which in the last days had been ousting Rhodes from his head.

Ella paid no attention to what he said. Her normal self had never had any truck with irrationalism, even with D. H. Law-rence – although, of course, it was the decriers of Lawrence who were 'perfectly foul'. Her neurotic self had no need for generalized irrationalisms, on such a plane she believed in her 'own system'. 'If half of what they say is true,' she pronounced, 'she ought to be prosecuted.'

'And no doubt will be, as the Lancashire witches were, or the Kentish lady who produced rabbits for George III, or anyone else who's in touch with Life in this dead land. Only I rather fancy Mrs Curry's a bit too smart for them. She's a very wise old woman, you know. One or two of the little games she plays hit against some of the *tabus* of that great Christian classical up-bringing I've been burdened with. But the older I grow, you know, Ella, the less satisfied I am with the compound of Christ and Cicero which Father instilled into us.' It was improbable that Bill was in any way influenced by the tenets of his father's teaching, or indeed had been for thirty or forty years, but the theme was useful to his present discourse, and he excused the invention to himself by considering the family link it made with his sister. 'Tully, no doubt,' he went on, 'was an excellent gentleman and certainly a very desirable check on gentle Jesus. . . . '

Ella soon felt that she could decently abstract herself from the discourse. She had been reminded by Bill's references to her father of a long session with an analyst – that Bavarian, Dr Wengl, who made you draw pictures – in which they had got stuck at her father's deathbed. Dr Wengl had insisted on her visualizing the scene – the noises, her father's pallor, his incontinence – but they had got nowhere; all she could recall vividly was the intricate square of iron work at the bedhead. As Bill talked, she began to rearrange these iron tubes into fresh patterns. Every now and again Bill's phrases came to her as though through pads of cotton wool. He was aware by now of her abstraction, but in his total absorption with his new interest he allowed his thoughts to wander, clothing them as he went along in that historically allusive, pseudo-encyclopaedic language which he considered literary. He had indeed constructed a very penetrating analysis of Mrs Curry's *milieu* in these few days of growing intimacy, so that he had found even his deadened, ego-bound moral sense jabbed and torn by what he uncovered. But he had set out from the pub that afternoon to find the Wife of Bath and he usually ended where he had begun. Through the anaesthetizing filter of his stupefying mass of words he passed all that he had learnt, and felt the wounds of outraged conscience slowly numbing; healing no doubt. When a man had seen as much of the seamy side, you know, as Bill, it could hardly be expected that he was going to get upset at the diverse ways by which those curious beings, men and women, burned out their brief candles. So the phrases rolled out, passing here and there into Ella's iron designs – 'roguery, that is an admirable expression, an errand boy's cocked snook at all this highminded superior sort of Pecksniffery by which our rulers try to persuade

us that a lot of damned bad food is all for our own good';
'wonderful gift of cant – as old as Jonathan Wilde – throwing the
stinking, creeping-Jesus talk of the age back in its own throat';
'perfect subject for Joyce Cary'; 'healthy morality of *Moll
Flanders*'; 'minors, perhaps, but curious how the old sacrifice of
the virgin goes on, atoning for the burden of sin . . . '; 'look at
little St Hugh of Lincoln'; 'And who's to blame? Those fools
who think the dark gods can be kept down?'; 'lid of the Kettle';
'very few sins that aren't as old as time'; 'D. H. Lawrence,
though he could never break through the prison of D. H.
Lawrence, at least saw that, when he deified the loins'. Across
and through the complicated iron patterns which Ella was busily
rearranging, letters and words began to weave themselves –
Minors, Lincoln, loins and then again minors, minors.

'It's quite simple, Nicholas. You tried to make toffee in the
kitchen, when you were told not to, and you burned your arm.'
Sonia's voice was as cool and deliberate as the quick despatch
with which she wound the bandage round the little boy's arm.
'That, of course, was why we told you not to do it. You must
learn to obey.' She cut the ends of the bandage and tied them
dexterously. She turned to the French girl, who was still shaking
slightly from the sight of the accident. '*Et maintenant, Berthe,
vous pouvez passer chez Mlle Snagg lui payer les comptes. Nicholas
vous accompagnera. C'est la meilleure chose, oui, je crois que c'est la
meilleure chose.*' There were moments when talking in French to
Berthe almost broke Sonia's patience, but it was a discipline she
had set herself, and she was determined to keep it.

James was at home preparing a difficult brief; but no difficulty
under heaven could stand in the way of that moment he and
Sonia so valued, when they took a glass of very dry sherry before
luncheon. It was the one thing that they missed on those many
days when James was away in court. Starting with a few words
on general topics of politics, current books, or theatre, they
usually passed to some aspect of James's career, and then dealt
coolly and expertly with any worry or anxiety, that in another
household might have fretted or fussed its way through the

business of the whole day. It was Sonia's recipe and, like her excellent cuisine, James felt he could never repay her for its healthy effect after the muddle of his childhood.

'What had Hubert to say?' asked Sonia. She sat, as usual at this hour, on the arm of James's chair. The restraint needed to deal with Nicholas's accident unemotionally had tired her. She allowed herself the refreshment of running the side of her little finger down her husband's cheek.

'Oh! only Saturday's council meeting,' said James. 'He's very much against our using financial grounds to oppose the Bradley scheme. I quite agree with him. Labour'll only make use of it. Besides there are plenty of other grounds. He hated *Ghosts*. "Reminiscent of a Sunday-school treat", you know the usual Hubert stuff.'

'Yes,' answered Sonia, 'I know. He probably didn't see very much of it. He's always too busy thinking of what he's going to say. Your father will know if it's any good. Not that I should want to go.' She thought of the emotional excess which most people seemed to prefer in their conduct of life. 'I admire Ibsen's stagecraft, but I find it more and more difficult to sit through hours of life in the raw.'

'Yes,' said James, 'like those documentary films. We'll go to the new Anouilh, darling. It's period 1913, so we can have a real wallow. Not,' he added, 'that Ibsen doesn't hit the moral nail on the head every time. Far too often for Hubert's liking.'

'I don't think,' Sonia said, she spoke slowly, drawing little lines with the tip of her finger just above James's ear, 'that Hubert's brilliance has got enough stamina, do you, James? I was amused how quickly Lord Howlett dismissed that speech of his the other day. "I suppose, Mrs Sands",' Sonia turned down the corners of her mouth in imitation, ' "that that fellow Rose will tell us the point of it all in his continuation". You know how the old man speaks. As though he'd just heard that he'd only another week to live.' Sonia twisted a strand of her husband's hair round her finger. 'He liked *your* speech, darling.'

James did not answer this point, though his dark eyes flashed up at his wife for a second. 'Hubert's extraordinarily valuable,' he said with judicial fairness. 'He's the F. E. Smith type really. They've done wonderful things for the party, of course, men like that, but they're not the mainstay, and they *can* be a great embarrassment at elections or anything of that kind.'

'Yes,' Sonia replied. 'I shouldn't think really that was the sort of thing Central Office wanted in a near dormitory constituency. But so much depends . . . ' She and James were great Edenites.

'He saw Father at the theatre. He said he looked very ill.' James sipped his sherry. 'He had some young poet with him. Hubert was very quick to say that he imagined it was one of Vardon Hall's new tenants. Corduroys and sandals, he said.'

'Oh, yes,' said Sonia. She had her own ideas about Bernard's young friends, but it was not one of the anxieties that she intended to straighten out at sherry time.

'Perhaps,' said James hopefully, 'Father won't feel up to this awful opening ceremony. If the scheme has to go through, the more quietly it does so, the better.'

'Oh I don't agree, darling.' Sonia removed her caressing hand. 'It's most interesting how everybody's coming round to it, now that it's inevitable. And, of course, it *is* a very remarkable achievement of your father's. All sorts of people have congratulated me. I don't think it's a glory to be sneezed at, you know,' she gave the little giggle with which she always attempted to palliate any cynicism, 'even if it *is* reflected.'

James said nothing. It took him longer to work round to new points of view than his wife: after all she had not the same personal jealousy to contend with.

'I think I shall take Nicholas, at any rate,' mused Sonia. 'It'll please your father and it really is something Nicholas ought to be able to look back to.' Fearing, perhaps, that she was wounding James's pride, she added, '*We'll* have to work very hard, darling. It's so important on a public occasion like that to see that the right people meet the right people. And I will say for Bernard that he knows how to get hold of people that one wants to meet. I'm not terribly good at all that unfortunately, but *you* can make all the difference if you want to.'

'I shall do what I can, of course,' said James, 'if only for Mother's sake. She'll hate it so much.'

'I think it's *quite* silly for her to come,' said Sonia. 'She'll only make herself ill.' She spoke as though Ella would eat too many meringues.

James needed a little revenge for his wife's praise of Bernard, so he said, 'Well, that's not really in our hands, is it?'

'Lunch! darling,' cried Sonia, jumping to her feet. She preferred to reserve her opinion.

It was with the greatest impatience that she received Bill's telephone call half an hour later. He called, he said, to tell them that Bernard had come home ill, a heart attack, but no occasion for anxiety. James, of course, could not leave his brief, but Sonia decided to drive over. 'Somebody must see that the poor man isn't worried into a *real* heart attack by Elizabeth and Ella. You know how they fuss, James. Of course, it's nothing to do with the heart, really, just over-excitement about the ceremony.' She set off determined to see that Bernard had a nice rest and a wash so that he didn't get overheated before the party, and as for Ella, well, really it wouldn't do her any harm to be put to bed, she'd only over-eat herself if she *did* go.

Ella was clearly not at all ready to be put to bed. She had a bustle in her movements and a flush on her ravaged, sunburnt cheeks that would have suggested a dangerous elation in anyone else. In her, it merely seemed as though she had at last come to life, a zombie with its soul restored.

Bill had gone down to the village, after being rebuked by the two women for bringing Sonia on their heads. Sonia, left alone with her own sex, could only comment on the situation by drawing Elizabeth aside. She disliked her sister-in-law very little less than her mother-in-law, but she had to say something to someone. 'Do you think she ought to be rushing about like this? She looks as though she's working up for trouble,' she said. Sonia's references to Ella's illness always implied some directly purposeful misbehaviour.

Elizabeth, who was going back to London by the next train,

said, 'Leave the poor sweetie alone. She's as happy as a sandgirl, dear. It's years since she's been able to wash the nappies out like this.'

Sonia thought, with satisfaction, how old maids always used phrases like that. 'Bernard's the last person to be fussed over,' she decreed.

'Oh,' replied Elizabeth, 'Bernard isn't taking any *notice*. But he *likes* it. They both do. It's rather touching, and it's definitely, dear, where you and me make our little exit noiselessly from the left.'

Sonia sat down and wrote some names on a piece of paper.

When Ella came into the room, she smiled at her daughter-in-law. 'You shouldn't have interrupted your shopping, dear,' she said, looking at Sonia's list; 'Bernard's quite all right really. It was very kind of you though,' she added, smiling again.

'This,' said Sonia, ignoring her mother-in-law's foolishness, 'is a list of some of the people that I know to be coming on Thursday. I expect Father's worrying about it all.'

'Oh, I don't think so,' said Ella; 'he's reading a book about Sickert. We used to know him, you know. And I've given him a rug and a hot-water bottle. He doesn't want them really. But we're both such comfort-lovers. No, dear, *I'll* take your list up to him,' she added, intercepting Sonia at the door. 'He'll be very interested.' A few moments later, she called down the stairs, 'He's very pleased to have the list, dear, though he did know it all already.'

Sonia stood for a moment, fingering a spray of syringa in a vase on the hall table. Elizabeth looked up from the paper, and said, 'All already, dear, that's what she said.' Sonia turned and walked out of the door. She knew that she was never at her best off her home ground, especially if the opposing team consisted of other women, but she was determined not to lose her temper. She stood for a moment in the porch and watched a nuthatch – Ella's most boasted visitor – peck at the coconut shell hanging above the bird table on the lawn. Picking up a pebble from the drive, she threw it. The bird's alarmed flight, however, did not appease her mood. She remembered Nicholas's infuriating tears in front of Berthe. Anger at the selfishness and irresponsibility of her family welled up in her. She put her head round the front door and almost shouted at Elizabeth, 'If you stop Bernard from being at the opening, you'll ruin the rest of his life. I hope you realize that.' Then she turned away and walked rapidly down the drive, her trim little figure still shaking slightly despite her cool, determined carriage.

Elizabeth merely called up the stairs to her mother, 'She's gone, darling. Is there anything *I* can do before I leave?' Ella came and leaned over the banisters. There was a natural down-rightness in her mother's behaviour that reminded Elizabeth of her childhood days. It had, then, spelt an apparent insensitivity which added as much to the smoke screen of shyness that cut the children off from their parents as did Bernard's inept arti-ficiality. Elizabeth remembered this all too clearly, but never-theless it cheered her as a symptom of real recovery in her mother.

'Heavens, no,' said Ella, 'he's not ill, you know, just tired. Come down early on Thursday, dear, we're counting on you quite a lot.' She had taken charge of affairs on Bernard's arrival, partly because she wished to banish the well-meaning fussing of others, partly because it relieved her nagging conscience of its endless charges of neglect of her husband. She was, however, most anxious to return to her own life, not least because the suc-cessive effects of forced contact with Bill and forced concern over Bernard had driven into her a stronger, more total realiza-tion of the objective world than she had known for years. She could not but feel that this new vision would alter radically her approach to her inner problems, though she was too aware of past false starts and failures to be other than agnostic of what that change might prove to be.

Bernard sat in a deep armchair in his study, looking at the Sickert reproductions, and musing. He had left the rug over his knees where Ella had placed it, although the day was sultry. He did not wish to check her attentions. The hot-water bottle, how-ever, he had discarded. He was, for once, sufficiently confident of his wife's restoration to believe that she would view her ministrations comically enough to permit at least that excess to be ridiculed. Ella, indeed, immediately showed herself open to this degree of his confidence. Nothing could have been more like her old behaviour than her half-conscious continuance of the joke in picking up the hot-water bottle by its burning steel top and at once dropping it again with a loud, 'Blast!'

'I shall go and cope with that damned clematis Mrs Rankine gave us,' she said. 'The thing was almost certainly diseased when she sent it.'

'I'm not really surprised,' said Bernard, 'but is it worth saving?'

'Once the wretched thing's here, one's rather committed,' replied Ella.

'I see,' said Bernard; 'you don't feel like giving it a further push on its way to the rubbish heap?'

To his pleasure, his wife considered for a moment before she answered. She found such an idea difficult to fit into her daily existence of ordering and constructing.

'No,' she answered at last, 'I don't think so, Bernard. Gardening always seems to mean keeping things alive and getting them to grow. Perhaps I'm not ruthless enough.'

'With weeds?' he asked in his old Socratic quizzical manner.

'Well, only because they stop the right things from growing.'

'You're very sure about the right things,' he commented.

Ella laughed. 'Well, yes,' she answered, 'I suppose I am. But I don't follow *quite* blindly, you know. Some flowers are absolutely foul. Double begonias, for instance, or prize dahlias. Any of those fat, waxy things. But then I never have them in the garden.' She paused for a moment. 'Of course, it's quite true that I did all I could to keep that wretched euphorbia going,' she added, 'but I was really awfully pleased when it died.'

Bernard made a decision. 'Don't you ever get a kick when you forget to water those precious gentians of yours and *they* die?' he asked.

Ella looked surprised. 'I never *do* forget,' she said. 'It's far too difficult to get them to grow at all in this wretched garden.'

Bernard sighed. 'Yes,' he said, 'yours may not be the conventional approach, but it is, after all, the proper exercise of authority.' Behind his open book he shrank into his chair, as though determined to emphasize his remoteness from her.

CHAPTER TWO

Life-loving Ladies

CELIA CRADDOCK preserved most of her old evening dresses of brocade, of real lace or of the sort of velvet you don't see now. She seldom wore them, indeed she seldom had occasion to do so. On Eric's birthday, she put on the rose and silver brocade, because he had always loved it so as a child. If she suddenly felt that life was very good, a mood that came upon her quite genuinely but which she soon theatricalized out of reality, she would wear the grey-blue watered silk or the crimson velvet. Increasingly the dresses had become objects by which she could revive memories – memories that grew more sensitive, more nostalgic, more literary as time passed – dwell a little sadly on the lost hopes of the past, and end with a little hard core of bitterness about the present. She did not take them down from the hangers deliberately; but, going to her bedroom on some other errand, she would look at them, touch, stroke them and eventually would find herself seated on the floor, surrounded by the billowing pools of rich material. Eric, too often, on such occasions would find her in tears. 'Mimi darling, don't,' he would cry; and then, raising her lovely eyes so that the light would catch her tears and each would shine like a raindrop in sunshine, Mrs Craddock would smile and say, 'No, Eric, don't feel sad for me. They're happy tears, dear, the nicest kind, that lie very near to laughter.' Alan had always been too manly a child to concern himself with her clothes, nor would she have wished it otherwise. Like his father, he had that masculine blindness to what she wore, that made the occasional gruff compliment so strangely important to a woman when it came. But Eric had always been different – a funny little boy who knew everything she wore, shared her excitement over new dresses, touched and caressed the materials as she did. It had made them – sometimes she felt wrongly, but a lonely woman cannot always bear in mind these psychological dangers – such close companions when he was a child: two strange children, almost, in love with beauty. In these last years, it was true, Eric had begun to forget her dresses in a passionate interest in his own untidy clothes – an interest that somehow irritated her; it was, she felt, a little unmanly, but no doubt only a passing phase. Nevertheless it almost seemed that tears were needed before Eric's old love could be aroused.

On this hot June afternoon, the pretty rose-coloured bedroom, with its lovely pieces of old silver reflecting the sunlight here and there, seemed almost too enclosed, too stifling, for the recapture of the customary mood. Sweat mingled with Mrs Craddock's joyful tears, Eric's mood of gay solicitude was broken by the mopping movements of his handkerchief; it was as though they were really wearing the greasepaint for which the scene might well have called.

Nevertheless, 'the nicest kind, that lie very near to laughter,' she said as usual and jumping to her feet. 'Oh how *wonderful* it is to be alive, Eric,' she cried. 'Don't ever lose the power to feel that.' ·

Her son's histrionic imagination was soon awakened to her call. 'I shan't, Mimi, I shan't,' he said, measuring a flowered brocade dress against her; 'that *was* the dress, I *knew* it was,' he cried, 'the one you wore when you went to see Massine in *Tricorne* and I cried because I was too small to go with you, and you gave me the jade pig that had lost one eye.'

Mrs Craddock folded the dress and put it on the little white chair with the embroidered seat. 'Yes,' she said sadly, and then, 'but your happiness mustn't always look backwards, darling. Too many people are like that. They only believe in joy when it's over.'

'That's what Bernie says,' Eric remarked. 'But I don't think I could feel that. Perhaps it's an easy trap when you're old, but not when you're young. In any case,' he added, anxious to efface this impression, 'how could I live in the past when you and Bernie are so good to me all the time?'

Celia Craddock walked over to the window and stared out at

the garden. 'Bernard Sands is a very good man,' she said solemnly. 'It is generous and typical of him that he should tell you to find your happiness in the present. Only people, I think, who know what great unhappiness means are capable of that advice.' Eric made no comment; he began to put the dresses away in the walnut wardrobe. 'I hope your company will give him some of the compensation for life that it has given me,' Celia said.

'You speak as though I was going away from home for good,' Eric remarked.

Celia did not notice the interruption: 'And less, perhaps, darling,' she said, 'of the disappointments.'

'I don't suppose I shall grow wings just because I spend the week-nights in London,' Eric answered, 'and in any case I'm going there to be on my own, not to take up Bernie's very busy time.'

Mrs Craddock sat down at the dressing-table and began to polish her nails – she never used varnish. 'I think you're very wise, darling,' she said; 'it doesn't do, you know, to live other people's lives. One finds oneself suddenly left behind, and then it isn't always very easy.' She turned and looked at her son. 'I wonder how life will treat you,' she said. 'It isn't going to be very much more in my hands, so that I *can* just sit back and wonder. You *could* follow a road that would make you a rather important kind of person. Oh! I don't mean materially,' she added hastily; 'I'm afraid you're far too like me to be a "success". And you could . . . ' She broke off and stared into space. Eric said nothing.

When Mrs Craddock spoke again, it was in a lively, interested voice. 'I do wonder what sort of a wife Alan's going to bring home one of these days, don't you?' she asked. 'I shall probably make all the mistakes. Poor Gran! I shall never forget the first day Gerald took me to Cromwell Road. She tried so hard to like me, poor dear, and she was *so* careful to say the right thing. But she stared and stared at my skirts – they were just beginning to get *really* short you know, and I had a creation that I thought was everything that's lovely, a hideous thing all beads and fringing – and I knew from the look in her eyes that we'd never really make it work. An American, you know, she could never quite forgive it. Poor darling! She was an incurable snob; she'd never got over marrying into service circles. In the Croydon world of 1900, you know, that must have been the height of ambition. At any rate, Alan's wife, whoever she may be, won't be able to feel that I'm anything grand or imposing. No, no!' she laughed in gay diminuendo. 'I'm afraid it'll be moral snobbery I shall suffer from. Alan is sure to choose someone terribly good and serious – all child clinics and Peckham centres – who will disapprove terribly of my useless life. At any rate, he'll have a supporter at last. How anyone so serious and good and straight ever got born to me, I don't know. He ploughs *such* a lonely furrow. I'm afraid he'll never know how much I've admired his courage. Because, you know, darling,' she looked so deep and straight into Eric's eyes, 'it's the ploughers of lonely furrows who get there, who matter, and, yes!' she flung out her arm, 'who suffer less in the end. I do so hope, darling, that all you've got to give the world won't be frittered away in sidetracks and bypaths. The normal inevitably seems so boring to the young and talented, but it is unfortunately in the end so rewarding. But let what will be, be.'

Eric recognized that the housemaster's talk on the facts of life, which he had so long anticipated, had at last arrived. 'I think perhaps that one can only live as one is,' he said, and then added, 'at least that's what Bernie says.' Confronted at last with his mother's spoken disapproval, he could not resist the refuge in others that he had always sworn to avoid.

'Does he?' said Celia. 'He's right of course if one can be sure what people are. I wonder though if it's quite so easy to tell, especially with the young. Poor dear! how he must wish that it is so. Because, of course, if it's not, he's in for such a lot of terrible unhappiness. Youth can be very cruel, especially to those who've asked more of it than it can give.'

Eric felt curiously elated by the sense of power which her analysis gave him, especially as he normally feared, with some reason, that it was he who would be left on the shelf. 'I don't

think Mimi,' he said, 'that I would wilfully hurt anybody.'
Curiously, the operas, the concerts, the opportunities for study
and reading that London usually spelt for him had receded,
leaving only a prospect of emotional recrimination and guilt,
that was half alluring in its drama and half disgusting in its anticipated exhaustion.

Celia walked over and kissed his forehead. 'No, darling, I
don't think you would,' she said. 'If I seem to have thought so,
it's only because a side of me – a quite selfish side – will miss you
terribly. When one gets older, it's not very easy to keep one's
standards up, if there isn't anybody about who matters enough to
do it for.' Mrs Craddock's face twitched slightly as she said this.
A horrible vision of the reality of what the words might
mean pierced the drama with which she had surrounded
herself.

'I shall always be here at week-ends,' cried Eric, 'and in the
week, too, of course, if you want me particularly.'

The surrender made his mother feel guilty. Was it, perhaps,
only an audience for the tears near to laughter that she was
demanding? 'No, darling,' she said, 'it's all settled. I wouldn't
have you give it up now for worlds. You need the opportunity
it offers you – to see more of what's worth seeing, to meet
people, and,' she smiled kindly, 'to have less excuse for neg-
lecting your studies.'

Eric received the statement literally. 'Oh! I wouldn't give the
idea up,' he said; 'it's too important to me. There's so much
that we'll both be able to get on with on our own, so much,' he
added, putting his arm round her waist, 'that we'll have to
discuss on those week-ends you refuse to believe in.'

Mrs Craddock never made rough, abrupt movements, but
her waist seemed to shrink away from her son's arm and her
voice when she spoke was dead and flat. 'May be,' she said,
'may be. We shall see. Shall we go out into the garden? This
vie de boudoir is a trifle stifling.'

They passed the magnolia tree, around whose base lay the last
fallen petals, brown and cracked with the sun's heat. Poor brown
dried-up little Missie Magnolia! Where now is the tender young

girl in her muslin ball-frock listening so shyly on the verandah to the distant spirituals of the happy, adoring coloured folk?

The dear mulberry tree, so old, no one could say how old, seemed unlikely to bear fruit this year. One can fight and fight to keep a tradition, a way of living going, and then, suddenly, why, one asks oneself; what for?

And the Judas tree? Why! Mrs Craddock could hardly forbear to cry out, 'Look, Eric, look! The Judas tree!'

Eric was unable to support the constrained silence any longer. 'Come and look at the Bolshies,' he cried. It was his mother's own time-honoured name for the Muscovy ducks. They had chosen the poultry so carefully together; as Mrs Craddock said, 'If I am going to rear creatures for profit, at least I insist that they shall be decorative.' And there they were, on the other side of the two beech trees, so decorative in their subtle colours and strange shapes that Eric could never see them without feeling gay – the flat, waddling Muscovy ducks in their white and green-black plumage, with their scarlet wattled beaks, the black glistening feathers of the Minorcas, shining with red, green, and gold lights all at once, the shimmering speckled Plymouth Rocks and, above all, the absurd Silkies, white or grey-buff, with their frilly Victorian drawers and their fringes of soft, soap-suddy feathers.

Mrs Craddock threw them a handful of scraps from the box that hung on a nail at the side of the fowl house door. She watched the frothy scurrying of feathers, the craning necks, the gobbling beaks; she watched, too, the delighted twists of her son's willowy figure. 'I can't have it done here,' she cried. 'Dodd will have to take them to his own yard. I can't have such a disgusting, messy business done here.'

'Mimi!' cried Eric in horror, 'whatever do you mean?'

'Well, you can't suppose, darling, that I can look after them when you're away.'

'But Dodd will look after them. He's coming twice a day on purpose. I've arranged to pay him specially.'

Mrs Craddock smiled wearily. 'I'm sorry, dear,' she said, 'but looking after the house will be just as much as I can manage.

I can't have the extra responsibility of worrying whether Dodd's doing this or that for the fowls.'

'But there won't *be* any responsibility, Dodd has always fed them in the morning. It's only a question of his coming in the evening too.'

Mrs Craddock put her arm round her son's waist, but it was now his turn to break away. 'Oh dear! oh dear,' she said, 'you don't like paying life's price, do you? But I'm afraid you'll find that there won't always be an adoring mother to take the edge off the blows. It's just one of the prices of growing up,' she laughed on a loud, hard note. 'You go to Bernard Sands and London, the Bolshies go to their heavenly home. Shall we call it all the massacre of innocence?'

Hubert Rose had to meet all sorts of people in the pursuit of his career. If it could not be said that they ever liked him, they always went from his company satisfied that they had acquitted themselves well with so clever, so rising a man. Only, perhaps, those who were so securely entrenched in their position that they did not conceive of any mischief being done them could afford to regard his cleverness and assurance with complete distaste. Other men, even though it might be they who were conferring favours or bestowing benefits, felt faintly grateful to him for allowing them to escape with their self-esteem comparatively undiminished. Hubert was always affable, yet always showed that he had sharp claws; his affability appeared so much greater when he did his associates the favour of keeping the claws sheathed. Though he could not entirely conceal his contempt for them, he made great play with his goodfellowship in not revealing it more. On the rare occasions when he flayed his victims, he did so in public as a general warning against mutiny.

It was all the more surprising, then, when he turned on the junior partner of the principal contractors in Roddingham, the large South Midland industrial town to which Hubert's affairs often took him. There could not have been less feeling of insubordination in the air. They had discussed during the morning a neat plan for flooding a small competitor, who had seemed recalcitrant about selling his business, with orders beyond the power of his commission. It had been a scheme close to everyone's heart, and they had adjourned to the Metropole for drinks in a haze of *bonhomie*.

'If things go on as they are,' said the senior partner, 'we ought to be in power by the spring. What do you feel about it, Rose? You always know what's afoot.'

Hubert took the compliment as his right. 'Oh, my dear fellow,' he said, putting a thumb into the pocket of his canary waistcoat, 'I say what the Gallup Poll says, you know. What's the use of all these marvellous scientific systems, if we aren't going to believe 'em. All the same, I wouldn't be too optimistic. The great voice of the people can make itself heard in such damned silly ways.' He implied a slight rebuke of the speaker's facile optimism, yet somehow bestowed an encouraging pat for his loyalty in maintaining it.

'Do you think you'll put up yourself?' asked the borough surveyor.

'Simply can't say, you know. Everything's a bit in the melting pot. Wouldn't mind having a bash, if the election wasn't such an infernal bore.'

'Question of a good agent, isn't it?' asked the senior partner.

'Oh, we've got a first-rate man,' said Hubert. 'No, I simply meant all the answering of a lot of idiotic questions that have nothing to do with the issues at stake.'

The junior partner, who always supplied the note of good-natured chaff, said, 'Oh, I don't know, think of all the fun you'll have kissing the kiddies. That's the thing to win the working woman's heart.'

It could not have been solely the somewhat antiquated conception of electioneering implied by the joke that annoyed Hubert so much.

'Have you ever spoken to a working woman?' he asked.

The junior partner was understood to say that he had certainly intended no disrespect to a courageous body of women, immense sense of responsibility, greatest check on their menfolk in times of industrial unrest.

'Most of that,' said Hubert, 'is cant. But whether it is or not, that sort of joke is peculiarly ill-judged at a moment when national unity is, to put it very mildly, a life-and-death matter.' He replaced his glass on the bar counter. 'Joe Chamberlain,' he said, 'did the Conservative Party a very doubtful service when he saddled us with the experience and integrity of the great English trading community.'

Of course, it was all dissipated in good-natured chaff and sound good sense, but as Hubert passed through the swing doors of the Metropole after luncheon he left his colleagues with an impression that he had relinquished them to a suitable background in the second-rate opulence of that vulgar hotel.

As he walked through the tram-ridden streets under the shadow of the great edifices of Bankers' Georgian, he seemed like a gentleman-farmer in for market day, in his tweeds, his brown shoes decently darkened with use, his canary waistcoat. Only perhaps the slightly excessive length of his hair above the ears might have suggested artistic interests – a collection of Lowestoft, perhaps, or some interest in the harpsichord. No destination could have seemed more appropriate to him than 'The Lamb', so solid and quiet in its alleyway retreat, an ordinary-panelled old inn, with no ostentation of beams or warming pans, but still serving a good Cheshire or Stilton, and still delighting visitors with its knowing old cockatoo that filled the narrow hallway with chuckles and guffaws.

Mrs Curry was waiting for him in the lounge. Even the huge chintz-covered armchair seemed inadequate to contain her billowing body, yet she was by no means voluminously dressed. She, too, was on business in Roddingham. Ron had driven her over in her old-fashioned Daimler, and when she motored, Mrs Curry liked to dress for motoring. She wore, in fact, a neutral-toned tussore dust-coat over her grey linen dress, and her natural yellow straw hat had a great deal of mauve muslin veiling. Her only ornament was a small opal cross on her ample bosom. It was a costume, perhaps, more appropriate for preserving an antique tradition of motoring than for serviceable use in a closed car.

She made it clear from the start that graciousness was to be the mark of her relations with Hubert Rose by the gesture of her little dimpled hand that waved him to an armchair beside her.

'Such near neighbours,' she cooed, 'and we always seem to meet so far from home. I've got such good news for you, Mr Rose. Dear Mr Potter's had a long talk with little Elsie's mummy and she's taken such a sweet, sensible view of our little treat for the child.'

Hubert laughed. He had, from the start of his relations with Mrs Curry, decided to take her words at their lower level. 'That's all right, then,' he said.

'Yes,' said Mrs Curry, her blue eyes gleaming through their liquid veil, 'dear little Elsie Black. She's such a little parcel of love, and quite a simple little soul, too. She was playing on her swing when I saw her the other day, and she seemed more like ten than fifteen in her little peach-coloured party frock. Anyone who wins *her* love has got such a lot to make up to her for not having a real daddy. You should have heard her the other day, "I had a lot of daddies in the war," she told me. "A G.I. daddy and a Norsky daddy and a Polsky daddy. But they all went away." Poor little thing, she's quite simple. Oh it *will* want a lot of making up for.'

'We've already agreed on all that, I think,' said Hubert.

Ron, who had been sitting stiff and unnoticed upon the sofa since Hubert's arrival, crossed his legs and said, 'There's a lot of work goes to this kind of thing, you know.'

Mrs Curry considered for a second. She would have enjoyed discomfiting Hubert with Ron's presence, but she conceded the priority to keeping Ron in his place.

'I shan't want the car until five, Ron,' she said; 'you'd better go to the cinema.'

The dark skin of Ron's temple flushed with red. 'I'm not sure I don't . . . ' he began, and then hesitated as he caught Mrs Curry's eye.

'Not sure you don't what, Ron?' she cooed. 'Hurry up, dear, you'll be late for the film. I expect it'll be all passion and kisses. Not like the kisses of a kiddie, all the same, are they, Mr Rose?'

Hubert realized only too clearly his inability to deal with Mrs Curry's use of this phrase as sharply as he had with the junior partner's. He had coped with Mrs Currys, Mr Potters, and Rons before in his frenzied search to regain those wondrous secret childhood games beside which all the pleasures of the adult world were dust and ashes in his mouth. He had learned to sit tight and watch every movement of these obscene creatures as they nosed a way for him through the underworld maze that led to the dark oblivion he sought. Rigid with watchful fear, spattered with foul, degrading innuendo, he must seek his return to innocence, be faithful to his childhood tryst – his sister's remembrance of it, perhaps, confined to a yearly Christmas card – an art reproduction of Greco or Goya – from the Embassy in Madrid. Hubert was much given to such self-pity. He understood his needs so well, and felt so deeply that they should be satisfied.

'I expect it was quite a surprise to you, Mr Rose, to find that the lady you wrote to in Brighton was such a near neighbour after all,' said Mrs Curry. She carried against the heat a jade green parasol with a parrot head top, and, as she talked, she demurely traced little patterns upon the scarlet Turkey carpet with the ferrule.

'I rather think,' replied Hubert – he made perhaps too nonchalant a play with his amber cigarette holder – 'that we're both a bit too old to be surprised.'

'Oh no!' said Mrs Curry, her great eyes all harmony and peace. 'I love surprise. Every minute of life has some new surprise – the blue skies when you wake in the morning, the first aconites, the birds making love outside my window, a little child laughing – they're all things we've seen a hundred times, but every time they're a surprise. It's what makes me love life so. All the funny little things. I always say to Ron, when we go to the cinema, "I'll have a nice little snooze, dear, and you can wake me up for the Silly Symphony". All the pretty little tiny things in those cartoons, the naughty little bunnies in their frillies getting smacked where Nature intended, or dear old Pluto catching his nose in the chamber pot.'

'And what,' asked Hubert, 'about the dear little spiders eating their flies and the sweet little mice running over the food?' His mouth twisted slightly with disgust.

Mrs Curry laughed with delight. 'Oh dear,' she cried, 'all you men are the same – you only love the big things in life, big ideas, big ambitions. Mr Pendlebury's just like you, he sees the world on *such* a big scale. But I'm afraid he's a wee bit bitter all the same, things haven't quite turned out as big as he hoped. I said to him only yesterday, "You have such large views, Mr Pendlebury, but I wonder if you haven't missed a little of life, because you haven't seen the importance of the tiny things around you". I'm not a clever woman at all, but I've always noticed little things – people's little ways, you know, and their funny little fads – and life has been very kind to me really.'

'Pendlebury?' said Hubert, glad to cast off from the dangerous shoals of Mrs Curry's penchant for life's *minutiae*. 'You mean Bernard Sands' brother-in-law? I heard he was in Vardon.'

'Do you know him?' asked Mrs Curry.

'I've met him casually once, I think, but I don't *know* him.'

'Oh he's *such* a clever man,' said Mrs Curry, 'he comes to see me a lot. I think he finds it a wee bit gloomy at the Broad House, with his sister being so poorly. I'm only so glad that he finds my little cottage a happy refuge. There's no clever talk, I'm afraid, but we're always cheerful. Poor Mrs Sands, it's very sad. She cuts herself off from life's joys so dreadfully. I'm afraid Mr Sands must be very lonely, although he's so famous.'

Hubert smiled. 'Oh, I think life has its compensations for him,' he said.

Mrs Curry was delighted. 'Do you?' she cried. 'You think so? Oh I'm so glad. Some companionship, perhaps?'

'Yes,' replied Hubert, 'the companionship of youth might be said to fit the case.'

'Oh really,' cried Mrs Curry. 'Of course, that would be it. Youth is so important to any artist, youth of one kind or another.'

'Oh, definitely one kind, I think,' said Hubert. 'A *protégé*, I believe, is the term. I met him the other evening with some young poet.'

Mrs Curry smiled at Hubert. 'How good you all are to young people. And then they say there's no love left in the world. A young poet!' In her delight she could no longer restrain from her more vernacular, less ethical speech. 'A nice young chum!' she cried. 'Oh, I should like to meet him. I expect he could tell us all sorts of things that Mr Sands would be far too modest to say of himself. Perhaps he'll be at Vardon Hall on Thursday to see his friend's triumph. There's always a little hero-worship in these things, isn't there? I do so hope it's a fine sunny afternoon, it would be awful if it was showery.' The word seemed to appeal to her, for she repeated, 'Oh yes, a showery afternoon would quite spoil the fun.' She glanced at the black marble clock on the mantelpiece. 'How absurd of me to go on talking like this to you,' she cried. 'A man in love only wants to hear of one thing. Dear little Elsie! She's such a pliable little thing. . . . '

Mrs Curry sat in the front seat and ate chocolates – large, expensive ones with soft centres. After each, she licked the ends of her fat, sticky fingers to which the chocolate had adhered. Ron kept his eyes fixed to the road and drove at an average of fifty. He whistled 'Ghost Riders in the Sky' between his teeth, slightly off key, pitching the tune a little louder each moment that Mrs Curry failed to notice his bad temper.

'Mr Rose has met Mr Sands' little friend,' Mrs Curry said, rummaging amongst the empty frilled papers.

Ron changed to 'Water'. 'Don't you listen, Dan, he's just a lying man,' he sang in rather loud Cockney-American.

'A poet, he said,' Mrs Curry remarked.

Ron made a special snarling noise which signified 'Oh'.

'I daresay it was the same little friend you met in St Albans,' Mrs Curry continued, undoing a box of peppermint creams.

'Oh, you do, do you?' said Ron. 'Well, excepting that that one wasn't a poet, it might have been, I suppose.'

'Somebody's got a little black dog on his back,' said Mrs Curry playfully.

'Somebody's got a bloody cheek,' answered Ron. 'You put the muckers up on the bastard, didn't you? But you wasn't going to tell me nothing about it. You and your bloody "love".'

'Silly boy!' cried Mrs Curry. 'I didn't quarrel with Mr Rose and I'm not going to quarrel with you. He was very grateful for the little help we've given him. And I'm very grateful to you, Ron. I want to give you a nice present.'

Ron relented a little; he turned and flashed the old one two at her. 'All right,' he said, 'I'll buy it.'

'What do you say to two new suits at that tailor's I showed you in Sackville Street?'

'That's easy,' Ron replied. 'I'd say, "F — off."'

'Do you remember,' Mrs Curry asked dreamily, staring out at the blowsy summer countryside, lush with vegetation, yet dry and dusty at the end of the day's heat, 'that old pin-stripe suit you were wearing when you were sent to me for that little job last year? You'd creased the trousers so carefully and then it split at the knee when you sat in the drawing-room. And your poor, funny shirt with the hole under the collar. Oh dear! I'm afraid you weren't at all at ease. A good-looking boy like you always wants to be nicely dressed.'

'I can get the clothes whenever I like,' said Ron. He slowed down and taking a comb from his breast pocket with one hand, he ran it through his hair. 'That blonde piece at St Albans is proper nuts on me. Wanted to give me a signet ring and all.'

Mrs Curry's silvery laugh was as hard as metal. 'Poor Mr Potter will be getting quite jealous,' she said.

'Yeah, Potter?' said Ron with contempt.

Mrs Curry recognized the effects of drink and the cinema when she heard them. 'Poor Mr Potter! He's such a baby. He'll run and tell Jack Winter.'

'The big shot, eh? So what?' Ron asked. He held up his index finger close to the next one. 'Jack Winter and me's like that.'

'Oh dear! Oh dear!' Mrs Curry laughed. 'Jack is such a

child. He's always trying to pull my leg.' She fumbled in her bag, then putting on her horn-rimmed spectacles she began to read from a letter, ' "The truth is I'm not accustomed to entrusting my affairs to little fools like Wrigley that can't keep their mouths shut. So if you and me's not to quarrel, Vera, and for old time's sake, take the advice of an old pal and keep your fancy bits out of business.'' I took him seriously and wrote him such a rude reply,' Mrs Curry laughed. 'He *will* have the laugh on me.'

The production of a piece of paper mentioning his name, and that unfavourably, acted like magic upon Ron. He felt surrounded by hidden enemies. Though he prided himself on trusting no one, he always accepted at face value any friendly gesture that was offered to him. 'I don't care nothing about Jack Winter,' he said, 'nor for the bloody lot of you for that matter. Here's one little boy that can look after himself.' He was at once the lone wolf and the boy who got to the top though everyone tried to kick him down.

'Silly,' said Mrs Curry, 'but I do care for you, dear, when you're nice and cosy. You don't have to be naughty with me. I was pulling your leg about the suits. That was just the beginning, Ron dear. I want you to have a nice time and money in your pocket to play with. You'd like that, wouldn't you, dear?'

Ron turned and looked at her. The look in those large blue eyes seemed to satisfy him, for he stopped the car and, putting his arms round her, he gave her a very passionate kiss. 'Like *that*?' he asked.

Mrs Curry gave forth a mooing sound. 'You can be a very loving boy when you try, can't you?' she said.

They stopped for drinks two or three times on the way home, and when they entered the cottage Mrs Curry's red head was on Ron's shoulder. 'I can't give you anything but love, baby,' she sang in her rich voice, 'that's the only thing I've plenty of, baby.'

Ron pinched her broad bottom. 'A bugger for that tale,' he said. 'What you got out of Rose?'

'Naughty Mr Rose,' Mrs Curry lisped. 'I told him spring

flowers come expensive out of season. But he's very understanding, he doesn't mind what he pays for his bunch of violets.'

' 'E's playing a funny game,' said Ron, 'messing about with kids.' And, imitating a favourite film star, he added, 'That's bad, that's awful bad.'

Mrs Curry's squeeze was like a sudden incursion of the sea. 'Who said it was bad for us?' she laughed.

To Bill, awaking from sleep in an armchair in the sitting-room, the conversation came as the continuation of a nightmare. He had failed again; the story of the Great Mother, Rhodes' mother, was untrue, false, the villagers themselves had laughed it out of court, and now the village children were crowning him with a mock wreath – roses and violets. Bernard looked at his manuscript. 'That's bad, that's awfully bad,' he said, and the children, laughing, danced round him in a ring, 'Bad, bad, bad,' they sang.

Whatever Mrs Curry's feelings when she found Bill in her sitting-room, she cooed with delight. 'Well,' she said, 'who's been asleep in my bed?'

Bill, dazzled by the light, sat like a great moon-faced bear, blinking his eyes and swallowing the bile of a hangover sleep. 'I've been to sleep,' he said. 'I took the key from under the mat and made myself at home. I had a tin of your sardines, too, I hope you don't mind.'

If Mrs Curry had been more sober she would have minded very much, both at his finding the key and at the sardine oil on the little marqueterie table; as it was, suspicion and pride were dissipated in a cloud of power. 'You lazy old thing,' she said, and tousled Bill's hair. 'You won't know how to do without me soon.'

Bill, feeling at a disadvantage, took refuge in words. 'When,' he asked, 'have we been able to do without you? Samson couldn't you know, nor David. Put ye Uriah in the forefront of the battle. Actium and an Empire lost might have satisfied you, but, no! to Ann Hathaway my best bed.'

If this hymn to her sex passed a little above Mrs Curry's head, it was not the less gratifying to her. She dearly loved a scholar and a gentleman at her feet; and many a one, with her understanding of humanity's funny little fads, she'd had. 'That's all right, dear,' she said, 'you'll get there in the end.' With her instinct for man's inner yearnings, she always answered Bill's unintelligible flights with general reassurances.

For Ron, Bill's range of historical allusion had less magic. 'What's he want hanging around here?' he asked. 'You ought to be more careful what you do with your key.'

Mrs Curry's smile of rebuke was slow and kind, and her hand as it ran down Ron's arm was slow and kind too. 'There's always a tiny corner for the lonely here,' she said. 'You make yourself comfortable, dear,' she told Bill. 'Ron and I have got a little business to talk over.'

'We've talked enough business with him hanging around,' said Ron. 'How do you know what he's up to?'

Mrs Curry's eyes hardened a little. 'Dear Mr Pendlebury, he wouldn't bother himself about our little secrets. Would you, dear?' she asked, and she pulled the lobe of Bill's ear ever so slightly.

To Bill's horror, the whole of their conversation pieced itself together in his mind in clear detail, and with it, so much more of what he had heard in the past week slipped into its monstrous place. How could he travel light, when other people projected their lives upon him like this? 'My dear lady,' he said, 'a far wiser man than I once said, "The misfortunes of other people sit lightly upon our shoulders." Like La Rochefoucauld, I never make the mistake of considering anyone but myself.'

'Well,' said Mrs Curry, 'I'm sure that's fair enough. And nor you should, the way luck treats you. Oh well, unlucky at cards, you know. All the same, dear, I only hope the ladies have been kinder to you than the naughty horses.'

'It's just a question of following up your losses,' said Bill.

Mrs Curry smiled. 'Well, dear,' she said, 'you've got plenty to follow. But never mind, old Mother Curry's always there to help. It's a good thing you've fallen into the right hands, you old baby. Later on, dear, maybe you'll be able to help me in some of my little business troubles. It's often very helpful to have

a gentleman at one's side, and one with such a lot of book learn-
ing too.' She turned to Ron. 'We don't have to have any
secrets from Mr Pendlebury, dear, he wouldn't want to upset
me, I know.' She went to the sideboard for the whisky decanter,
but before she had opened the cupboard door, it came upon her.
She sat quite still on a chair, with her eyes closed, looking like a
huge and obscene parrot, and let them pass – Bill, and Ron, and
Hubert Rose, and Elsie Black and her Mummy, and a long line
of others. What, will the line stretch on to crack o' doom? All
the love-starved and the needy, and all on bended knee.

CHAPTER THREE

Up at the Hall

THE Thursday on which Vardon Hall was officially opened proved to be the hottest day of the year in the South of England. Indeed the temperature recording at midday was higher than that for any of the previous ten years. Already at seven when Mrs Curry, who always rose early, looked out of her bedroom window, the heavy white heat mist was subsiding and the cattle were tossing and twitching against the assault of the summer flies. As she stood by the open window, drawing in great draughts of the morning air, Mrs Curry closed her eyes in ecstasy at the prospect of fun offered by such superb weather on so interesting a day.

Nobody afterwards could say exactly why everything got so out of hand as it did, though there were many who claimed some premonition of disaster. Mrs Craddock, for example, who habitually spent the morning hours in her bedroom with pots of tea and Fortt's Bath Olivers and never came downstairs until eleven, declared that she had only left her bedroom under protest; though Eric, looking back to the morning's events, was inclined to think that Mimi's disinclination to make the early start necessary for their attendance at the ceremony had been the result of a lassitude induced in the whole family by the stifling, moist atmosphere of their home which, on such a morning, was like some cooling crater of primeval times. Mrs Rankine, too, was witness to a more local sense of unease. 'Vardon,' she told her husband at breakfast, 'has so many moods for those who know it well. But I have never known it so angry. It's as though, darling, something terribly primitive in the place has not been appeased.' Her husband remembered her premonition afterwards, and told a group at the golf club that he ought to have known Stella well enough by now to have taken notice of what she said. It was not really clear what he could have done; indeed a less naïve person than Ralph Rankine, who had known Stella Rankine so well would have remembered the innumerable occasions on which, possessed by Mrs Dalloway, Mrs Ramsay, and Mrs Ambrose all at once, she had been seized by an awareness of evil even more striking than this. Bill Pendlebury, too, with his mind so full of the Great Mother, was impressed by the challenge of some pretty deep forces when he awoke at ten, indeed he refused to meet the challenge and returned to sleep until midday. Bill, however, had both a bad hangover and the remembrance of his new financial anxieties to urge him from the day's bright sunlight.

Of course, the general crumbling of good manners and lifting of emotional lids, which seemed to beset the visitors to Vardon Hall – both local people and those from afar – towards the end of the afternoon's ceremony, can easily be explained by the cumulative effect of a long, hot afternoon of speeches and standing, and fractious children. This general peevishness was certainly not assisted, as will be seen, by the chaotic inadequacy of the arrangements for refreshment and the disorder due to the presence of so many builders and workmen. The primitive state of the reconstruction operations alone was a great shock to many who had expected a running organization, with tame poets and artists, to spring full grown before their eyes. Exhaustion and disappointment undoubtedly accounted for many of the little scenes and rows which spread like heath fire through the crowd after four o'clock, not only illuminating the central figures of the ceremony in a lurid glow, but lighting many a fierce little family feud that had seemed dead driftwood the day before.

Nevertheless, though the situation deteriorated as the afternoon wore on, the premonition-mongers were not wholly without justification. There was a general sense of strain, of emotional conflict and of hostility anxious for justification among a large number of the visitors from the very start of the afternoon. It was unfortunate, of course, that the morning papers should have carried news of one of those periodic worsenings of the world situation, which, however familiar, necessarily crack the uneasy paste of hope and optimism of which so much confidence is compounded, and destroy the overglaze of social manner. The confluence of world crisis and lovely weather, in particular, threw into sinister highlight the sense of individual impotence, as though both personal happiness and personal disaster burst unannounced from outside, like the fair promises and curses of the Mosaic Jehovah.

Isobel Sands, in particular, was almost hysterical over the news after she had read the auguries of ten leading daily papers in the train to Vardon. For her companion, Louie Randall, of course, the possibility of-playing Cassandra among the heedless crowd – for so she imagined all bourgeois gatherings – was not only a dialectical duty but a rôle, prophesying atomic disaster as threatening to herself as others, which peculiarly satisfied her. Nor were the non-political untouched by the headlines. Terence Lambert, for example, who rigidly eschewed all reading of the news, was especially susceptible to political crises which spread beyond the newspapers into general conversation; his intense, solipsistic world of personal ambition was broken in a moment by the chance overheard remark of a carriage companion, and, behind the façade of his usual competent social manner, he was intent all the afternoon on securing confirmation or denial of his fears from one of the many celebrated people 'in the know' who were present at the ceremony.

But beyond all the maleficent effects of chance – of burning sun, cold war, absence of tea and sandwiches, ubiquity of workmen and planks and buckets of paint – there were certain mischievous happenings which could not be entirely explained without the introduction of conscious hostile human agency. The obstinate behaviour of some of the builder's men, for example, appeared to go beyond a certain natural annoyance with the visitors who invaded the scene of their labours. It was remembered afterwards, with some misgiving, that Ron had spent many evenings in the pub at Crowther, to which the vagrant Irish workmen went from their nearby camp. Some of the rows at the tea tents too seemed more violent than was called for by the inadequate and slow service, which is not, after all, so unfamiliar a feature of modern life. Certainly Mrs Wrigley's inefficient bulk appeared to dominate the urns and teacups more completely than might have been expected in an enterprise carried out by a well-known firm of caterers. Whether or not, in fact, there was some concerted plot, however humble and amateurish, to assist the fates in their accomplishment of Bernard's disaster, it is impossible to say, but as the afternoon wore on, some of those most concerned – Elizabeth, Sonia, Terence, even Bill – became convinced that there was deliberate enmity at work, and this conviction did not assist them in remaining coolheaded.

Bernard himself undoubtedly saw all the fragments, the threads of evil which had been weaving in and out of his thoughts during the preceding weeks, work together before his eyes, in the hard bright colours of the afternoon sunlight, into a huge tapestry of obscene horror. As the little patterns of hostility, of violence, and of cruelty took shape in rows and scenes and personal shame, they always seemed to coalesce around the saturnine arrogance of Hubert Rose's sneer, or the blond malice of Sherman's 'camp' chatter, or the gracious jealousy of Mrs Craddock's careful charm, or the enveloping hatred of Mrs Curry's sweet cooing. Yet it was not an external picture of concerted enemies that he saw, but the reflection of his own guilt, of his newly discovered hypocrisy, his long-suppressed lusts. Whatever happened here, whatever collapse of his humanistic ideals, whatever disaster to those he loved, seemed to him now the price of all that had been revealed in his thrill at the arrested man's horror. Against its inevitable issue in his own destruction he could not, must not, raise any protest. Among this whole crowd – the respectable, the successful, the great ones on the platform who had accepted the proper use of authority with its tempered, considered cruelty, or the crooks, the disappointed, the psychopaths who were committed to the open warfare of emotional bullying, undermining of the weak, trickery, and physical violence – he thought himself alone, the coward who had refused to face the dual nature of all human action, whose resplendent, eccentric cloak of broadminded, humane, individual conduct had fallen to pieces in one moment under the glaring neon searchlight of that single sordid test of his humanity in Leicester Square. He had failed the test and must take the consequences.

Certainly, Bernard's inadequacy, his unexpected apathy on his 'great' day had a good deal to do with the bad impression of the whole enterprise that was formed by the *important* visitors. They had travelled obligingly from London, or Oxford, or Cambridge in the discomfort of the day's great heat and they had expected, not unreasonably, a grateful reception from the man whose scheme they had come to honour. Few of them remained after the speechmaking; but the poor impression made by Bernard's speech, and by the general flatness of his behaviour, upon those who left early, was a fertile soil for the strange rumours and distorted stories of those who stayed long enough to witness, if only as observers, the odd scenes and quarrels that marked the end of the afternoon. There was no general condemnation, let it be said, certainly no impression so bad that it could not have been repaired by energetic conduct, but the tenor of opinion at College High Tables and in London clubs or literary parties during the subsequent week suggested that the whole scheme had been too easily accepted and that open support should be withheld until time could allow of a reasoned judgement. The rumours, too, if not conflicting, seemed unconnected. Thus a well-known novelist might find himself agreeing with a Professor of Literature that Bernard, if not a fellow-traveller, was certainly the perfect material for Communist propaganda; though the novelist's own belief had been that the scandal lay, not in the political field, but in an indefinable, though very definite, impression of sexual indiscretion, of the unnecessary crossing and dotting of t's and i's, which were perfectly well known, but not to be advertised. It did not take long, however, for these different rumours to coalesce, so that Charles Murley, who had been unable to attend at the ceremony, received a serious enough impression of Bernard's danger from the conversations he heard to feel it necessary to write letters that were to have great importance for both Bernard's and Ella's future. As for local opinion, that was far more condemnatory; for without the excuse of trains or distance, most local people were forced to stay to the close and so witnessed the unfortunate events that ended the afternoon.

Bernard and Ella entertained twenty of the more important guests to luncheon before the ceremony. On the whole the meal passed off well. The firm of caterers, which was to prove so inadequate in the tea marquees, did creditably in the provision of food and drink. A meal of smoked salmon, cold duck and *praliné* ice, with champagne or hock, satisfied the appetites of the distinguished guests, who were hungry after the journey, whilst allowing them to patronize from the backgrounds of college or club kitchens. 'An exceedingly adequate, unpretentious meal,' the great Sir Lionel Dowding said to his neighbour, with his special brand of humour. 'Exactly the thing before a country romp of this kind.'

Bernard, perhaps, was already a little too fatalistic about the future of Vardon Hall to satisfy the importance which his guests naturally attached to an enterprise that demanded their presence. 'If it's really needed it will survive,' he said, and turning to a somewhat sad young poet who had been invited to represent 'the coming young writers' for whom the scheme was devised, he said, 'If it turns out to be of use to you, you'll fight for it. If it doesn't, clear out before the weeds start to grow in the paths, and the springs of the chairs get lumpy.' As Sir Lionel said, 'Sands gives us the nicely balanced alternatives. But one can't help thinking that the ringing, if strident, tones of an Arnold or a William Morris crying "This place will be what I make it" would have encouraged the wretched young scribblers more.' However, apart from the topic of Vardon Hall, Bernard was an amusing, easy host, anxious to see that his last official contact with his distinguished colleagues should pass urbanely.

Ella, too, was at her best, recalled for a short while to life by the presence of one or two friends from the past; and, if at moments she seemed abstracted or was over-excited by Professor Graham's account of his ascent of Kilimanjaro, the general opinion was that she was still a charming, astute woman, whose illness had been grossly exaggerated. Ironically, however, it was the success of the luncheon which indirectly led to the first faint notes of discord in the afternoon's performance. It was a little after a quarter to three before the principals arrived at the Hall, although the ceremony had been advertised to begin at ten past two promptly. Sonia's over-zealous efforts had, in any case, persuaded most of the local notabilities to arrive by two. It was therefore an impatient and peevish crowd that awaited the speakers. It was also far too large a crowd. Here again Sonia's missionary activity was much to blame. Bernard, in the' days of local hostility to the scheme, had expected little support from the neighbourhood, and his recent apathy had done nothing to repair this out-dated estimate. As a result the two main rooms and the great entrance were already filled to capacity half an hour before the speakers arrived, and the suffocated, packed crowd were not altogether friendly to the notabilities who had to force their way through to the platform. Indeed it took some uncomfortable minutes before it was realized that these new arrivals were not just latecomers attempting to reach the front seats. Cries of 'If you don't mind, sir, I should be very glad . . . ', or 'I don't know whether you're aware that you're pushing this lady,' were mingled with more direct complaints such as, 'Any bloody fool can see there's no empty seats' and 'It's easy enough to knock children over, you know.' There was even some purely physical skirmishing from which an authority on the literature of the twenties emerged rather battered and a brilliant woman broadcaster without her glasses.

Outside on the terrace and the drive the crowd was even more dense. Though gossip later undoubtedly exaggerated the numbers, there were certainly sufficient to overflow on to the lawns, and it was thus that the first serious altercation arose between the crowd and one of the builder's foremen, who had received particular instructions from a Georgian-loving member of the committee that the lawns were to be held sacrosanct. An improvisation of amplifiers was quickly arranged to allow those outside to hear the speakers. It was, perhaps, unfortunate that this was not a total failure, for complete inaudibility would have allowed the visitors to stroll through the grounds, hold picnics or depart for home. As it was the speeches were clearly heard for five minutes at a time, then became indistinct or inaudible, then deafening, and, worst of all, were given forth in strange, sub-human explosions that provoked a suppressed, hysterical laughter.

The effect of luncheon upon the speakers was most satisfactory to themselves. Isolated upon the comparative cool of the plat-form, with the scents of the summer garden coming in from the open windows on each side of them, they lapsed into a gentle, mellow, if somewhat boring, delivery reminiscent of more spacious garden parties. This was in some degree satisfactory to their audience who expected the speeches to be comfortingly platitudinous where they were not incomprehensibly learned. If they too, like the speakers, had been able to dream away among memories of the cluck of croquet balls, of the wafted scent of heliotrope and the murmurous haunt of flies, for which indeed, in their Ascot hats and gowns and well-cut flannel suits, they had come dressed, they would have been well content; but for those inside it was more like some terrible indignity of the Japanese upon the white rulers of Singapore, and for those outside, a heaven-sent chance to relax ruined by sudden, nervewracking assaults upon their ears. For the few who could hear with com-parative ease and in comparative comfort, the Oxford speech, despite its somewhat difficult passage of Pushkin, was judged the wittiest; the Cambridge speech, despite its Aeschylean demand upon a largely non-existent knowledge of Greek, the noblest. The theological flavour of the two prominent writers who spoke was accepted for its resemblance to the customary political exhortations to stand firm in face of peril; whilst the Under-Secretary, who lent some air of Governmental support to the occasion, was liked for his many poetic quotations which he pro-nounced in a manner happily reminiscent of a popular radio preacher. Had the seating and auditory arrangements been more adequate, the speeches would have been a great success; as it was, the importance of the speakers was sufficient to flatter the audience into benevolent toleration.

A clear, humorous, highminded speech from Bernard would have saved the occasion. Indeed it was expected from his reputation as a fluent, witty yet astringent speaker. He seemed, at that moment – so distinguished, so wise and sad, so familiar a figure – to be the county's own ambassador to the great world outside, the link between a live and important district with all that was best in English life to-day, a barrier between a tranquil, age-old countryside and the muddy flood of modern life outside. He was almost a symbol of the commuting trains that took so many of them each day to play their part in the busy life of London and brought them back to replenish their souls with the keen breezes of field and hill. If he was presenting Vardon with a great cultural enterprise, he was also giving the world of culture a much needed breath of Vardon's wholesome air.

Bernard made no mention of this local aspect of his scheme. He could not, he said, but consider deeply the motives that had led to the inauguration of the new Vardon Hall. The needs of the arts in an age poised between private patron and state, the difficulties of housing, of leisure, of solitude in England to-day, the gulf between scholarship and creation, the absence of a meeting ground for writers, the dangers of coterie art, the hopes for a new humanism, all these seemed so clear, and yet, and yet . . . Motives were so difficult, so double, so much hypocrisy might spring from guilt, so much benevolence from fear to use power, so much kindness overlay cruelty, so much that was done didn't matter. If the scheme failed, if the young writers ceased to write, it was of small account in time; better failure than deception, better defeat than a victory where motive was wrong. He seemed quite unable to leave the subject of motive, so that the more inattentive of his audience got the impression that they were involved in a discussion of some mysterious crime. He seemed to eschew all humour for fear of bitterness, though occasionally he fell into unconscious Freudian *double-entendres*. 'So much that has been written would have been better left unprinted,' he said. 'One can pay too dearly for what one picks up in the Charing Cross Road, and not only in cash, but in more lasting ills.'

153

Sherman, who was very drunk, screamed loudly, 'Gracious!'
And his friends, who were fairly drunk, tittered wildly.

Bernard declared, 'If I seem to be warning poets against an
eternal valuation of their work, do not please suppose that I do
not value a single verse of it more highly than anything any one
of you here is ever likely to create. We are not given many
chances of justifying our existences, but respect for the poet
is one. If you are lucky enough to meet a young poet, love him
very much, hold him very close to you, you may yet be
saved.'

Mrs Curry whispered loudly to Ron, 'What a loving, passionate man he is!' and the noise of Ron's guffaw quite broke the
trend of the speech.

Occasionally, too, Bernard seemed to reach a personal level
that held no communication for his audience. 'There is always
the possibility,' he said, 'that our most heroic self-sacrifice –
and the conviction if it comes is a horrible one – may only be a
comfortable evasion of duty.'

Mrs Craddock, in the front row, laid a hand on an arm of each
of her sons, between whom she sat so proudly, and cried, 'Oh
how dreadfully true! How dreadfully true!' But her moment of
drama seemed only to underline the meaninglessness of Bernard's
words for other members of the audience. For the rest, the
speech dwelt mainly on defeat and the saving power of evil.

'No culture that reposes on resistance and strength alone can
survive,' Bernard urged. 'No culture that doesn't accept its own
decadence is real. I trust I shall not be convicted of false *mystique*
if I dwell on the sweetness of the forces that oppose us, on the
renewed life that may come from capitulation to their primitive
power.' An outburst of clapping from Louie Randall and a loud
'Bravo' from Isobel seemed to remove the sentiment from its
mystical cloak and reveal it in its true political colours, for
Bernard's sister was known to most as a confessed fellow-
traveller. The most unfortunate aspect of the speech, however,
because the most public, was its effect on Ella. A few moments
after her husband began speaking, she seemed to be galvanized
into life, and followed every word with an earnest, almost lip-

reading attention, which coming so suddenly upon her apathy during the earlier speeches lent an unhappy effect of pantomime to the group on the platform.

It was, in fact, a disastrous speech, and it was also an unsuitably long one. Bernard apparently realized this, for when he had finished he bent for a moment's conversation with other members of the platform. It was only when the young poet struggled to his feet that the audience realized that an item had been cut – and *that* item the speech of the only local councillor invited to sit among the great. As one stockbroker's wife said to Hubert Rose, 'Poor old Vardon isn't getting much of a show!' and Hubert's reply did not really salve the wounds of local pride. 'Well, after all, dear lady, these highly important men have found their way down to the damned place. It'd be asking a bit too much to make 'em hear all about the local amenities, don't y'know?'

The poet, whose blue serge suit and row of fountain-pen heads in his breast pocket were all too reminiscent of the bank clerk of Hubert's earlier warning, had not been mellowed by drink like the other speakers. He was less accustomed to it. He spoke very fast, with a stutter and a tendency to sudden falsetto. Few of those inside the house, and none of those in the garden, ever fully grasped that he was reciting from his own works. The words that came to them were therefore peculiarly incomprehensible. At intervals the amplifiers carried strange phrases to the tired crowd, adding to their sense of isolation or provoking hysterical giggles as a defence against their embarrassment. 'Hyaena false or more', 'and artery for rice exchange', or 'Unloved, unsired, Nestorian stripped' were teasers that even the most competition-minded preferred to greet with philistine laughter under such blazing sun. If it was for this that their largesse of spirit and pocket had been asked, there were few that did not feel the great cause to be undeserving.

Nevertheless there was still enough element of awe, of incomprehensible glory, attached to the great figures who had come among them to have won the crowd's favour when the speeches were over; enough self-satisfaction among the great themselves to have secured their attachment to the enterprise to which they had already showed favour; certainly enough relief on both sides that the speeches were over, to have saved the day had the arrangements for the entertainment which followed been less completely deficient.

An attempt was made to prevent the unexpectedly large crowd stampeding to the tea marquees by a microphone request that some part of the visitors should inspect the house and grounds before seeking refreshment. It was an appeal that probably saved some lives, but did little to repair the ensuing confusion. Large numbers of people, it was true, were only too anxious to explore. Among the commuting gentry, those who had already visited at Vardon Hall wished to exhibit their familiarity, those who had not were urged on by social snobbery; whilst the visitors from London, especially Sherman's small but vocal smart set, partook of that general contemporary passion for displaying a 'sense of period' which the National Trust has so successfully encouraged.

It was one of Sherman's more outrageous friends who led the rush to the upstairs rooms, which were still largely derelict. 'I must see how they managed the upstairs loos,' he cried. 'Do you think they'll be the push or the pull, or the wonderful old pull up kind?' Local visitors would have been daunted by the ropes which were intended to cut off the upper apartments, but Sherman's friends were not, and soon a miscellaneous crowd began to drift upstairs after them.

There was no question of drift, however, where Sherman's party was concerned. They scampered about the corridors and empty bedrooms like so many mating mice. It was somehow, they felt, Edwardian – and what could be nicer – to behave rather badly in the bedrooms of a country mansion. Terence's attempts to control them were voted entirely po-faced.

Sherman himself was too drunk to care if Terence minded. 'Oh hell!' he cried. 'If you think I'm going to sit still and play noughts and crosses, after listening to all that dreary crap, you've bloody well got another guess coming. You go down and join all the Girton girls in a little eurhythmy on the lawn, dear, we'll just finish our Bacchic rout and go home.' In and out of the cupboards, up in the attic and even under the baths they chased one another. It was break-up day at St Monica's and no punches pulled.

Mrs Curry, attracted by the girlish screams, faced the effort of the stairs to join in the fun, and was only the slightest degree put back by the unaccustomed nature of the fun she found. 'Like a lot of boys let out of school,' she said. It was only failure to bring her cards, one felt, that prevented her from advertising a rival tuckshop. 'The boys', too, adored her in her pale mauve muslin dress and her 'wonderful period hat' with its osprey. 'You'll never get under the bath, duckie,' they said. She was, perhaps, a trifle put out when one of them cried, 'My dear, I *do* believe she's the madam! Old world, that's what it is!' But she soon saw it was all just fun, and really she felt quite proud of Ron's adaptability – he was giving the old one-two look left and right. 'He's such a loving boy,' she told Sherman.

'You're telling me, dearie,' he replied in cockney.

The other visitors, however, began to drift downstairs again, determined not to put two and two together lest they made four. One solicitor's wife, having opened a bedroom door on the oddest embrace, cried loudly, 'There's nothing *here*, to see anyway.' The general impression was not good.

In a short while one of the contractor's foremen and a party of assistants were on the scene protesting against this invasion of their still-undecorated territory. Mrs Curry seized the occasion of the general hubbub to remove herself from a scene that threatened at any moment to become unloving. If the reception of the workers by Sherman's party was rather more mixed than the disregard they had shown for the local bourgeoisie, the judgement of the local labouring class was, with one or two unfortunately sophisticated exceptions, far more openly censorious. There was almost an open fight; though the foreman's statement, after Sherman and his friends had retreated, 'We're not 'aving any of *that* muckin' about up 'ere,' was tactfully vague in its application.

Those who had chosen, on this lovely day, to confine their explorations to the garden, were exposed to other less purely moral perils. Although, at first, the grounds were uncomfortably crowded, the heat, the exhaustion that followed the speech-making and the obvious impossibility of getting near the tea tents soon caused the less determined to leave. Those who remained were left to enjoy the hothouses, the herbaceous borders and the shrubbery with no more discomfort than is usual in viewing such things on public days. It was more than comforting to find the famous vine so small and fruitless, the delphiniums so inferior and the shrubbery no more than a tangled mass of dusty St John's Wort. There was general conviction among the visitors that they could have done better at home. They settled down to an after-noon of satisfied disappointment.

Sonia, whose high hopes had been so sadly deceived, was in that overcharged, childish state which she had prophesied for her mother-in-law. Her social equilibrium was easily upset at large gatherings; her competence to cope with any particular group was constantly being disturbed by her fears for the others that were outside her direct control. With her little bird-like face flushed and excited, above her trim, cool figure in a simple, lemon-coloured silk frock, she attracted more than one of the elderly great. She was not, unfortunately, in the mood to give them the undivided attention they asked, and hopped from group to group, pecking little introductions at them like a mother bird feeding her young with worms. Sir Lionel Dowding, however, was almost importunate and resisted all her attempts to involve him with other guests.

'Please,' he said, 'allow me to have had my fill of platitudes. If we sit down on those two very inviting chairs we can supply all these distinguished men and beautiful women with the bril-liant romantic remarks that should, but never will, emerge from their lips. That handsomely built woman over there – if I was introduced to her, of course, I should immediately think her grossly fat – is telling that charming slim youth – once known, of course, he would give all the appearance of a rabbit – of the night when, beneath a hunter's moon – let us hope, poor rabbit, that the expression does not alarm him too greatly – she slid from her mullioned window down the rope that led to the runaway match which so astonished the county.' Into the whimsical twinkling of his faded old eyes he began to insert the faintest suggestion of a leer. 'Ah!' he continued, as the rabbity young man began to speak, 'see how hotly *he* is pressing his suit. "Repeat the adventure," he is saying, "and with me." But she is uncertain, she is held by the sacred bonds of marriage.' As Sonia made no answer, he continued, 'You don't believe me, you think her hesitation is due to increased weight.'

Neither the elaborate whimsy nor the leer were to Sonia's taste, but she reflected on Sir Lionel's position, not exactly political but 'in everything'. 'I was only thinking,' she said, 'how delightful it would be if we could persuade you to settle here and transform Vardon's dreary round.'

A quarter of an hour later she was happily absorbed. 'My dear Mrs Sands,' Sir Lionel was saying, 'I will pay you out for introducing me to so many bores. You must dine with me and meet your hero in the flesh. Don't blame me if it shatters for ever your charming faith in the party whose cause you support so warmly. Of all bores, let me assure you, the political bore is the greatest. Your hero, when I last saw him, was concerned with meat, so prepare yourself to talk of meat, or rather to listen to talk of meat – meat in all its aspects, imported, exported, undersold, oversold, beef, pork, mutton, and veal. You've prepared your own doom, you know. The only compensation I can offer is that I will serve you only the finest poultry at dinner.'

It was a doom that Sonia had long sought, and she set herself quickly to clinch it with an exact date.

Bill Pendlebury seemed more than ever bursting out of his best pinstripe suit when he interrupted them. Sonia found it difficult to believe that such vulgarity could accompany advancing years.

'Something's gone sadly awry with the gay whirl,' he said. 'The funeral baked meats taste a bit ashy in the mouth, don't you think?'

Sonia said coldly, 'Sir Lionel Dowding, my uncle, Mr

Pendlebury. The twenty-fourth,' she went on, 'would suit *us* very well.'

But Bill had felt neglected all the afternoon and was working round to be snubbed. 'Have you ever heard the gods angry, Sir Lionel?' he asked. 'Take my word for it, they are this afternoon. The Vardons were the darlings of the gods – wild, lawless and proud as the devil,' his invention ran ahead as he spoke, 'murder, rape, incest, the whole bag of tricks. And this afternoon we've come along and defiled the holy places – a lot of nice little ladies and gentlemen with our culture and moderation, my brother-in-law's humanism and the bishop's Christian virtues. I don't fancy these young writers' chances of getting anything written in this scene of sacrilege, even if they could write.'

Sir Lionel was furious at the interruption; he lay back in the deck chair and closed his eyes. 'My imagination,' he said, 'unlike your uncle's, Mrs Sands, refuses to function in the heat.'

'My husband's family,' said Sonia, 'will bore even Hell by their fancies.' She calculated that direct rudeness to Bill would increase Sir Lionel's good opinion. To moderate her remark, however, she smiled up at her uncle. 'Get us some ices, Uncle Bill,' she added, 'and we'll hear all your gloomy prophecies unmoved.'

Bill was on the aggressive. His huge frame looming over Sir Lionel, he swayed uneasily from foot to foot. 'Perhaps,' he said defiantly, 'you think I despise these young fellows because I'm jealous. But it isn't that at all,' his speech was jerky, yet slurred. 'I can't write for toffee, I know that, but I know what it ought to be like. Like your father's, you know,' he said, turning to Sonia.

Drink and self-pity combined with a reverence for his own sudden sincerity to bring tears to Bill's eyes. Sonia prayed to God that this disgusting drunken old man might die where he stood.

Sir Lionel took out his cigarette case. He offered it first to Sonia, then to Bill. 'Will you have a cigarette, Mr Pendlebury?' he asked. 'The flies seem unusually troublesome this afternoon. I hope Sands has laid in an adequate store of "Flit" to keep his protégés free from their attentions.'

Sonia said, 'He's found the most superb Italian cook to look after them. Everybody round here will be brushing up their culture to get invited to dinner.'

Bill leaned forward unsteadily and took his niece's hand. 'I'm sorry,' he said, 'unpardonable outburst. Curious, you know, how the soul finds need for expression. Call it confession, call it free association, call it "sharing" or just the truth drug: Dostoyevsky was right, we all need a spiritual purge now and again.'

Sir Lionel's long yellow fangs gleamed maliciously at Sonia as he turned to her. 'Has your uncle no Sir Andrew to support his carousals, Mistress Olivia?'

Bill's tears rolled down his fat red cheeks. 'I've behaved disgracefully,' he said, 'and there's no catch that I can sing that will make up for it.'

'You can make up for it best by going home to bed,' said Sonia.

Bill kissed her hand and began with great care to walk off. He had hardly moved a yard when Hubert Rose descended upon Sonia.

'My dear Sonia,' he said, 'how insufferably dreary the old place seems without the Vardons.'

Sonia's relief was great. 'Sir Lionel Dowding, Mr Rose,' she said.

'I was to have met you last week at the Russells, Sir Lionel,' began Hubert, when he was suddenly confronted by an enormous red-faced old man who stared at him like an owl.

'You agree with me about the Gods, don't you,' said Bill. 'I know you've got *your* little sacrifice tucked away. I wish I had, but she's left me. For manicuring, you know. Be careful of that.' Then looking very knowing, he added, 'But yours would hardly be of the age for that. Oh for God's sake,' and he looked quite comically anxious for Hubert's approval, 'don't think I'm censorious. Just the opposite. As I told my sister. Older than time. Little Saint Hugh,' he began to mumble incoherently, then ended loudly, 'All the same, you be careful of them – the Christians and the respectable – remember that millstone.'

Hubert's long heavy body shivered slightly. But with quizzically raised eyebrows directed at the others he said very seriously, 'My dear Sir, of course I agree. Both about the gods and the millstone.'

'That,' said Sonia icily, 'is James's uncle. He's drunk and we *had* hoped he was going away.'

Hubert took Bill's arm. 'Come and have a long talk to me about these interesting phenomena.' His *savoir faire* seemed to Sir Lionel a combination of ostentation and arrogance, but it delighted Sonia.

Unfortunately Mrs Curry's roving eye had seen the undesirable confluence and her large mauve form bore down upon them.

'Hullo, Mr Pendlebury,' she cried; 'enjoying yourself? Oh dear! I do believe the dear old boy's a wee bit tiddly. You come along with me, dear, and join all the boys and girls.' When Bill drew his arm away from her, she added sharply, 'Now you do as you're told, my lad.'

Sonia rose from her chair. 'Mr Rose is looking after my uncle, thank you,' she said. 'Pull yourself together, for God's sake, Uncle Bill.'

Mrs Curry smiled graciously. 'You're quite all right, aren't you dear?' she said to Bill. 'Old soldiers never die. You mustn't speak to them like that, dear,' she said to Sonia. 'The gentlemen never like it. Naughty old thing, I expect he's just merry because he's in love. He'll come with me all right. We're old friends, business friends,' and she led Bill away.

Sonia turned to Sir Lionel. 'I must go and find my son,' she said, but Sir Lionel had closed his eyes in pretended sleep and he did not intend to open them.

Nicholas held his grandmother's hand very tightly. 'I shouldn't think anyone knows the names of *all* the flowers, should you?' he asked.

'Oh yes,' said Ella. She was always very polite with children. 'I expect some of the people at Kew do.'

'All the flowers in Africa and Asia and Australia?' Nicholas asked.

'Yes,' said Ella, 'I think so.'

'And in the North Pole and the South Pole?' Nicholas urged.

'There aren't any flowers at the Poles, Nicholas,' said his grandmother, 'only ice. Thousands of miles of ice. It breaks away in square blocks, but it leaves clear edges.' Her pale blue eyes gazed washily away over thousands of miles of ice. She tried to imagine the blocks of ice as equal squares, each floating away across the grey water, each the same in size and colour.

'That's a pretty flower isn't it, Granny?' Nicholas cried.

'No, dear,' said Ella, 'it's a coreopsis. It's rather ugly.'

'*I* like it very much,' said Nicholas. 'I like it better than all the other flowers. Mummy,' he cried to Sonia, 'Granny doesn't like this flower, but *I* do.'

'Perhaps Granny doesn't like daisies,' Sonia said.

'It isn't a daisy,' Nicholas cried. 'It's a . . . What is it Granny?'

'A coreopsis, dear,' said Ella.

'Well, whatever it is,' said Sonia, 'it's time for you to go home, Nicholas,' and she took the boy's other hand. Nicholas clung to his grandmother, protesting tearfully.

'We were going to see the shrubbery,' said Ella. 'There used to be a cage of silver pheasants. I think Nicholas would like their long lace tail-feathers.'

'Nicholas,' replied her daughter-in-law, 'would like anything that will excuse him from doing what he's told.'

It was with difficulty that Ella produced a smile of appeal for herself through her ravaged features and watery eyes. 'It makes me very happy to have him with me,' she said.

'Will it also make you happy to see him grow up spoilt and whiney?' Sonia asked.

Ella sighed and disengaged her hand from her grandson's. 'Bernard's speech was so good. I have such a lot to think about,' she said, almost addressing herself.

'I'm glad you found it so,' said Sonia. Pulling Nicholas by his arm, she moved away. 'Berthe had no right to leave you wandering about on your own like this,' she said; then turning her head she almost shouted at Ella, 'It was the *most* appalling bilge that ought never to have been spoken in public.'

Ella picked a coreopsis and began methodically to pull the flower to pieces, petal by petal, then stamen by stamen.

'Our Constitution,' said James, and he bowed his fine head to the level of the little man beside him, 'is surely a perfection of checks. In removing the University vote, they've removed one of the principal of these checks – the check of educated opinion.' The weight of his father's disgraceful speech seemed to lift from him in the flower-scented air of the garden. Walking beside the Master of his late college, he felt himself almost an undergraduate again, only, of course, more assured.

'Yes, yes,' said the little man, 'but the constitution can't be petrified. It must grow, you know, like any living organism.'

'Grow,' said James, 'but not shrink.' He felt pleased at the judicious and adult manner in which he could now face the learned, the sheltered.

The Master's beetling sandy eyebrows drew together in a frown. Too many of his young men seemed filled with this illiberalism. 'So you propose to give us all back our little extra vote?' he said.

'Certainly,' James replied. University representation was one of the peculiar duties he had laid upon himself. Contact with important academical men like the Master would be a good card in his play for adoption as candidate. 'With more than three-quarters of undergraduates receiving state aid, there's no question of class or privilege, you know. Merely the reward of talent.'

The Master looked at the crumbling steps of the terrace. The peacocks would not be missed, he thought, while James strutted there.

'Your father,' he said gruffly, 'knows how to reward talent. We have finer things at Cambridge than all this,' and he waved his hand across the terrace and garden, 'but your father plans to give talent leisure, and of that we have a very shrinking supply.'

Before James's eye the garden was transformed as in a quick

motion film – leaves turned brown and withered with the jerky speed of automata, flowers lost their colour, the air grew dry and scorching.

'My father,' he said grimly, 'has King Midas's touch.'

The Master raised an eyebrow. 'I wish,' he said, 'that I could turn my young men into gold, it's better than the dust of vocational education.'

James strove to silence his bitterness, but, 'My father's dreams,' he said, 'seem incomplete to a younger generation. I find it difficult not to remember that golden girls and lads all must, as chimney sweepers, come to dust.'

'Oh yes!' said the Master. 'I think your father understands *that* very well. It was, after all, the burden of his speech.' He put out his hand. 'Good-bye,' he said, 'we shall look forward to receiving our suffrage again from a member of the college.'

The voices of the local gentry as they talked their way through the shrubbery and the Dutch garden came as a pleasant relief to James after the raven's croaking of the Master's dying liberalism. Never more perhaps for him; but for the strong and the determined an infinite period of Burkean experienced administration.

The chatter of the local gentry exploring the hothouses came to him on a tonic wind – the voices of experience, competence, good sense, and reliability.

'Well, I don't suppose it will do any harm,' he could hear one woman saying. 'They may be a bit wild and woolly when they first arrive, but they'll soon settle down. And if they don't, they'll be gone before this time next year.' She had said the same of the Lithuanian maids, the billeted civil servants and the visiting Australian cousins.

Mrs Rankine's voice answering her was, perhaps, less reassuring. 'I could never settle down, I'm afraid,' she was saying, 'in a place so full of ghosts – ghosts of happiness and miseries. Personality, and especially a family personality like the Vardons, is so persistent. It will be too strong for our poor poets' imaginations. I had a great fear for it before, and now, I feel sure. Unless, unless,' her voice mused away into the distance and then reappeared. 'They might, you know, and then of course all traces of the Vardons would die away.' Pretentious woman, thought James, it was that sort of dissatisfied, aspiring person that weakened the solid middle classes of England.

But the words of the other woman seemed a reaffirmation. 'My dear,' she said, 'you can't kill stock like the Vardons just by taxing them out of their homes.'

James sat down on the terrace step and watched a small cock-chafer making its way through the forest of the stonecrop leaves. He felt happy in the reassurance of those words and in the sun flowing over his cheeks like warm water. It was only in those moments of watching the activity of small things – birds or insects – that he escaped for a moment his biting ambition; in those moments, and in Sonia's embraces. Suddenly the soft air and the comforting buzz of chatter were broken by a shrill scream and the noise of arguing, angry voices. He moved in quick strides round the corner of the house to find a small but growing crowd of visitors collecting around a hunched, seated figure.

Poor Mrs Rankine! Her premonitions had been all too completely realized. Absorbed by her interesting emotions she had trodden on an insecure duckboard and fallen seriously to sprain her ankle. Already, as James approached, the visitors and the workmen were dividing into hostile camps.

'Well, all I can say,' Ralph Rankine was declaring, 'is that somebody's been damned careless.'

'It's perfectly clear, sir,' the foreman retorted, his mouth set belligerently beneath his tooth-brush moustache. 'Visitors are warned to keep away from the constructional operations. I'm very sorry for the lady, but it's entirely her own fault.'

'I'm not concerned with your opinion about . . . ' Ralph began, but the foreman interrupted him.

'Ah, but I *am*, sir,' he said. 'I have to protect my men from . . . '

'You'd be a great deal better employed protecting the public from this sort of . . . '

'If members of the public choose to disregard the notices put up for their benefit . . . '

Voices began to chime in from every side. Poor Mrs Rankine

moaned with pain, as the district nurse, for whom the accident made the afternoon one of the most enjoyable of her life, directed the two young stockbrokers who assisted the injured lady to one of the many cars drawn up in the drive.

James suddenly felt a murderous hatred of the workmen, who appeared as conscious agents of his father's mischievous misrule. He strode up to the foreman, his handsome face pink with fury.

'Will you kindly make adequate arrangements to fence off this dangerous area,' he shouted, 'and then get your men out of the place before they succeed in killing someone.'

'Perhaps it would be better, sir,' the foreman replied, 'if you were to mind your own business.'

'It happens to be my business. I'm Mr Sands's son.'

'I can't help it if you're the son of old Joe Stalin. I'm working for the contractors and I take my orders from them.'

'The contractors,' said James, 'if your limited intelligence can grasp it, are working for the committee of which my father is chairman.'

The foreman turned his back on James. 'Come on,' he said to the workmen who were standing near, 'we've got a job to do. We can't stand all day listening to this little lot blowing their tops off.'

It was only the restraining hand of Hubert upon James's arm that prevented him from physical assault. Hubert's sardonic grin was affability itself, as he said, 'Dear old boy, no, definitely no.'

Mrs Craddock was *delighted* by Bernard's speech, delighted by *all* the speeches; it was a field day for her, of course, and only made her realize why Eric was so anxious to be with his friend, and why it was so important that he should be. She told Eric and Alan so a hundred times and rather loudly. She hadn't perhaps got all the points, but then she was out of touch with – she had almost said modern *jargon*, but that wasn't the right word at all, of course – modern *ethos* would be better. Now Eric, of course, who had such opportunities of soaking himself in the thought of the day, could probably explain what Bernard – she felt she almost must call him Bernard now – had meant by such and such. But when Eric suggested a tentative explanation, she really could not resist a delicious little laugh. No, she couldn't really say she *did* think that was what Bernard had meant. Smiling, she put her hand on Alan's arm, confidentially she whispered, 'What sort of picture the child makes out of the wonderful world he's been taken up into, one really slightly shudders to guess at.' Gradually, and with many gracious halts to admire this prospect of the house or to note that charming vista through the elm trees, she guided her somewhat unwilling sons until they had reached the group in which Bernard stood.

'I'm not, you know,' she said, 'going to say anything, because it's all clearly been said a hundred times before, a hundred times better, by a hundred other people. But it *was* very, very fine. It was something that we, or at least Alan and I – for Eric, thanks to you, is going on to richer and richer treasures – will have with us always.'

Bernard, introducing Celia Craddock to the company, attempted particularly to attach her to Elizabeth. Safe from the presence of the great, he hoped that she would feel less nervous, more free to shed her affectation.

'Your father was wonderful,' said Mrs Craddock in a stage whisper, 'but he looks so dreadfully tired. Can't something be done to save him from all of us? To let the poor darling rest?'

Before Elizabeth could reply that she saw no immediate means of doing this, Mrs Craddock signified by a smile and a shake of her index finger that 'the poor darling' was listening and their little intimacy must end.

'This,' she said proudly, 'is my son Alan, and this, my son Eric, whom your father has so wonderfully helped with his friendship. It is, I'm afraid, our only excuse for being here on this distinguished occasion.'

Elizabeth looked at Eric. There was, she thought, something infinitely dreary in his 'tousled mop' of hair, his emerald shirt and brick-red tie. She almost forecast a nasal, cockney accent; and compared him unfavourably with Terence.

'*Distingué*'s the word, surely,' she said to Mrs Craddock with a smile. 'I'm afraid it couldn't be less my cup; as the pansy general said, when asked about the war,' and she turned her gaze on Eric, ' "My dear, the *noise* and the *people*." '

Mrs Craddock gave the laugh she used to put awkward people at their ease; and Elizabeth flushed pink to the base of her throat.

'Does all this,' asked Mrs Craddock, and she waved her arm with its bracelet of antique charms, 'pall so easily for those who've always had it? Will *you* get tired of it so quickly, Eric?'

Her son gave a squeak of laughter. 'I shan't have terraces and hot-houses in my bed-sitting room, Mimi darling,' he said, 'though I might have a silver pheasant.' With his eye on Elizabeth he turned to Bernard. 'Could I, do you think, have a silver pheasant in Bramham Gardens, Bernie?' he asked.

'Certainly not,' said Bernard; 'vile incontinent creatures.'

'It'll have to be the koala bears then,' cried Eric. '*They*'ve been house trained for years. Bernie,' he continued, turning to Elizabeth, 'thinks woolly bears on the mantelpiece horribly middle-class. What do you think?'

'Not my column,' said Elizabeth savagely. 'You want the March issue on those little things that make all the difference to your boudoir.'

'Elizabeth works on one of our great women's papers,' Bernard said, 'making important contributions to the evolution of English prose.'

Mrs Craddock looked quite wide-eyed. 'If the comparison does not appear too blasphemous, I should like to say that, for an ordinary woman like myself, this is uncomfortably like meeting God. Miss Sands, my dear,' she turned to Alan, 'is probably that very terrifying young lady whose columns remind me of my painful duty to my appearance every time I sit in the dentist's waiting-room.' She smiled at the general absurdity of Elizabeth's presence among so many fine minds.

Elizabeth smiled too. 'I hardly think so,' she said; 'my little racket is advising the *older* woman on how to look her best.'

Mrs Craddock tried to feel above such ordinary bitchiness. Turning from the juvenile sphere, she placed her small hand in its black lace glove on Bernard's arm. 'You turned us all over to the button-moulder this afternoon, my dear friend,' she said.

'Poor Peer Gynt! poor humanity! We got the trouncing we deserved. I wonder,' and she seemed the bovine Madonna looking out on a sinful world with great, compassionate eyes, 'I wonder how many of us understood. I wish I could feel sure that I had.'

Bernard made no direct answer. 'I'm afraid,' he said, 'that much of it was an interior monologue. If you'll excuse me, I must speak to my sister. Elizabeth dear, get Mrs Craddock some tea.' Celia Craddock's gaze at his retreating figure was quite stony.

Bernard, remembering his confidence to his sister, was disturbed to see her in animated conversation with Terence. He need have had no such fear; whatever Isobel's political indiscretion, she had the honour of a schoolgirl where affairs of the heart were concerned. She would have blabbed state secrets, had any state been so foolish as to entrust them to her, to the first spy she met, but let the least emotional confidence be locked in that ample bosom, and, cross her heart, might she die if she sneaked, no dormitory bully or prying fellow don would ever get it from her.

When Bernard approached, Terence was deep in attention to a political harangue from Louie so that Isobel was able to draw her brother aside and whisper, 'That's your friend, isn't it, Bernard? I *knew* I was right. He's a very distinguished young man, dear. Louie likes him very much.' Indeed Louie was delighted; she had not been listened to so earnestly by anyone outside the Party since MacArthur's dismissal. She had carefully preserved her Left Bank student get-up for this bourgeois gathering, substituting only a pale sulphur silk square for the jade green scarf. For Terence, her boyish appearance was outstandingly more attractive than that of any other woman present.

'Liberty's the most sickening claptrap of all,' she was saying. 'Liberty to conscript, Liberty to keep millions on starvation level, Liberty to sit back on solid dividends and pour out woolly-minded platitudes.'

'I couldn't agree more about the woollymindedness,' said Terence. And as to liberty, he reflected, it was economic necessity that was throwing *him* into Sherman's unsavoury arms.

'Never mind,' said Louie with a laugh, 'we'll soon have the liberty to be blown to pieces.'

'You think all these talks will come to nothing?' He could not remember exactly what talks, but there were always some going on.

'When they've served Uncle Sam's propaganda purposes. Of course,' said Louie.

Terence felt a *frisson* almost of pleasure. In his neurotic search for expert opinion, he had at last found one voice that gave no hope and that put the guilt squarely on the shoulders of his own world. There *would* be war. She had pronounced it. His stomach constricted, and yet, at the same time, he found a relief; war was the final horror, here on the very doorstep, and yet it was quite unreal; meanwhile to dwell in panic on its presence shut out the dreary immediate reality of his decision to live with Sherman.

'Bernard thinks,' he said, 'that the Government are a restraining influence.'

Isobel had to join in Louie's laughter. 'You like the Walrus better than the Carpenter, because he sheds tears,' she said.

'I don't like any of them,' said Terence. 'I'm a sort of spiv, like any other artist. I just want to be left alone to design for the theatre.'

For the first time that afternoon, Bernard felt his despairing acceptance giving way before anger. Terence's hard clarity was one of his last rocks and he could not bear to see it crumbling.

'I imagine,' he said, 'that spivs, however artistic, receive very short shrift in Russia's great freedom to work.' Looking Terence up and down, he added, 'A little training, you know, would soon give you the physique needed for more immediate tasks than *décor* for *Aida*.' Terence winced at this stab in the back. Leicester Square, thought Bernard. But thrill and remorse were swept away by the rush of the ladies' expostulations.

'Really, Bernard, you've no right,' said Isobel. 'No country respects . . .'

But Louie took the platform as by right. 'Do you *know* any-thing, Mr Sands,' she asked, 'of the Soviet theatre? Of the high position that artists occupy in Russia? The care to ensure them quiet and spacious accommodation to work in?'

'Yes,' said Bernard. 'I only wish I could take it at its face value. But it seems to me so horribly like the bourgeois liberty you were deploring. Liberty to create under dictation, or liberty to sit back and express their feelings on large salaries given them at the expense of others' poverty.'

It was Terence's turn to stab. 'Oh! my dear,' he said, 'give me the large salary and I'll risk the remorse. I'm a bit sick of all this highmindedness if it's simply leading us to a nice high-minded atom bomb.'

Louie was saved the difficulty of sorting out so difficult an ally by the approach of Eric and Alan.

'Bernie!' cried Eric, 'Mimi's found a wonderful old woman serving at the tea tent with a cropped head and they're having a tremendous thing about children's undutifulness. Meanwhile hardly any tea is forthcoming.'

'I'm afraid,' said Alan laughing, 'that Mother is very deficient in sense of responsibility to the community.' Now that the burden of his mother's demands had been shed for a while, he was ready even to smile at his own customary priggishness. It was the highest mark of happiness he could show.

Terence walked over and shook Eric's hand. 'Let's go and look at the water-lily pond and see if it's as suburban as the rest of this dreary stately home,' he said. Noticing Bernard's alarm at this unexpected move, he attempted to make amends. 'My dear,' he said, 'I'm sure you're perfectly right and I'll see it all clearly as soon as I get into the shade. Politics and the sun to-gether always put me into a mad tizzy. I would,' he added, looking at Isobel and Louie, 'have made Mrs Pankhurst's silliest militant suffragette.' And, smiling at them all, he led Eric in the direction of the Dutch garden.

'You've just arrived in time,' said Bernard to Alan. 'The Welfare State's on trial for its life.'

'It couldn't have a more brilliant counsel for its defence,' said

Alan. He felt more and more that it was he who belonged to this world, not a child like Eric.

'Nor I'm afraid a more disingenuous one,' said Isobel. She noted Louie's growing disgust with distress and apprehension. 'My brother throws out a few vague charges against the Soviet Union and then pleads that we were attacking the Welfare State. I can't make you out, Bernard,' she went on, 'after the understanding you showed in your speech.'

Alan's boyish lieutenant smile changed to his usual tight-mouthed disapproval. He had found the speech distastefully decadent and irresponsible.

'My speech, Isobel dear,' said Bernard, 'related to the soul, and I apologize to you all now for treating you to so unsuitable a topic.'

Isobel and Alan tried to look as though they recognized that the soul had its place, and respected the deep seriousness that must necessarily underlie Bernard's light manner of speaking of it. Louie had no such scruples.

'You're fooling yourself, you know,' she said. 'You see as clearly as anyone that all this,' and she waved her hand around the garden, 'is death. You're just frightened to take on the job of living, that's all.'

'I hardly think,' said Alan, 'that an enterprise like the new Vardon Hall backs up your diagnosis.'

'No, no, Louie, give Bernard his due,' cried Isobel.

Louie smiled defiantly. 'I judge trees by their fruit,' she said.

Bernard narrowed his eyes as he addressed her. 'And I by their shape,' he said.

'Oh Lord! Art for art's sake. Thank God! you *aren't* going to speak at the Peace Meeting, with your personal messages and your personal morals.'

'Louie dear,' cried Isobel, 'that's Bernard's own responsibility.'

'It's every intelligent person's responsibility to let the people know the truth,' cried Louie.

Bernard noticed uncomfortably that numbers of nearby visitors had stopped to listen to the excited group.

173

'I should have thought,' said Alan, 'that the responsibility of intelligent people was to back those who know the facts.'

'That I reject too,' said Bernard. He could see Hubert and Sonia among the crowd who were collecting; a sense of inevitability urged him to stoke the senseless fire he had lit.

'I'm sorry for that,' said Alan. 'The more one is concerned with Education, the more one sees that people need a sense of direction if Communism is not . . . '

'Really,' said Isobel, 'it's too easy to label anything you don't like Communism.'

'If you had waited for my point,' said Alan, but Louie stamped her foot with anger.

'I don't know who you are,' she said, 'but it would be a very good thing if you didn't keep interrupting.'

'Mr Craddock is a friend of mine,' said Bernard, and turning to Isobel he added, 'I really think, Isobel, that Miss Randall would feel more comfortable if I left you. It was nice of you to come and I'm glad you liked my speech, though I'm sorry you got it wrong. . . . ' Isobel's trembling lip showed that she was on the point of tears, but this final indignity was spared her by the sudden irruption of James into their conversation.

'I don't know whether you realize,' he said in the kind of controlled, angry voice that carries, 'the exhibition you're making, Father, with this little Marble Arch debate, but, believe me, you'd be far better employed keeping all those damned workmen of yours under control.'

Hubert, standing a short distance away, turned to Sonia with mock admiration. 'The dear boy,' he said, 'is *always* ready to act on the spur of the moment.'

Terence took out a large crimson silk handkerchief from his trouser pocket and spread it on one of the stone seats by the large lily pond.

'You don't want those trousers to spoil,' he could not forbear to say, as he looked at Eric's bottle-green corduroys.

'Do you hate them?' asked Eric.

Terence, who was anxious to keep all the good behaviour on his own side, was rather annoyed at this disarming honesty.

'Well, they're certainly not me at all,' he said, 'but I expect they're ever so comfy.'

'Yes,' said Eric, 'but *I* got them because I thought they were rather beautiful.' He had determined on his honest line as they walked to the pond, and he was going to stick to it. 'Bernie looks awfully ill,' he said. This remark, too, annoyed Terence, since it removed the main lead from him in the conversation he had designed. Oh! well, he thought, I shall just have to give up all hope of handing it out, and let him have his nice, cosy, all-girls-together talk.

'That's just, my dear,' he said, parodying the conversation he imagined Eric wanted, 'what I wished to have a little get-together about. Did he tell you about his heart attack?' He tried not to be angered at Eric's genuine look of anxiety. 'It's not madly serious, but he *has* got to be careful,' he said.

'How did it happen?' asked Eric.

'Well, I don't know *how* it happened, if you mean about the blood circulation and the arteries and all that.'

Eric giggled, 'What a funny thing to think I meant. No, I meant where did it happen and what caused it?'

'Well, to be honest, my dear, in Bernard's flat one night last week with me. And as to the cause, he'd got into a sort of state about seeing somebody arrested for trying to pick people up. Only I still don't quite know *why* he got so upset about it.'

Eric looked very surprised. 'Wouldn't *you* get upset?' he asked.

'Oh! my dear! I was livid with anger, but there was something more with Bernard.'

'Oh,' said Eric, 'do you think that's why he made that sad little speech?'

'Well, it wasn't very little, and I didn't find it sad, only rather shaming. But yes, I do,' answered Terence.

'What do you think *I* can do to help?'

'I don't know how you go on,' Terence drawled, 'but that's why I told you. Because if you do go on too much or anything, then you couldn't say you hadn't been warned.'

'What a nasty way of speaking,' said Eric.

'Is it?' Terence replied. 'I'm afraid it's the only one I've got.'
There was silence for a few minutes.

'Will his family be any good?' asked Eric.

'I really don't know,' answered Terence. 'At least, I do, his daughter's very nice. I want to see her if I can this afternoon.'

'She wasn't very nice just now, when she was being rude to my mother.'

Terence felt sure that Elizabeth had been quite justified. 'How awful for you, my dear,' he said, 'but I'm afraid I shall have to see her all the same.'

Eric giggled again. 'I didn't think her rudeness to Mimi would alter your decision.'

Terence looked at him curiously. 'I see why Bernard likes you,' he said suddenly. 'You've got what's called a sense of the ridiculous. It's a kind of whimsy I've never been able to manage.' He got up from the seat. 'I'd better go and look for Elizabeth now,' he said.

'Shall we be friends, do you think?' asked Eric, still the little boy.

Terence considered for a moment. 'I shouldn't *think* so,' he said. 'I can't see why we should ever need to be. But I haven't got a mad thing against you, if that's what you mean.'

Eric, on the other hand, felt quite sure of his dislike for Terence; but he said nothing.

Eric strolled slowly back to the lawns, the young son of the old Philistine Lord Vardon – was he a marquis or an earl? – who had fought at Culloden Moor – was that possible? – and who now lay in old, old age on his death bed. At last he would be free from this foxhunting tyranny; all Vardon would be his, he would throw aside convention and dress in a simple black velvet jerkin and hose, and entertain the young poets, who were also breaking through the conventions of the age – already they were coming to be known as the Romantic Movement – Keats with his ringlets, the pale, beautiful Shelley and the handsome Byron who had smiled at him so sweetly and so strangely. . . .

Eric was standing and wondering whether it was he who had

brought the pampas grass to Vardon Hall and if so, why, when Bernard, breathing very heavily, came up to him.

'Bernie dear,' said Eric, taking his arm, 'you mustn't run about so.'

'I haven't really,' said Bernard, 'but my sister and I have had a silly political argument and I lost my temper. I'm very fond of my sister and it's upset me.'

'You must go and apologize,' said Eric.

Bernard ignored the suggestion. 'I'm afraid your brother didn't get a very good impression of us. I'm sorry because he seemed so much nicer to-day.'

'He was rather happy,' said Eric, 'but you needn't worry, he's never very happy for long anyway.'

'I'm glad you said that,' Bernard replied, 'because I don't think I *am* going to worry much these days whether people are unhappy or not, even you, Eric. Or at least I shan't do much about it.'

Eric realized suddenly that the future frightened him. All of it, with or without Bernard's help, with or without being Lorenzo's page or the young Lord Vardon. As though to point the moral, Ron, in his best dark-grey suit, pale peach shirt and silver tie, came across the lawn towards them.

'Hullo,' he said, 'I wondered if I'd see you here, seeing as you was such a good friend of Mr Sands.'

'This is Ron,' said Eric. 'I never told you, Bernie, about meeting him at St Albans.'

'No,' said Bernard, 'you didn't.'

'He told me he lived at Vardon, and I told him that I knew you.'

'Yes,' said Bernard, 'I see that you did.'

'Well, it's all gone all right, hasn't it, Mr Sands,' said Ron.

'Yes,' said Bernard, 'it's nearly over now.'

Ron fiddled with his belt and moved from one leg to another, but neither Bernard nor Eric spoke.

'You're lucky to have a pal like Mr Sands,' Ron said. 'I haven't got a pal.'

'I remember,' said Eric.

'You been to St Albans again?' asked Ron.

'No,' said Eric.

'You never seen the Abbey what you'd come special to see, not after you met me, did you?' Ron winked.

'You work for Mrs Curry, don't you?' asked Bernard.

'Don't hold that against me,' said Ron. 'I'd like to work for a man really.' He was sweating with the effort of getting his point across. As no one answered, he peered at Eric's tie. 'You like bright colours, don't you?' he said. 'He looks all right in them too, don't he?'

It seemed inconceivable that Mrs Curry's huge form could have been hidden behind a rather small azalea bush, but nevertheless she appeared so suddenly that Bernard got that rather unpleasant impression.

'Good afternoon, Mr Sands,' she said. 'I didn't know you knew Mr Sands, Ron.'

'This is his pal what I told you about what I met in St Albans.'

'How do you do?' said Mrs Curry. 'You write poetry, don't you, dear? Love lyrics, I expect.'

'No,' said Eric, 'I work in a bookshop.'

'Selling Mr Sands' books, eh?' Mrs Curry smiled. 'Quite a labour of love. Well, Mr Sands,' she went on, 'so we know one poet at least who'll make use of the new Vardon Hall. Very nice, too. I should have been so glad to have had you as a guest, dear, if I'd been able to run the hotel. Sitting about writing your love poems and Mr Sands coming up to see you, whenever he wanted.'

'You've got it wrong again,' said Bernard smiling. 'As Eric already said, he doesn't write poetry.'

'I expect it's because he *looks* so poetical,' said Mrs Curry; 'like Lord Alfred Douglas.'

'You go a long way back for your parallels,' said Bernard. 'One can see, I'm afraid, that you're not on your usual ground.'

'You dress like a poet, anyway, dear,' said Mrs Curry to Eric. 'You like a bit of colour, don't you? I expect you like a bit of something else too, although you look such a quiet boy. But then they often go together, don't they, Mr Sands?'

Eric's giggle broke the tension. 'What a funny thing to say,' he said. 'I shouldn't ever call you delicate, just because you're wearing such a delicate shade of mauve.'

Mrs Curry gave her brutal laugh. 'You've got the ready answer ready, haven't you?' she said. 'We'll have to see more of each other, I can see.'

'Thank you,' said Eric, 'but I'm afraid I must go now to find my mother. I left her at the tea tent talking to an extraordinary old woman with cropped hair. I'm sure she was tiddley. Only, of course, Mimi never notices things like that.'

'Christ,' said Ron, 'that sounds like *my* mother. You been giving her something to drink?' he asked Mrs Curry.

'She seemed so tired, poor old dear,' said Mrs Curry. 'I gave her a bottle of whisky to keep her on her feet.'

'Well, she won't be on 'em long,' said Ron. 'Nice sort of night I'm going to have.'

'I'll help you to put her to bed,' said Mrs Curry. 'I'll come along with *you* now,' she told Eric, 'and see how she is.'

As the squat mauve figure walked off with her chin pressed close to Eric's shoulder, they reminded Bernard of Alice and the Duchess. It's love, he thought, that makes the world go round.

'You haven't got no special pal in Vardon, have you?' said Ron.

'I haven't any pals in Vardon,' Bernard replied.

'No!' said Ron. 'Mrs Curry don't like you.'

'I'm sorry for that,' Bernard answered.

'If I was your pal, I could tell you lots of things about her what would make it easy for you to deal with her.'

'I doubt if I shall have to *deal* with Mrs Curry,' said Bernard.

'Course I wouldn't meet you in the village,' said Ron, who was 'sexing' with his eyes to an almost painful degree, 'but I might see you in Bantam.'

'I shouldn't think so,' said Bernard. 'I hardly ever go there.'

'Your brother-in-law's got in proper with Mrs Curry. He better know how to look after himself.' When Bernard did not reply, Ron said archly, 'I don't seem to appeal to you.'

'No,' said Bernard, 'I think we might bring the conversation to an end.' He walked across to the drive, where the last motor cars were making their departure. As he crossed the lawn, he was met by a drunk Sherman with his band of friends.

'You old horror,' Sherman said, waving his hand towards the direction of Ron, 'always getting what everyone's after. But still we mustn't be grouchy, after all it *is* your big day.' Sherman's friends were too awed by Bernard to do more than sway lightly; but peals of giggles came to him, after he had left them.

Hubert Rose was standing on the steps of the Hall as Bernard entered. He crossed over and stood for a moment looking at Bernard, his dark face embarrassed and agitated.

'I liked what you said. Perhaps since all this has been so bloody, you might care to hear that.' He spoke without his usual drawl, quickly and jerkily. 'I'm glad that you should see how deeply one must go under in order to come up again. I hope that you meant it. Actually, of course, I know you did. You are the only completely respectable man among us, you see. I'm not respectable to myself, but I can respect others.'

'I'm not respectable to *myself*. I hope I didn't convey such an idea.' Bernard was puzzled.

'No, no. I understood that. That's why I can speak to you, because it *seems* as though we were the same. But in fact, we're not. I can know that, at least. But I'm with you against all the others, if understanding counts, and I would like you to know it, and how much respect I must feel from that very fact.' He took Bernard's hand and held it for a moment. Then he smiled ironically and said, 'You'd better not make much of me, though. It's probably only a piece of theatricalism caught on what, if I may say so, my dear fellow, has been a damned bad afternoon of amateur dramatics.' He turned away, but before he finally left Bernard he added, 'I'm afraid your daughter-in-law found it all rather a strain, which is one comfort.'

Sonia was to find it all even more of a strain before the afternoon finally ended. Things had gone from bad to worse at the tea tent. Mrs Curry's liberality to Ron's mother had exceeded the one bottle of whisky to which she had confessed, and Mrs

Wrigley had found great pleasure in bountiful distribution to the mixed body of local helps and hired waiters who were charged with dispensing refreshment. The earliest effects, operative when the crowd was at its greatest, had merely appeared in a somewhat jolly and offhand inattentiveness and muddle. Soon, however, Mrs Wrigley had fallen into a very talkative, complaining state. It was at this stage that she had taken such a fancy to Mrs Craddock.

Celia, of course, prided herself on her 'common touch', particularly with 'characters' like Mrs Wrigley; in Esher her 'friends', she was always most emphatic in stating, were the dustman, the milkman, and the old woman who dealt in second-hand clothes. She could speak to them, she always found, on a level of reality that suburbia simply did not understand. It was, she implied, an old Virginian tradition.

' *You* look after your pretty figure, my dear,' said Mrs Wrigley, as she handed Celia a cup of washy tea and a battered cream bun.

Mrs Craddock was delighted. 'My dear,' she said, 'I promise you I will.' She spoke very seriously and emphatically, as though to a child, and with that roving glance at the assembled company which usually accompanies serious conversations with children.

'Don't ever have no babies,' said Mrs Wrigley.

'Gracious me,' said Mrs Craddock, 'I don't think that's very likely now.'

'Children are that ungrateful,' grumbled Mrs Wrigley. 'I got eleven of them. Won the *News of the World* tray for it. But much good it's done me. Three's in Aussie, and my daughter over Ipswich way's got the television. I might be dead for all they care.'

Mrs Craddock's lovely eyes glowed with the rich comedy of life. She put an arm round both her sons. 'There you are darlings,' she said, 'you have been judged.' It was after this that Alan and Eric slipped away.

If there was some discontent among the waiting customers during the next quarter of an hour, Mrs Craddock was oblivious of it. She laughed and agreed; and caught Mrs Wrigley's rich little phrases and played with them like bright juggling balls. It was all the fullness of Françoise and Mrs Gamp, Mr Doolittle and Slipslop for a woman like her. Perhaps Mrs Wrigley showed signs of getting a bit obstetrical, but any true, genuine humour is after all worth its salt.

'Dead drunk he was all the night,' said Mrs Wrigley, 'and little Ron come buttocks first.' She looked at her new-found beautiful friend. 'Don't let them do it to you, dear,' she said, 'there's ways and means. Now, if you was to take a rhubarb root regular. . . .'

Mrs Craddock's laughter became a little more strained. 'I really don't think,' she said, 'that there's much you can teach *me*.'

Mrs Wrigley's scaly hand seized at her delicate wrist. 'Shameful, that's what it is,' she said, and though she began her reproach with a merry twinkle, her new friend's attempts to remove her hand seemed to change her mood. 'Lot of whores that's what you all are now,' she said. It was lucky for Mrs Craddock that the old woman's attention, so quickly diverted, suddenly became aware of the disapproving, though dwindling, crowd. 'Gloomy lot they are for a party,' she said. 'I wish I had my gramophone.' Mrs Craddock, who had contemplated a rather shameful flight from life's racy humour, felt able to retain her amused position, though at a slightly greater distance.

She even hummed a tune, as Mrs Wrigley bawled, 'But in spite of all temptations to belong to other nations, He remains an Englishman,' though she did not feel prepared to vaunt her Virginian blood, when the old woman glowered menacingly in front of her and said, 'We're all English here, I hope.'

It was somewhat of a relief, however, to see Eric approaching, accompanied by an enormous smiling woman in mauve.

'Funny old thing,' said Mrs Curry, 'she's having a real larkey do. She's not worrying you, is she, dear?' she asked Celia.

'Good heavens, no!' Mrs Craddock replied. 'No one who's happy worries me.'

'This is my mother,' said Eric. 'This is Mrs Curry who has the *most* peculiar ideas.'

'He's a naughty boy,' said Mrs Curry, 'but it's easy to see where he gets his pretty looks from. Come along, dear,' she added to Mrs Wrigley. 'We'll get Ron and have a nice comfy evening, just the three of us.'

It was at this moment that Sonia appeared. She had been warned of the unsuitable scene by a number of the local gentry, whom she had met as they were leaving. Such embarrassment, coming on top of a row with Berthe and Nicholas, was more than she could stand.

'Get out of here at once,' she cried to Mrs Wrigley. 'How dare you encourage this disgusting exhibition,' and her accusation took in not only Mrs Curry, but Mrs Craddock also. 'I have no intention of letting this be forgotten,' she said.

Mrs Curry smiled at her. '*You* don't want to make a fuss, Mrs Sands,' she said. 'It wouldn't do at all for you with all your position here to think of.' She took Mrs Wrigley's arm, and the two fat old women waddled away.

Sonia turned on Mrs Craddock. 'How perfectly beastly!' she cried. 'Why can't you stay in your own home?'

'What a very rude lady,' said Eric.

Mrs Craddock raised her great eyes to her son's face. 'No darling!' she said, 'just dear English democracy, bless it!'

'I don't know why you're here,' said Sonia, 'but you'd much better go. It's getting very late.'

At the sound of Sonia's hysterical voice, Elizabeth detached herself from her mother. 'Control yourself, Sonia,' she said. 'I'm so frightfully sorry, Mrs Craddock, I'm afraid my sister-in-law's had too much to do. It was terribly sweet of you to come so far. Would you like me to get you a car?' She was glad to repair her earlier rudeness.

Sonia rushed up to Ella. 'You realize the appalling scandal these wretched people have caused,' she cried.

'No, dear,' said Ella, 'I don't know who they are.'

'This is Mrs Craddock and her son, Mummy,' said Elizabeth loudly; 'they're great friends of Father's.'

'How very nice of you to have come,' said Ella. 'I'm afraid it's been a very tiring afternoon.'

'I've enjoyed every minute of it,' said Mrs Craddock, as she and Eric departed.

'Sonia, dear,' said Ella, 'you oughtn't to have spoken like that to Bernard's friends, or to anybody for that matter.'

'Friends!' cried Sonia. 'Just another of his fancy boys by the look of him.' And when Ella made no reply, she shouted, 'Don't pretend you don't know. Everybody knows. You don't care, that's all. You don't care a damn how it hurts James and Nicholas.'

Ella's head trembled, and she murmured, 'Of course, I know, dear.' But Elizabeth towered in rage over her sister-in-law.

'You bloody little bitch,' she said, 'if things don't turn out just as you want them, you'll hurt anybody to get your own back.' Sonia was quite frightened by her sister-in-law's manner. She literally ran away. Ella began to cry. It was at this moment that a young reporter with rather too long dark hair and a high-necked sweater appeared.

'I just want to get a last photo,' he said. Elizabeth sprang towards him in her rage. 'What bloody cheek!' she cried, 'how dare you?' She seemed about to knock the camera to pieces. It was Terence who held her back.

'My dear Elizabeth,' he said, 'I've been looking for you all the afternoon. Don't take on so, duckie. It's all right,' and then as she began to sob wildly, 'Dear, dear Elizabeth,' he said, and kissed her. He led both mother and daughter weeping from the grounds.

The picture of Ella appeared in that week's local paper, headed, 'Novelist's wife weeps at husband's triumph.'

It seemed to Bernard a fitting end to the day's agony when Bill came into his room that evening. 'I'm pushing off now,' he said. His eyes were very bloodshot and his speech was still slurred. 'I made a bloody exhibition of myself this afternoon, I'm no bloody good to anyone, Bernard.'

Bernard laid his head back against the armchair and pulled at his cigarette. 'Being good to people,' he said, 'is a dangerously complicated process.'

Bill swayed slightly on his huge legs. 'Those young chaps who are going to live up at the Hall,' he asked, 'can they write?'

'*I* think so,' said Bernard.

'Yes,' answered Bill, 'I thought so. Even that poet that talked all that balls. I *can't* write, you know. I like doing it. They say that's the main point, but it isn't. I expect I write too much, but I'm always thinking of things. That's good work you're doing, then, giving them a place to work in.'

'It's done and over,' said Bernard. 'It's theirs now, or, perhaps, somebody else's. Certainly not mine.'

'*You* ought to be writing, you know,' said Bill, 'that's what you're good at. You wouldn't be feeling like this, like all that you said up at that place, if you were writing.'

Bernard smiled. 'You know as well as I do, Bill,' he said, 'one writes what one has to say. At the moment, I see Nothing behind nothing.'

Bill sat down and stared at his brother-in-law. 'All this isn't just because you like boys, is it? You don't want to take any notice of what all these little people say, you know. *Chacun à son goût,*' he said, and, though he had not meant to, he gave a salacious chuckle. Bernard, hearing it, said nothing. 'I'm no good,' said Bill, 'no good at all and, as you well know, I don't even get a kick out of admitting it any more. I'm badly in debt again,' he added, 'to that old bitch in the village. I talked a lot of cock, you know, about her – Earth Mother and all that. She's only a cheap crook, really, a bit off her rocker, but that doesn't make her any more than a crook. I always fall for any line that people shoot; I suppose I see the story in it. Ought to have been a journalist, really. I probably only swallowed it though because she gave me the chance to gamble.'

'I'm sorry the debts are to Mrs Curry,' said Bernard. 'It's put them in with a great deal of Danegeld, and I've not decided yet whether I must pay Danegeld. If I do, rest assured they'll be paid.'

'Don't be frightened of the old cow,' said Bill; 'she's got far too dirty a record to turn nasty over anything. She tried to pump me about you, but I wasn't having any. She's doing something damned nasty for that chap Rose at the moment. Little girl under age or something. I suppose any decent man would have taken action about it. But I travel light, you know,' he explained. '*You* could get them on it, Bernard, though. They've nothing tangible against you, have they?'

'No,' said Bernard, 'nothing. Perhaps, if they had, I should be more free to live. I have it all, Bill, against myself. And so, you see,' he added, 'I, too, have to travel light.'

BOOK III

CHAPTER ONE

In Sickness and in Health

IN the weeks that followed the opening of Vardon Hall, Bernard lived a strange, confused existence. Night, through long hours of sleeplessness, became mixed with day; events that were separated by but a few days seemed months apart, as his weary consciousness was forced to live through the hours of darkness. Dreams, peculiarly vivid in the short periods of sleep that forced themselves upon him at the least expected moments, were inextricably mingled with the real world around him. A restless overflow of nervous energy would drive him to long, exhausting walks through the countryside, from which he returned too tired to sleep, eager only to escape the confinement of his bedroom in turns about the garden at those death-still, moonlit early hours when the trees cast great shadows across the level lawn.

Ella had retreated far into her world of shapes and figures, and lay for hours in bed, weeping as the threatening darkness seemed once more to close in upon her, swallowing up her personality in a sea of unrelated fears. They might have been two different species, brooding, prowling in the narrow limits of their private hells, each as little concerned with the other's trapped existence as a restless, pacing leopard with a she-bear sunk in torpor in a nearby cage.

Meals, in such circumstances, were irregular and neglected. The house fell under the tyranny of the servants' care. Bernard, for whom whole aeons seemed to be passing, wondered constantly that the garden was not choked with waist-high weeds and the house not buried beneath the century's dust. Yet every morning the mowing machine and the vacuum cleaner brought

187

unwelcome evidence of a world still fighting corruption, rank-
ness and decay, a world still demanding decision, choice, and
affection. Every morning, too, he felt his stock of these com-
modities dwindling before the sudden rush demand upon his
tired will.

The demands arrived most usually by the morning mail, for
even Sonia had been daunted by the death-like response her visits
had received. Terence had telephoned during a Soho meal with
Elizabeth, and Elizabeth after a visit to Kew with Terence; but
this unexpected and repeated combination produced no more
than a wearied register from Bernard, while Ella only found in
Terence's name another obsessive word to distract her energies
from their determined fight.

For Bernard, tramping resolutely in stout brogues and heavy,
high-necked sweater through the light, misty rains that had followed the intense heat of the preceding month, the familiar
countryside had become a desperate need, an opiate urgently
craved to dull the pains of the human conflicts that were wrack-
ing his exhausted mind. Conflicts, so carefully brought out, so
lovingly delineated in his novels, where they so inevitably and
easily led to the climaxes and resolutions that released him from
the strain of creation, now seemed an enveloping mesh of personal memories and guilts that offered no conceivable solution
that could ease his soul. It would have been simple, of course, to
have retrieved and recomposed the fragments of his stable
existence, scattered in the morbid moods and unfortunate events
of the last weeks. He had met far more difficult practical situations with resolution in the past. A little positive affirmation, a
few decisive actions would quickly dispel the atmosphere of mistrust and scandal that had gathered around him. The very
activity required for rebuilding confidence in his direction of
Vardon Hall would have gone far to dispel his depression and his
distrust of himself. Eric and Terence needed guidance no less
because he now distrusted his own motives in giving it; the
difficulties of providing such help were but little increased by the
collapse of those screens around his private life which, in any
case, comfort rather than honesty had urged him to preserve.

The vulgar threats and innuendoes of Mrs Curry's petty Alsatia could not stand for a moment against a well-directed retributive stroke. It was even likely that, with his old life once more firmly established, the ugly, dirt-smeared corners in the dark twisted passage of his will, which he had glimpsed again and again in the preceding weeks, only to see so clearly in the neon lighting of Leicester Square, might then have been cleared and scoured to take their place in the daylight world of his conscious existence. But he found in himself no belief or will adequate to support the task.

The surging rustle of the wind as it swept the oats, the strange loud popping of the rain as it beat upon the dry wheat ears, fat furry caterpillars found upon the shining wet roadway, the sudden bigness of an owl in a countryside of small creatures, the tropical giant white convolvulus trumpets among the depressingly modest wayside flowers of England – such sudden and intense visual and aural contacts seemed his sole defence against the human flood that surged about him. Yet the countryside, too, had its Wordsworthian threat of moral stirrings. Through wood, hedgerow, and field alike, memory found its way to menace his security. The beech trees echoed with the loneliness of James's and Elizabeth's childhood as the wood-doves cooed their mourning. The distant whistle of a train or the far-off bark of a farmyard dog – so often, in the past, faint, sad sounds that yet drove home the happiness of solitude – now seemed only to speak of the false comradeship with which he had protected himself from his children's hearts. The sudden harsh shriek of a jay mocked at his pride in his fearless candour with his lovers. He could trace now no kindness in his teasing exposure of Eric's ignorance, or in his witty rebukes of Terence's vulgarity; he could see only the white, frightened face of the arrested young man changing to the pink flush of Eric's embarrassment or the wincing tick of Terence's cheek, and could detect only his own answering shudder of pleasure. He found bunches of willow-herb and campion dying by the roadside where some children returning from school had idly picked and dropped them; and he instantly longed to take magic flight to London that he might offer to Isobel the love and apologies that might revive their dying intimacy. He would startle the rabbits from the lush, rain-soaked fields, as with a cumbrous, unconvincing jauntiness he climbed the gate bars – for he felt a constant need to assure himself by movement that the machine of his body was not grinding to a standstill. Seeing their headlong flight – all ears and quivering white scuts – he would wonder if so to watch the young poets and writers scamper and quiver in dismay as he told them that their hopes were at an end, their trust in him ludicrous, Vardon Hall a play that would not be put on, could perhaps calm for ever his fevered need to smash the images of love and kindliness before which he had worshipped so long in self-deceived, conventional homage. Once, in defiance of his body's long-learnt urge to save the weak, he forced himself to stand by while a weasel sucked the brain from a quivering rabbit. What was one more rabbit compared to the satisfaction of the snakelike creature's tensed lust? But he could find no bond of kinship that recalled the brotherhood seal of Hubert's handshake. Perhaps, he reflected – for he did not spare himself his customary mockery, though its sting made no impact upon his present mood of dramatic hysteria – the rabbit, like Hubert's small girl victim, had too little appeal to his paederastic taste to make its suffering a test of the true source of his humane ideals.

He found his greatest peace far up on a distant hump of the downs among scabious and trefoil. There, by the iron railings of a dewpond, he would lie and gaze into the sky and lose himself for a while in the hurrying blanket white clouds above him; until one afternoon he found a solitary duck, swimming in rapid crazy circles upon the small pond, and instantly he was reminded of his life with Ella, alone and yet never alone; and the hill peak, too, became closed to him.

Nowhere seemed closed to Elizabeth and Terence during those weeks. They went everywhere together. At first, their meetings were designed to discuss 'the Bernard situation' – the meetings of two hard, competent minds, content to accept their ultimate antipathy in a common effort to solve a practical problem. As the weather was fine, it seemed foolish to be stuck indoors, and when the rainy days followed, it was somehow an additional impetus to competent discussion to brave the wet in long rides on the tops of buses or on the river steamers to Greenwich or Hampton Court. Elizabeth played truant from her office and Terence let important contacts go unheeded. There was so much to report, of someone's colourful story of Bernard's sex life and of someone else's chance remark that 'Communists like Sands were at the root of a lot of the trouble'; there were discussions of how to counteract this rumour and how to give the lie to that; there were analyses of Bernard's problems, which inevitably led to reminiscence. Imperceptibly the discussion changed to more personal questions – of whether Terence was really 'queer' and if so, why; of whether Elizabeth need be bound by her childhood unhappiness. Terence would point out how much happier she was when she was not being 'bright', and wasn't that nice? Elizabeth would retaliate with how much happier he was when he was not being 'camp' and wasn't *that* nice? They enjoyed analysing and converting each other; and they delighted in pointing out that each was far too tough and sophisticated to be really influenced by anything but clear thinking and hard, enlightened self-interest. They enjoyed, too, showing each other little-known aspects of London – an Italianate Methodist Chapel in Lewisham, a strange formal garden in Highbury, open to the public but visited by no one, the arty horror of Church Street and the chic horror of Beauchamp Place, Ethical Churches and Christadelphian meeting houses – and they found even greater pleasure in visiting all the tourist's haunts that neither had ever seen before – the Elgin Marbles, Frogmore, the Dome of Discovery, the armour at the Tower, Kensington Palace, above all the Fun Fair. In a little while they saw the conventional 'romance' aspect of these jaunts, and then they enjoyed guying it. 'Thanks for the memory,' Terence would sing, 'of sounds of London's bells and queues at Sadler's Wells. How lovely it's been.' Elizabeth was a little slower in assuming a mood, but soon she was responding with 'The rush hour buses passing Hyde Park Corner, a visit to observe the Zoo's new fauna, a quick look round Pontings, these foolish things remind me of you,' only she tended to continue her parodies to a point where Terence became slightly embarrassed. Yet now that the barriers he had so long set up against whimsy were breaking down, he seemed almost to delight in the embarrassment that followed.

After their first night together, Terence said, 'Darling Elizabeth, you can't imagine what a relief it is that sex has at last reared its ugly head,' and Elizabeth agreed. For Terence, at first at any rate, it was strangely pleasant to feel released from the need to disguise guilty motives of main chance by shows of technical efficiency. For Elizabeth it was wonderful to be free from the melancholy secretiveness of her previous relations with married men – 'I might have known,' said Terence, when she told him, 'it would be a lot of dreary father-figures that have messed your life up.' – Yet it was not ultimately sex that gave them their fullest content, but the first sense of equality in age and affection. They guyed the 'sweetheart' aspect of their intimacy, but for Elizabeth, certainly, the mockery was only a self-protection against an onrush of love so deep that she was afraid of it. At first it was Terence who insisted on holding hands in the cinema and the park. 'Stop being so damned refined,' he said. 'What's the good of walking out if you're going to spoil it all by being stuffy and Kensington.' But it was Elizabeth who refused to smoke a cigarette unless it was shared with Terence; riding on the top of a bus, with her head on his shoulder, she would take the cigarette from his mouth and puff at it, her eyes closed with happiness, until Terence really began to wonder if he would ever smoke a cigarette of his own again. 'Don't act so common, dear,' he would say, but Elizabeth would only giggle in reply, and then, 'Oh dear! I never knew a girl could be so happy,' she would sigh. Arrived at Kew Gardens or Hampstead Heath, they would feed the jostling, snapping ducks with bits of cake and buns from a paper bag. Lying there, watching the glittering green heads and wagging tails, they felt themselves part of the holiday crowd around them, free at last from the rack of self-advancement and of self-pity, free at last from solitude.

Eric's solitude, as he stood among the gobbling 'bolshies', seemed complete. The return from Vardon Hall had unleashed all the dormant hostility and jealousy which Alan's injured pride had suppressed since he came home from the War to find his young brother securely embedded in the heart of his mother's affections. Throughout Alan's childhood, Mrs Craddock's aloof beauty and triumphant femininity had raised her above filial devotion to an adoration that he felt to be beyond word or gesture. She was woman enthroned, the symbol that urged man on to face all dangers, the purity that saved him from all cheapening act or thought. Isolated in his seriousness from his contemporaries, he had woven a picture of the deep love between them – the deeper because it had never been uttered – only to find that Eric's easy acceptance of her, his very despised effeminacy, had broken down the exalted temple and the holy places, and built of them a cosy, gossiping women's parlour, from which an ordinary man like himself felt excluded. What he could do by hard work and decent living to win her regard he had done, but the fires of resentment had continued to smoulder.

The blaze when it broke out on the return from Vardon was fierce and crackling. He had seen enough and heard enough, Alan cried, to know just what sort of a midden Eric had got himself into. He only hoped, he said, that Eric realized the sort of way that kind of thing ended up. Oh! he knew all the cant about art and self-expression that people of that kind used to excuse themselves, but when Eric was a little older he would see the difference between second-rate poseurs and people of real greatness. Habit, he warned Eric, was the most dangerous master. Could he not see the tragedy of Sands' own life; every word of his speech showed it, let alone all that hysterical mob of fellow-travellers and God knew what that had gathered round him. It had really been an eye-opener to him, he said, to see what went on, when he thought of the distinguished men who apparently were either too cynical or too flabby to protest. Such a cleansing of the stables as he could see was needed, no wonder the nation was so slack. What he disliked most, he declared, was the pretence of highmindedness that people like Sands adopted.

193

If Alan appeared to forget his progressive standpoint entirely in his anger, Eric's gaiety, frivolity, and irreverence also seemed to vanish. If Alan had so little human sympathy, so little under-standing of anyone's nature but his own, it was disgraceful, Eric shouted, that he should have any authority over youth. It was typical of anyone so completely small-minded, so totally without sensitivity, that he should be frightened of men like Bernie who lived by a larger code. He could hardly expect that anyone so essentially self-centred and mean as his brother would appreciate that one could care so deeply about someone greater than one-self that one would give them anything, yes anything, that would make life happier and fuller for them.

The louder they both shouted and the more red in the face they got the higher the moral plane they felt it necessary to ascend to, until only physical violence could have brought them down to earth. Since a certain sense of dignity still restrained them from a return to nursery fighting, there was nothing left for them but to retire to their respective rooms in sulks.

Mrs Craddock behaved superbly. She never allowed the slightest gesture to show her awareness of the scene, though she came into the room once or twice during the quarrel to fetch a book, her glasses and the *Radio Times*. But her finest hour came later in the evening when each of her sons in turn tried to enlist her allegiance.

'Eric, darling,' she said, when her younger son attempted to raise the subject as they were washing up after dinner, 'don't look so pompous. It's all right for Alan, darling, because, ssh! don't tell a soul,' and she put her finger to her lips, 'he feels important and grand and dutiful, but it doesn't do for you and me, we're much too irresponsible. Tell me all about this silly business, if you really have to, but don't expect me to be serious about it,' she put her arm round Eric's waist. 'I value the gay relationship we have far too much to let it get involved in a lot of huffing and puffing about nothing. You see, darling, how selfish I am,' she ended. 'Whenever people start to look important about themselves, I always begin to giggle.'

With Alan, however, she didn't giggle at all. She looked up so seriously from her pillow when, pacing male and clumsy about her bedroom – the very temple of feminine delicacy to him – her elder son began to speak his heart. Then, patting her rose-coloured quilt, she indicated to him that he might sit there. 'I can't have you prowling, darling, however serious it is,' she cried.

'It *is* pretty serious,' Alan replied. 'I don't even know whether I can talk to you about it.'

Mrs Craddock took his hand and looked very steadily into his eyes. After a pause, she said very deliberately, 'Then don't. Not because it isn't probably something that I don't know already, but because our relationship is built on trust, Alan. Trust and silence. There are so many things we don't talk about, you and I. Things that perhaps we couldn't talk about without twisting ourselves into shapes we don't want to be. But that doesn't matter, I know, and I think and hope you know, that we're on the same side, on the side of decent, clean things.' Then, kissing her son on the cheek, 'Now go to bed, darling,' she said, 'and remember that Eric's awfully young, and you know as well as I do, with all your experience, that young people need leading, not driving.'

It was a chastened, serious, more progressive Alan who began 'leading' Eric the next day. He was afraid, he said, that he must have seemed very pompous the day before. Eric must not misunderstand him. He had not read Bernard Sands' books; but he had heard enough of them and seen enough of the man to realize how easily he could command a younger fellow's devotion. Sands was clearly a man of outstanding ability and unusual breadth of understanding, though personally he could not help feeling, a tragic figure. In any case, he had not lived twenty-eight years without realizing that we were not all cast in the same mould. He had only been trying to say – and making a mess of it, he was afraid – that perhaps this was not the happiest road for Eric to follow. It might seem all right now, but one had to think of twenty years hence. Everyone went through certain phases – when they were at school, for example. But one had to grow up. He offered to pay for a psychoanalyst for Eric, if that would help. He had been immensely struck, he said, in the Army, with the

number of first-rate men who shared his brother's difficulty –
interesting and often good men, but a bit more highly strung
than the rest – and there was no doubt at all, he assured Eric, of
the immense good that psychiatry had done for them. He ended
by reminding Eric how remarkably lucky they were in the
mother they had – so extraordinarily unusual and courageous, so
well worth trying to live up to. He felt sure that Eric, who
understood her in many ways far better than he could – it cost
Alan a lot to say this – would be the last person to wish to add to
the pretty grim way in which life had treated her.

Unfortunately Mimi's advice had affected her younger son as
much as her elder. Eric was determined not to repeat his mood
of solemnity. He thanked Alan very much – he was, in fact, quite
sincerely moved – but Alan mustn't take him so seriously. He
often doubted if he had what was usually called a personality yet.
Certainly he had not acquired any fixed aim or way of life. He
was probably, he giggled, going through what was called 'a
phase'. As Alan himself had said, we were all very different. He
supposed that he had that exceedingly bogus thing – an artistic
temperament. In any case, he had got to work it out for himself.
No doubt he would find what he believed they called his feet in
time. Once more he giggled. He ended by agreeing with his
brother that so unusual, so lovely a mother – he inserted this
adjective as his own personal appreciation of Mimi – must be
their first consideration and care. For fear of hurting Alan, he
forbore to say that he also believed her to be completely aware
of his way of living.

They parted with mutual respect and an even greater mis-
understanding of one another.

It was then that Eric, in panic, began to bombard Bernie with
letters and telephone calls. From public call-boxes in the lunch
hour and secretively from the bookshop he rang the London flat
and got no reply. He hesitated before ringing Vardon, for fear of
causing Bernie domestic difficulties. It was only after he had
received no answer to three letters that he felt justified in risking
Bernie's peace. But the contact only added to his anxiety. Yes,
Bernie said, he had received Eric's letters. He was deeply

ashamed not to have answered them, but a reply was on its way. His affection was not in any way altered but, as Eric would see from the letter when he got it, there was much to consider besides affection, or rather much to consider within affection. In short Eric must follow his own judgement most carefully. In answer to Eric's pressing questions, he added that he saw no reason why any of the plans about London should be changed, any help he had promised to give he would give – and be glad to give, he corrected with a break in his voice – but Eric alone could decide.

The letter, when it came, had clearly been written after this telephone conversation.

My dearest Eric, it read, *you are right to be angry with me for not replying to you, but you are not right to be anxious. If you want my help in getting to London and in studying, you have it. You know that. If you want my very deep affection, you have it. You know that too. I cannot, at the moment, give you guidance or counsel. You have complained once or twice of my moralizing influence. You were quite right. My influence must of necessity be 'moral', I thought that my motives too were 'moral', now I have no such faith. Yours is a difficult enough life without the added danger of my motives; so I think, my dear, you must avoid that danger. I hope, but with no conviction, that I am simply 'ill' – sickness of the soul is a convenient piece of high-sounding cant – if so, I shall know that I am well again when I can take your curious mixture of irreverence and happiness and seriousness as they should be taken – with gratitude. Until then, rely on them to form your own judgement. I would like to say something about your mother, but motive forbids.*
With all my love,
Bernie.

Eric had derived little comfort from this letter, less still, perhaps, from Mrs Craddock's determined easiness, the gaiety with which she met his depressed silence and mooching each evening after work.

And so, as he stood by the gobbling 'bolshies', he felt none of the usual thrill at their gay, glittering, shimmering colours. He was alone, the fair Antinous, careless of the ibises to whose warm scarlet plumage he had once been wont to draw the Emperor's attention, intent now only upon old Nile itself. Soon there would be but busts and statues and the grief of an Emperor. The tears of Hadrian would be too late, though he watered the whole world from Britain to Scythia. Damn Hadrian, and damn Bernie who by his moralizing and the mocking influence he was now so selfishly withdrawing had cut off even the refuge of daydreams.

He started from his reverie as Mrs Craddock placed her hand on his shoulder.

'Do peacocks make a hideous noise?' she asked.

'I don't know,' Eric replied in surprise; 'they're said to.'

'Oh dear!' said Mrs Craddock. 'Well, it was only an extravagant dream. I was thinking as I came back from the post that you might like to add to the "bolshies". Something exotic to gladden our sad days together.'

Bernard received Celia Craddock's letter at breakfast. The handwriting sprawled and jerked across the thick, rough-edged paper.

My dear friend, he read, *I have so long rehearsed this letter that it cannot but seem lifeless and secondhand to me. I can only hope that your generous spirit and penetrating sympathy will pierce the empty words to the sincere distress which makes me write them. Eric is sad and puzzled! I am not so fond a mother as to think it extraordinary that a young man should be so. All humanity worth its salt is often sad, all young people should be, must be, puzzled. But there are sadnesses of growth, moods that come and go with the awakening consciousness of passing time – or so it seems to me, though I am appalled to think of writing my poor reflections on mankind to you – these are puzzles, necessary puzzles that lead on to new views of life. Eric's are not. His sadness is ingrowing, it may lead to bitterness. His puzzle may end in the boring eternal question mark of the premature cynic.*

It is because you and I alone see and value his unusual quality of natural gaiety and strange impudence to life's pomposity – an impudence that I always think comes neither from ignorance nor from cynicism, but from a deep seriousness – do you agree, I wonder? – that

I have determined to write to you what might otherwise seem a cruel letter. I know that it must seem cruel to you, and I know also that you will take it and accept it far below the surface of its immediate unwelcomeness. (She had written here and then crossed out, *Is there such a word? Oh! how awful it is to write a letter to a great writer.* The letter continued.) *You will accept what I write not only because you are the very remarkable man you are, so that any words from me would be impertinent, but because you have been and have the power to be more, so much more, to Eric than I can ever be. Oh, yes! it's true, my dear friend. You have, I think, believed that I minded. And in face of such a judgement I have of necessity searched and searched the truth of my mind as far as we poor creatures can know it. But for once I think you are wrong — do you perhaps occasionally fix people a little in moulds that are oh such clever moulds, but that don't just quite fit? I am far too selfish, far too exultant in myself and all that surrounds me to be the possessive mother you novelists so delight in. But just because I love life so much myself, I must want my son to grow up loving it too. As I have watched his delight in you and all you could give him, I have tried so hard to stand aside. Pulled affections are so cruel, and* whatever else *we must not be cruel.*

You described yourself once — was it to me or in some newspaper? when people are famous, it's so difficult to know — as a humanist. It is to the humanist then that I appeal. Eric is sad because his idol has feet of clay. There, I have written it at last and it has hurt you. You will know of course that I do not point to any real defect in you, but only to the impossibility of anyone with a large life, large interests, large sympathies like you being the central core of any young person's existence, as Eric in his youthful egotism had expected. I had thought before that he was adult enough not to expect it — I believe you have thought so too — but alas! he is not.

Vardon Hall was the collapse of the very sky above him. Oh! not the project, the future of Vardon Hall, that is and will be fine. *But your speech, my dear friend, your sad, despairing speech — for me it was human and good of you to speak what we all fear to say, but for Eric it was a tumble of bricks. And then the foolish little fracas and squabbles which were, of course, simply the result of those over-hot afternoons with which England tries to make up for her wretched climate, were a quite disproportionate agony of shame to him. He is far too loyal a friend, of course, to have said any of this to me. But Alan who is a simple blundering old Dobbin – do you hate Amelia Sedley as much as I do for her treatment of Dobbin? – rushed in where angels . . . and then there were words and anger; and I saw my Eric divided as I have always wished him not to be. I am glad to say, that with a little help from me, the silly quarrel is now over, and they are once more the good friends they must always be. But Eric is still lost and unhappy. He wants so much to rebuild his dream of his importance to you and he wants – bless him! – to be honest with himself.*

Only you can help. Be cruel now to be kind. Break his idol completely. Tell him now – or let your silence tell him – that he is not ready for a life and a friendship so far outside his achievements. It will hurt – if it comforts you, let me say it will hurt deeply for a while – but he is young, and that is not just the comforting phrase of middle age. It will also, of course, mean the end of a life in London, at any rate for the time being. Later, perhaps, I may manage something, but I repeat that he is young, younger, as I see now, than I had supposed. I have thought even that we might try to get him work nearer here. It would save the tiring journeys and give him more time for those studies, which you have made us see are so important. But whatever and however, with your co-operation, your silent co-operation, we can help to rebuild his self-confidence.

Forgive me, my dear friend, for writing what perhaps many mothers would have written long ago, and, since we shall not meet again, accept my sincere gratitude for all you have done – this sad end to it cannot diminish that by one jot – and my every good wish for your noble *enterprise.* That *demands all your faith and energy now.*

Yours,

Celia Craddock.

The tree of love was so thickly entwined by the vast hairy trunk of power's ivy, the roots of conscience so overlaid by the lush weeds of self-deception, that who could blame Celia Craddock if she offered so rank a bouquet? Who could condemn her if she took the crown of thorns which she had worn so gracefully and with such loving care for all these years and planted it firmly upon her own son's brow? Only herself, Bernard decided, and no doubt she was already enjoying the painful thrills of guilt's embrace. Certainly, *he* could not offer to prune and weed, though Eric choked, whilst his own garden was so thick with briars. He returned to his breakfast, but the coffee and the Oxford marmalade had lost their savour. He fetched an ashplant and a cap, and set off on a long walk.

Though Bernard's hours of walking had been sad and solitary, there was another figure who had shown himself only too ready to make them lighter, more companionable. Ron seemed somehow ubiquitous during these weeks. Like some spiv-dressed satyr or dryad in a modern ballet, he would appear suddenly now by this hedgerow, now from that copse, winking, smiling or with sly deferential touch of his head. Bernard, in his guilty preoccupation, almost welcomed these appearances as a concrete, less terrible manifestation of the phantoms that beset him. Nevertheless, he never spoke or smiled in response to this battery of winks and nods. Horror at his inertia before Eric's distant drowning, however, made him resolute now to save that other unknown victim from the waves.

As he left the last row of village council houses behind him and ascended the hill, he saw Ron making his way from his hovel. His padded shoulders and draped hips made a curious contrast with the meadows and woods. He had cut a switch from a hedgerow and as he walked he lashed the heads from the straggling blackberry trailers beside him. Bernard turned his course and walked deliberately over to him.

'Hullo,' said Ron. He had expected this. He knew Ron Wrigley never wanted something he didn't get. That was how the stars worked out for him. 'I seen you about a lot lately.'

'And I you,' said Bernard. 'It has been in my mind to help you. And now I've decided that I must.'

Even Ron was surprised that his 'old one two' was quite so compelling. But he only smiled and said, 'I wouldn't take no help and give nothing in return.' He clothed all potential situations in the most brilliant colours, but as he had not the faintest conception of what relations with a man in Bernard's sphere of life might offer, he had limited his visions to an endless horizon of drape suits interspersed with an occasional signet ring.

'Don't worry on that score,' said Bernard. 'Any help I gave you would mean a considerable return from you.' Then he added, startling Ron, 'I want to know all about your little job for Hubert Rose.'

As Ron began to bluster and expostulate, Bernard once more surprised him with a short statement of how much he had already learnt from Bill. 'It's enough, you know,' he said, 'to have you put away for a long time – but for me, the mixture of motives would be indecently complicated, so I'm willing to help you.'

'I shouldn't talk too much about putting away, if I was you,' said Ron. 'Your sort aren't very popular with the cops either, you know.'

Bernard smiled at this. 'You know exactly how much notice I shall take of that,' he said. 'I'm not supposing you feel anything against giving Mr Rose the little help you've been giving him, but I'm not supposing, either, that you're getting any special kick out of it. If you tell me enough to caution Mr Rose,' he went on, 'you'll none of you hear any more of it. You can say it's because I'm frightened, but it won't be true.' Bernard was surprised at his own sudden renewal of vigour, the disappearance of his burden. If he was to claim Eric from the net, he thought, he must release the other rabbit first.

'What if Mr Rose has *had* his little party?' asked Ron.

'I was afraid of that until I spoke to you,' said Bernard, 'but now I know he hasn't.'

'I don't want no trouble with Mrs Curry,' said Ron, looking down at the ground and switching the hedge angrily.

'You don't want *any* sort of trouble,' said Bernard, 'and that's why you're going to help me. Mrs Curry won't know,' he added, 'and if she does turn funny, let *me* know. *You* don't seem to do so well out of her anyway,' he said, looking Ron up and down.

'I could go places if I wanted to,' said Ron.

'Yes,' said Bernard, 'and I think you should. A bright boy

like you. But not to prison. That's where Mrs Curry will put you one of these days.'

'I can look after myself.' Ron was mumbling now.

'Oh, you'll get by all right,' said Bernard. He fought to prevent himself making promises, offering money, anything to make up for this use of force. 'When was this little party to be that won't take place?' he asked abruptly.

'I never thought it was right, you know. Not with kids. But you don't know Mrs Curry. . . . '

Bernard waited while the self-justifications that must precede the facts were over. He imagined that Ron must be fighting self-disgust at his betrayal of a cinema-learnt code of crooks' honour. He was wrong. Ron was quite soon as happy in the rôle of the 'decent' crook for whom some things – messing about with kids, for example – went too far.

When the whole confession had ended, Ron drew himself up like a soldier at attention.

'That's the honest truth,' he said, straight and decent.

'Yes,' said Bernard, 'thank you.' As he turned to go, he found himself saying, 'By the way, you needn't bother about "appealing" to me any more. I prefer to take my walks alone.'

Once again he realized that the little knife had appeared from nowhere, and with it he had thrust home to hurt. There was no amends that he could see, but he turned and called to Ron, 'You'll get by, you know. Don't worry.'

His encouragement was unnecessary. As Ron continued his walk, he soon forgot any duress under which Bernard had placed him, as he thought of the central part he had played in cheating Mrs Curry and Hubert of their gains. One, two, he switched at the briars, and Mrs Curry fell to the ground with a resounding bang.

It was the pathos of Hubert's setting which Bernard had not expected, against which he had to fight so sternly in order not to throw in his hand. How could he have known that the inner sanctum into which Hubert had led him for their private talk would have revealed not the lavish display of Edwardian gentleman's taste that marked the main living-rooms, but the deathly hygiene of an operating theatre? He would have liked nothing so much as to have cut short his demands, to have risen from the deep armchair and, crossing the vast desert of Hubert's studio, to have left behind for ever that sad functional glass tank.

The high, steel-framed windows, through which the faint light of a wet summer afternoon shone like the last fading gleams of a cooling planet, seemed to offer no concealment to Hubert's self-pity. An infinity of space hung above Bernard before his eye could rest upon the endless stretch of ceiling, an infinity of stone flooring seemed to lie between him and that other armchair in which Hubert had submerged his lanky form. Every object from the complicated radiogram to the carpentry bench and the drawing board seemed determined to reveal its mechanism, to lay bare its inner organs, as though the owner's fear of being charged with any positive assertion either of taste or personality had forbidden him the use of all covering which, by design or ornament, might be used as evidence against him. Not even the frightened disclaimer of English good taste had been allowed – no trace of colour in the neutral chair-covers and distempered walls, no evidence of form that could not be explained by function. Only the desolate moonlit horror of a single Samuel Palmer summed up in coherent statement the world of its owner – the empty hopelessness of a desert universe which had almost wound down to its end.

The conscious assertion of old English gentlemanhood that sounded in Hubert's affected Edwardian tones only further emphasized the desolation of the scene.

'All this understandin' then, this goin' about like a cross between St Francis and Thomas More comes to nothin' then, when it doesn't happen to be your particular little fad,' he said.

'I make you a present of the failure of humanism, if it consoles you to believe that my despair makes yours less,' Bernard answered. 'They are, in fact, two despairs and they can help neither of us. Nor, for that matter,' he added, 'do they say anything about what other men may do with the same things –

other humanists or,' and he looked round the room, 'other disciples of negation.'

'Oh! my dear fellow,' Hubert laughed. 'I'd forgotten how little the room must be to your taste. Nothin' of the human about it and less still of that special devitalized human which you Greek-love boys need so much to make life seem safe. No Murillo shepherd-boys or Michelangelo heads to make you feel lovin' and good. No little Greco-Roman indeterminates to bolster the itchin' palm up with a bit of culture. Not even one of those etiolated mad scarlet sins to make you feel naughty and different. Just man in his proper place among a lot of bigger things that serve their purpose.'

Once again Bernard thrust back immediate compassion. 'Don't make me add impertinence to necessary interference,' he said. 'I'm not here to point out the arrogance of your assumption of man's smallness. If your despair does not lend you compassion, then I can only limit its field of devastation.'

Hubert jerked a hand towards the long windows. 'Your own house, you know,' he said, 'has quite a lot of glass in it, and a well-aimed stone would make an unsightly havoc.'

'Since the day of Vardon Hall's opening, I have accepted the possible collapse of everything I have constructed,' Bernard replied. 'I have no more care for what you or anyone else may do to bring about its ruin. That was the purport of the speech you so much admired.'

'My God!' cried Hubert, 'you talk about compassion, you creeping-Jesus Karamazov. I attempted to meet you on the level below good and evil which you profess to live on, to speak to you directly out of our despairs and desires, and you throw it back in my face.'

'No,' said Bernard, 'I believe that your gesture was sincere, though many might have thought it indulgent self-abasement. You have quoted Dostoyevsky at me. All right! He knew two kinds of abasement: Myshkin, the divine idiot's, and Lebedev, the professional clown's. Yours, I think, was Lebedev's.'

'And you,' Hubert cried, 'are Myshkin, I suppose.'

'No,' said Bernard, 'God help me. But because we recognize

each other's failure gives you no brotherly claim on my acquiescence. I accepted your handshake as recognition, not as a pact to silence.'

'You bloody prig,' said Hubert, 'and you bloody fool too. All this because a girl who was born into a world with nothing to offer her is going to part with something she'll be giving away to Tom, Dick, and Harry in a couple of years, at an age when an ignorant society prefers to think she's bathed in childhood innocence instead of slum smut. And you, the man outside convention, put that above sensual needs.'

'Yes,' said Bernard, 'even above the *emotional* needs of so unhappy and lonely a man as yourself.' He rose from the armchair. 'Remember,' he said, 'I know quite enough to act if *you* do.' From Hubert's silence, he felt confident that he had won. It was only as he walked down the gravel path between the rhododendron bushes that the pain in his side told him of the strain of the interview. He took out a digitalis tablet and crushed it between his teeth.

Ella, in old felt hat and goloshes, was very active in the garden during these rainy days. She had fought through a week of crying and trays of scrap ends of food, the dreary prison of luminal sleeps and an over-hastily made bed. She had fought, too, through the sudden revelations of Bernard's despair, and of Elizabeth's humanity. She had absorbed the humiliation of Sonia's public declaration of what she had so long guessed at. But the calm and confidence of her renewed attack on sprouting weeds and untidy shrubs was built upon more solid ground than the usual recurrent emergences from neurotic flight. She had come closer, in the days after the opening ceremony, to losing herself in a land of rocks and ice than at any time since her breakdown. She had walked on the edge of crevasses and bridged icy torrents that threatened to engulf her personality, to swallow her up and save her from her dilemma by cutting her off for ever from the sane. Yet, at the most hideous crisis of her fears, when even the living death of madness seemed a longed-for peace beside her ghastly fancies, she had suddenly known that if Bernard feared life and sought death, she faced a living extinction because she feared to relinquish her hold on life. Surely and deliberately, in her symbolic world, she had braved the annihilation of crevasse and icy ocean, had stepped out from the safety edge into the void, and remained herself. Beside the terror of that step, the surrender of her will, the deliberate courting of annihilation, life, when she returned to it, seemed a small problem. Her will and her power, she knew, were equal to anything it might offer. As she cut back the honeysuckle bush and pruned the roses, she wanted only an object, a task, a duty or a call on her love to live again fully in the world around her, and with fresh sources of strength derived from her long battle that seemed exhaustless.

Mrs Curry's visit was not, perhaps, the call on her love that Ella sought; nevertheless, it proved a step on the road. Had she known those round blue eyes and soft pink features better, she would have detected both anger and uncertainty. As it was, she was only surprised that someone so famed for their evil power should prove so ill at ease. Her reaffirmation of life had aroused an intense curiosity in its external manifestations. She blinked at the huge figure before her in undisguised interest, taking in every detail of the broken veins around the nose and on the cheeks beneath the layer of powder, the old-fashioned shoes with pointed toes, the flesh forced into bulges around the corsets, 'Evil power' indeed, she thought with scorn. How typical of Bill to make up all that nonsense about Earth Mothers. Why! she was just someone's cook dressed up, certainly dishonest and probably a secret drinker.

Mrs Curry, in her turn, was surprised to find the old looney, as she thought of Ella, so spry and tough. She let her weight with caution into the rather small Chippendale chair that Ella indicated, and spread her little mouth in a sweet smile.

'We don't really know each other, Mrs Sands, do we?' she said, accepting a cigarette. 'But we're not strangers. We're neighbours and neighbours must help each other.'

Ella got up and stood by the fireplace looking down at Mrs Curry as though she were a new chair-cover sent on approval. But she spoke no judgement.

'If neighbours can't go to each other with their little difficulties who can, dear?' Mrs Curry asked. 'I wanted to have a
nice little talk to you, as woman to woman.'

'Oh,' said Ella, 'why?' Though she spoke loudly there was
no hostility in her voice, only a questioning.

Mrs Curry took refuge for a moment in licking her little lips,
then she said, 'So that there shouldn't be any silly little mis-
understanding. I like life to be happy and cosy, you know.'

'Do you?' said Ella. 'Well, I'm afraid it isn't.'

'It can be if we make it. It's just a question of live and let live,
really, isn't it?' Mrs Curry reproved.

'I've been rather out of the world for some time,' Ella
replied, 'but I'm afraid I've found it more a case of die and let
die.'

'Oh dear!' said Mrs Curry. 'Things would get to a pretty
pass if we all looked at it that way. I'm sure I don't know what
would have happened to dear Mr Pendlebury if *I'd* thought that
when he came to me in his troubles.'

'I can answer that,' Ella said. 'More troubles. My brother
goes regularly from one trouble to another. But he always
manages to get out of them.'

'Perhaps that's because there are people who believe in a
loving world, to help him,' Mrs Curry smiled. 'Not that I
regret the little bit of help I gave him. He's such a dear old
gentleman. He enjoys a little flutter, like we all do, and if he finds
himself in Queer Street now and again, I'm sure no one would
grudge him his bit of fun. I love to help sporty gentlemen. I was
only too glad I happened to have a little nest-egg by me at the
time. Of course I know the world, and I dare say he'll forget all
about it, now he's gone away; but then Mr Sands will see to it
that things are put straight.'

'I shouldn't count on that,' said Ella. 'If Bernard paid all
Bill's debts, we shouldn't have a roof over our heads.'

Mrs Curry's smile was so sweet as she answered, 'I think he
would, dear, for me. We understand each other so well. Only
I'm afraid Mr Sands takes poor Mr Pendlebury too seriously.
He's a dear old gentleman, but he's a terrible fibber.'

Ella laughed loudly. 'He's quite incapable of telling the truth, if that's what you mean,' she said.

Mrs Curry stroked her lap rather demurely. 'Nobody minds a little tarrydiddle now and again,' she said, 'so long as it doesn't do any harm. But I'm afraid your brother's been telling dreadful stories about me to Mr Sands and now Mr Sands has gone and made a lot of trouble for me with Mr Rose. I thought of going to dear Mr Sands myself, but then I thought perhaps it would be better if I came to you.'

'Oh,' said Ella, 'why? I thought you said that you and Bernard understood each other so well.'

'Yes, dear, we do,' said Mrs Curry, 'but he's made me a little angry believing such silly stories, and I might say something I was sorry for.'

'I see,' said Ella. 'What are the stories?'

'Nasty little stories about poor Mr Rose,' said Mrs Curry, 'just because he's so fond of kiddies.'

'I see,' said Ella again. 'Very nasty. I had no idea that Bill had turned into such a dirty old man. I'm quite sure, though, that Bernard would never listen to such tales.'

Mrs Curry put her tongue into her cheek and gave Ella quite a hard look, before she answered. 'I'm afraid he's not quite himself,' she cooed. 'It's such a pity, because of course they're just the sort of nasty little stories that I've been so angry hearing about *him*. I'm sure he wouldn't like it if I was to repeat all the silly little village gossip about his young friends. But then I don't believe in scandal and disagreeableness, and I'm sure he'll see how silly he's been when you tell him what I've said.'

Ella moved over to the door. 'I've no intention of telling him a word of it,' she said, 'and if you decide to tell him yourself, I should be glad if you would do so somewhere else than here. I don't wish to see you in this house again.'

Mrs Curry waddled slowly out of the room. She turned at the door and stared at Ella.

'Well!' she said, 'if poor Mr Sands does make the little slip we all expect him to, I shall know who's to blame.'

And now, thought Bernard, as he opened Charles's letter, the Voice of the Great World outside.

Dear Bernard, he read, *I regretted so much that I could not be at the opening of Vardon Hall, but government, perhaps my last mistress, is also the most insatiate. Your speech was, from all I hear, an exhibition of pyrotechnics that has certainly lit fires still burning in many quarters I know of. Seriously, what were you at? At a guess, the old game of making people think for themselves. I wonder if you realize quite what a dangerous process it is. To revive the last faint embers of thought in the Master of St Botolph's deadened mind, or in the lichen-encrusted stone of the Bishop of Beckenham's brain, was an act of incendiarism that would have graced a last-century nihilist. They won't easily forgive being set alight so painfully. And to what end? So that those who have conscientiously tried to disguise from themselves the feeble little show they make as they strut on the stage of high office, who have tried, after all, if they can do no good, to limit the harm of their stupidity by sleeping comfortably, should be woken by your cries of 'dust and ashes'. As if they didn't know it, as if we all didn't know it. Why do you imagine they rallied to your support? Don't you see that they recognized as I could have told them all along, that here at last someone in their petrified world – a petrifaction, mind you, that works for the best in everyday matters – was doing something a bit outside the routine day-to-day business, a bit of extra, Sunday fancy-work which was both imaginative and practical? And what do you cry about yourself? Stinking fish.*

Well, you've got your stinking fish all right, and even from this distance it smells pretty high. Your morals are not my affair, but surely there was no need to put a seraglio on as part of the afternoon's entertainment. Your politics, if you have any, are to my knowledge enough of the cocoa-and-high-thinking brand to have delighted dear old Beatrice Webb herself. But, like that courageous old simpleton, you seem to have got yourself caught up with the most unseemly mob.

I don't like artists in public life, and when the artist is as good at his art and as old a friend as you, I hate it. Not only because you inevitably mess things about, but because I don't like to see you burn your fingers. But it isn't too late to save the whole thing, if you'll only come up to London and put on a show as I know you can. Come and dine with me and Lionel Dowding. He has a lazy mind and a showy one, but he likes saving causes rather than destroying them, once he's associated with them; and he's brilliant at forming what they call now 'climates of opinion'. If you won't come for your own sake, buried as you are with guilt enough, in that Rosmersholm of yours, to keep an analyst working for a lifetime, come and help these wretched young poets you made all the fuss about. Will it move you if I tell you that Greenlees was almost in tears when I saw him on Tuesday? You persuaded them all to trust you with your 'News from Nowhere': you've no right to leave them standing, or worse still at the mercy of some careerist charlatan. What's the good of seeing how good Greenlees' stuff is — you were quite right about it, by the way — if you're only going to dangle Utopia in front of his long nose and then whisk it away because your own soul is sick?

If you can lunch on Thursday or Friday I will guarantee to get Lionel Dowding and any others you think you would like.

I used to think you were the only one left of us who still had some sense of using life for happiness, I wish I had been right.

Bernard folded the letter carefully and replaced it in its envelope. Sitting down in the large armchair by the hall staircase he began to cry.

When Ella came in from the garden she was at once appalled to see her husband's distress and quite unable to deal with it. In the years before her illness they had approached each other's grief by gruff or ironical overtures, almost exaggerating their shyness in order to compel an atmosphere of conventional self-control. With the situation once 'in hand' and all external emotion banished, they would then settle down to a sensible, comradely discussion. The most that Ella would have permitted herself was to stroke Bernard's hair, the extreme of Bernard's demonstration would have been a hand on his wife's waist and an 'It's all right, my dear.' In the years of her illness she could not have eased his grief, for she could not have fully realized it. But now the sight of that long-familiar grey head bent in private and uncontrollable grief seemed like an assault on her own existence.

She was paralysed by an onslaught so different from those she had been fighting over all these years in her fantasy world. Picking up a letter from the hall table, she moved like an automaton to the lobby, taking refuge in routine performance of acts she would have carried out had there been no weeping Bernard to confront her.

Bending to remove her goloshes, she caught sight of herself in the mirror over the little antiquated wash-basin with its single tap; she noted the untidy, straying, bleached hair, the lined face and the stocky, spreading hips in their old tweed skirt. She realized with interest rather than emotion that she was not going to cry. Crying had become so automatic with past years that she found the change embarrassing. She opened the letter to distract her mind. No one but Elizabeth ever wrote to her and she felt genuinely puzzled by the unusual event. Charles, she thought, as she turned to the signature, that was no solution, she knew at once no one and so many who might be 'Charles'.

Dear Ella, the letter began, *I don't know whether you like to receive letters. It is so long – too long – since we saw each other. Perhaps this world and its happenings are not to your taste. Robin Ferris and Lionel Dowding, however, both told me you were wonderfully well when they saw you. I hope so much that they were right. For you and for Bernard it is so important that you should be yourself. I remember well your directness and good sense in the bad old days when we all had such a good time. I find it difficult to convey to anyone now how good it was. As a result I find myself cherishing memories and links like an octogenarian, but really one might be eighty for the contact one has with the pleasure-haters of to-day. Many of our old friends, too, have been caught by the sourness, the hatred of life that seems so operative now. So few are left, but you miss nothing in not seeing them – most of them like poor Evelyn or dear sweet Alice Lowndes have clung to their little bit of fun until it's sucked them under. I'm sometimes afraid that I'm getting prim, but drugs and nymphomania and all the rest of the* détraqué *habits do depress me. I cannot tell you how pleasant it has been to see Bernard holding all our old values and going steadily on coping and more than coping with life at the same time. That it should have been one of the old lot who organized the Vardon Hall scheme was a wonderful knowledge, especially when one thinks of the appalling arrivistes who usually get hold of any worthwhile ideas to-day. You will imagine, then, how sad I was to hear that Bernard had lost heart in the scheme, indeed had given the impression of not believing in it. To be honest, the impression that the opening day and his speech made on people was disastrous. I'm sure they've completely misunderstood. But he really must repair the damage, not only for his own sake, but for the many young writers who have counted so much on his help. I have written to ask him to dine with Lionel Dowding. One dinner would set things right again, I feel sure. Do urge him, my dear, to step out of his mood of exaggerated conscience. If he doesn't use the authority that becomes him, all the little jacks-in-office and the ignorant arrivistes will sin. Do more than urge him to life; make him live again.*

Ella read the letter through carefully twice. Then she looked at herself in the mirror and made a little gesture of disgust. She walked back into the hall with deliberate, rather jerky steps.

'I've had this letter from Charles Murley,' she said in her loud voice. 'I should like you to read it.'

Bernard read the letter through and handed it back to her.

'Charles's concern is touching, but not very relevant,' he said, and then added, 'or rather, it is only relevant to his need to compensate for his own disappointment.'

'Is he disappointed?' asked Ella in surprise. 'I thought he had everything. People must have changed while I have been away.'

Bernard looked up in surprise.

'Oh! yes,' said Ella. 'I have been away really as much as if they'd shut me up. But I'm back now, I think, for as long as I can see ahead at any rate. There's an awful lot that wants doing, Bernard,' she added.

'A lot of thinking,' Bernard commented.

'A lot of action, I should have supposed,' his wife said, and as though to emphasize the need she began to stump about the hall, altering the position of ornaments and re-doing the flowers. 'That Mrs Curry mustn't come here again, for example, and then we must see that you get to London and settle all this bother without tiring yourself too much.'

'Has Mrs Curry been here?' Bernard asked with anxiety.

'Yes. She's perfectly foul, Bernard, like that nurse we had for James and Elizabeth who told them those beastly stories. What was her name?'

'Ellis,' said Bernard smiling. 'Mrs Curry's not a stupid woman, you know, Ella.'

'Low cunning,' said Ella sharply. 'They always overreach themselves in the end.'

Again Bernard smiled. 'She has,' he said. 'I've checked her for a while, I think. But she's got a fertile imagination for evil.'

'She'll end up on the wrong side of the law,' Ella remarked.

'She's never been on the right side,' Bernard replied.

'Then somebody must see that the law takes action.'

'Sides of the law,' Bernard said bitterly, 'are hardly an issue on which *I* can take up a strong position.'

Ella crossed to the mantelpiece and altered the position of a photograph of James and Elizabeth as school children. 'You've never done anything foul,' she said, in a voice that was somewhat unnaturally direct and easy.

'The law would think so,' Bernard said. 'When I have imagined speaking to you of it, these were not the circumstances I saw.'

'We are not children,' said Ella, 'to believe that we have no pill to swallow because of the jam in the spoon. Created circumstances cannot last. I know what you want to tell, at least as much as I want to know, and I suppose I shall always hate it, but the dead have no claims on the living, the resurrected must prove their right to restake a claim in life. In any case, you have sought and found affection which you needed, and I know that for you that must mean new duties and loyalties which you have to fulfil.'

'They would be accounted curious loyalties by most women,' Bernard said.

'Most women don't indulge themselves by marrying children,' Ella said sharply. Bernard winced. 'Oh! my dear,' Ella went on, 'you have told me so often in the past that I took a romantic view of artists. There you have it. Besides, before the children were born, and even after, you were never exactly the usual man in your tastes.'

Bernard was silent, then, 'I had no idea of your seeing it.'

Ella laughed harshly. 'The ship's boy at Lowestoft and that student in Montpellier,' she said.

'In eye and thought,' Bernard said, 'but never until these last days more.'

'In practice I hate "more",' said Ella. 'It's something that happens to me physically and I can't help it. But in theory I know it's all the same – thought or deed. The theory's right and I must bend the practice to it.'

'Has that been with you all these last years. Has it, in fact, been the cause of them?' Bernard's sunburn was fading to grey.

'No,' said Ella. 'At least not directly.' She paused and then said abruptly, 'We failed badly with the children, Bernard.'

'Yes,' said Bernard. 'Perhaps I was jealous.'

'Of their youth, perhaps,' Ella replied, 'and I was jealous of their putting a stop to our fun together. I wanted you to be the small boy as much as you did yourself.'

'We tried,' said Bernard, 'to be natural with them, not to be the conventional parents. Do you think now that we were wrong?'

'No,' said Ella, 'only in motive, at any rate. Sonia's disgusting with Nicholas and *we* were right. But I've come to think, Bernard, that we did the right thing for the wrong reason. That's what you said in your speech.'

'I had been thinking of other motives and other acts,' said Bernard, 'but you are right of course. With James and Elizabeth too, I feared to be cruel, or rather I feared to be responsible . . .' He was going on, but Ella interrupted.

'Yes,' she said, 'we feared responsibility.'

'I, perhaps,' said Bernard, 'but you were so sensible.'

'Oh! yes,' said Ella bitterly, 'about cod liver oil and wet shoes and piles, but they wanted love, not good sense. They were and still are lonely.'

Bernard sighed. 'I had not thought you cared.'

'I didn't,' said Ella. 'I don't know that I do even now, for James. He has measured his small stature by finding Sonia enough. But Elizabeth need not have been the lonely, bright bore that she is.'

'She has found companionship now, I'm afraid,' said Bernard.

'Oh!' said Ella, 'with that friend of yours. I ought to have seen, but new facts are still hard for me to grasp. But why afraid, Bernard?'

'Because,' said her husband, 'Terence is as you say that friend of mine.'

There was a long pause. In his descent to the grave and in her rising, such sustained effort had exhausted them. Grey and trembling, they seemed like ghosts.

Ella deliberately walked to the window and turned her back on Bernard before she spoke.

'I see,' she said. 'Ours has not perhaps been the ideal advertisement for such a union, but also it has been very happy, Bernard. If Elizabeth is as happy as I have been . . . '

'I was thinking of Terence,' said Bernard.

Ella's voice seemed to come across a desert of separation. 'Are you jealous, then?' she asked.

'Oh! no,' said Bernard. 'All that is over or nearly so. But Terence is a very respectable person. He treads a safety line of decency with great courage. He is clearheaded and hard. I don't think he can compromise, or if he does, he will be broken. Even in these last weeks he's been contemplating,' Bernard paused for a moment, 'going to another person, a very worthless man, and I've been frightened of his being sucked down.'

'Then,' cried Ella, 'what could be better than this with Elizabeth?'

'For Terence his own course, for Elizabeth another man,' said Bernard.

Ella considered for a moment. 'I think,' she said at last, 'we are not the people to judge. If they want one another, we must want it for them.'

Bernard rubbed his eye wearily and wiped the sweat from his

forehead. 'I suppose so,' he said. 'As you say, how can I know my motives?'

'Oh!' cried Ella. 'I don't try to suggest that good men like you should not take action. Who else if the fools and knaves are not to beat us? Charles is right there, you know.'

'I took action to-day,' he said sadly. 'God knows if I was right.' And he told her the whole story of the intended seduction of the wretched Elsie Black.

'My God!' cried Ella. 'How perfectly foul. But, Bernard, how can you know if they won't go on with the beastly business, all the same?'

'I don't really,' said Bernard, 'but they won't. Hubert Rose is a frightened neurotic ruled by superstitious fears, and I touched the centre of those fears.'

'H'm,' said Ella, 'you're right, of course, because that's why that woman was so angry. She was frightened too. But they ought to be punished, Bernard. You must act against them.'

'I?' said Bernard. 'My dear, I am the last man with a right to act or to punish others. To protect the girl I have taken all the action that I have right to. A limited action, I know, but the only one that I can justify. I am not with the authority of the law, you know.'

'You're not frightened of what they can say?'

Bernard looked hurt. 'Can you think that?' he asked.

'No, no,' Ella answered. 'You're tired and ill, that's what it is. I must take action. I'll get hold of Bill and make him tell me what he knows. He deserves to pay for his lazy selfishness.'

'People *pay*, that's all,' Bernard said sadly. 'Don't let us start talking of *deserving* to pay.' He lit a cigarette with trembling hand. 'If you insist on taking action I shall, of course, have to play a part in helping you. I wish though that you did not.'

It seemed to Ella a long time before he spoke again, for she knew instinctively of what he was going to talk, and she tried in vain to stop her gorge rising. 'You see,' he said at last, 'I too have my superstitious fears. I had to save that innocent, but I do not want to take vengeance. How do I know where that action may lead or who it may hurt far beyond my control? And I too

217

have my innocent to save, but God help me! I cannot hurt those
he loves for although I know their motives to be wrong, I cannot
fight them while I am unsure of my own.'

Ella sat on the high-backed chair by the hall table. Her mouth
twitched as she spoke. 'Tell me,' she said.

When Bernard had done with the story of Eric, 'Give me the
letter the mother wrote to you,' she said. 'Yes,' she said after
she had read it, 'she hates you a lot. It's strange, I ought to be on
her side. While you told me about her, even, I was. But the little
knot that binds us is very tight. I fight for my own, if they're
hurt, and she must already have hurt you so much to be able to
write as she does.'

Bernard protested, 'We can't like each other, it's true. The
situation can't allow it. But I see that she may be thinking she's
doing her duty. I know that it isn't so, that her motives are fear
for herself. But she may not know it. I can't hurt her because of
that. But I also know that she will suck Eric down and I ought to
stop that. But how can I, when my own motives may be worse
than hers?'

'That may be, yes,' replied Ella. 'You're probably right, as
far as the boy's concerned. I'm afraid I can't reckon with that.
But she has hurt you and that I do mind.' There was a pause and
then, 'Yes, Bernard, we must help the boy to get away. If
necessary we must show him this letter.'

'Oh,' cried Bernard, 'I couldn't hit people like that.'

'It would be quite justified. She has no right to expect you to
co-operate in such underhand treatment of him. If she believes
he should not leave, she should have the courage to tell him so.'

She walked over to her husband and put her hand on his arm.
'In any case the main point is to help him to get away.'

There was for the first time a false note in her voice. Bernard
stifled his awareness of it. Everything, he thought, was all right,
she was on his side. He smiled up at her. 'Thank you,' he said.

'And now,' said Ella, 'what are you going to do about this
letter of Charles's?' She had pandered enough, it was clear.
'You can't let all these people down. These young men depend
on you.'

'They should depend on themselves,' said Bernard. 'Vardon Hall is theirs now.'

'Yes, but they need your help and direction. At first, at any rate, to keep out the unholy army of climbers and jacks-in-office.'

Bernard smiled wearily, for the first time he sought refuge in his body's ills. 'You forget that I'm a sick old wreck,' he said.

'You can't do it all, I know,' Ella answered. 'You'll need someone else. Someone intelligent and honest who understands you.' She considered for a moment. 'What about Charles?' she asked.

'Charles is a very busy civil servant,' Bernard answered.

'You also said he was unhappy,' Ella replied. 'This would give him something. Between you both you could do it. You must, Bernard.'

With a deep sigh, he answered, 'I'll do my best, dear.'

'Write to Charles to-night,' she said. She bent over and kissed him. 'We have a lot to do,' she said. He put his arms around her and held her for a moment in a close embrace. Then, 'I'll make you a mushroom omelette for dinner,' she said.

Bernard went to his room early after the meal. He felt heavy and exhausted with the programme of common activity that lay before him. Ella had returned to give him safety and comfort, but his conscience, his beliefs, his tattered humanism were now compounded through and through with alien motives and decisions.

He sat for a time at his desk in the great beamed bedroom that lay under the thrall of the vast flickering shadows thrown up by the firelight. He had the letter to Charles to write.

Taking up his pen, *Dear Isobel*, he wrote, *I have been so sad that our meeting should have ended on such an unhappy note. It was dear and good of you to come down and to wish me so well, and it was very foolish of me to let an unimportant argument prevent me from expressing my gratitude.*

If I cannot believe as you do, you must not think that I have ever ceased to be on the side of the oppressed, the weak and the misfits. I have lived long enough to know that many of them are so from their own doing, that many of the strong and fortunate are finer people, but still I must stand with the unfortunate. We shall not see anything of what we wish come in our lifetime, and, of what happens after we are gone, we are free to make what pleasant dreams we will. If I am right about those you believe in, you will be the first to denounce them, I know. If I am wrong, you will forgive me and understand why.

I have thought so much about you and how wonderfully you have coped. Neither you nor I were born to be teachers. By the lucky fluke of being able to write, I got out. Surely it is time that you did the same. Your life is a very full one, full enough to do without the grind of work that has gone stale on you. If you should think of retiring, perhaps we could start your new life by a trip abroad together. I should like that.

I am tired now and cannot write sensibly. Let us meet soon. My good wishes to Miss Randall, if she will accept them.

> *All my love,*
> *Bernard.*

When he had addressed and stamped the letter, he padded downstairs and left it for the postman to collect in the morning.

It was dark in the room when he woke in bed, only the dying embers of the fire showed life. The folly of eating mushrooms possessed him as he felt his way across to the washbasin for his soda mints. A sudden violent thrust of pain through his side brought him to a standstill. He moved back towards the table by his bedside to reach for his digitalis tablets. But as the pain lashed across his chest and filled his throat, as he sank back into red-hot darkness, he was content that he had not kept the tablets in his pyjama pocket as the doctor had told him.

CHAPTER TWO

Epilogue

THE day-time had become almost a pageant of histrionic rôles for Celia Craddock. Every movement of her body, every tone of her voice, combined to fortify her in these rôles which her emotions invented in their fight against her conscience. Whatever doubts she had of her sincerity in her letter to Bernard, whatever distaste she felt for the underhand scheme she had proposed in order to hold him and Eric to her will, were blurred and lost in the intensity of her play-acting. She moved simply, graciously, about her household tasks – a mother who, despite all her healthy desire to live for herself, had courageously pushed aside her lazy distaste for interference and her hatred of circuitousness in order to save her son from unhappiness. If she put on a kettle, it was done quietly, a little sadly for the shabby tricks to which life forces us to descend, but radiantly, proudly, for the strength and the wisdom in her that had allowed her to accept such little shabbiness where life had become too big for her poor human conscience. If life, in fact, had proved too big for her moral values, she had at least proved as big as life by setting them aside. As she made flaky pastry for the chicken pie – she would at any rate spoil Eric a little in these hard growing-up days when a mother had to stand by silent and see him suffer – she was Elizabeth Tudor or Catherine of Russia who, with a little *moue* of disgust for the smallness of humanity, set scruple aside in the greater cause of statecraft.

But night was not so kind. With the early morning light of four or five o'clock, she woke to a world in reverse. Now she saw only a mother who, from her own selfish grasp on life, had stooped to dishonesty and indulged her sense of power to keep from her son what she had missed for herself. In vain she told herself that she was a woman of the world, not a Buchmanite to harp on unadult dreams like absolute honesty. In vain she told herself that any other mother would long, long before have revolted against so unhealthy a relationship for her boy. Her will, her ego, were too exhausted in those early hours to play their daytime rôles. She knew that a conventional outraged mother would have spoken directly and honestly in her anger. She knew, in fact, that she had herself long accepted the 'unhealthy' relationship, but that she had never been willing to resign the future to her son.

As noises from the outside world told her that day was beginning again, her will would once more begin to come to life, and in those early, in-between hours a compromise would be effected between conscience and desire. If, perhaps, her motives were selfish, we can none of us examine motive too closely; if she did not feel the conventional mother's antagonism, that did not make the assumption of it the less necessary. In a little while the scheme would have worked – Bernard would not have written, Eric, after the miseries of life's lesson, would have accepted the future. Her motives would then be buried beneath the issue, the happy issue of a son saved from moral danger. God – if one could believe in Him, she thought with a little laugh – would once more have moved in mysterious ways His wonders to perform.

She had unfortunately planned without considering one important thing – Eric's own feelings. If Bernard could be restrained, she had taken it for granted that the child would act according to her scheme. But, as Eric mooched in the garden, or dealt with the bookstore's customers in a haze of unhappiness, as his daydreams failed him and his night fears increased, he became seized by a hysterical desire to see Bernard, to demand his reasons, if necessary to force from him a confession of that lack of loyalty and affection which his silence seemed to declare and at which Mimi hinted.

He got on his bike on Sunday morning; and all Mrs Craddock's cares over the chicken pie and mayonnaise were wasted, for he was not back for lunch, and he was still not back at dinner.

Ella was pottering in the garden when he turned in at the drive. Bernard's death had left her with only one possessing thought – to carry out the plans they had devised together on that last evening – only so, she knew, could she absorb the agonies of regret and sorrow and fear that were inside her. But to do so she had to escape for a while from the family sympathies and hostilities that had filled the house since he had died.

It took a few moments for her myopic gaze to recognize Eric in the sweating, flushed, wind-blown figure that descended from the bicycle. For a moment physical nausea threatened to engulf her as she thought of his place in Bernard's life; and then she dwelt with determination on the misery that Bernard had felt at that woman's letter, the things he had hoped so much to do for the boy.

'Oh! how do you do? I want to see Mr Sands,' Eric cried on a high, excited note. 'I've heard nothing from him and I was afraid he might be ill again.'

'He was,' said Ella. 'He was very ill.' Curiously, she found herself angry that the boy had not written to Bernard in those last days. 'He died,' she said in a hard voice, 'last night.'

Eric's flush rushed from his face, his hands trembled, the bicycle fell into a lilac bush. When he rose from picking it up, he was crying.

'I had so much I wanted to talk to him about,' he said.

'Yes,' answered Ella, 'so had I.'

They both stood for a moment in silence. Then Ella said abruptly, 'You've ridden here too quickly. You need a rest and some food. In any case, I want to talk to you about all the things Bernard intended to do for you. He was very fond of you, you know,' she added lamely. 'We can't talk in the house,' she went on, 'it's full of family. Put your bicycle round the corner there and wait a minute. I'll get the car and we'll go in to Bantam. I don't think it's too late for the "Crown" to find you something to eat.'

They sat in silence as the car sped along the country roads, and even when the food had been ordered in the too-oak dining-room, Ella said, 'I don't want you to talk until you've had something to eat.' The result was that Eric, in his shyness and anxiety, ate the cold ham and brawn far too quickly and got indigestion. After he had drunk a cup of bluish coffee, Ella began to tell him of what he must do. She spoke quickly and firmly to prevent him from interrupting. She felt that any intrusion of his personality might antagonize her and so prevent her from carrying out Bernard's aims. Bernard, she understood, wished him to live in London. That was, of course, quite right; it never did for children to live with their parents. In addition, she believed, he needed extra qualifications to get a job suitable to his ability. Bernard had thought highly of his ability. Extra qualifications meant evening study, and that could never be done with the strain of long train journeys. What financial help Bernard had offered would, of course, be forthcoming. She made an effort not to appear too formal; she would be glad to give it, she said. The sooner the better, she went on. He must get his room at once. Had he a bank account? It would be better so, then there would be less financial dealings.

Eric sat quite still, as though he feared that, if he stirred, the whirlwind of her determination might blow him out of the room.

'Well,' she said at last, 'I don't think there's anything more, except addresses and that sort of thing.' She tried once more desperately to be humane. 'Where will you live in London? I should think Bloomsbury would be good. It's reasonably cheap and near your place of work, and near to theatres and concerts, too, which is even more important.'

Suddenly Eric came to life. 'Why didn't Bernie want to see me in these last weeks?' he said in a tense voice. 'What made him so unhappy?'

Ella said nothing for a moment. Then, lighting a cigarette, 'I think you'd better see this letter,' she answered, and she handed him Mrs Craddock's note.

When Eric had read it through, he gave an odd giggle. 'Mimi has got herself in a stew, hasn't she?' he said. Then he laughed bitterly. 'Thank you,' he went on, 'I shall accept your offer. I shall try to leave for London to-morrow.'

Ella nodded with pleasure at his decision. 'It's a foul letter, I'm afraid,' she said.

Eric did not answer directly. 'It was none of it true, of course. Bernie would have realized that,' he said.

It cost Ella a lot to confirm Eric's trust in Bernard, but after a pause, 'Yes,' she answered, 'Bernard knew you were on the right side.'

'But why didn't he ask me?' Eric persisted.

Ella felt too much was being demanded of her. 'What makes you think *I* should know?' she asked.

'I'm sorry,' Eric replied. 'I must be going.'

Ella announced, 'I don't think you'd better cycle back. I'll put you on the London train, and send your cycle to-morrow by rail.'

When they reached Bantam station, Eric held out his hand, but Ella began to adjust the car window. 'Good luck in London,' she called to him.

'Thank you,' he said. 'Perhaps I can come and see you sometimes.'

She fiddled with the gears. 'You'll be very busy, you know,' she said gruffly. 'Bernard expected that.'

Eric suddenly saw life without Bernie or Mimi. Ella noticed his upper lip trembling, she started the engine and was gone.

To her pleasure, she found on return that James and Sonia had left. Elizabeth was writing copy in the drawing-room.

'Where *have* you been, Mummy?' she cried. 'Aunt Isobel phoned to say she would come down for the funeral.'

'Oh! yes,' said Ella in a disinterested voice. She did not answer the question. 'Has Bill phoned?' she asked.

'No, darling,' Elizabeth replied. 'You surely don't mind, do you? We've had quite enough of his fragrant presence for a while to come, I should have thought.'

'Of course, I don't mind,' Ella answered, 'but I've got to see him quite soon. It means I'll have to go to London. I must anyway to see Charles Murley, now that he can't get down.'

'I think Terence Lambert wants to come for the funeral,' Elizabeth said. 'Is that all right?' She had told Terence that only with him there could she support it.

'Of course, dear, I'm glad,' Ella said. 'You *will* explain to
him that I shan't be much in evidence, won't you? But it doesn't
mean I'm not glad to see him. I shall always be glad to see him,
you know.'

'Did Daddy ever talk of Terence to you?' Elizabeth asked.
She felt that she had no right to be putting such a question, but
she desperately wanted to know what Bernard had said, and she
desperately wanted to talk of Terence in any case.

'A little,' said Ella. 'He admired him very much.'

'Terence admired *him* greatly. I wish *I* had understood Daddy
as he did.'

Ella smiled. 'You mean you wish you had *liked* Bernard,' she
said, and when Elizabeth was about to protest, 'No, no, dear,'
she said, 'these questions are bound to crop up now. Bernard,
you know, hated having failed so badly with *you*. We both did.
We hated to see you getting lonely and bored.'

'I know,' Elizabeth said. 'Daddy tried to tell me once. You
mustn't worry. I've got the mag, you know.'

'Elizabeth dear,' said Ella, 'don't be silly. That wretched
paper's been more than half of our worry for you. That's why I
was so pleased that you got on so well with someone Daddy
admired so.' There was a pause. Ella walked across the room and
straightened a picture on the wall. 'How fond are you of
Terence Lambert?' she asked.

'Very fond,' said Elizabeth. 'He's helped me so much. It's
all different.' She hesitated. 'I think I've been able to help him
too,' she added.

'Why don't you marry? You do believe in marriage, don't
you?' Ella asked.

Elizabeth laughed loudly. 'Of course, darling,' she cried,
'we're not living in 1911 or something. But marriage with
Terence . . . it's so difficult to say.' She gave a high-pitched
laugh. 'He's what's called "not the marrying kind", I suppose.'

Ella came and stood by her daughter's side. 'Bernard wasn't
the marrying kind,' she said.

'And were *you* happy?' Elizabeth's voice was suddenly very
hard.

'Yes,' said Ella, as though she had supposed her daughter too intelligent to have such conventional doubts. 'Oh!' she cried, 'you're thinking of these last years. That wasn't because your father was as he was. No, that was *my* jealousy and weakness. You see I thought I had nothing. I hadn't got you or James, because I'd been too frightened of losing Bernard if I gave in to motherhood. And then after Bernard became famous, I think I got frightened of losing him too. We'd been so happy with the school and in his early days of writing. Or perhaps I was afraid of losing myself, I nearly did, you know, later. At any rate, Bernard was so wanted everywhere, and there didn't seem much point in me. He had his work and his friends.'

'But darling!' Elizabeth cried. 'What nonsense! You were adored by all those masses of people that came to stay. James and I hated them. You seemed to be mother to everyone but us.'

Ella laughed. 'Oh yes,' she said, 'I was happy in a way. The jolly, commonsense mother to all Bernard's set, the one who saw that they changed their socks and ate good meals. With one or two like Charles, I suppose I really flirted and enjoyed it. It was something I could never have had with Bernard. But then the war came and that all seemed to smash up.' Once again there was silence for a few minutes. 'But that's quite different with you and Terence. You're not so demanding as I was. And then you say you have helped him, that he's fond of you. My dear, you'll be very wicked – wicked and stupid – if you bother about what his life *has* been. If you really love him and let him go, you'll deserve to be as lonely as you probably will be.' To have thought otherwise would have been a blasphemy against the whole of her own life with Bernard. She took her daughter's hand into her own for a moment. 'I'm going to write some letters,' she said.

The morning after the funeral, Ella went to London. Although she was obsessed by the details of the schemes to which she was committed, and although deeper still there lay the horror of her resurrection to a life without Bernard, she felt nevertheless, for the first time since her recovery, scattered evidences of a pleasure in life itself that she thought had gone for ever. To be going to London at all was an event, to be going to lunch with Charles Murley was a peculiarly pleasant prospect. She regretted that she had no coat and skirt of which she really approved. She attempted a new hair style and even contemplated getting a new shade of lipstick before meeting him. The streets of London seemed all cleanliness and vigour after the green prison of the country in which she had so long been confined.

Charles found her appearance horribly aged, but in no time her charm had reasserted itself. She ate with gusto at the quiet Soho restaurant he had specially chosen for her, though she would much have preferred Claridges or the Berkeley.

It was only when they had almost flirted their way through luncheon and she had agreed to a brandy that she felt free to make her demands upon him. She had never been able to take any man but Bernard seriously, and although she was happy to flirt with or mother any of them if they liked it – even, on occasion, herself enjoyed doing so – she had usually ended by getting from them what Bernard needed. To-day's meeting was therefore a return to such relationships undertaken on Bernard's behalf, if it was also the last.

'Charles,' she said, holding the great brandy glass in her small, freckled hands, 'I want you to take Bernard's place on the Vardon Hall Committee.' And when Charles began, 'Ella darling, above all things, you know, I should adore to serve you, but . . . ' she said, 'No, Charles, wait until I've finished before you ask to be excused. Bernard's greatness, what people will know of it long after we're both dead, lies in his books. But this scheme was a good thing to have done, it was the last thing he did and he cared about it. These people, too, the younger writers, depended on it, and in a sense, I should think, it's one of the few useful things done for literature in England to-day. It mustn't fall into the hands of those foul people – the tuft-hunters and the formal deadheads. Bernard wanted to let the people who worked there run it for themselves, and if he'd lived he'd have seen that they did. The rest of the committee are far too lazy or too frightened. They'll appoint the first petty tyrant who wants to make a name for himself so that they don't have to worry any more. Charles, it mustn't happen. If you go on the committee – and they'll be glad to have you – you can see these younger men through the first year, and then they can cope on their own.'

'My dear, even if I had the time, I doubt if the committee would have me for a moment.'

'Give me some of their names, Charles,' she said, 'and I'll see that they do.'

'Darling Ella,' he cried, 'I believe you would.'

Ella smiled. 'Of course I would,' she said.

It was enchanting, Charles thought. He had no idea how he could possibly fulfil such a promise, but to be brought back in peace to his past like this, and by one of the figures whom he had long struck out of existence; he could not resist it. Probably she would cease to be so concerned with it in a few weeks, she had clearly not yet come to grips with her grief; meanwhile, it would make her happy.

'Very well, darling,' he spluttered. 'I'll see what I can do.'

'Thank you, Charles,' she said. 'It will be so nice to see something of you again.'

It was only when they parted and he bent from his great height to kiss her, that she remembered his tiresome habit of disarranging one's hat.

Her next errand lay in a very different quarter of London. It was only after ringing for ten minutes at the door of the peeling stuccoed house off the Vauxhall Bridge Road, that a pouchy-eyed woman with peroxide hair opened to her.

'I want to see Mr Pendlebury, please,' Ella said.

'Second floor up on the right,' the woman was suspicious.

Ella had never seen the more sordid aspects of her brother's life. She realized, as she climbed the stairs, that it had been easier to imagine and then to dismiss them. Conscience, in these few minutes, bit rather fiercely, as she remembered her periodic affirmations that Bill's belief in his writing was justified. It had been pleasant to assert one's faith in one's brother to sceptical audiences; and easy too to agree with a little shrug of realism that he would never fulfil his hopes. She dreaded the remorse that the actual appearance of the squalor to which he had descended might bring to her.

The trays of half-eaten meals, the litter of crumpled newspapers, the cigarette ends and the stale air that filled his room brought her, however, not remorse, but remembrance. This was nothing new to her, only the echo of her own past neurotic misery.

In her surprise, she could find no approach save a return to their youth. 'Hullo, my dear,' she said.

Bill's histrionic sense was more alive to the occasion. He sprang from the broken armchair in which he was buried beneath books, newspapers, and ash.

'My God!' he cried, 'this is my lowest point. That you should have to come up here to see me, and I haven't even had the decency to write. I can't expect you to believe me, I know, but it's knocked me harder than I would ever have believed. One doesn't meet so many men of stature in this puking little world, and his greatest thing was that he never made one feel small.'

Ella swallowed her disgust. It was not impossible, she thought, that Bill might even have felt something of what he said. He was getting old and death might well have touched what little nerves of feeling the years of selfishness had not insulated. The familiarity of his excessive speech, however, hardened her resolve to make her demands of him.

'Well, Bill,' she said, 'I'm afraid you'll have to put your sympathy into action. I need your assistance and I intend to have it.'

'Good God,' Bill cried, 'if you came here to kick me on the bottom, it wouldn't be more than I deserved.'

'That would be easier, I think, than what I'm going to ask. I want you to go to the police and tell them all you know about Mrs Curry and Hubert Rose and their friends. And if you don't know enough about that, tell them anything you know that will put as many of those foul wretches in prison as possible.'

When Bill began to protest, she sat on the side of the huge brass bedstead, swinging her legs.

'No, Bill,' she said, 'you've got to do it. I realize now that you knew this bloody story about the wretched girl when you were with us last week. You tried to tell me something about it mixed up with a lot of nonsense.'

'I told Bernard of it quite directly,' said Bill, 'the night I left you.'

'I see,' said Ella. 'Well, tired and ill as he was, he did something about it. We agreed the night he died that it was not enough, that we must do more. But you, Bill, you hadn't the guts to do anything. You could have done it your own way, but you didn't. You've lost that right now; you must do it my way. You must tell the police and after that, whatever they want you to do, you'll have to do.'

'I don't think Bernard had quite your admirable British love of the law,' Bill said. 'Perhaps he knew men and women too well to believe that shutting them up was going to cure the world's evils.'

Ella had been thinking with anxiety of this view which she and Bernard had always held so strongly; its statement in her brother's mouth so sickened her that she dismissed it finally from her mind. Her next approach was indicative of her growing distaste for Bill.

'I shan't let your help go unrewarded,' she said. 'You can't go on living like this, you know, Bill. It is something I ought never to have allowed. Bernard's will has left me well off, far too well off for my plain needs. You must let me give you an income. It's what you've always needed if you're to write as you want. I believe in your writing, you know, so that it won't be insulting you. Of course there's a limit to what I can do, and if you decide to let the money push you further downhill I can do nothing to stop you. But you must do what I ask you now.'

When Bill told his story to the police inspector it was amazing, in fact, how completely he entered into the rôle of the public-spirited man. Perhaps it was the little income that was now assured to him that made him see the attraction of travelling through life with rather more luggage.

Mrs Curry was arrested in the act of sending some cosy snaps of ladies with wooden legs to one of the more lonely and love-needing of her correspondents. Such struggling emotions of fear, of anger and of thwarted power boiled and swirled within that huge bulk that an unaccustomed shivering shook the great mountain of flesh, as with difficulty it was fitted into the police car. Nevertheless by the time she reached the station her sweetness had been restored. Throughout the long dreary weeks of trial and appeal her eyes once more shone forth to recall to the dusty sordid courts a happier, sweeter world of sunlit skies, of bluebell woods and of quiet, dignified gardens with delphinium borders. Somehow, however, the court atmosphere proved sadly resistant to the messages of love and beauty which were offered. Sweet wood-doves cooed in her voice, quiet lakes rippled in her smile, but the story of threats, of lies, of cheating, and of cruelty flowed on. Love, it may have been, had brought together the collection of pimps, of blackmailers, of greedy shopkeepers and bribed garage mechanics: it was fear, however, that made them speak in court. Mrs Curry had always been fond of that music-hall song in which a judge addressing a young lady says, 'You're a bad, bad woman, but you're damned good company.' The judge's address to the jury was sadly different. It might have been, he said, that the sickening exhibition of sanctimoniousness and moralizing which the accused had offered them from the witness box had prejudiced some of them against her. They must, however, put all that out of their minds. The facts, and the facts alone, must form the basis of their verdict. Never, perhaps, had judge had so ample an opportunity for moralizing.

It was only when the sentence – a sentence that by its severity surprised even some of the lawyers present – was passed and the touch of the wardress's hand on Mrs Curry's arm urged her below, that a look of such hatred came from those liquid blue eyes as to disturb even the judge's excellent digestion.

Ron was taken in the heart of his shrine, trying on a new knock-out suit that Ma Curry had just given him for his loyalty. It was difficult to persuade him to leave his worship. He clung to his

bed in hysterical screaming and kicking. During the trial, however, he was all that justice could have required, anxious to tell
all that he could, difficult only to stem in his voluble incrimina-
tion of all and sundry. He was rewarded for his co-operation
with a far lighter sentence. It was only when he left the box
that his somewhat restored spirits allowed him once more to
indulge the old 'one two' as he looked up at the judge.

Mrs Wrigley took it very badly. Hers had been a respectable
family. She could hardly believe it, when she thought of the way
in which she had been so regular at chapel as a girl. She even took
out the 'Good Book' from a dusty cupboard and set it on the
table as a testimony to the godliness of her home. It only showed
the ingratitude of children. One worked and slaved to give them
a good home and this was the result. However, after Ron's sentence she sold his suits – the very demons of his temptation – and
after that she felt better. Two new records of *Patience* – bought
with part of the proceeds of the sale – helped to solace her new
loneliness.

Hubert was arrested in the rich, Ouida-esque setting of the chic
drawing-room in which he usually received visitors. His
behaviour to the police was as polite, as insolent and as Edwardian as to any of his ordinary callers. His calmness was superb.
Despite the seriousness of the charge the police felt justified in
not opposing bail. It was in the functional desert of the studio,
however, in which he had received Bernard, that he was found
dead the next day, hanging high from a hook in that vast ceiling.
He seemed a curiously lonely figure in his Edwardian tight
trousers and brocade waistcoat, swaying in so ungainly a manner
amidst the vast stretches of steel and glass.

James and Sonia only learnt by chance from Bill of the active
part that Ella had played in this mass dealing-out of justice. He
revealed it to them in a patronizing interpolation to his great
eulogy of his own part in the proceedings. Even Sonia had to
agree with James that his mother had behaved with admirable

competence and public spirit. They could find no two expressions of higher praise, but then there were few things they so delighted in as primitive retribution. They bombarded Ella with invitations to play with the children; and Sonia did not even openly interfere when Ella told Nicholas that God was a person whom lots of people made up stories about because it made them feel better but that like Rumpelstiltskin and Humpty Dumpty he wasn't a 'real person'. She merely laughed and said didn't Ella think that Nicholas must judge that for himself when he got a bit older.

Both James and Sonia kept advising Ella about the best means of coping with the large estates that Bernard had left outright to her with the request that she provide for the children and grandchildren on her death. Should she not, they said, invest in this, or sell that, security? Should she not get rid of the house, so big and difficult to run, and buy something smaller, more comfortable and modern? After all – and they reiterated this a hundred times – she had only herself to think of now; the money was no good unless she made sure she got exactly what *she* wanted out of it. Ella would have liked to talk of her satisfaction at Bernard's legacy to Eric which relieved her of a responsibility that she hated. She would have liked also to have regretted that nothing had been left to Terence, which would have helped on her schemes for Elizabeth. She realized, however, that any mention of either of the young men would have upset James and Sonia greatly. They all found it possible to compromise by wondering at the legacy to Isobel – an elderly single woman, with a good salary; really! it was rather coals to Newcastle.

James and Sonia felt no embarrassment, however, in discussing the Curry case. The enormity of such things having happened in their village seemed particularly to impress them.

'You have supplied, Mother,' James said, 'the link that is so peculiarly weak in our judicial system – the public-spirited citizen. The public as a rule consistently assists the offender in this age of sentimental values.'

'The rot, of course,' said Sonia, 'set in with that stupid play of Galsworthy's. He completely falsified the dilemma by making his convict a gentleman.' She had conveniently forgotten her previous social admiration of Hubert.

'I only did it because of the little girl, you know,' Ella said.

'Yes, yes,' said James pompously. 'No woman can be expected to act from abstract motives. But it only shows that if the occasion is well chosen, the general principle will be upheld.'

'I wish,' said Ella with a sigh, 'that one could act in single things without involving so many others. Such a lot of wicked things get mixed up with any good one does. Bernard understood that so well; but then he didn't only act in particulars, he maintained what's important in his life itself.'

Sonia really could not forbear giving a hard little laugh, and was about to protest verbally; but she caught James's eye and forbore. Ella's natural feelings so soon after her bereavement must be respected.

'I can hardly bear to think of Hubert Rose,' Sonia said. 'One knew that he was vulgar and superficial, but one couldn't guess that he was degenerate also.'

'I can hardly bear to think of him, too,' said Ella. 'I feel as though I'd killed someone myself. What sort of a home can the wretched man have had?'

There was an awkward pause. 'The local committee are well out of it,' said Sonia. 'Supposing this had happened after they'd selected him as candidate. Not that they would have done anyway, darling,' she added, taking James's hand.

Ella looked at her son to see if he would protest, but he was purring like a cat, so she picked up her handbag and walked out of the house.

Elizabeth would have been glad to comfort her mother in any way she could, but she was nevertheless relieved that Ella was so competent to console herself. It allowed her to spend all the time she wished with Terence. At the very moment that Ella left her son's home, Elizabeth was waiting impatiently for his arrival in a funny little 1870 pub all coloured glass and gay vulgarity that they had adopted for their own. Terence's habit of arriving late was growing, she reflected. It wouldn't matter, of course, if she didn't always feel so certain that he had been knocked over by a bus. He obsessed her thoughts so completely in these last days that a mention of 'Lambeth' in an article she was proof-reading had set her daydreaming by its likeness to 'Lambert' and she had almost destroyed a column about a new theatrical designer because she felt so angry that Terence's great talents were not yet recognized. She had almost begun to hate this obsession, this longing for his physical presence because it made her so unable to be the amusing companion that she knew he wanted.

'Here's your pink gin, darling,' she greeted him when at last he arrived. Terence made no reply.

'Elsie's boy friend's got a new motorbike. Isn't that good?' she said. Elsie was the barmaid. Terence said, 'Is it?'

Elizabeth's stomach turned over a little, but she found herself going on exactly as she wished not to. 'Of course it is. Jolly D. They're going for a dainty spin out to Elsie's Ma's.' When Terence said nothing, she lit a cigarette. 'Shall it be one good dish or a real blow-out?' They had long agreed that these were the only two possible kinds of dinner.

'If I said I was going home now,' said Terence, 'it would be bloody, and if I stay I shall almost certainly be bloodier still.'

Elizabeth summoned all her strength to cope. 'No, darling, if you really would rather go home, it wouldn't be bloody at all. It would be silly not to,' she said.

'No,' said Terence. 'Please don't try to be understanding and put it all off. It won't help either of us really. I know I oughtn't to have let it happen, but I also know that I can't stand it much now and soon I shan't be able to stand it at all. The same cosiness every evening, the same little warm jokes and happy matinées. I feel I could almost scream.'

'Have you met somebody else?' Elizabeth asked. 'Some boy?' she added with difficulty.

'Some boy?' Terence echoed scornfully. 'You've got sex on the brain.' He checked himself. 'I'm sorry,' he said, 'that was silly and rude. But you see . . . '

'No,' said Elizabeth, 'this means a lot to me, Terence. I'm not going to let a sudden mood of yours destroy it. I might fight for it. Surely, what's gone up to now is worth fighting for?'

Terence looked suddenly very hard. '*I* shall have to fight then,' he cried. Then putting down his glass he said, 'Look Elizabeth, I'm to blame, or at least, let me be honest, I blame myself more than you. Not for the beginning, which is really what you mean by "what's gone up to now". We wanted it, we enjoyed it and we ought to be glad about it. But for the way it's drifted, I am to blame. I should have seen what you were making of it. In fact, of course, I did, but I did all the usual silly hoping and excusing. But I'm not going on with it. It's not sex, or only partly so; I've liked that and it's given me confidence. I've not been "changed" or whatever they call it, but I know now I'm not completely one-tracked. It's what I want in life and the way I've got to go about getting it. Oh, this is squalid and tedious.'

'My dear,' Elizabeth cried, 'I'm not going to get in the way of that. I'm not asking for any more than we've had already.'

Terence was silent for a moment. 'No, duckie,' he said at last, 'I don't think you are, or rather you'll make yourself put up with it. But you'll always be hoping and watching, and you'll begin to hate it fairly soon. And even if you didn't, I like you too much to want to see you a good-scout queen's woman rooting pluckily in the background with a double gin for her fairy prince.'

Elizabeth grimaced with disgust.

'You see,' said Terence, 'it won't do. All I can do to help is not to say "What can I do to help?" I can't, except by getting out now.'

Elizabeth laughed hysterically. 'Mummy,' she cried, 'was saying how we ought to marry. Isn't *that* silly?'

'No,' said Terence, 'or rather, only because she shouldn't have said so without knowing me.'

'What will you do?' asked Elizabeth.

'What I was going to do before, I suppose,' said Terence. 'It was partly fear of Sherman's cesspit that led me into this.'

'Thank you for "this",' said Elizabeth bitterly.

'I'm sorry,' said Terence. 'I shall go now, because otherwise I'll say a lot more such things.' When Terence had left Elizabeth took herself off to a cinema and cried her eyes out.

As the last of the committee were leaving the flat, Isobel put a hand on Louie's arm. 'Stay and have some coffee with me,' she said, 'there's something I want to tell you.'

Louie sat on the kitchen chair, while Isobel brought the good, strong coffee to the boil.

'Verreker's impossible,' she said. 'I'd like to get rid of him, only the Pacifists are rather important.' Isobel made no answer. 'Margaret Tasker has no conception of when to raise things,' Louie went on. 'Of course, we all agree that the Women's Guilds aren't of the slightest . . . ' Isobel was making so much noise with the cups that she stopped in the middle of the sentence. 'What was it you wanted to tell me?' she asked with a sigh.

'Oh nothing important really,' Isobel was clearly agitated, 'only something purely personal.'

'Oh,' said Louie flatly. 'What is it?'

'Well,' said Isobel, 'I've decided to resign my chair.'

'Resign?' said Louie. 'Good heavens! whatever for? You've got five years to go yet.'

'Yes,' said Isobel, 'that's why it seems worth while. If it was only two years it would only be a sort of gesture.'

'But whatever are you going to do?' asked Louie.

'I thought,' said Isobel, 'that we had agreed there was infinite work to do at the moment.'

'Yes, of course,' said Louie, 'but yours is rather an important position. You're not just a lecturer like me.'

'I know,' Isobel replied, 'but that seems to make it worse. I simply haven't any right to use my position to go on teaching young people what should be important and alive, when it's been dead to me for so many years. Especially when there's so much I think more vital.'

'It's taken you a long time to make up your mind,' commented Louie, laughing.

'All the more reason to act quickly now,' said Isobel. 'You see that I'm right, don't you? Think of all I shall be able to do now. I shall be free to speak completely as I wish.'

Louie blew on her boiling coffee. 'Quite honestly, no, I don't think you're right,' she said. 'I understand what you mean. God knows I should get sickened wading through all that stuff. But. . . . Well, look, you say how much more you can do, but what you do won't carry anything like the same weight. On the Peace Committee, for example, an *ex*-professor's not much, but a Professor's just what we need.'

'I see,' said Isobel. 'It's not what I do or say, then.'

Louie laughed again. 'You do believe in the personal element a lot don't you?' she said.

'Yes, I suppose I do,' Isobel replied. 'At least I try not to do useless, dishonest things when I realize that they are so.'

'I should have thought giving the weight of your position to the Committee was useful enough.'

'And killing the enthusiasm of the young?'

'English Honours students?' Louie laughed.

'I thought,' said Isobel, 'that you believed so much in Education.'

'Of course,' cried Louie, 'one can't emphasize enough that the failure to implement the Act is one of this Government's most shocking betrayals.'

'I see,' said Isobel slowly. 'Perhaps my brother was right.' She was silent for a moment. 'I'm sorry you don't like my decision,' she added, 'but I've got to stick to it.'

Eric left the bookshop at six exactly. He carried his bathing trunks rolled up in a towel. He had been working so hard in the past few nights that he felt a certain moral satisfaction in the indulgence of a free evening. Life in London had acquired so strangely self-defensive a character from the beginning. It was like, he thought, all the Kiplingesque phrases which his headmaster had used in leaving-day speeches, phrases which Bernie had called the 'cheerless athlete's conscience'. He was forever 'proving himself worthy' of Mrs Sands' kindness and trust, 'living up to' what she had said Bernie had expected of him; above all, refuting Mimi's sarcasm and laughter in the 'painful' scene which had ended his life at home by 'showing he had the guts' she had refused to grant him.

Her hostility, her rancour, ate into everything he did. They hung like a cloud of duty over his studies, robbing them of all the intrinsic interest which Bernie had revealed in them. They banned him from all the concerts, shows, and parties to which Bernie's friends or his own colleagues at the bookshop invited him. They drove him to casual contacts in vain to break his loneliness, although he had determined to avoid such a casual life as frustrating and time-wasting; yet only among strangers could he get away from the memory of her unhappiness, her collapse before the lies of the letter she had written, her pleas that she had been denied life's pleasures, her charges that he was about to take them at her expense.

If, he reflected, Mimi had been driven to deception by her jealousy of Bernie, her greater hostility to Mrs Sands' intervention had broken her into a pathetic figure of tearful appeal and impotent anger. If he was to survive, he had been forced to resist both appeal and fury, yet he had seen too clearly the pathos of her wasted life in that 'scene', and its memory clogged his own hard-won freedom. Eric was ill adapted for 'hard winning', for refusal to answer letters of appeal, for tenacious opposition. If only, he thought, Mrs Sands had not shown him that letter, he would have effected his escape without the violent wrench of Mimi's silver cord; or would he? Bernie, at any rate, would never have brought it about so violently. Bernie, too, would have dissipated the gloom of his life in London with giggles and mockery. He missed Bernie every hour. Death was indeed a final thing.

The Reverend Bill MacGrath sat on the edge of the swimming bath and waved to Eric. He was, of all Eric's new casual acquaintances, the one who looked most like sticking – the one, at any rate, who was most determined to stick. Backwards and forwards they swam – three lengths of the baths in race – despite the Rev. Bill's forty-five years, his strong overarm crawl won him victory. *Mens sana in corpore sano!* And would old Eric like to come back for a cold supper at the Rev. Bill's flat – only a cold supper, mind, none of the delicious fleshpots that he was used to with his swell friends, but a bit better perhaps than the sort of scraps a chap was liable to make-do with in digs. Eric did not listen a great deal to what the Rev. Bill said, but he felt cheered by his determined kindness. The supper, he reflected, when they sat down to it, was really only very little better than he *would* have got for himself. But now the Rev. Bill, in pinstripe suit and no dog-collar, was getting down to some good talk. Athlete though he was, the Rev. Bill was very keen on things of the mind. Not, of course, that he pretended to be an alpha man himself, but he enormously admired them. Not only thought but the arts – literature, perhaps, not so much, he had so little time for reading – but music – Eric and he must 'do' some symphony concerts together – and painting. Italy had opened the Rev. Bill's eyes and ears, there was no doubt of that; opera – Verdi and Puccini – out of doors, that was so grand. Eric should have seen some of the fellows out there, great tough chaps, lapping it up. For the Rev. Bill was first and foremost an ex-chaplain of the Eighth, with plenty of talk about the Desert Rats. But when the talk turned to the visual arts, the Rev. Bill's tone changed. What did Eric think of this, for example? Only a reproduction, of course. But wasn't the figure absolutely splendid. Some people said there was nothing more completely right – artistically right, you know – than the figure of a young boy. Certainly these really big chaps, like Donatello and Michelangelo, seemed to think so.

'But Michelangelo was queer anyway,' said Eric.

The Rev. Bill's laugh was a little hollow. Of course he knew Eric didn't mean anything by it, but didn't he think that word was rather a pity, implying as it did something abnormal. He meant to say that love between man and man, or he would prefer to say the companionship of an older chap and a lad could be such a damned fine thing. A kind of complement, if he was making himself clear – a harmony of body and spirit. David and Jonathan, he went on, and Achilles and Patroclus, and Shakespeare and Southampton, too, you know. The truth was that, although the Rev. Bill was a very modern parson, his technique of seduction was derived from his own original experience and issued from a very old-fashioned world of Edward Carpenter and the *Shropshire Lad*. He couldn't help thinking, he said, when

241

they'd been stripped down at the baths and going all out to win against each other in that race – and by Jove, he'd enjoyed the contest, every stroke of it – that Eric reminded him of a little statuette he'd seen at Urbino, or was it Cremona?

But here, unfortunately, Eric began to giggle helplessly until tears ran down his cheeks. 'I'm terribly sorry,' he said, 'but I'm afraid you ought to have met me some years ago before I knew Bernard Sands. You see he used to do an imitation of that particular approach which was so terribly like all you've been saying.'

After that there was nothing to do but leave. But when Eric got home, he felt suddenly as though Bernard's death had not left him completely alone. He even felt sure enough of himself to write to Mimi. If she would like it, he said, he would come home for the week-end. Everything was going very well in London, he emphasized, but he would like to see her and put an end to this foolish quarrel.

It had taken Terence some days to get used to living the desultory, malicious and calculating existence that Sherman's *ménage* demanded beneath the excessive ecstasy of saints' eyes and the writing sensuality of martyr's limbs. But the *manieristi* held the day and whatever held the day took first place in Sherman's house. Nevertheless, though there were moments when Terence longed to hang up a reproduction of a Cézanne apple, little though such an object would have been to his taste, the first weeks went smoothly enough. The important guests, it is true, tended to treat him rather as a new appendage to Sherman's furniture, and Sherman himself carefully underlined the golden-cage aspect of the relationship, but Terence felt that patience and tenacity would have their reward. It was quite suddenly that his resolve broke down. The incident arose, to his surprise, over Evelyn Ramage. He had already realized that Evelyn was among the many aspects of his life over which Sherman would demand revision; he had decided, in fact, on a compromise by which he would continue to visit her, but would resist her attempts to visit him in his new splendour. It was not a pretty compromise, and he realized that his fear of Evelyn's suffering at Sherman's hands if she came to Hill Street was only an attempt to palliate one more unpleasant decision into which his life had led him. What he had not expected was that Sherman would himself ask Evelyn to dinner. She came, she saw and she was genuinely enchanted. What was more, Sherman made full use of her enchantment. He dangled every hope before her eyes; he suggested that her return to prosperity and café society would be his especial care; he asked her advice and her help for Terence – after all she had been a mother to him in his time of need and Sherman could never forget that; he appealed to her good-scout sympathy for his own loneliness – if she had thought him hard and cruel, he would like to tell her something of his early years, of the way life had thrown him up; he even encouraged her to patronize him. Terence, by every desperate effort he made to warn her, only succeeded in appearing ungrateful. Before the evening was over she was snubbing him and moralizing on the slender basis of his foothold in Sherman's house.

Sherman was in quite a purring mood when she had gone. 'Poor old dear,' he said, 'you did give her the works, but if we're going to her house, we've got to ask her back, you know.'

'*You*,' said Terence, 'don't have to go near her house. You only came there to keep an eye on me anyway, as you damned well know.'

'Yes, dear, that's what I said,' Sherman laughed. 'Poor old Evelyn! How she did enjoy a good square meal. I think she likes me, dear, you know. She promised to keep an eye on you for me and it promises to be quite a jealous little eye. Of course, if you feel you want to leave the seamy past behind, we can always cut such cables. I don't know which I shall enjoy more, manoeuvring them or cutting them. It sounds quite nautical either way, and a sailor's life is my favourite thing.'

Evelyn, it seemed, was to be on Sherman's side or go. Terence told himself firmly that he would not give her up. It was only quite suddenly in the night, in the darkness that hid the luxury of his Louis Seize bedroom, that he counted through all his friends

– the only safety that he possessed outside the rocky ocean of his new chosen life – and realized that those who did not drop him would become Sherman's friends. He cursed Bernard for dying on him. He even regretted Elizabeth's cosiness. But by the morning he remembered only Bernard's warnings, and, after a row that nearly broke the glass bathroom with shouts and flying bottles, he left to take up his complicated fight alone once more.

The first two months in prison Mrs Curry found very trying. It was not at all a loving, and certainly not a cosy, world. She found herself more and more possessed by psychic visions in which wardresses and judges and Ella Sands and Ron underwent the most appalling misfortunes. But after a while her sunny nature reasserted itself. Her beautiful thoughts got over to the chaplain and through him to the governor, and through her to many of the wardresses. Her huge bulk and advancing years fitted her only for such light duties as bookbinding and the prison organ. Soon, too, her loving and enterprising nature made her the centre of quite a group of young girls among the inmates, and when, after two years, she was released as a result of her good behaviour, she had really formed a most useful group of loving, dutiful girls through whom she could bring snugness and cosiness to respectably lonely gentlemen.

Ron, too, though he much disliked the hard work of prison life, found in so monastic a community that success with the 'old one two' which had been so consistently frustrated in the course of this story.

It was one afternoon in late August, when Ella was sitting among the half-packed suitcases which signalled her departure for a holiday abroad with Elizabeth that she received her first visit from one of the new literary residents of Vardon Hall. She was pleased to see young Mr Greenlees for she had heard so much of him from Bernard.

'Well,' she said, 'how are you running yourselves?'

'It's all going very well really,' Mr Greenlees told her. 'The builders have, thank God! at last vanished. To that extent the new axe has brought us peace.'

'New axe?' Ella asked. 'What new axe?'

'There's been a need for economy apparently,' said Mr Greenlees. 'The committee were most reluctant, as usual in these cases –' He spoke with a bitter twinkle of the eye.

'But the money was all arranged,' Ella cried.

'Not, it would seem, with sufficient prudence,' Mr Greenlees replied. 'I regret only the chef. The new cook has had only too telling experience of institutional cookery.'

'My God,' cried Ella, 'how the hell has Charles Murley let all this happen?'

Mr Greenlees looked quite surprised. 'I think,' he said, 'Murley was one of the movers of the economy. It's true, you know, that we must step carefully at first. Bernard had done wonders, but the cost of living, you know, does rise so. They've got a very good man now though to manage the estate. It saves the cumbrous machinery of frequent committees.'

'What man?' Ella cried.

'Well, I've only seen him once. He used to be a publisher and then he ran some government-sponsored scheme for information exchange. He's quite young and very pushing. He's already decided on a summer programme to attract foreign visitors.'

'Foreign visitors?' Ella's face was purple.

'We shall all contribute,' said Mr Greenlees. 'Sir Joseph felt it was the most satisfactory way of giving us contacts with foreign publishers.'

'And what did you say? The writers, I mean? Did you have any chance to put forward your views?'

'Oh yes,' said Mr Greenlees, 'we have an elected member on the committee. Murley insisted on it; he pointed out how Bernard would have wished it.'

Ella looked at him closely; she was unable to tell if he was being ironical. At last she said, 'And you're all quite satisfied?'

'Oh yes, I think so,' said Mr Greenlees. 'It's so difficult to know how any new enterprise is going to turn out, isn't it?

Bernard, you see, would have known how to let it grow, but without him . . . '

It was when they were on the aeroplane to Nice that Ella made her attitude clear to Elizabeth.

'I've got a mass of introductions,' she said. 'There should be people to visit almost everywhere.'

'I'm coming to be with you, darling,' Elizabeth said, 'not to visit people.'

'Yes, I know,' said Ella, 'and I'm very happy, dear. But I want to be on my own sometimes and I want *you* to meet new people.' She sighed. It seemed so conventional and trite an answer to her daughter's unhappiness, which she so longed to ease; but she had not got very far with her earlier, less conventional advice.

Later, when the little trays of luncheon had been laid before them, Elizabeth suddenly said, 'I've been reading *The Player Queen* again. It's even better than I remembered.' She had decided that to talk of Bernard to Ella was the right thing to do. 'It seems strange that his books will have such influence when in his life he got so little done. I suppose it's because you were always the doer.'

'My dear,' Ella replied, 'doing doesn't last, even if one knows what one's doing, which one usually doesn't. But Bernard *was* something to people – lots of people – me, for example – and that has its effect in the end, I think.' She turned away to the window. It was really easier to concentrate on the clouds moving above and below like great golden snowdrifts.

Thorley, 1951